THE SHADOW TRACER

This Large Print Book carries the
Seal of Approval of N.A.V.H.

THE SHADOW TRACER

MEG GARDINER

THORNDIKE PRESS
A part of Gale, Cengage Learning

GALE
CENGAGE Learning·

Detroit • New York • San Francisco • New Haven, Conn • Waterville, Maine • London

GALE
CENGAGE Learning

LIBRARY OF CONGRESS CATALOGING-IN-PUBLICATION DATA

Gardiner, Meg.
    The shadow tracer / by Meg Gardiner. — Large print edition.
      pages ; cm. — (Thorndike Press large print thriller)
      ISBN 978-1-4104-5967-1 (hardcover) — ISBN 1-4104-5967-5 (hardcover) 1.
Large type books. I. Title.
PR6107.A725S53 2013b
823'.92—dc23
                                       2013018896

Published in 2013 by arrangement with Dutton, a member of Penguin Group (USA) Inc.

Printed in Mexico
1 2 3 4 5 6 7 17 16 15 14 13

For Sheila Crowley
and Deborah Schneider

1

Under the wind, snow needled Sarah Keller's face. She ran, slipping on leaves and mud. There was no path. The forest swelled around her, thick with fir and Ponderosa pine. In her arms, the baby stirred.

Sarah tugged the blanket around Zoe's tiny shoulders. "It's okay." She whispered it raggedly. "Shh."

Branches loomed in front of them, camellias flowering red. Shielding the baby, she pushed past. Her foot snagged on a root.

"No —"

She pitched to her knees and slid, cradling Zoe. "Dammit."

She caught herself. In the rush of wind, her voice would carry. *Christ.*

She struggled back to her feet. Zoe's face screwed up and her hands balled beneath her chin. Her little cotton watch cap had come askew. Sarah rearranged it.

"It's okay, it's okay, shh."

Mud from her hand streaked Zoe's cheek. The little thing opened her eyes, mewled, and turned away from the sting of the snow.

"Quiet, quiet." *Please.* She wiped Zoe's face. And stopped. Her palm had smeared the baby's cheek with blood.

She turned her hand. "Oh —"

She was cut, a long slash along her palm. For an instant it startled her, a raw gash, sharp and numb, before the pain grew thorns and stung.

She looked over her shoulder, past the grasping roots, up the trail she'd crashed through the forest. Beyond shivering branches the house sat still and dark in the strange, shadowless morning. Sarah blinked, from shock and pain and tears.

It looked unexceptional and hideously wrong. Doors shut, shades down: abandoned. Though her coat was pulled up to her ears, the cold bored through her. The house looked like its soul had been stolen.

She turned away from it and from everything in it. *Gone.* She, Zoe, everything — gone. Chest heaving, she plunged through the trees.

Her truck was a quarter-mile away, parked on a switchback. An instinct had warned her when she drove up the mountain earlier, an eerie undertone that sighed, *Don't pull in the driveway. Keep driving. Someone's there, watching.* This place was a backwoods idyll, secluded in the coastal mountains south of San Francisco. It was lonely and wild and studded with redwoods. California dreamin. A waking nightmare.

And it was snowing. Goddamn snowing, ten miles from the beach. The wind drove flakes against the baby's face. She squirmed and let out another mewling cry. Sarah pulled the blanket up.

"Shh. I gotcha."

Six weeks old. Barely old enough to grasp Sarah's finger and smile. And now this.

Why? Why now? They'd just gotten home. They'd had a safe trip. They'd run the gauntlet and come out untouched. Everything was okay.

Except it wasn't. The hairs on the back of Sarah's neck prickled. She glanced back again. Screened by the pines, barely visible now, the house wore a wraith's face. Windows, its blank eyes, watched her.

Veiled beneath the wind, another sound rose, a dark flow that seemed ready to take solid form. Shivering, she turned and aimed for the switchback.

The man appeared directly in front of her. He seemed to materialize from the gray recesses of the trees.

"Jesus." She jerked to a halt, breathing hard, and pulled Zoe against her chest.

He moved silently into her path. He was dark-eyed and somber, his face raw from the wind. His voice was low.

"Don't move."

Her chest heaved. "You're too late."

Behind her rose a crackle. The ashen light of the woods flickered and turned orange. It burnished the snow and reflected in his eyes. The house was burning.

He stood between her and the truck. Zoe let out a tiny cry. Sarah backed up a step, trying not to look toward the switchback.

He raised his hand, gesturing *stop.* "Don't."

She shook her head. "I'm not staying here."

With a glass chime, the windows of the house blew out. He tensed. Eyes on the distance, he reached inside his jacket and drew a semiautomatic pistol.

He held it as though it ended all arguments, as though it answered any question she could possibly ask. But the wind shook the trees and the snow blew harder. Around them ghosts seemed to rise. She held still. Because the forest was deep, and he wasn't the only one carrying a gun.

2

Five years later: Present day

9:03 A.M. Outside the memorial, Sarah snapped a photo and slid her phone into her jeans pocket. On the cyclone fence, mementoes fluttered in the spring breeze. Photos, flowers, miniature flags. Teddy bears. She stood alone at the gates, but as long as she looked solemn she'd be taken for a tourist, not a threat.

Not a stalker, and never a thief.

The morning was warm, the sky porcelain blue. On Harvey Avenue, rush-hour traffic rolled downtown. Across the street, the vintage red Porsche was parked, locked, and unguarded. The driver had been gone eleven minutes. He hadn't noticed Sarah. He flicked the remote and walked away, preoccupied, leaving the 911 sitting there like a 300-horsepower lollipop. She paced along the fence.

Fifty yards away, a group of schoolchildren

11

clustered outside the entrance to the museum. They bounced and giggled while their teachers and parents shushed them through the doors.

Let 'em laugh, Sarah thought. The sound seemed to skip off the reflecting pool. Let it echo and fill this place with life.

She continued along the fence. She'd gone full rodeo this morning: low-slung jeans and a belt with a hefty silver buckle; a plaid work shirt knotted over a ribbed white tank; city-girl cowboy boots. It was straight from the Barrel Racer Calendar, and around here, this disguise worked better than a sniper's ghillie suit. Her brown hair hung halfway down her back in the warm sunshine.

A jogger ran by, earbuds leaking Muse. The man she was tracking, the driver of the Porsche, had disappeared into an apartment high-rise down the street.

She glanced again at her watch. How much longer? Maybe she'd miscalculated. Maybe they were playing Trivial Pursuit, or making insane love, or figuring out who had set them up and why.

A police car cruised past. The officer at the wheel glanced at her.

At the museum, the kids' silvery voices ebbed. In the resulting quiet the sunshine seemed to hum from the Field of Empty

Chairs — 168 of them, 19 smaller than the rest.

The pines stirred. Beyond them one corner of the Murrah Building had been left after demolition: concrete and twisted rebar, plaster charred black by the heat of the explosion. City skyscrapers looked out over the memorial park, a beautiful and heartbreaking view.

On the cyclone fence, key chains glinted. Beside them hung a pair of baby shoes. Sarah stopped. Tiny Mary Janes, dangling from the fence.

Sarah glanced again at the museum entrance. Zoe had a field trip this morning too. Her kindergarten class was climbing on the bus about now.

The last of the parent chaperones shooed kids through the doors. The woman laughed quietly, staring at her phone.

That phone probably had GPS turned on, and would broadcast the woman's position to all her social media accounts, so the planet could know exactly what time she and the kids would step onto the grounds of a terrorist atrocity. Sarah never activated her phone's GPS. She knew where she was: in the center of a block drenched with ghosts, in the middle of Oklahoma City, completely on her own.

OKC was a big city, the metro area more than a million people. Sarah had found that, with effort, she could remain comparatively anonymous. Nobody got suspicious if she protected her privacy. But the place was unpretentious. Folks were friendly. They tried to take care of each other. Perhaps because of what had happened in 1995, near the spot where she stood, when Timothy McVeigh parked his Ryder truck, lit the fuse, and walked away.

The baby shoes on the fence were black patent leather. She touched them and turned away from the morning sun.

The driver of the Porsche emerged from the apartment high-rise and stalked along the sidewalk toward his car.

His name was Derek Dryden. He was a physician, a fast car nut, and an adulterer. He rented his mistress an apartment in the Cadogan Towers, and if Sarah was playing things right this morning, he'd just had a flaming argument with her.

Dryden looked harassed. He glanced around, acting exactly like a man who didn't want to be spotted.

Showtime. Sarah checked traffic and crossed the street, heading in his direction.

Her Glock was in the pickup, secure in a stainless-steel lockbox. But in her messenger bag she had a spring-lock military knife. She didn't know Derek Dryden, and planned to take no chances. A stethoscope didn't guarantee he'd be nonviolent.

The sidewalk radiated heat. The street was prairie flat, with pale grass struggling to cover red dirt, studded with a few hardy oaks; a sun-drenched and exposed walk. She and Dryden were the only people on it.

Two things had given him away: a speeding ticket and his trash. Getting him here had taken a week of Sarah's time, two hundred miles of driving, and a few pairs of latex gloves. Now came the endgame. Dryden didn't know he was being played — she hoped. Because Dryden wasn't her target. His mistress was.

Kayla Pryce had the hard body of a workout freak. In photos, she looked as though she could crack a man between her thighs like a nut. And she had a heart of acid-eaten steel. She had worked for a children's hospital charity in Houston. When its bank account turned up empty, the charity's director of finance was charged with embezzlement. The day after the cops took him in, Kayla Pryce skipped town.

The finance director was about to stand trial. His attorney planned to defend him by putting the blame for the missing money

where it truly lay: on Pryce. The defense
had issued a subpoena compelling her to
testify. She was ducking it.

Sarah intended to change that.

But the trial was only four days away. The
defense attorney was scrambling. *Find Pryce,*
he said. *We don't have much time left.*

The problem was, he didn't have much
information either. Just Kayla Pryce's full
name, her date of birth, and a rumor that
she was in Oklahoma City.

Sarah's initial digging came up empty. No
address, no phone number. A criminal
background check turned up nothing.
Pryce's car was registered in Texas and her
credit report gave Houston as her last
known address. She'd canceled her rental,
canceled all utilities and her cell phone account, and blown town without a forwarding address.

People on the run, people attempting to
hide, stayed out of the sunlight. Often they
couldn't be seen directly. But they left
shadows. And that's what Sarah traced.

Kayla Pryce was sly, but she was also careless. Like most twenty-first century Ameri-
cans, she suckled at the cyber-teat and
couldn't wean herself from social media.
Instead of deleting her accounts, she
changed her settings to Private. But that

didn't block Sarah from seeing her Friends list. And those friends talked to her, and about her, and eventually one shared a photo Pryce had posted, for all the world to see.

It was a photo Pryce had snapped of herself — standing by the side of a rural highway, loitering while her date got a speeding ticket. It showed her Texas hair, gym-sculpted shoulders, and duck-lipped pout. It also showed a corner of the car: a vintage red Porsche. Plus a highway marker: U.S. 62 West. And the bottom portion of a sign: ELCOME TO KIO.

The tagline: SO CLOSE TO THE COUNTY LINE.

That was enough. It told Sarah the Porsche had been ticketed where Kiowa and Comanche counties met. And that sent her to the courthouse nearest to the line.

Most people didn't realize that speeding tickets were public records. It took her two hours, but she found it: the citation for a 1976 Porsche 911, clocked doing 93 mph. The ticket bore Derek Dryden's name and his address in Oklahoma City.

His house was a mock-Tudor mansion near the country club. When Sarah staked it out, she discovered that Dryden cheated on his wife but faithfully hauled the trash can to the curb every Wednesday night.

The trash can was where she grabbed the Hefty bag that contained a receipt for the wide-screen television Dryden had purchased — the one he'd had delivered to the Cadogan Towers.

Unfortunately, the receipt was torn. The apartment number was missing. Sarah had called the store, trying to get the apartment number. No luck. She called the front desk at the Cadogan Towers, pretending to be the store, and asked if the TV had been delivered to the correct apartment. Got no joy.

So this morning she had walked into the lobby of the apartment building, carrying two dozen red roses.

"Delivery from Moonflower for Kayla Pryce," she said.

The receptionist smiled. "Aren't those gorgeous?"

Sarah walked past her toward the elevators. "And it's apartment number . . ."

"You can leave them with me."

"That's okay. I can take them up —"

"I'll see that they're delivered."

She left them. Ten seconds later she was back on the sidewalk, walking toward the memorial. She'd hoped the flowers would get a reaction out of Kayla Pryce. She wanted them to bring Pryce down to the street, chasing her for information. After all, she had signed the card: *For my one, my only, my incredible Janelle. Love, Derek.*

But Pryce hadn't appeared, or phoned the number for Moonflower — which was a spoof number that would be forwarded to Sarah's phone. However, ten minutes after Sarah left the roses, the Porsche had pulled up and Dryden had gone into the apartment building. Now, thirteen minutes later, he was returning to the car. Alone.

Kayla Pryce was everything Sarah hated: a cheat, a leech, a thief. She was cunning, devious, and remorseless. Maybe Derek Dryden knew what she was. Maybe he didn't care to know. Either way, he wasn't Sarah's concern.

Sarah watched him stomp toward his car. He looked back once at the apartment tower.

Perfect. He feared that Pryce was watching him. He wouldn't do that unless her apartment faced the street.

Sarah put on her game face. She walked up to the Porsche. Slowing, she admired it a moment, then leaned against the hood. She crossed her feet and waited for him, as if she owned the thing. Or the guy driving it.

Dryden huffed up to her, annoyed. "What are you doing?"

"This machine is a work of art." She ran her hand along the car's flank as though stroking a thoroughbred. "It's a seventy-six, isn't it?"

"Yeah. Get off."

"I'll give you 10 percent above Bluebook for it."

"Not for sale."

"Cash. Or cashier's check. I can have the money for you in twenty minutes."

He neared, hands out, gesturing *shoo.* "What did I just say? Move."

"Fifteen percent over Bluebook. It's a beauty."

"Am I talking to a wall? Get your cowgirl ass off my car."

He was four feet away. Not yet within arm's reach but close enough to set her tingling with apprehension. He was six-two and looked fit, as if he worked the weights and maybe a heavy bag. He smelled strongly of cologne and sweat.

Steady. She stood up. "I represent a collector who will pay top dollar for vintage cars like this. Let me know what it will take. At least let me give you my card."

She reached toward him — suggestively, she hoped.

He brushed past her. "Forget it."

He got in and slammed the door. She went to the driver's window, leaned down, and put one hand against the glass, plaintively.

"If you change your mind . . ."

He fired up the engine, set his hand on the gearshift, and paused. His head flicked around. His gaze clouded.

Uh-oh.

He threw open the door. "Who the hell are you?"

"Whoa." She raised her hands and backed away. "Sorry, mister."

He got out and stepped toward her. "Did you send the flowers?"

She kept backing up. "What flowers?"

He reached for her arm. "What kind of bullshit game are you playing?"

She didn't need to feign alarm. She batted his hand aside. "Don't."

He stopped himself, seeming to realize he'd crossed a line. He jabbed a finger at her. "If I find out . . ."

"Forget it. Keep your car. I don't want it."

She continued to back down the street. His pointing finger hung in the air a second longer. He shook his head in seeming disgust, climbed in the Porsche, and screeched away. She stood in the street, hands at her sides.

Well, that was fun.

On the sidewalk was a mailbox. She walked over, wound up, and kicked it. Reminded herself: *Showtime. This is why you wore the hard-toed cowboy boots.* She kicked it again. Wiped her nose with the back of her hand. Then she walked, slowly and in open view, to the coffee shop on the corner. She went in and slumped in a seat by the window.

Sarah was no game player. She was a hunter, a manipulator, a professional liar. She was a skip tracer. She looked out the window at the Cadogan Towers, waiting.

3

"Everybody on the bus."

The kids climbed the steps and scattered down the aisle, backpacks bouncing. Outside the door, Zoe Keller paused.

The teacher, Lark Sobieski, smiled and said, "Come on, honey."

Zoe stayed put. "Do the cheetahs have room to run?"

"We'll find out."

Zoe's face was grave. In the morning heat her cheeks were as pink as the giant strawberry on her shirt. She was a thoughtful child, dark-eyed and observant. She sometimes saw things sideways, things none of the other kindergartners noticed or even imagined. She was dexterous, one of those kids whose fine motor skills developed before their gross coordination. She'd suffered plenty of playground scrapes — Lark kept a box of Band-Aids in her desk that could be labeled *Zoe's*. Some days, Lark thought Zoe would be an astrophysicist, or a shaman. Other days, when she smiled, bottom teeth missing, she just seemed like a little girl going to the zoo.

"I hope so," Lark said. "Go on, honey, get a seat."

Zoe watched her a second longer, as if checking for signs of untruthfulness, before she took a big step and climbed aboard. At the top of the steps she turned back.

"Because if they don't have room, they need a place. In Kenya. Or a park. But with a fence."

The driver, busy texting, said, "Can't argue with that."

Zoe leaned toward Lark and whispered, "You're not supposed to be on the phone when you drive."

Turning, she skipped down the aisle and hopped up on a seat next to Ryan Fong.

Lark hung in the doorway. Unsettled, she said, "Sir?"

The bus driver looked up sheepishly and set his phone on the dashboard. "All set?"

"Ready to roll."

He fired up the engine. Lark took the front seat. The door closed slowly, easing shut with a pneumatic hiss that left her inexplicably ill at ease.

■ ■ ■ ■

Sarah was halfway through her second cup of coffee when the door opened and Kayla Pryce walked in. Pryce was in full makeup, with sugar-frosted curls, wearing a black velour track suit and a Rolex that could double for brass knuckles. Sarah set aside her cup and checked that she had a clear path to the exit.

She had been warned that Kayla Pryce liked three things: doctors, diamonds, and sharp objects. Pryce had once, she'd heard, defaced the portrait of a love rival by stabbing out its eyes with an ice pick. She had scratched a woman in the face in a dispute at the gym over a Thighmaster. And at a designer dress salon, she'd gone after a seamstress with a pair of scissors for remarking that her new gown needed to be let out in the ass.

Sarah clenched and unclenched her fist. The long gash in her palm had healed to a white weald of scar, a slice that made her lifeline untraceable. Luckily, Your Morning Joe didn't set out real cutlery. If Kayla Pryce wanted to slash, stab, or carve her up, she'd have to use toothpicks and bendy straws.

"You."

Pryce's voice rang like a school bell. Sarah reached into the messenger bag as though hunting for her car keys, and stood up.

"You. Janelle."

Around the coffee shop, conversation stopped. Peripherally, Sarah watched Pryce approach.

A skip tracer couldn't show fear. As an old hand put it, skip tracing was a dark business: Every time you found someone, you made an enemy. You had to be confident, tenacious, and crafty.

"Don't ignore me."

Sarah turned. Pryce was taller than she'd expected, by half a foot. And that didn't count her hair. The duck lips had been plumped to new extremes. She stamped up to her like a furious ostrich, and for a second Sarah thought Pryce planned to peck her face off.

"Sorry?" Sarah said.

"Why were you talking to Derek?"

Sarah looked around, as though for an invisible friend. "I'm here by myself."

"Outside. You were all over him." Pryce flapped her hands. "His one, his only Janelle."

"Not even close."

"Don't play innocent."

Nearby a barista watched anxiously, a coffeepot in her hand. "Ma'am . . ."

Sarah raised a hand. "It's okay."

Pryce said, "Look at me when I'm talking to you. Stay away from Derek."

"I don't know any of these people you're talking about."

"So who the hell are you?"

"Priscilla, Queen of the Cowgirls. Who are you?"

"I'm his fiancée," Pryce said.

Sarah cocked her head. "Kimberly?"

"I'm Kayla. Who the hell is —"

"Kyla? You're Kyla DeMint?"

Pryce's ostrich lips parted. "Kayla Pryce. Jesus, who are those other women?"

Sarah seemed to hear a sound like slot machines paying off. Pryce had just identified herself, and in front of twenty witnesses. From the messenger bag Sarah pulled the manila envelope that contained the subpoena.

"Maybe this will explain."

Pryce grabbed it. As she tore it open, Sarah said, "You're served."

Pryce gaped at it. Then, as though it had turned into a silverfish, she threw it on the table and jumped back. Sarah turned for the door. Rule number one for service of process: Once you get what you're after, don't hang around. Get your ass gone.

27

Pryce shoved a chair at her. "You bitch."

Sarah stopped the chair with her boot. Pryce blocked her path.

The barista came toward them, trying to be conciliatory. "Ma'am, if you don't mind . . ."

Pryce grabbed the young woman's arm and yanked the coffeepot from her hand.

The place erupted. People would happily watch a catfight, but scorned women and scalding coffee made for bad juju. Sarah hoisted the chair in front of herself.

The coffee flew first, a hot spray. Then Pryce smashed the glass carafe against a table.

"This is about the trial in Houston? You're their hound?"

The glass swung near Sarah's face, gleaming like broken teeth. She felt a white spark of fear. She hated sharp objects. And hated being part of a scene. She raised the chair.

"Take it back," Pryce shouted. "I refuse service."

That was like refusing gravity, but Sarah didn't bother to explain. The barista had ducked behind the counter. She came out, face flushed, and this time she wasn't holding a coffeepot.

Sarah lowered the chair to ensure that Pryce's eyes were on her. "Enjoy the flowers. In jail you'll get cavity searches, not roses."

Pryce lunged at her. Sarah ducked and raised the chair.

And the barista stepped up behind Pryce and Tasered her.

Pryce jerked, hit herself in the head with the broken carafe, and toppled to the floor. She hit with a thump and lay there twitching.

The barista said, "She shouldn't have done that."

Sarah set down the chair. "I'll say."

Pryce barked like a little dog and flailed at the barista's ankle with her nails. The barista scooted back.

Sarah groped some cash from her wallet and jammed it in the barista's hands. "Cupcakes for everybody. On me."

She rushed out the door. *Got her,* she thought. *By knockout* — a clean win. It took her two blocks to realize that she was running. In cowboy boots.

Ten minutes later, as she sat in the truck filling out the Proof of Service, her heart was still pounding. Her ears had barely stopped ringing when the phone started.

4

The emergency room at St. Anthony was
racked with noise. Kids were crying. Nurses
in scrubs called to each other. Parents
shouted into phones. Sarah rushed in and
found the teacher, Lark Sobieski, sitting
with her arm around a little boy. His shoulders bobbed with sobs. Lark's forehead had
a bloody gash.

"Where's Zoe?" Sarah said.

Lark glanced up, scattered.

"Zoe," Sarah said.

Lark pointed at the examination area
down the hall. Sarah took three quick steps
toward it and turned back.

"Everybody here?" She couldn't bring
herself to phrase it any other way.

"A minivan cut us off," Lark said. "The
bus slid into a ditch."

"The kids?"

"Most of them walked away." She cuddled
the little boy under her arm. "Everybody's

here, yeah."

"You okay?"

"It's nothing." Lark touched the gash. Her fingers came away bloody.

Sarah squeezed the young woman's shoulder and hurried to the desk. Her eyes stung. She tried to speak and her tongue felt thick.

"Zoe Keller. She was on the school bus."

The nurse said, "You family?"

Sarah nodded and fumbled to pull her wallet from her messenger bag. Lark called, "She's Zoe's mom."

With trembling fingers Sarah took out her driver's license. The nurse read it. "Your daughter's being examined."

"Is she okay?"

The nurse called a hospital volunteer, a woman in her seventies who wore a red vest. She led Sarah through double doors into the fluorescent bay of the ER. They passed kids from Zoe's class. Doctors. Mothers Sarah recognized. At the far end of the room, a nurse leaned over a hospital bed.

On it Zoe sat cross-legged, watching the nurse take her blood pressure. She focused attentively on the inflating cuff.

The floor softened beneath Sarah's feet and the walls seemed to shiver with light. The volunteer put a steadying hand beneath her elbow.

"Thanks, I'm okay," Sarah said.

She wasn't, she couldn't even spell *okay,* but she was back from the brink. The volunteer patted her arm and headed off.

Zoe looked up. "Mom, they're squeezing my blood."

With her two bottom teeth out, Zoe whistled when she talked. Sarah grasped the railing of the bed. "I see."

For the first time in five years, she felt herself praying. Not with words, but with a clear singing tone that seemed to spin around her and infuse the air. *Thank God.*

"How you doing?" she said. She eyed the nurse. "How's she doing?"

The nurse tore off the blood pressure cuff. "She's all right. Just shaken up."

Zoe's brown hair, bobbed short like a flapper, was held off her forehead with a clip. It had a big fuzzy bumblebee on the end. No unicorns or kittens for Zoe. She went for things that sting.

"The bus turned on its side," she said.

Sarah's throat locked. She put a hand on Zoe's head and kissed her, shutting her eyes to hide her tears. She felt a bandage on the back of Zoe's scalp.

The nurse took Zoe's pulse. "She has bruises and she complained of a sore neck — we got some x-rays."

"What did you find?"

"No neurological signs of head trauma, only abrasions and minor lacerations." She set Zoe's hand down. "The doctor will speak to you about her results."

Zoe eyed Sarah soberly. "On the bus, grass and dirt came in the windows. Like a cheese grater, only we were on the inside."

"I'm so sorry, pup."

"Ryan Fong fell on top of me. Then we crawled out the emergency door. Miss Lark busted it open with a little hammer."

Sarah lowered the rail, sat on the bed, and pulled Zoe into her arms. "You're going to be okay."

"I know."

At that, Sarah smiled. This child.

To the nurse, she said, "When can I speak to the doctor?"

"He'll be here in a few minutes."

Zoe said, "They took blood." She held up her arm. A cotton ball was taped to the crook of her elbow. "With a needle, and I didn't cry."

"You were very brave."

"I saw the van crash into the bus."

Once again Sarah's nerves crackled. She stroked Zoe's hair. "I'm sorry it was scary."

"It zoomed around the curve." She pulled her knees up and hugged them. "The lady driving the van was drinking a soda and talking on her phone."

Great. Her little eyewitness, prepping for testimony. The nurse raised an eyebrow.

"You saw that?" Sarah said.

"She yelled at the phone and threw it at the windshield. She was talking to her boyfriend, I think."

The nurse looked wry.

"Maybe . . ." Sarah stopped. Her own phone was ringing. She excused herself.

It was her boss. "Danisha," she said.

"Keller. Did you serve Kayla Pryce?"

Danisha Helms Legal was an attorney support service. The business handled service of process, court filings, document research, and Sarah's field, skip tracing. The company's name was both simple and canny: people would hide in a closet if they knew a process server was at the door, but they'd drop the chain and open up if they heard, "It's DHL."

"I served her," Sarah said, "and I'm at St. Anthony. Zoe's school bus was in an accident."

"Oh my God. Is she okay?"

Bless the woman. Cool and ruthless and always looking like she wanted to reach for a Marlboro or a .45, Danisha Helms could soften like a lullaby.

34

"Cuts and bruises. They took some films, and she may need stitches, but not in a place that will leave a visible scar," Sarah said.

No distinguishing marks. That was always the goal. "I'll bring the proof of service as soon as I can."

"Sugar, you stay there and take care of that little girl. Don't fret about the office," Danisha said.

"I'm not."

"Your voice is shaking. I'll be right there."

Sarah thanked her, grateful, and ended the call.

The nurse said, "Mrs. Keller?"

It was Miss Keller, but Sarah didn't correct her. She kissed the top of Zoe's head. "Don't know about Zoe's accident reconstruction. Kids see the world in creative ways."

Zoe was an inventive little girl. Wonderfully so, 95 percent of the time. The other 5 percent, the freaky five, the wild beasts of her imagination would see a mirage and conjure it into a hurricane.

The nurse just looked bemused. "It's not that. It's her test results."

"Is something wrong?"

"The attending physician will need to speak to you about her x-rays."

All at once she felt chilly. "What about her x-rays? What are you talking about?"

The nurse's expression had gone flat. She eyed Sarah up and down in a way that made her feel naked. "You'll have to speak to the attending about it."

"No — tell me. Please."

A man's voice stopped her dead. "Is this some kind of sick joke?"

Sarah turned. Standing there was the attending physician, Derek Dryden.

5

Sarah's internal alarm system flashed straight to Red.

So did Dryden's face. "What kind of game are you playing?" He pointed at the nurse. "Call Security."

Sarah raised her hands. "Stop. This has nothing to do with the subpoena I served on Ms. Pryce."

"You have to do better than that. Nancy, call them."

The nurse bustled to the wall and picked up a phone.

"Please, don't," Sarah said. "This is about Zoe. The nurse said you need to speak to me about her test results."

"You're her *mother*?"

Zoe said, "Of course she is."

Go, Zoe.

Dryden inhaled so sharply his nostrils flared. For a second, Sarah thought he would throw the chart to the floor and stomp out. Instead, he retracted his anger behind a neutral expression. He smoothed his tie. He headed for the hallway, jerking his head for her to come along. The nurse hung up the phone and trailed after them.

The double doors closed behind them. Sarah said, "Dr. Dryden, I'm sorry we got off on the wrong foot earlier."

"Is that what you call your little piece of street agitprop?"

"Is Zoe all right?"

Dryden crossed his arms and held the chart against his chest. "That depends."

"On what? Please, is she okay?"

He stalked down the hall to Radiology. Inside, he turned on a light box, pulled an x-ray from Zoe's chart, and jammed it up on the wall.

Sarah scanned it. "What's wrong? What am I looking at?"

He tapped the film. "That."

The x-ray showed Zoe's skull and spine. Between her shoulders, buried deep, was a white spot no bigger than a grain of rice.

"Why have you microchipped your child?" Dryden said.

"Jesus."

It tumbled out before she could stop herself. Dryden turned toward her, slowly, pivoting like a mummy. He eyed her for a long moment, seeming to check for signs she was gaming him again. His gaze slid over her shoulder to the nurse. The woman took it as a silent signal. She left the room.

"That's an RFID microchip," he said. "And you didn't know?"

Radio Frequency Identification. RFID chips were essentially sophisticated bar codes. Next gen product identification. The chip was a tiny transmitter.

Sarah's nerves began to pop. RFID chips were used in industry — to track cars on the assembly line or drug inventories in pharmacies. And pets and livestock sometimes had tags injected for identification. They were twenty-first-century cattle brands, scored into chattel with a hypodermic needle instead of a red-hot branding iron.

And one had been injected inside Zoe.

Sarah steadied herself. *Don't lie. Not if you can help it. Not yet.*

"No. I didn't know that," she said.

"Excuse me if I find that bizarre."

The implications coursed through her. Bad. Worse. Unbelievably awful.

Dryden stared. *Say something.*

"Her father," she said.

"What about him? You're saying he had the chip implanted?"

"He must have." She stared at the x-ray. "I can think of nobody else who would have done this."

He examined her with open suspicion. "Where is Zoe's father?"

"He's not here."

"Can you contact him?"

"No. And it doesn't matter whether he had the chip inserted."

"I take it you two are no longer together."

She held her hand up, gesturing *stop.* This was nearing dangerous territory. Her instincts told her to tread gingerly. They told her that one slip could be fatal, and that everybody was out to trip her up.

"I want it removed," she said.

She wanted it burned. She wanted to grab Zoe and get out of the hospital before this went nuclear.

"Now?" Dryden said.

"I never gave permission for that thing to be implanted, and I want it the hell out of her."

"Very well, but it's not a medical emergency. Who's her pediatrician?"

Cool it. She disliked the nosiness behind his question. "If she's got the all clear, I want to take her home."

His voice turned neutral. "Once we finish her paperwork."

He glanced out the door at the hallway. And Sarah understood where the nurse had gone.

"Oh, no." She rushed out of the radiology suite.

"Wait," Dryden called.

The pounding of her heart seemed like a warning bell. She ran back to the ER. On the bed sat Zoe, knees bouncing, while the nurse examined her with an electronic device that looked like a bar code reader.

"What are you doing?" Sarah said.

The nurse looked past her at Dryden. "Doctor, come see this."

Sarah had to get Zoe out of there *now*. "Is that an RFID reader? You were scanning . . ."

She stopped. Zoe was staring at her.

Bright-eyed, Zoe said, "The nurse waved it over me. It's like a Star Wars gizmo that looks inside and sees what's going on."

The nurse had almost certainly borrowed it from the hospital pharmacy. She handed it to Dryden. He read the display.

"Your name is Sarah Keller, correct?"

"Yes."

"And Zoe's father is named Nolan Worthe?"

Zoe turned to him, her eyes abruptly huge with curiosity.

"Yes," Sarah said. It was the first time she'd ever admitted that in public.

Dryden peered at the display, and at her. "Then who's Bethany?"

Sarah remained silent.

"Ms. Keller. This readout says Zoe's mother is Bethany Keller Worthe. So who the hell are you?"

6

Sarah fought the urge to grab Zoe and run. She had to get out of there, but Zoe was curled in the bed with a damn hospital ID bracelet around her wrist. The nurse was glaring at her. And Dryden stood between her and the door.

He looked again at the RFID reader. "The information encoded in the chip lists this child as Zoe Skye Worthe. Father, Nolan Asa Worthe. Mother, Bethany Keller Worthe." He lowered it. "Again, who are you?"

She checked her voice. "I'm Zoe's mother."

Zoe stared at her, wide-eyed. Dryden said, "You need to do better than that."

"I don't use the name Bethany. With good reason, but it's not for public discussion." Sarah stepped to the bed and took Zoe's hand. "And I'm taking her home."

"She's not going anywhere," Dryden said.

"You told me she's ready to be discharged. So we're leaving."

Worthe. The chip actually listed Nolan's last name? Not even Zoe's birth certificate did that. A sheen of cold sweat rose on her skin.

In the nurse's pocket, a phone beeped. She checked a message. "Bloodwork's back from the lab." She glanced at Zoe. "She's O pos."

Dryden said, "And?"

Turning to Sarah, she said, "Your blood type is on file here as well. From the blood drive."

"That's right."

She had donated, along with everybody from work, when a call went out for blood after a multivehicle wreck on the interstate. Nobody had hesitated to give. But now her heart sank.

Dryden read the message. "AB positive. You have a rather rare blood type for a Caucasian woman."

"That's why I donated," Sarah said.

"Type O blood results from a recessive gene. But AB is a dominant genotype. A parent will always pass it along to his or her offspring. A Type AB parent cannot give birth to a Type O child."

Sarah desperately wanted to talk to him in

private, out of Zoe's earshot. But she sensed that she shouldn't leave Zoe's side. She didn't want to move beyond arm's reach, and certainly not out of sight.

Dryden said, "You're not this girl's mother."

Zoe said, "She is so."

Dryden eyed Sarah with grim triumph. "Explain. And skip the bull you shoveled at me earlier today."

Zoe kicked off the covers and climbed to her knees on the bed. She looked fierce. "She is so my mother."

Sarah put an arm around her. "I don't owe you an explanation. I'm going to take Zoe home now."

The double doors opened and a uniformed security guard walked in.

Dryden looked pleased. "You're not going anywhere."

"You have no right to keep us here. The guard can't stop us from leaving."

Dryden said, "The police can."

Only seconds, Sarah thought — that's all she had. It was coming down to this.

From the moment five years earlier when she'd escaped a dead house primed to burn, the moment she'd run with Zoe, she had wondered if this day would come.

She said, "Sorry. Let's take this down a

notch. I can explain, but I don't want to discuss this in front of my daughter."

"Then you shouldn't have a problem stepping right outside," Dryden said.

Son of a bitch.

Zoe said, "Mommy, I want to go home."

"Soon, kiddo."

Reluctantly, she led Dryden and the nurse away from the bed and into the hallway. The security guard followed.

Sarah said, "Zoe's my adopted daughter."

Dryden's expression was as flat as plywood. "All I've heard from you today is lies and distortion. I'm not taking your word for anything. You're going to produce adoption papers. And we're going to contact the people listed as her parents." He nodded at the nurse. "Get a social worker down here. And have her alert Child Protective Services."

"No." Sarah grabbed his arm. "Don't."

He went rigid. She removed her hand.

The nurse said, "Already called, when I alerted Security."

Sarah's palms were clammy. Child Protective Services would be a disaster. She couldn't let anybody separate her from Zoe.

She seemed to feel the cold air of the forest, and the tiny warm life that had beat against her chest as she ran through the snow. That day she had held onto Zoe, against every fear and heartache, and she had to hold onto her now.

"Let me state this very clearly," she said. "If you attempt to contact Zoe's birth family, you will put both her and me in danger."

Dryden shook his head. "This gets weirder by the minute. What, you have a restraining order against them? You'd better produce that too."

"If you'll let me explain —"

"Your explanations only muddy the waters. If Zoe has a 'birth family,' why is her mother's maiden name the same as yours?"

"Sarah."

Coming across the entryway was Danisha Helms. Sarah felt a wave of relief.

Danisha wore a nose stud and dreadlocks halfway down her back. Some process servers might disguise themselves as meter readers, or Mary Kay saleswomen. Danisha was five-foot-ten, African-American, an ex-Army NCO. She wore a straw cowboy hat and enough turquoise jewelry to start her own mine — around her neck, on both wrists, and on the belt that cinched her hip-hugger jeans. Danisha didn't blend. Never had, never could, so she never tried.

She took in the tense atmosphere — the

doctor, nurse, the security guard. "How's Zoe?"

"She's going to be fine." Sarah took her hand. "She's by herself. Will you go stay with her?"

"What's going on?"

"There's some confusion. I need to sort it out and it's not the kind of thing Zoe should hear me talking about."

"Is this about insurance? Zoe's fully covered as a dependent."

Dryden said, "This isn't about insurance."

Danisha's eyebrows went up. "Keller?" She gave the people around them a cool stare. "You want me to stay?"

Sarah squeezed Danisha's hand, digging her nails in. "No. I want you to take care of Zoe. Please."

Carefully, Danisha said, "Are you sure Zoe's all right?"

"She's A-okay. She's ready to be discharged." She looked at Dryden. "Correct?"

"Not until I sign off on her chart," he said.

"But physically Zoe is absolutely fine to go home."

Reluctantly, he nodded.

Sarah squeezed Danisha's hand again. "You go on."

Danisha headed into the ER. Just as she passed through the double doors, a woman in a blue suit stepped around the corner.

"Dr. Dryden," she said.

It was the social worker. She introduced herself as Amelia Winston. Dryden gave her a rundown.

She turned to Sarah. She had a motherly air and guarded eyes. "You want to explain?"

"I shouldn't have to," Sarah said. "My daughter just survived a school bus crash. I want to get her home."

Dryden said, "She's playing you for a sucker, Amelia. She's been following me. An hour ago she tried to lure me into a trap. She draped herself across my car like some hayseed Lolita."

Winston frowned. "What?"

Dryden pointed at Sarah. "Don't believe a word this woman says. She laid in wait for me, then poured out an insane spiel of lies to trick a friend into revealing private information."

Sarah said, "Private information — her name? That's garbage. She isn't a covert agent."

The color flooded back to Dryden's cheeks. "You're a minx, you know it? You thought you got me. Bad news: We've got you."

Winston said, "What's going on?"

Dryden said, "She's a stalker."

Sarah said, "I'm a skip tracer. I've been trying to serve a subpoena on his girlfriend, and today I managed it."

Dryden nearly jumped. "Jesus, shut up."

"Not my fault you're having an affair with a thief."

Winston's phone rang. She answered it curtly and listened, gazing at the floor. Her eyes flicked back and forth. When she hung up, she said, "I don't know what's going on between you two, but refereeing he-said, she-said isn't my job."

Sure it is, Sarah thought. She bet it was a huge part of the woman's job. Her internal alarm buzzed again, a low drone. Who had been on the phone, and what did they tell Winston?

"Ma'am," she said, "you just need to understand that I am Zoe's mother. And if you attempt to contact her father or his family it could provoke a violent response."

"It was an acrimonious separation?"

It wasn't a separation at all. And Sarah got the feeling the woman knew it.

Sarah's impulse was to lie. It was an impulse she'd trained into herself over the past five years, as ruthlessly as she'd trained herself to hunt down debtors and fugitives, and to run a mile in six minutes, to go for a man's knee or for a woman's eyes. But she sensed that lying wouldn't work, not here, not now.

She composed herself. "Ms. Winston, I apologize if I seem on edge. Zoe could have been killed in that bus crash. And now Dr. Dryden has discovered that at some point before I became her mom, she was micro-chipped. It's bizarre and, frankly, scary."

The woman's expression didn't change. "Those aren't the issues."

"Here's the issue. I came to this hospital because my daughter was injured in a high-speed collision. And instead of comforting her and discussing her medical care, I'm being interrogated about my love life and family history." She was genuinely angry now. "Is this how you treat every parent when a physician has an unrelated beef with her?"

Winston finally looked disconcerted. "Your circumstances are highly unusual."

If you only knew. "Zoe is ready to be discharged. You have no reason to hold her, or to make demands upon us."

Dryden stirred. "She's threatening to slap you with legal papers. It's her specialty. Ignore her, Amelia."

The social worker glanced at him disapprovingly. "If Zoe is not your child —"

"If you think adoptive mothers aren't real

parents, God help you," Sarah said.

"I think that in such an exceptional situation —"

"You can corner me? Harass me? No. I need to get my little girl home. Not to stand here . . ."

Winston held up a calming hand. Sarah told herself: *Chill.* Then she heard a radio squawk. Two cops walked into the ER and approached the desk.

They knew.

Dryden exhaled, a triumphant half-laugh. "Try lying to them. See how that goes."

Sarah turned on him. "Stop acting like this is a pie fight."

Winston held up a hand. "Enough."

Sarah put her fingers to her temples. "Sorry. I don't mean to snap at everybody. But this is all too much — it's crazy." She pressed a fist to her mouth. "Please give me a minute. Where's the women's room?"

Winston pointed down the hall.

"I'll be right back."

She trudged down the hall, scraping her fingers through her hair, and pushed open the women's room door as though it was leaden.

Inside, pearled light filtered through a window. She grabbed her phone from her messenger bag and texted Danisha.

Where r u?

She scanned the room for a surveillance camera. Saw none. She checked the door: the dead bolt could only be locked with a key. She dragged the trash can in front of it. It wouldn't stop someone from getting in, but it would slow them down.

She hurried to the window, flipped the lock, muscled the pane up and stuck her head out.

Outside was the ER driveway. An ambulance was parked under the portico. A police cruiser was parked behind it.

Throat dry, she told herself: *No going back.*

She knew what it meant if she climbed out the window. Everything she'd built, everything she'd braced herself against, would be blown away. Part of her clung to the burning desire for normality. *You can explain.*

Her legs locked. Go out the window, and that option vanished.

But she could never explain, not to the police. If they were here, everything was already blown.

She wavered. She had come to love her job. She had, against every expectation, come to love Oklahoma — the big skies, the red-dirt prairie, the twangs, the fat-saturated foods, the rodeos, football, big hearts. She and Zoe had become part of the place. They'd become a family, and found a home.

And she saw: Those things were already gone. The cops were at the hospital. By staying, she was behaving like a dead thing that didn't yet realize its heart had stopped beating.

Her phone pinged. She read Danisha's text message and took a hard breath.

Rolling.

She boosted herself out the window and ran.

7

Sarah ran across sun-heated asphalt to the truck. If she could get out of the parking lot, she'd be a step ahead of them.

Some of them. Not the worst.

She jumped into the hot cab of the truck, fired up the engine, and forced herself not to squeal away. A CCTV camera covered the exit. Burning rubber would tell a damning tale. And in about ninety seconds she would need every advantage she could eke out.

She eased past the camera onto the street. The morning sun reflected from the hospital's windows. Each seemed like an eye, studying her.

The watchfulness of the modern world was inexhaustible. She now had to evade it, somehow — and fast. Before the word spread. The lies, and the truth, and the hatred that would follow like a burst dam.

She tried not to see it all again. She

focused on the road. Oaks overhung the street, dark green. The humid air was growing heavy, mirages beginning to swim on the asphalt in front of her. She stopped at a traffic light.

Zoe Skye Worthe. Bethany Keller Worthe. The words made her dizzy.

Her phone rang. She already had it in her hand. "Danisha?"

"No, Mommy, it's me."

Her heart leaped. "Hey. Where are you, honey?"

Zoe's voice moved away from the phone. "Where are we?"

Distantly, Danisha said, "Northbound."

The light turned green and Sarah pulled away. "I'll see you soon. Can you put the phone on speaker for Danisha?"

"Okay."

Sarah reached a corner and aimed for the interstate. Her heart felt like it was turning as fast as the engine.

Danisha came on the line. "Keller. Want to tell me what's going on?"

"Meet me at Arcadia Lake. I'm on my way."

"This a skip tracing problem? Somebody after you?"

"You have no idea."

She accelerated onto I-35.

■ ■ ■ ■

Derek Dryden said, "She should be back by now."

Amelia Winston was reading a news article on her phone. She checked her watch. It had been four minutes since Sarah Keller left for the women's room.

The social worker gestured to the police officers. "Come with me."

When she pushed on the bathroom door it barely budged. She stepped back and one of the officers put his shoulder against it. From inside came an almighty clatter.

"Trash can's blocking it."

He goaded it open. Winston and Dryden followed him in. They saw the open window.

Dryden said, "She split? You must be kidding."

In the doorway the ER nurse appeared, out of breath. "The little girl. She's gone."

Winston said, "What?"

"I can't find her — or the woman with the dreadlocks."

They rushed back to the hall. Dryden said, "Why wasn't somebody watching them?"

The cop turned to Winston. "Ma'am, is this a law enforcement matter?"

"Yes. Find them." Winston scrolled again through the article on her phone. Her stomach churned. "Sarah Keller may be a kidnapper."

Dryden said, "Are you serious?"

Grimly, Winston scrolled through the article. "The woman named in the microchip as the child's mother, Bethany Keller Worthe — I can't find that exact name online. But Bethany Keller died five years ago. Her body was found in the burned-out remains of an arson fire at her house. Her boyfriend and her infant daughter disappeared and have never been found."

Dryden said, "Until today, you mean."

One of the cops said, "Keller."

"Sarah is Bethany's sister." Winston looked up from the article. "I think she killed her and stole her baby for herself."

8

Sarah raced down a back road along a barbed-wire fence surrounding a field dotted with grazing cattle. She glanced at the dashboard clock. By now the hospital had to know that she and Zoe were gone. The cops were probably after her already.

She needed to dump this truck sooner rather than later. She needed to keep Zoe out of sight. She felt, for a fearsome second, a bottomless despondency.

She parked and cut through a stand of redbud trees with pink blossoms turning to green leaf. The air hung thick around her. The alley behind her house was empty. She slipped through the back gate and in the kitchen door.

Inside, the house was cool and still. From Zoe's closet she got the go-bag, the ever-ready backpack packed with clothes. She grabbed Zoe's favorite stuffed animal, Mr. Mousie, and jammed him in a side pocket.

Down the hall in her room she slung her own go-bag across her shoulders, grabbed her laptop, and swept toiletries into her messenger bag.

Outside the front window, a police car cruised by the house. She stepped back into the shadows until it passed from view.

They weren't there for her. Not yet. The police didn't know she lived here.

She rented this place from a retired couple who were currently touring Canada in an RV. But her official street address was an office in a half-deserted strip mall five miles away. She had convinced the property management company to let her rent one room there — a room with a mail slot — for fifty bucks a month. That ghost address was listed on her driver's license, truck registration, and Zoe's school forms. The police would find it soon, and when they did, they'd hunt for her all the harder. She couldn't linger.

From the bookshelf she took her copy of *The Great Gatsby.* She opened it to check on the photos stashed inside.

They were old and fading. Her and Beth as kids, with their mother at Fisherman's Wharf in San Francisco. Her and Beth on the beach at Half Moon Bay as teenagers, rough surf behind them, hair flying in the wind. And the ancient black and white photo, curling at the edges, of family she had never known and still couldn't identify. Europe, 1930s. It was the photo her mother had given her the day she died, the photo from before the war.

She slid them into the messenger bag. The photos were the only way she could hold onto Beth anymore. And they were all she could show Zoe, her only way to bring to life the mother Zoe didn't even know about. Her throat tightened. When she exhaled, the sound startled her. The house was so quiet.

So quiet. The house seemed too hushed.

She'd thought the same thing when she got into Beth's house that day and called her name and heard nothing, no voices, no music, just an oppressive hush that presaged disaster. *So quiet.* Until she reached the kitchen and found her, Beth barefooted on a snowy day, her blond hair tumbling wildly from a long braid, her eyes round with despair. Then there was no more air, only Sarah trying not to scream.

Now she hoisted her gear and hurried to the kitchen. At the back door she paused. This was just a little place on a quiet road, where the oaks dropped acorns on the roof on windy mornings and the cicadas droned like an electric symphony on summer nights. It was a place with a tire swing and Zoe's Big Wheel and her finger paintings stuck to the fridge with alphabet magnets. It was a bolt-hole that had become a home. It was about to be gone, maybe for good. The rent was paid for the next month. Sarah couldn't think about what would happen after that. She simply had to get through the next hour. And the one after that.

She left as silently as she'd come in. Ninety seconds later she was in her truck, raising red dust as she floored it toward Route 66.

9

"There. Stop. That's her."

In the Security office at St. Anthony, Derek Dryden pointed at the screen. "That's Sarah Keller, in the Nissan truck."

Crowded in the office, Dryden, Amelia Winston, and the uniformed cops had been joined by police detective Fred Dos Santos. The hospital's CCTV surveillance cameras had not picked up Danisha Helms leaving the premises with Zoe Keller, but now they had video of Sarah Keller behind the wheel.

Dos Santos leaned toward the screen. The truck's license plate was readable. He smoothed his goatee. "I'll need a copy of the video."

Dryden said, "What's next?"

"We'll put out a BOLO."

Dos Santos called it in: Be on the lookout for a late-model Nissan pickup. Driver wanted for questioning in relation to a possible kidnapping. Caucasian female, late twenties or early thirties, approximately five-foot-six, brown hair, brown eyes. May be in the company of a five-year-old girl, Zoe Keller aka Zoe Skye Worthe.

They'd already run Sarah Keller's name for wants and warrants and come up empty. They had little to go on, aside from the weird microchip, the news article the social worker had found online — and the fact that, confronted with these things, Sarah Keller had fled, and her friend had disappeared from the hospital with the child.

The five-year-old article was the most damning piece of information. Fire had consumed the cabin south of San Francisco where Bethany Keller's body was found and no usable forensic evidence had been obtained: no fibers, no fingerprints, no extraneous DNA. The article did not list Bethany Keller's cause of death. Her boyfriend, the article said, "could not be reached for comment."

But the fire was arson, and Dos Santos suspected the same thing as the social worker: Sarah Keller was responsible.

He looked at the screen. "We'll find her."

Sarah coasted down the hill and pulled off the road at Arcadia Lake. In the late-morning sunshine, white cumulus puffed in the sky. Gravel crunched beneath the truck's tires. Danisha's red Dodge Ram pickup was already there. When Sarah parked, Zoe hopped down from the cab and skipped toward her.

Sarah got out and scooped her into her arms. "How you feeling, munchkin?"

"The scrapes all sting."

"Bummer." She smoothed Zoe's hair off her forehead. "You okay?"

Zoe considered it for a moment. She nodded.

"Good." Sarah kissed her forehead. "I love you."

Zoe put her arms around Sarah's neck and squeezed. Danisha sauntered over.

Sarah said, "Thank you. You don't know how much."

Danisha crossed her arms. "Happy to help. Want to tell me what we're doing here? 'Cause this doesn't look like a picnic."

Sarah set Zoe down. "Why don't you get your things from Danisha's truck?"

Zoe skipped back and clambered into the cab. She looked steady and sturdy and unperturbed by everything that had happened in the last two hours. Sarah wondered how long that would last.

To Danisha she said, "You've done nothing wrong, and nothing illegal."

Danisha's expression was astringent. "And the cops at the hospital?"

Sarah felt caught. If she divulged one detail the rest might be discovered, but leaving Danisha in the dark would be a betrayal.

"It's about Zoe's father. His family. I've been hiding from them," she said. "I need to get Zoe out of sight. A shitstorm is about to erupt."

"Was your breakup that bad?"

"I was never with her father. Ever. I adopted Zoe."

Danisha's lips parted in surprise.

"Zoe's birth mother was my sister, Beth." Her head throbbed. "But she died when Zoe was six weeks old. Now I'm Zoe's mom, and I'm all she has."

Danisha took her hand. "But why . . ."

"Because nobody knows she's with me."

Almost nobody. An image brushed past her memory, of the man in the forest, stepping into her path from the trees. Dark-eyed, well-armed. Lawless.

Danisha said, "Her father —"

"Beth's boyfriend. They broke up three weeks after Zoe was born."

"Does he want custody? Is he stalking you?"

"His family does. Dani, they microchipped Zoe for identification."

Danisha was tougher than baling wire. And she was speechless.

"I can't stay here. If I do, the cops might arrest me. Then Child Protective Services would take Zoe to foster care. The authorities would look for relatives to take her while they sort this mess out, and they'd start with the name on the microchip. It's *not* her name — Keller is on her birth certificate, but they'd go searching for family . . ." She breathed. "They'd contact people who should never lay eyes on her, much less hands on her."

Beyond them, past rolling green countryside, the lake was glassy blue. Danisha's face was half-shaded by her straw cowboy hat.

"Why is this so tangled? Can't you show the authorities the adoption paperwork?" she said.

"There is none."

Danisha, to her credit, didn't flinch.

In the truck, Zoe was bouncing on the front seat. Sarah said, "Beth had no will, no guardianship plan. But she put Zoe in my care."

"Then why . . ."

"It's a nightmare. Her father's family . . ." Her face heated. "They're dangerous. They killed Beth. And if they find out Zoe's alive and I have her, they'll kill me and take her."

67

Danisha grasped her hand. "God, Sarah. What are you going to do?"

Sarah breathed. "Run."

"Honey, no."

"Yes. And now."

"There has to be another way. Let's call A.J. He can go with you to the police and explain."

A.J. Chivers was DHL's attorney. He was a plainspoken and shrewd lawyer. But Sarah shook her head. "I will not go to the cops."

"Why not?"

"Because law enforcement didn't protect Beth. I can't count on them to protect her child."

At that, Danisha stiffened.

Sarah felt the panic rising again. "I can't risk staying here. If Nolan's family gets Zoe, they'll destroy her."

"Who are these people?"

"Look up the name *Worthe* online. It'll explain."

"More than you have time to tell?"

"More than I can bear to talk about," Sarah said. "I gotta go."

Sarah grabbed Danisha and hugged her hard. Danisha inhaled as if she were fighting back tears. That nearly made Sarah lose it.

Sarah said, "If the cops come calling, tell

them everything. Be honest. It won't hurt me, and it'll help you."

"Where are you going?"

"I can't tell you."

"When will you be back?"

"I don't know."

Bye bye, job. Bye bye, hope. She broke from the embrace and walked toward her pickup.

Danisha said, "Wait."

She dug in her pocket and pulled out the keys to her truck. She tossed them to Sarah. "Take it."

"Dani . . ."

"It's a company vehicle. And until you come back, I consider you to be on company time. So don't scratch it."

Sarah clutched the keys. "Thank you."

"Get it in gear, Keller. I will be royally pissed off if you get arrested and I have to bail your ass out of jail."

"If the cops catch me driving your truck —"

"Don't worry about me."

"I never do." She whistled at the truck. "Zoe. Buckle up."

10

Sarah gunned Danisha's truck up the hill, past farmhouses and pastures and gullies dense with oaks. The engine was big, responsive, and reassuringly loud.

So quiet. The house seemed too hushed.

It got to her, even now — the way that muted stillness could open to chaos; how she had walked into a world of shadows and fire through a silent door.

That day, she'd spent the morning finishing a project, packing up her desk, writing a memo so the team at Past Link Software could keep up with her work while she was away. Ahead lay three months on the road, freedom, adventure. She was so stoked that she practically bounced around the office waving her arms overhead like a Muppet. She almost missed the call.

"Sarah, thank God. Can you come get me and Zoe?"

Her sister's voice had sounded faint, and

not just from the poor signal.

"Beth, what's wrong?"

". . . car won't start. Please — I don't want to stay here. I'm scared."

By then Sarah was moving toward the door. *"What's going on? Is it —"*

"Them."

That was when she broke into a run.

Now, from the back seat of Danisha's truck, she heard a little voice. "Mommy?"

Sarah eyed Zoe in the mirror. "What, honey?"

"I'm thirsty."

She handed a bottle of water over her shoulder. "This will hold you."

"When we go home I want chocolate milk."

"We're going out for lunch."

"Chuck E. Cheese?"

"Afraid not." She would cross the threshold at Chuck E. Cheese when the rivers ran with blood and frogs rained from the sky. So, maybe tonight.

She doubted the Worthes knew she was in Oklahoma City. She wasn't even certain they knew she existed. But she had to assume they did — that Beth had told them she had a sister; that they were already hunting for her.

"I'm coming, Beth. What's the matter?"

71

She had raced out of the parking lot in Cupertino, shouting as she drove. Cold rain was spitting down.

"Something . . . shit. Something happened in Arizona," Beth said.

"I thought the trip out there put an end to everything. You said — closure, you said."

"I meant for it to . . ." Beth's voice broke. "That family's a freak show. I mean scary bad. Nolan never told me. They believe men and women . . ." The sound faded to a hiss and returned. ". . . Sarah, I want to get out of here."

"You didn't let Nolan come back, did you?"

"He came by to talk. But no. No way."

Dammit, Beth. "I'm coming."

"I keep seeing an SUV drive past."

Sarah's heart began to drum. "You mean they're watching?"

"Could be."

"Get out of the house. Take Zoe and get the hell out."

Beth's voice sharpened. "Where, the woods — with a baby? It's snowing."

"Then call the cops."

"Absolutely not. They'll only make things worse."

Then, she hadn't understood. Now, gunning the truck toward Edmond, she understood all too well. It didn't matter whether the Worthes had known Beth had a sister. By nightfall, the police would let everybody know.

Scary bad. This morning, she had been given an x-ray view of what that meant. *Zoe Skye Worthe.*

No way. Not then, not now, not ever. Nolan Worthe may have fathered her, but Zoe was a Keller.

But Sarah knew the Worthe clan saw it differently. They were the ones who had microchipped Zoe. They had *claimed* her.

Throat dry, she pulled in at the Mail Box Store, got Zoe out of the truck, and headed inside.

She didn't use P.O. boxes, because the Patriot Act required her to provide the Postal Service with two forms of ID and her real home address. Besides, as a skip tracer, she often tracked down deadbeats through P.O. boxes. People invariably rented boxes in the ZIP code where they lived — and with a ZIP code she could search for phone, utility, or cable TV accounts, and pin down an address. Then the skip was done. Roasted.

But in four years of skip tracing Sarah had not found anybody who hid behind a series of commercial mail agency drop boxes.

She'd never managed to charm a skip's home address from the manager of a mailbox store. And what worked for sneaks worked for her.

From the box she retrieved the two manila envelopes she'd stashed here. One contained five prepaid credit cards. The other contained three prepaid cell phones. She stuck them in her messenger bag.

This box was her main drop. She had two other boxes in OKC, set up to forward mail and packages in a daisy chain to this one. The box was paid up through the end of the year — a heavy bit of insurance that had just paid off.

Holding Zoe's hand, she walked out. The young man behind the counter was busy sealing a package with strapping tape. "You have a nice day, ma'am."

"You too."

Zoe gave him a little wave. "Bye."

He smiled. "Bye, sweetie."

Sarah counted that as planting a marker, one that would start pinging like a beacon before the day was out.

Back in Danisha's truck, she headed south through town.

"That was our street," Zoe said.

"We're not going home right now."

"Where are we going?"

"On a trip."

"I knew it."

Sarah looked in the rearview mirror. "You did, huh?"

"The big trip. The one you're always packing for."

Sarah felt uneasy. "We'll see how big it is."

She put on her blinker and accelerated onto I-35.

11

At the entrance to the Oklahoma City Police Department's Will Rogers station, Curtis Harker paused, appraising the noise and motion inside. The station was humming with energy and apprehension. A big case buzz.

The desk officer straightened at the sight of Harker's charcoal suit, the white shirt and thin black tie, his *Mad Men* haircut. And a face that looked like it had been hit with a frying pan — and shattered the pan. He always went Full Metal Fed.

He held up his badge wallet. "FBI."

Ninety seconds later, Detective Fred Dos Santos arrived. Harker shook his hand and said, "Let's talk about Zoe Keller."

When the station's detectives gathered around a conference table, Harker leaned on his fingertips like a sprinter in the blocks.

"Everything you think you know about this case is wrong," he said.

Dos Santos said, "We know that Sarah Keller climbed out a bathroom window at St. Anthony, a few minutes after the child she's been calling her daughter walked out of the ER. We know Keller's Oklahoma driver's license lists a home address that's an empty office at a strip mall on the north side. Is that wrong?"

Another detective, a woman named Bonnie Bukin, said, "What's the Bureau's interest in this matter?"

Harker straightened. "Aside from kidnapping and murder?" Nobody responded. "Before this morning, Sarah Keller was last seen five years ago, driving to her sister's house in the coastal mountains south of San Francisco."

Dos Santos said, "Bethany Keller was found dead in the burned-out house. We know."

"Bethany Keller didn't die in the fire. She was killed by a stab wound to the chest, administered with a tactical knife."

The detectives stopped fidgeting.

"From the position in which her body was found, she died trying to reach the phone and call for help. She never made it."

"And the child?" said Bukin.

"Zoe Keller is the daughter of Nolan Worthe." Harker eyed each of the detectives in turn. "That name should make you pay attention."

Bukin crossed her arms. It gave her the glowering air of a bison. "You've got our attention. What else have you got?"

Harker opened a manila folder and pulled out a photo. The mug shot showed a man in his sixties. Behind his stubble and grandfatherly glasses he looked impatient and implacable. His hair flared into wings along the sides of his head.

"Eldrick Worthe," Harker said.

Dos Santos stirred.

Harker said, "Currently a resident of the United States Penitentiary, Florence ADX, south of Colorado Springs. He's serving thirty years for meth trafficking, mail fraud, and RICO violations."

"And?" Bukin said.

"He's Nolan Worthe's father."

"So he's a con. A career criminal."

"No," Harker said. "He's a prophet."

12

Sarah rolled south through Oklahoma City. The interstate was a stripe of bright concrete slicing the endless prairie. Above, cumulus clouds marched across the horizon. She checked her speed: at the limit. Checked the mirror: no cops.

In the back seat, Zoe played with Mousie. Sarah's gaze lingered on her.

She looked so much like Beth. Zoe had the Keller eyes and wiry frame, and Sarah's own overdose of attitude. But Zoe had much more, and Sarah wondered if it came from the others, from her father's people. Strange things, the kind of things rational people whispered about, things that seemed both inherited and otherworldly.

She thought of Zoe's father, Nolan. For a brief hour he thought he could repudiate the family by telling them *no*. By telling them *good-bye*. He thought he could escape to California, build houses, and play guitar in a bar band. But to the Worthes, *no* and *good-bye* were booby traps, code red, words that sent a silent alarm to the heart of the clan and triggered a ruthless response.

That family's a freak show. Scary bad. The Worthes cooked meth and inhaled their own private brand of hellfire. And more: *"They're polygamists,"* Beth had said. *"Fucking, Big Love polygamists."*

Nolan had rejected all that, but never broke free. When he left, the Worthes shunned him — but expected him to come crawling back. And he had. After Zoe was born, he told Beth he wanted to make peace with his family. He convinced Beth to bundle up the baby and go with him to visit them in Arizona.

The visit finished off Beth and Nolan's shaky relationship. When they got back to California, she told him to move out.

At the time, Sarah had felt relieved. Now, she knew that by breaking it off, Beth had painted a bull's-eye on her chest.

That day she had reached the cabin to find the lock on the front door splintered. The house was trashed, Beth's paintings torn off the walls. She found Beth in the kitchen, inside the pantry. The shelves had collapsed, as though from a fight. Beth lay crumpled on the floor, covered in blood.

"Oh God." Sarah dropped to her side. "What happened?"

"Nolan . . ."

The room seemed to tilt sideways. Blood was chugging from a stab wound in Beth's chest.

"Did he do this?"

Beth's chest rose and fell irregularly. "Worthes. Came."

A stab wound, gaping and ugly, a thing that happened in movies or back streets. *Right there.* Sarah pawed through the mess on the pantry floor, found a dish towel and jammed it against the wound. Beth moaned at the pain.

"Where are they?" Sarah said.

"Gone."

"You sure?"

Beth hesitated. No. She wasn't sure.

Sarah's heart beat like a sewing machine. "Nolan?"

"He was in the driveway when they drove up, he . . ."

"Nolan brought them here?"

"Don't know."

Sarah fumbled her phone from her pocket. No signal. She started to rise but saw the phone in the kitchen ripped from the wall.

"Where's your nearest neighbor?" she said.

"Too far."

"I'll get the truck." She took Beth's hand. It was cold.

Beth said, "They thought they killed me. Left because they thought I was dead."

"You're going to be okay. Where's Nolan?"

"Gone. He got here just before they drove up. I looked outside, he was trying to calm Grissom down, but . . ." She started to cry. "Grissom and those girls, they . . ."

A cold gust of fear passed over Sarah. "The baby."

"They wanted her," Beth said. "That's why they came."

Now, Sarah felt the heat of the sun through the window of the pickup truck. In the fast lane an eighteen-wheeler rolled past, loud and close, startling her. She hadn't seen it coming in the mirror.

Gotta stop that, she thought. *Situational awareness, Keller.* She had to be alert and oriented times five. She was the only one available to stand watch now. She sat straighter behind the wheel. Downtown skyscrapers flashed past.

Oklahoma City sat like a belly button in the center of the United States. Freeways crisscrossed it like the bow on a Christmas present. It was a great American road trip just waiting to be opened. East lay Arkansas and the Deep South. North lay a thousand miles of plains, Chicago, and Canada. South was the Mexican border. And in all directions, for days at top speed, it was wide open, a horizon that ever beckoned. A country she'd been hiding in, a strange land.

She left the freeway and pulled into a Love's Travel Stop. At the pump she stuck the nozzle in and surveyed nearby vehicles. Half a dozen eighteen-wheelers and twenty cars and pickups were filling up or parked in front of the minimart.

She topped off the tank and grabbed her messenger bag. She found an old cowboy hat in the back seat and popped a sun hat on Zoe.

"Come on."

They headed into the crowded store. The aisles were stocked with candy and beef jerky, deli sandwiches and Thunder T-shirts. Sarah loaded a basket with food and counted CCTV cameras. One covered the pumps, another the door, a third the cash registers. The hats were a half-assed disguise — like putting sunglasses on Sasquatch.

In a corner was an ATM. Sarah withdrew the maximum, $300, with one of the prepaid cards.

Prepaid cards could be purchased without a credit check. They weren't connected to her bank account. And because funds were front-loaded onto the card, her transactions were never reported to credit agencies.

It wasn't foolproof. If someone found out that she owned a particular card, they could try to burrow into her account and track her through her purchases. But doing that took power or money. It took the government or a wealthy stalker.

Today she had to count on both coming after her.

A young mother with a baby and a squirming toddler walked past her into the women's room. Sarah took Zoe's hand and followed the woman in.

The mother slung her diaper bag onto the counter and ushered her little boy into a stall, saying, "Hold on, hold on."

Sarah told Zoe, "You go."

When Zoe locked the stall door, Sarah turned to the diaper bag. She had only a few seconds. She took out her phone, set the ringer to silent, and activated its GPS.

The diaper bag was stuffed with the complete baby field kit. She stuck her phone inside and covered it with spit-up rags and toys.

Thinking: *Apologies, honey. But kids come first.*

Zoe finished up, washed her hands, and

they hurried out. Sarah paid for their gas and food with cash. Outside, she told Zoe: "Hop in and buckle up."

From her go-bag Sarah got a roll of duct tape. She removed the portable satnav from the dashboard. It was registered to the network and would be linked back to her, though officially it was the property of DHL Attorney Services.

She surreptitiously checked the big rigs parked at the diesel pumps. She picked one with Minnesota plates.

Casually she walked to the rear of the rig. Nobody was watching. She pulled off a long strip of duct tape, tore it with her teeth, and ducked beneath the rig. Underneath, it was hot and cramped and smelled of oil. The axle was coated with greasy dirt. She reluctantly wiped it with one hand. She set the satnav on top and wound the duct tape around and around the axle, sealing it like a larva in a chrysalis.

She scuttled out from under the trailer and hopped back in the truck.

"You buckled up?" she said to Zoe.

"What were you doing, Mommy?"

Sarah dug for a grease rag on the floor. She wiped her hands. "Playing a game."

It was called *Sorry,* and would be played by all. With luck, it would be played two thousand miles from here, in all the wrong directions. She started the engine and pulled away from the pumps. Behind her the city rose out of the prairie, shining in the sun. She checked the rearview mirror and kissed it all good-bye. She pulled onto I-40 and headed west.

13

Special Agent Curtis Harker held up the mug shot so the OKCPD detectives got a clear view.

"Eldrick Worthe is the head of a criminal family that extends across four Western states. He has enthusiastically practiced stealing, bearing false witness, coveting his neighbor's wife, and killing — strangers, rivals, and his own flesh and blood whom he thinks have betrayed him. He is the patriarch and self-proclaimed prophet of the Fiery Branch of the New Covenant."

Detective Dos Santos said, "I've heard about Worthe. The Holy Spirit descended on him while he was smoking crank and cleaning his shotguns. After that his every order became divine revelation. Great way to keep his family in line."

"He demands their complete obedience," Harker said. "People who opposed him became 'obstacles to the work of the Lord.'

So he removed them. His vendettas became 'blood atonement.' His prophecies read like a cross between the King James Bible, Hallmark Mother's Day cards, and slasher lit."

Harker held up another photo: Worthe in court, in an orange jumpsuit. His hair was a gray tangle of Last Judgment proportions, rising above his skull like flames. He appeared to be shouting.

"This was at his sentencing. He called the judge a man-whoring tapeworm whom God will strike dead with lightning to the skull."

"Charming," said Detective Bukin.

"Judge Partyka has been guarded by a protective detail from the U.S. Marshals Service for the past six years."

Dos Santos said, "What does this have to do with Zoe Keller?"

"She's the patriarch's grandchild. The daughter of an apostate. The clan will want to bring her into the fold."

"Why?"

"Perhaps so they can marry her to one of Worthe's lieutenants when she turns twelve. Perhaps so they can sacrifice her to atone for her father's betrayal."

"They'd kill her?"

"They'd slit her throat and let the blood run across the floor," Harker said.

The detectives around the desk went quiet.

"The Worthes are white trash mafia who got a bad dose of God. They're the twenty-first-century's version of moonshiners, but more violent and egomaniacal. They think it's them and the Seraphim against the Man — and the Man is you and me and anybody who participates in government of the people, by the people, for the people."

Harker slid a new photo onto the table. The detectives shifted and one looked away.

The photo showed the aftermath of a courthouse bombing. It had been taken six years earlier when two pounds of dynamite and nails and ball bearings exploded outside the United States District Courthouse in Denver, where Eldrick Worthe was standing trial. The bomber had placed the device in a brown super-size fast-food bag, dropped it beside a bench in the plaza outside, and walked into the courthouse.

The glass front of the building was shattered. The plaza was blackened and pitted from the high-velocity impact of nails and shrapnel. Near the courthouse doors lay two splayed bodies.

"The bomb was remotely detonated by cell phone as Assistant U.S. Attorney Daniel Chavez and FBI Special Agent Campbell

Robinson approached the courthouse," Harker said. "It was a targeted assassination. The clan executed them and called it a cleansing act of retribution."

Bukin said, "Christ."

Harker held up a new photo. "This is the man we believe built the bomb. Grissom Briggs."

Briggs was white — as white as it was possible to be without becoming invisible — with ropy muscles, drowsy eyes, and the buzz cut favored by men who cried *Sieg heil* in private.

"He's the Worthe family's shattering angel. A sword of righteous destruction, if you believe the tattoos. A sociopathic thug if you don't."

Harker brought out two more mug shots. "These girls are Briggs's posse. Reavy and Felicity Worthe. They're Eldrick's granddaughters. Briggs calls them the angel's wings."

The girls had a wild light about them. Teenagers — one blond, one dark-haired — they glared at the camera with disdain and utter confidence. They looked like they wanted to fly at the police photographer and bite through his jugular.

Dos Santos said, "Why are you here, Special Agent Harker?"

"To warn you. After the courthouse bombing, the Worthes scattered to the hills. The bombers have not been apprehended. But if you splash Sarah Keller's name across the news, the clan will crawl out of the woodwork to seize Zoe. You'll find yourself facing a whirlwind, and you had better prepare for it."

Bukin said, "You're after the bombers."

Never underestimate the ability of people to think the obvious, Harker thought. *And to say it out loud, undermining any tactical advantage they might have had.*

He said, "Eldrick Worthe heads a family that includes 37 children, 112 grandchildren, and, at last estimate, 62 great-grandchildren. And at least 13 wives."

Bukin tossed her pen on the table. "Polygamists. Isn't that special."

"If you're Worthe or his sons or anointed goons," he said. "Eldrick's religious awakening was bred from drugs, mountain man paranoia, and narcissistic personality disorder. The point is, he has a large and dysfunctional family army that will go to war to carry out what they think are orders from Heaven."

Dos Santos said, "What's Sarah Keller's part in all this? You saying she's innocent?"

"Hardly. She left her sister dead of a stab

wound in a burning house and ran off with the baby. And the moment her deception was exposed, did she ask for police protection from the Worthes? OKCPD had officers right there in the ER with her. All she had to do was say *please.* Instead she crawled out a window and fled. No, Sarah Keller is complicit."

Bukin said, with a note of doubt, "Zoe Keller is not in the records of the National Center for Missing and Exploited Children."

Harker said, "Have you contacted the cops in California? I suspect they thought Zoe's father had vamoosed with her. Or that they were both dead. But we now know that's not the case," he said. "Maybe they botched the investigation. Maybe they're withholding evidence. Either way, they got it wrong. And you have the opportunity to put it right — if you get on it quickly, before Sarah Keller escapes your jurisdiction."

He gathered the photos and glanced at the clock on the wall. "Tick-tock."

Outside a minute later, walking to his car, he phoned the FBI's travel office. "Am I set?"

"You have a seat on the one-thirty P.M. Frontier flight to Colorado Springs."

"Excellent."

He got in the car and pulled out. The OKC detectives would get it. The photos of the courthouse bombing would drive them to act. Especially in this city, the deaths of a U.S. attorney and an FBI agent would sink in, bruising them like a body blow. They were brother cops.

Zoe Keller was alive. She was in range — like the charge at the center of a blast radius. She was with a civilian, her biological aunt, a woman with no law enforcement or military training, an amateur.

Sarah Keller was the pin in the grenade. Pull her loose and the entire thing would blow.

He drove toward the airport. The prison would be waiting for him. As would Eldrick Worthe.

14

The sun rode west, hauling Sarah toward the green horizon at 70 mph. In the back seat Zoe held Mousie and drowsily watched the miles flow by. The heated sky gleamed with anvil-topped cumulonimbus. They passed Weatherford, Elk City, and Sayre. *Drive,* Sarah told herself. *Foot down.* Her mind spun, revving so fast she thought it might spit gears like broken teeth.

There were right and wrong ways to disappear. She'd tracked people who tried to go off the grid and failed. She knew a dozen ways to do it badly.

One of the dumbest was to create a false identity. A fake driver's license wouldn't fool the police, Immigration and Customs, or the FBI. And a black market ID — one that came with a birth certificate and Social Security number — frequently also came with a bad credit score and even arrest warrants. Not to mention that false IDs weren't necessarily unique. Buy from a crook, and it was possible he'd sold the same identity to ten other people. Assuming a false identity was for spies and the stupid.

But creating new legal identities hadn't been an option for her and Zoe. *Keller* was on Zoe's birth certificate, and Sarah couldn't very well go to court and ask a judge to change it. However, she had informally altered the way she spelled her own first name. Neither her birth certificate nor Social Security card read *Sarah.*

Even dumber than faking an identity was faking your own death. People who tried it ended up in the newspaper and, frequently, in jail. Yet many found it irresistible. They pretended to drown while kayaking. They bailed out of a Cessna over the Sierras. There was even a name for it: pseudocide.

Only faking your death got Coast Guard helicopters searching the oceans. It got the NTSB wondering why the wreckage of the Cessna contained no body. It brought TV news crews and sobbing friends to the campsite where bears supposedly dragged you off into the woods. Faking your death sent up an emergency flare.

No. To disappear successfully you needed to diminish the shadow you cast in people's lives, so that when you vanished, few people would notice or care.

Sarah had forced herself to do that. She had given up the amateur soccer league. She didn't join social networks. She had stopped searching for the truth behind the photo her mother gave her the day she died. *Before the war* hovered there, beckoning, and she ached to know what it meant. She felt she was betraying her ancestors, leaving them suspended in a netherworld. But she didn't dare search for them. The dead could finger her.

The way to disappear was to hang onto your own identity and hide your location. You wanted to stroll out the door and melt into the crowd. And Sarah knew that today she'd done just the opposite. Against that, now she had to evaporate into the vast plains of the Southwest.

On the stereo she heard ringing guitar chords. Foo Fighters, "Wheels." She turned it up, and instantly regretted it.

"And everyone I've loved before flashed before my eyes . . ."

Her throat tightened and she blinked back tears. Mistake number three was the hardest for most people to avoid: sneaking home. But that wouldn't be her problem. Home didn't exist.

Her mother had not simply come from a

refugee family. Atlanta Keller declared herself a free spirit and rejected ties to place, dogma, and tradition. *Mother to two girls, daughter of the Earth,* she used to say.

Sarah never knew her father. Her mom would not talk about him or about what had happened between them. She said only that she loved him, he loved her, and he loved the girls. He was gone. But a dark longing hung over Atlanta, for lost love and a lost history that war and flight had cut her off from.

As kids, Sarah and Beth had imagined their family's past. They held adventures in their tree fort — fantasies where they were ancient horsemen or people running from the Nazis. Maybe fighting them behind the lines.

They always defeated the tree fort demons.

The knot in Sarah's throat felt like a ball of string. Her sister, who grew up to paint *Follow your bliss* on the nursery wall above Zoe's crib, and who tattooed *Free Spirit* across her shoulder in their mom's honor, had gone down fighting.

"Beth, where's the baby?"

Through her dread, Sarah had barely been able to get the words out. She knelt over

97

Beth in the pantry, hands bloody. The stab wound wouldn't stop bleeding.

Beth wheezed. "They told Nolan — get the kid. He didn't move fast enough. Grissom, those girls — broke the door down. Caught me coming out of the pantry."

Sarah put her hand against Beth's cheek. "Where's Zoe?"

Beth looked over her shoulder. "Behind the wall."

Hidden behind the pantry shelves was a crawl space. On the floor, under a pile of blankets, Sarah found her.

She scooped Zoe into her arms, warm and wriggling. Holding her close, she crawled back through the debris.

"She's fine. Look, Beth, she's safe."

In the light Zoe blinked like E.T. and pulled her hands up in front of her face, fists cocked like a tiny boxer. Tears rose in Beth's eyes.

You saved her, Sarah tried to say. The words wouldn't come.

She grabbed Beth's hand. "We have to get you to the ER."

Beth raised her head, grimaced, and dropped back to the floor.

Sarah eased her arm beneath Beth's back and tried to lift her. "We need to hurry."

Beth looked at her tiny daughter, then at

Sarah. "Get Zoe out of here."

"I will. Come on."

She can't. The words rang like a bell, clear and imperative, deep in Sarah's head. They seemed to come from the night world. It was close by, waiting to swallow her sister. She shook her head to clear it and tried again to lift Beth.

Beth pushed her hand away. "Go. Before they come back."

Sarah's grip tightened around Zoe. "The Worthes . . ."

"Not only them," Beth said. "Was supposed to be safe. Only went to Arizona because . . ." She struggled to breathe. "Nolan — the Feds came here. Before."

"The Feds. Federal agents?"

"FBI. Said they'd protect us."

"They wanted Nolan to go to Arizona? Why? To . . ." Dear God. "Inform on his family?"

"Agent — said we would be safe." Beth's eyes were sad and fearful. "I didn't understand. We were . . . tools."

Sarah felt like she'd been doused with ice water. "Come on. Let's go."

"You still don't understand. Get Zoe out of here. Keep her safe." With a brief rush of energy, Beth gripped Sarah's arm. "Don't let anybody take her."

"I won't."

"She's my life." Beth's fingers dug into her arm. "She's all I have now. She's everything."

Sarah nodded, dizzy.

"Take her, Sarah. Protect her. Don't let anybody else touch her. Nobody. You understand?" Beth pinned her with her gaze. "Do you understand? Say it."

"I understand," Sarah whispered. "I'll protect her. Nobody will take Zoe from me."

Beth looked at the baby. Sarah took her sister's hand and put it to Zoe's cheek. The little girl blinked and reached out. But Beth no longer saw her.

Sarah was still bent over Beth, shaking her, crying her name again and again like a litany, trying to fend off the night world and call her back, when she heard a heavy vehicle bump up the gravel driveway toward the house.

She scrambled to her feet. Panic, a sense of uncontrollable fear, hit her like buckshot. Holding Zoe, she grabbed Beth's arm and dragged her from the pantry into the kitchen. A slick of blood painted the floor in their wake.

She peered out the front window. An SUV was creeping down the driveway, lights off in the snowy morning. Fifty yards from the house, still rolling, the doors swung open. Dark figures emerged and loomed on the running boards.

Run.

She let go of Beth's hand and opened the back door. Clutching Zoe, she plunged into the storm.

In Danisha's truck, the music rose, plaintive and bittersweet. The lyrics echoed: *Been looking for a reason, man, something to lose.* Sarah glanced in the mirror.

Zoe had fallen heavily asleep, as children do — intensely asleep, as though it were work, their little bodies avidly consuming the deep rest they need to grow. Her face was pale and peaceful. Her long lashes lay against her cheeks. Mousie hung loosely in her fingers.

When Beth died, Sarah had thought nothing could be worse. How wrong she'd been.

The sun glared white in the windshield. The highway arrowed to the vanishing point on a horizon of wind-bent grass. She wiped away tears with the heel of her hand.

Disappearing was possible. Look at the FBI's Ten Most Wanted list. Those posters of sullen criminals showed men and women who had vanished. Some of them had been on the run for twenty years. If they could do it, so could she.

That's what he'd told her. *Get out of here. Run. Hide.*

Five years earlier she'd done exactly that. Now she was doing it again.

She blew past a road sign. WELCOME TO TEXAS, THE LONE STAR STATE.

15

The sun hung above the peaks of the Rockies, orange against dark crags and slicks of snow. In the high plains desolation of Florence, Colorado, the FBI car turned off the highway into the United States Penitentiary ADX. Neither the Colorado Springs resident agent at the wheel nor Special Agent Curtis Harker spoke. Florence wasn't the kind of place that invited conversation.

The building was redbrick with towering concrete turrets. Around the barren perimeter ran two parallel fences. Coils of razor wire filled the gap between them, a deadly garden of shining vines. Dogs patrolled the inner grounds.

Part of the Federal Correctional Complex, Florence was ADMax: an Administrative Maximum Facility, better known as a supermax prison. It housed felons too dangerous for maximum security institutions. Some called it the Alcatraz of the Rockies.

Here the government imprisoned men who had escaped from other facilities, or killed prison guards, or controlled criminal gangs on the outside.

Men like Eldrick Worthe.

At Florence ADX, cell windows looked out on walls, so inmates could not discern the facility's layout or their location inside it. Prisoners got one phone call a month with family, fifteen minutes, always monitored. Uncontrollable inmates were isolated in their cells up to twenty-three hours a day. Florence housed 9/11's twentieth hijacker, Zacarias Moussaoui, and the Unabomber, Theodore Kaczynski, and the leaders of the Aryan Brotherhood and the Gangster Disciples. A former warden described the place as "a clean version of hell."

They were expecting him.

In the front lobby Harker deposited his service weapon, phone, wallet, and credentials. The Colorado Springs agent said, "I'll wait here." Good choice. Otherwise, she would have had to remove her underwire bra. Harker signed in, had his hand stamped, and was buzzed through the sally port into the visitors' room. A prison official accompanied him.

Aside from the guards he was the only person there, but he bet the warden was watching him on CCTV. It was past normal visiting hours. He sat down at the Plexiglas barrier and waited.

The door on the other side clacked open and two guards escorted in Eldrick Worthe. He wore federal institutional clothing: a white shirt buttoned and tucked into white trousers, an institutional belt, institutional black shoes, and institutional shackles, hand and foot. The guards sat him down and chained him, clinking, to a steel ring cemented into the floor.

Eldrick's skin was flaccid and potato-white. His hair flew in gray streaks above his head, like a greasy crown. His wiry beard spread to his chest. His eyes, deep-set and steady, stared at Harker.

He said, "If you're here to confess your sins and beg for miracles, you need to get on your knees."

"Good to see you, Eldrick," Harker said. "It's truly good to see you chained to the floor and so deprived of sunlight that you might come down with rickets."

Eldrick continued to stare without blinking. "Begging wouldn't work, mind. She's still dead. She'll stay dead. The angels will not raise her up. The Lord will not breathe eternal life into a minion of the Beast."

Harker pressed his hands to the cheap

painted surface of the table. His pulse pounded in his neck. Then he sat back and tightened his necktie. "Don't you get bored, talking all day like a cut-rate Moses?"

"But that's why you're here, ain't it? To talk about redemption? About finding a way to atone?"

"I'm here to talk about the killing of Bethany Keller."

"Bethany died in the blood of her sins. Nothing to do with me."

"You could still be charged with capital murder for that crime."

"And you could find out the buzzing in your ears is blowflies hatching in your brain."

"Stem-winders count as solicitation," Harker said.

Beth Keller had died while Eldrick awaited sentencing in Denver, shortly after he smuggled a bloodcurdling sermon out of jail. Read aloud at his family's scrub-brush paradise near the Grand Canyon, the sermon ordered the Fiery Branch to remove all obstacles to their work, especially unreliable and disobedient women.

Eldrick sucked on his teeth and eyed Harker with disdain.

Part of it was an act. But much of it, Harker thought, was clinical narcissism steeped in fantasies of omnipotence. From what he'd learned through confidential informants, Eldrick's personality was organized around affirming his extraordinarily grandiose sense of himself. He was in Florence ADMax because, at another prison, he had paid an inmate to knife a female guard who dared to exercise authority over him.

Narcissists, the shrinks said, felt empty. That was why they craved constant affirmation. And perhaps emptiness stoked Eldrick Worthe's rage and hatred. His first wife left him and took the kids. He lost money in fly-by-night gold-mining schemes. He was arrested for selling drugs. And his reaction, in every case, was fury at the injustice done to him.

Narcissists who were not given adoration tended to lash out. They punished those who failed to offer it. And so it came to pass that one night, paranoid and high on methamphetamine, Eldrick heard the Holy Spirit giving him orders — which his family was to carry out.

Strangely, the Spirit never ordered Eldrick to tend the sick or feed the hungry. It ordered his family to render unto Eldrick whatever Eldrick wanted, and his lieutenants to punish people who crossed him. It directed his subordinates to give him their daughters in spiritual wedlock, to warm his bed and his sagging body. Few objected. Eldrick was heavily armed and most of his clan lived fifty miles from the nearest sheriff's department. It was the Holy Gospel of I, Me, Mine.

This led to a chain of slashings, shootings, the stocking of an arsenal for the clan's periodic showdowns with rival drug dealers and the DEA, and finally the courthouse bombing that killed Special Agent Campbell Robinson and federal prosecutor Daniel Chavez.

Harker took three photos from his pocket and fanned them on the tabletop.

Eldrick glanced at them. "So you've got my family album. What of it?"

Harker tapped the photos of the two young women, Reavy and Felicity. "I want to interview them. If you put me in touch, I can help you gain privileges."

"In my cell I have the intense freedom of solitude. I don't need your privileges. And is *interview* the FBI term for a takedown with a tactical assault team?"

"Very well. You tell me how to find them, we can arrange for them to surrender themselves safely. And I can keep them off Death Row."

"They fear not death, much less Death

Row. They are the angel's fiery wings. They will fly beyond any attempt to cage them."

Eldrick turned and spat on the floor.

Harker touched the third photo, thinking: *Grissom Briggs is no angel.* "Let's cut the babble. How about you keep your business from dissolving into a war of attrition between your brother, your sons, and your hired thugs?"

That got Eldrick to eye him, momentarily, sidewise.

"Who wanted Beth Keller dead?" Harker said. "Who did that serve — Nolan? He wanted to patch things up with the family. He brought Beth and their baby to Arizona to meet the relatives. But Beth wanted no part of the Worthes, for her or her child. After the visit she kicked him out."

Eldrick's eyes had a peculiar light. Maybe it was delusions of godhead. Maybe it was the fact that one eye was brown, one blue. Even to Harker, it was unsettling.

"Still, I don't get it," Harker said. "Nolan wanted to reconcile with you so bad, he brought the clan his child like a tribute, to be blessed."

"What of it?"

"Yet he never married Beth, and he let his daughter take her mother's name. He didn't legally recognize the child as a Worthe. Talk about a kick in the teeth."

Eldrick didn't react. But Harker knew what must be running through his mind. *Never married? Not a Worthe?*

Eldrick eyed him hard, maybe looking for a tell. Harker emptied his expression.

He didn't intend to reveal how shocked he'd been to learn that Zoe was living with Sarah Keller. The microchip had surprised them all.

Harker knew that Nolan and Beth had visited the Arizona box canyon where the clan had encamped. But he'd never known what happened during the weekend — he never got the chance to interrogate Nolan or Beth. Now he could only face Eldrick Worthe's hideous mask of godliness, and try to work his own dark magic.

"You might feel free in your monk's cell," he said. "But you can only see a two-foot patch of brick outside the window. You can't possibly control your entire extended family. The tribe is beyond reach. Even a prophet's reach."

Eldrick sat motionless, his hands loose on the table. Harker leaned forward.

"Your grasp has grown weak, Eldrick. Nolan escaped from you. Beth wasn't quick enough, but Nolan — he had some of your caginess. I don't know where he is, but he's not with the clan. If he were, his daughter wouldn't be in Oklahoma City."

Eldrick's breathing slowed. Harker smiled.

He said, "Where's Sarah Keller headed? Who's helping her?"

Eldrick blinked and shifted his shoulders.

Harker paused, taken aback. "You don't know."

He straightened, processing. "It's worse than I imagined. Your intelligence network has become slipshod. You can't even keep track of your own progeny. Sarah Keller's a lowly skip tracer and she probably knows more about the family than you do." He half-laughed and tapped the photos on the table. "And your Shattering Angel is sidelined. He and your granddaughters may be living on the Mexican Riviera — on your dime — but they're not keeping control of the clan the way you want. They can't."

Eldrick didn't speak.

"After the courthouse bombing, I know the family sent Grissom and the girls into the wilderness to evade arrest. But they've been exiled a long time now. They have to be lonely. And they're the ones whose lives are on the line. They'll look out for number one. When they run out of money, or when they can't stand their banishment one more second, what's next? They come to us for protection."

Harker leaned forward. "This is your last chance to help yourself. Your operation isn't going to last long. So what'll it be? You want to talk to me?"

Eldrick turned to the guard. "Take me back to my cell."

16

One phone call a month. Fifteen minutes, that's what inmates were allowed, but Eldrick Worthe hadn't taken his allotted call in six months. His family came to the prison on visiting days, one wife at a time until each had seen him, and that was enough. He didn't waste his energies making phone calls to women. If he needed to contact his brother, he wrote.

But ten seconds after he was escorted from the visitors' room, he told the guards, "I want my fifteen minutes. Today."

They led him to the pay phone. He raised his shackled hands and made a collect call to his brother Isom, at the trailer he kept behind a minimart in Winslow, Arizona.

Isom accepted the charges immediately. "Brother, it's good to hear your voice."

Isom hated him. Eldrick didn't care about that either. What counted was that Isom feared him mightily, and would do exactly as he said.

"Is your health holding? You sound like you're hacking up a hairball," Eldrick said.

"Can't complain."

"And the family? Tell me about each of them, down to the youngest."

Isom hesitated, but only a second. "The grands and great-grands are thriving. I swear they shine like gold coins under the eyes of heaven."

"Are they obedient?"

"If any act rebellious, they're reminded the Lord requires them to walk in his paths."

" 'This shall they have for their pride, because they have reproached and magnified *themselves* against the people of the Lord of hosts. The Lord *will be* terrible unto them.' Chapter and verse, Isom. Read to them from the book of Obadiah. The story of the Exodus. The lessons of Abram and Sarai, how they were given new names and lives because of their submission to the Almighty. And remind them of the gospel of Mark — the Lord at the house of the leper. It's your responsibility."

"I won't let it slide," Isom said.

"Give the littlest ones my love. I miss them so. The ones I've never seen . . . it pains me."

"I'm sure it pains them too."

"That's the greatest loss I experience. That those babes have been left to grow without my oversight. They should be found, and blessed, and brought into the fold."

"Amen."

Eldrick's shackled hands awkwardly gripped the phone. "You still like the Heat for the NBA title? 'Cause I think it's finally the Thunder's year."

Isom snorted. "Fat chance. Talk to you later, Eldrick."

Eldrick hung up. Isom would know that when the Thunder rolled, angels flew.

Four hundred miles away, Isom Worthe replaced the handset. He had already decoded Eldrick's message. It was damn surprising.

Zephaniah, Obadiah, Exodus. Jesus at the leper's house in Bethany.

Beth's child, Zoe, was alive. With a woman named Sarah. In Oklahoma City.

He got his cell phone and lit a cigarette and walked out of the trailer and down the steps into the sandy wash behind the minimart. He punched in a number he used infrequently.

It was answered on the tenth ring. "What?"

"I have exciting news for you."

"Isom," said Grissom Briggs, maybe in acknowledgment, maybe in acquiescence. News, in Grissom's world, meant a job.

"One of the lambs we thought was lost forever has been found."

Grissom waited. Grissom didn't like to talk.

"A babe," Isom said. "That you shall return to the flock."

When he ended the phone call, Grissom Briggs leaned on his shovel at the construction site. He took off the hard hat and wiped his brow. The sun glared in the empty California sky, shining on San Francisco's blue-glass skyscrapers and rickety Tenderloin hotels and the granite buildings near the Civic Center. This was the badlands — asphalt and junkies and lawyers, a proving ground, an almost biblical wasteland.

The foreman walked past, a walkie-talkie to his mouth. Grissom whistled and jerked a thumb over his shoulder. "Gotta hit the can."

The foreman nodded. "Sure" — he paused before the name came back to him — "five minutes, Barry." He continued toward the far side of the site.

Grissom dropped his shovel. He walked

toward the blue Porta-John and straight on past. He shucked off his orange safety vest and tossed it and the hard hat in a Dumpster. The vest and hat might be missed, but he wouldn't. He was casual labor, chosen from a line of men who waited every morning on a street corner, hoping for a chance to dig the office tower's sewer trenches. The foreman paid him in cash at the end of the day. Considering that the project was spitting distance from the San Francisco Federal Building and a mess of courthouses, getting paid under the table was the best part of the job, a middle finger to the government.

He walked off the site and down Mission Street. He felt as if he were stepping back into the world of eternity. The local tweakers who relied on him to provide meth from the Worthe family's fountain of crank, they'd have to survive their holiday weekend some other way. He'd just been given a new assignment — a greater, deeper mission. And it was urgent.

He phoned the crumbling hotel around the corner on Market Street. "Get to the airport."

"Just me?"

"Cinda can stay put. The room's paid up

through July," he told her. "I'll call your sister."

He pushed through the door into a coffee place called Tank Up. At the cash register, small and pale, Cinda was ringing up a customer. When she saw him, she jumped like a rabbit.

He frowned. She was seventeen — she should have been calmer. He waited until the customer left.

"Gotta hit the road for a spell. Keep the room at the Blue Angel."

She glanced out the window at the sun-bleached street and the Court of Appeals and the Federal Building. He could practically see her rabbit heart pounding, hear her thinking: *Police. FBI. U.S. Marshals.*

"You keep watching, just like that. You're safe at the hotel," he said. "Nobody knows your real name. And you got the fire escape onto the alley."

"Okay," she said, almost whispering. "Fine, Grissom."

Cinda would stay put. She was easily frightened. She was his wife.

"How long will you be . . ."

"Hush."

She closed her mouth.

He nodded at her SAN FRANCISCO: TANK UP T-shirt. "Get me one of them. This shirt's filthy."

She scurried to the back room. From the counter he grabbed a couple of TANK UP matchbooks, along with ten bucks from the tip jar. He phoned the storage locker south of town where his right hand was camped.

"The airport?" she said. "What's up?"

Cinda returned and handed him a white T-shirt. In black letters it said SFTU. He smiled. Close enough to what he wanted to tell the TSA.

He said, "We're going to Oklahoma City for the family reunion."

17

Past Shamrock, Sarah pulled off the highway at a rest stop. Thunderheads were piling up to the west, blindingly white anvil tops spread against the stratosphere. The sun glared gold from beneath them.

She killed the engine. "Okay, firefly, let's stretch our legs."

Zoe stirred, her face flushed, and looked around with the off-kilter bewilderment of someone roused from a heavy dream. Outside, a hot wind greeted them. Zoe rubbed the heel of her hand against her face.

"Is this Texas?" she said.

"Big, huh?"

Sarah got their groceries and they headed to a picnic table under a grove of low-hanging oaks.

Zoe looked around. "Where are we going, Mom?"

"We're camping," Sarah said. "We're going to stay here tonight."

Zoe still looked half-gone in the nether-world of sleep. The wind lifted her hair. "What are you scared of?"

Sarah froze. "Nothing, honey."

Zoe held her gaze. Her little mouth drew into a line. *Busted.*

Sarah sat down beside her on the picnic bench. "It's nothing for you to worry about. It's grown-up stuff."

"Am I going to miss school next week?"

Sarah felt a pang. "Afraid so."

"But it's my turn to feed the gecko. I'm supposed to."

Sarah smiled feebly and stroked a lock of hair from Zoe's eyes. "Ms. Lark will make sure the gecko gets fed."

Zoe watched her face. After a second, she stared down at the table. *Hmmph.*

They ate under the oaks, with the wind gusting and traffic sluicing past. When Zoe finished her sandwich, she climbed off the picnic bench and ran around collecting acorns. Sarah got one of her prepaid throw-away phones, fired it up, and went online.

When disappearing, a common mistake was to Google yourself. Fear and longing made people itch to know if anybody was talking about them. So they searched for their own name to see if friends had posted emotional pleas for their safe return.

121

It was often a trap. Skip tracers, cops, or stalkers could easily set up websites about missing people, begging for leads. Then they captured incoming IP addresses and traced their location.

So Sarah didn't search for her own name. She checked the headlines. The bus accident had made the NewsOK site. The story mentioned no names, and she felt a pinch of relief. Then she saw *Breaking: Child in bus crash may be baby from fire death case.*

"Oh, no."

The trees shivered and the grass bent flat beneath the wind. Sarah grabbed paper plates before they blew off the picnic table. The thunderheads were swelling into a charcoal mass above the plains. The sky beneath them was a slick of sickly yellow light.

Zoe ran over to her. She was holding the hem of her T-shirt turned up like a basket, full of acorns. "Mommy, hurry."

Sarah gathered their things. "It's okay, I don't see lightning."

Zoe tipped her head up and eyed the clouds. "It's waiting."

Sarah turned. "What?"

"Inside the dark. It's far away, but it's coming."

A coil of fear tightened around Sarah's

chest. She took Zoe's hand. "Let's go."

At the storefront office of DHL Attorney Services, Danisha Helms dropped into her desk chair and rubbed her forehead. She was the last one there. The computer screens that monitored dockets at state and federal courthouses were dark. The evening light slatted through the blinds. She was waiting.

She didn't know who she'd hear from first. In her secret heart she pleaded that it be Sarah, but she knew that was a fantasy. Girl was *gone.* Sarah might think she was coming home in a day or two, a little shaken, a little tired, apologizing and handing back the keys to the truck.

She wasn't coming back.

Whatever Sarah was running from wasn't a problem that could be solved with a weekend away. Pulling Zoe out of school? Telling Danisha she should speak honestly to the authorities? Heavy trouble was dogging Sarah's tail.

Across the room, Sarah's desk looked forlorn. Danisha stood and walked over to it. Sarah's taste was spare, but now she noticed how it was almost invisible: no photos, not even of Zoe. Instead Sarah had framed Zoe's kindergarten crayon drawings.

The frames covered Zoe's childish signature.

She thought of Sarah's gratitude and urgency back at Arcadia Lake. Uneasily, she pondered Sarah keeping a go-bag ready for a five-year-old.

How well did she really know her friend?

Well enough to love her. Not well enough to know what the hell had happened in the woman's life before she applied for a job at DHL.

Sarah had left a bandanna on the desk. Danisha picked it up. For a second the office seemed to echo with Sarah's melancholy laugh and the faint strains of music, "In the Arms of the Angel." Sarah had declared it *that damn song* because it made them both tear up, and because late one night, as they sat side by side on the floor in Sarah's living room, it nearly induced Sarah to open up. That line about being pulled from the wreckage. Danisha watched it bring pain to Sarah's eyes.

She said, "Who'd you leave behind?"

Sarah paused, beer bottle halfway to her lips. "You're getting sentimental, Dani."

"You have a kid. Had to be somebody, honey."

Sarah's smile looked both sad and savage. "If I told you the last time a man put his

124

arms around me and whispered in my ear, you wouldn't believe it."

Danisha held her gaze.

Sarah's smile faded. Quietly she said, "There's nobody."

The look in Sarah's eyes, fierce and lonely, lingered even now.

The office door opened and two police detectives came in. Both white, the man with a neat goatee, the woman hefty enough to tackle a refrigerator to the ground. Danisha stood waiting.

The man flashed his badge. *Dos Santos.* "Is Sarah Keller here?"

"No."

"Do you expect her back today?"

"No."

His twang bent so tight he must have learned it from the country music channel. He ran his gaze over her, head to toe. "And you are?"

"Danisha Helms." She handed him her business card.

"Do you know where we can find Ms. Keller?"

"No."

"When did you last speak to her?"

If the cops come calling, tell them everything. Be honest. It won't hurt me, and it'll help you.

125

But Danisha balked. Call it contrariness, or her ornery streak. She instinctively resisted people who waved the cudgel of Authority. Then she seemed to see Sarah in the corner, shaking her head and rolling her eyes.

"This morning," she said. "When she picked her daughter up."

"The child is not her daughter."

"An adopted child is still very much a daughter."

"So you know she's not the girl's mother."

Danisha raised her eyebrows. "Did you hear a word of what I just said?"

The woman, Detective Bukin, put up a hand to stop the conversation. "Do you have Ms. Keller's home address?"

"Why do you want to know?"

Dos Santos said, "We're the police. We need to speak to her. And her driver's license defaults to a ghost street address."

Bukin said, "She's suspected of kidnapping and murder."

"Sarah? That's Looney Tunes."

"There's nothing funny here. Considering you took the little girl from St. Anthony and handed her to Ms. Keller, you could be considered an accessory to child abduction."

The office abruptly felt cold. "Sarah asked

me to watch Zoe while she spoke to the hospital staff. The ER doctor had signed off on her discharge. I'm listed with Zoe's school as a designated adult who has permission to pick her up. Zoe even asked me the secret password, which I gave, in front of the nursing staff. So don't try 'accessory' on me." She crossed her arms. "Sweet Jesus, the child had been in a bus crash and spent an hour alone in the ER. She did not need to endure another minute there while her mom dealt with a family issue."

Dos Santos said, "Keller killed her sister. That's one hell of a family issue."

Danisha slowly, firmly shook her head. "I know about Beth Keller's death. I know it came at the hands of her boyfriend's family."

Bukin raised a hand. "Whoa. What?"

Danisha repeated what Sarah had told her that morning about the Worthes. "Beth asked Sarah to take Zoe, and she's been keeping her safe ever since. Sarah had no part in her sister's death."

The cops watched her for a moment. They glanced at each other. Then Dos Santos took a long, searching look around the office, eyeing the computers and file cabinets.

"Which desk is hers?" he said.

"Get a warrant."

Dos Santos stroked his goatee. "This is going to be a very big problem, very soon. You don't want it to be *your* problem."

"I play by the rules. I know you will too," she said.

After a frustrated moment, they turned to go. At the door Dos Santos paused. "It won't take us long. And when we come back, we'll remember how this office looked."

"I'll see you then. You'll have to bring your own confetti and party streamers."

The door eased shut behind them, the blinds clanging against the glass.

Danisha leaned back against her desk. *Jesus, tell me I'm doing the right thing.* The detectives hadn't asked about the truck.

Sunset spilled across the prairie, red sky bleeding onto red dirt at Oklahoma City's Will Rogers World Airport. Grissom Briggs stepped out of the terminal into a humid wind.

He paused to catch the scent of the land. The heat and weight of the air told him this place was infected. A jet powered up and roared down the runway into the deepening sky. Behind him the women approached.

"Feel it?" he said.

The girls stepped forward, one on either

side of him. The wind lifted Reavy's pale hair from her shoulders. She wet her lips. Her eyes, always suspicious, scanned the terrain. Far to the west, toward Texas, a line of storm clouds blackened the horizon.

"This place is lost. And they don't know it," she said. "That gives us the advantage. They won't be expecting us."

Fell's gaze swept past the airport control tower and the pecan trees where locusts thrummed, toward the smattering of lights in downtown skyscrapers miles away. Her near-black hair blew across her face.

She said, "The woman will be expecting us. Keller."

Grissom said, "So we don't go straight at Keller, do we?"

Fell shook her head. "From behind."

That pleased him. "Come on."

He rented an SUV, using an Arizona driver's license that said *Barry Briggs.* It belonged to his brother, who looked like him and who had a perfect driving record because he'd been dead eighteen months.

Accelerating onto the freeway, he turned to Reavy. "First stop?"

The glow from her phone lit her face, shadows around her eyes. "Half a dozen attorney services in the metro area. Two with

skip tracing capability." She looked up.
"Head downtown. Start with DHL."

18

The hailstorm came as they ran to the truck. Lightning split the air. The temperature dropped, the trees slashed under the wind, and the sky spilled a torrent of ice. Pebbles bounced off the ground and pinged Sarah and Zoe in the back of the neck.

"Oww, hurry," Zoe said.

They jumped in the cab and slammed the door. The hail turned to ice cubes and golf balls. The clouds seethed overhead.

They couldn't stay here. Couldn't possibly camp. This could turn into a night of tornadoes, and Sarah wasn't going to take shelter in a rest area bathroom with her child, while Danisha's truck flew away to Kansas.

The noise increased, the hail thrumming down.

Zoe said, "Mommy, go."

Sarah whipped out of the parking space. Hail stuck to the windshield wipers and formed a ledge of ice. She drove toward town, looking for a safe haven, listening for tornado sirens. She turned on the radio.

". . . Oklahoma City police have issued a bulletin about a possible child abduction. In a bizarre case, a kindergartner involved in a school bus accident this morning was discovered not to be the daughter of . . ."

Sarah lowered the volume.

Zoe said, "He's talking about my school bus."

Stupid. Inevitable. "Maybe."

"The child and the woman who claimed to be her mother have now disappeared. Sarah Kel—"

She turned the radio off.

You knew this was coming.

"Mommy, he was talking about you."

The hail clacked against the windshield. "I know, honey."

"Why?"

"I'll tell you when we get . . ." *Idiot.* "Let me get out of this hailstorm."

"But the clouds are everywhere," Zoe said.

At Will Rogers station, detectives Dos Santos and Bukin watched the TV news bulletin.

". . . Keller is believed to be driving a beige Nissan truck with Oklahoma

132

plates . . .”

On-screen flashed Sarah Keller's driver's license photo and the tag number of her pickup.

Bukin tapped her pen relentlessly against her desk. "It's a start, but it's not an Amber Alert."

Amber Alerts were intended to mobilize the public and rescue children kidnapped by predators. But before an alert could be issued nationwide, law enforcement needed to be certain a child had been abducted — and that she was in imminent danger of death or serious injury. In Zoe Keller's case, Bukin and Dos Santos weren't there yet. They were waiting to hear back from California officials, particularly the Santa Cruz County Sheriff's Department, which had investigated Bethany Keller's death.

In the meantime they had obtained Sarah Keller's cell phone number. They'd requested information from the phone company on Keller's recent calls and the phone's location. And they'd learned that Keller's skip tracing equipment included a satnav system — DHL had coughed up for a portable dashboard GPS whose location could be tracked. They were waiting for a callback from the satnav company.

Bukin tapped her pen. Dos Santos paced,

biting his thumbnail. Bukin said, "What else is eating at you?"

"Something's off about this," he said. "It should have been big news long ago."

"Meaning, a young mother's murdered, dad and the baby disappear — it should have made national headlines."

"The news channels, Court TV, tabloids . . ."

But it hadn't. On Bukin's desk lay a slim stack of news articles about Beth Keller's death. Their gist: "Bear Creek woman dies in house fire."

Dos Santos stroked his goatee. "Special Agent Harker was certainly gung-ho to point blame at Sarah Keller and light a fire under our feet. What's his real angle?"

"You're saying it's either a cover-up or a stitch-up."

"Either the California cops were completely clueless, or we're being played like yo-yos at the end of a string." He checked his watch. "Still business hours on the West Coast. I'll call the Santa Cruz Sheriff's Department again, try to talk to the investigating officer on the case."

"Detective?"

Bukin looked up. Across the room, the desk officer was waving at her. "Southwest Security's on the line — they've located the

Keller woman's satnav."

Three minutes later Bukin dropped her desk phone back in its cradle. "Sarah Keller's portable GPS is live and headed east on I-40. It just passed through Lonoke, Arkansas." She found the number for the Arkansas State Police. "I'll call the troopers."

As she punched the number, Dos Santos's phone rang. He answered, listened, and abruptly straightened. He snapped his fingers to get Bukin's attention. Into the phone he said, "Is that so?"

In the parking lot outside Burger King, the Topeka police officer put away the radio. The patrol car's lights flashed in the hot evening sun. Traffic rolled noisily along the road nearby. In the blue station wagon parked outside the restaurant, the family was hunched and nervous. A baby squalled in the back seat.

The mother stood beside the car, arms crossed, rocking back and forth. "Go on, search the car. I told you, that's not my phone. I don't know how it got into my diaper bag."

"Yes, ma'am."

The phone belonging to Sarah Keller was bagged and in the officer's hand. The baby in the back seat kicked and screamed.

"I have no clue what's going on," the mother said. "We're on our way back to Kansas City. My name's Kelly Hardwick. That's my crying baby and my two-year-old boy. I don't have a five-year-old girl. Jesus Christ, what is wrong with you people?"

19

The motel lobby was crowded. A bus carrying a high school marching band to a Memorial Day competition had pulled in, the driver and band director deciding not to risk the road in the thunderstorm. Around Sarah four dozen teenagers talked at high volume. Perched on a chair by the plate glass windows, Zoe took in the scene, backlit by headlights on the highway and rain blowing sideways in the wind. Another bolt of lightning sliced the sky. The teens gasped and laughed.

Sarah finally got to the desk. She handed the clerk a prepaid card in the name of S. C. Keller and smeared her signature.

"You've got your hands full," she said. "But better safe than sorry."

The clerk nodded distractedly and handed her the room key. "Enjoy your stay, Ms. . . . Keiler."

She parked the truck at the farthest corner

of the lot, front end out, hiding its Oklahoma plate. Motel owners sometimes snuck out at night to write down the license numbers of guests' vehicles, but Sarah hoped the manager might be unwilling to slog through pouring rain into soggy grass and weeds to copy down the number from the back.

Cops would be another matter.

The room décor was concrete breezeblock painted gray. The bedspreads were gold nylon. A placard said nonsmoking room, but a stale tang of smoke permeated the drapes and carpet.

Zoe hopped on a bed. "This one's mine."

"As you wish, Buttercup."

She drew the drapes and threw the dead bolt. Zoe set Mousie on the pillows and said, "I'm tired."

"Brush your teeth and put on your PJs."

While Zoe was in the bathroom, she turned on the TV news. *Movie star attacked by chimpanzee. Court to hear arguments in Second Amendment case.* Sarah no longer knew where she fell on the issue of gun control. Destroy all firearms, except the ones she needed to defend Zoe? *Bus crash child may be missing baby.*

"Authorities in Oklahoma have instituted an all-points bulletin for a woman suspected of child abduction. It's a bizarre and fast-developing case . . ."

She hit Mute. Her driver's license photo flashed on the screen. Next to it were her name, description, and *last seen*. It said she was traveling with a five-year-old girl who answered to *Zoe*. And up popped her daughter's class photo.

Her heart thumped heavy in her chest.

She wondered if Danisha was watching this. She wondered what the instructors at the Y's self-defense class were thinking about her. And the instructors at the firing range.

The bathroom light turned off and Zoe trooped out. She looked sleepy. She'd had a hell of a day. Sarah flicked the TV off.

When Sarah tucked her in, Zoe gave her the big-eyed, serious look, and Sarah waited for it. For questions about grown-up trouble, or about Nolan Worthe and Bethany Keller, the father and mother she had never once mentioned.

Zoe sighed. "Where are we going, Mommy?"

Sarah felt almost relieved. "To San Francisco." Why not?

"Really? To the beach?"

"Really." She kissed her good night.

Later, when Zoe lay burrowed in the covers with Mousie tucked lovingly under her chin, Sarah took her burn phone into the bathroom and shut the door.

Unless she got Zoe to real safety, Beth's sacrifice would be for nothing. And *Why not?* didn't count as a real plan. She paced, tapping the phone against her forehead.

She could call A. J. Chivers. That's what Danisha would counsel: Get DHL's lawyer involved. She brought up his number. Her thumb hovered over it.

Sarah knew what A.J. could and couldn't do. Even a shrewd lawyer had limited options. And in her case, they all involved going back to Oklahoma City. They all involved tabloid hysteria, and the cops, and Zoe being taken into foster care. She might as well paint a sloppy red X on the door as a target for the Worthes to attack.

She sat on the edge of the bathtub. She brought up a different number. She stared at it with trepidation.

"Screw it." She dialed.

She pinched the bridge of her nose and listened for the call to connect. Through the air, across thousands of miles, forging a bridge across the years.

He had promised this number would always be in service, that he would be there on the other end. She tried to work out what she was going to say.

It rang.

The phone rang on the coffee table in the darkened living room. He climbed down the stairs from the loft to get it. The evening dusk of the Cascades was tilting through the plate-glass windows. He'd spent the previous night on duty, caught a flight up here for the holiday weekend, and slept through the afternoon. Daylight was fading. The phone was insistent.

He picked up. "Lawless."

"Michael."

The voice sounded distant, and static flared on the line. Like the caller was phoning through an electrical storm.

He raised his head and gazed out the floor-to-ceiling windows. The eastern sky beyond the Three Sisters had fallen to a gray and purple night. The peaks of the volcanoes rose above the green boughs of the forest. The snow was tinged red with the sunset.

He walked to the windows. "What's happened?"

There was a pause. Had he gotten it wrong?

Then she said, "I'm blown. And running."

In her ashen voice, the anguish and the desperation came through clear, and brought it all back.

In the motel bathroom, Sarah leaned against the wall and spoke in a hush. "I'm headed west, with Zoe."

"She's all right?"

"For now."

"Are you in a safe location?" he said.

"A motel. Safe from one storm for the moment. Not safe for more than twelve hours, I'd wager."

He hadn't asked who it was. He heard her say his name, and he knew. It both reassured and unsettled her.

"What do you need?" he said.

"Help. Backup. A safe place to stay while I sort all this out." She pushed away from the wall. "A way out. Legal, illegal. A border. New documents. Something."

"Give me the story."

"Turn on your television, Lawless. I'm the story."

He paused. "You don't think I . . ."

"No. I don't think you had anything to do with this."

Not directly. Not in the last twelve hours.

But five years earlier, he had shifted her compass. Running through the snow, clinging to the baby, she had looked back and seen three dark figures emerge from Beth's cabin. A man and two women — *Grissom and those girls.*

She ducked behind a tree. Their voices carried to her on the wind.

"Nolan. Yeah, got to be . . ."

". . . baby. Here someplace. Keep looking."

They thought Nolan had run off with Zoe. Sarah stifled a sob. Her hands were seriously bloody. The snow pricked her face.

She peered fearfully around the tree trunk. She could see no sign of Nolan. The dark figures slid out of sight, headed away from her. This deep in the trees, the snow hadn't yet covered the ground, so her footprints had died out. Still, she took a breath and ran again, careless of all the things she would learn in the next few years: covering her tracks, leaving false trails. She tore through the forest, barely aware that the axis of her life had radically shifted to spin in dark new directions. She just ran.

Until he stepped from the trees into her path.

She drew up sharply. She felt charged with lightning, as if she could blow him out of the forest if he came one step closer. He had dark eyes. A scar ran through one brow and down to his cheek.

"Stop right there," she said. "Or I'll kill you."

And he said, "Wait."

In his right hand he held a pistol. In his left he held a badge.

"If you want to stay alive, let me help you," he said.

She said, "I need help."

Through the phone, his voice was calm. "Take it from the top and don't leave anything out."

It took her twenty minutes. He listened and asked only for clarifications. She wondered if he'd known about her life with Zoe in Oklahoma all along. They'd met only a few times, that day in the forest and in the fraught hours that followed, but he seemed to have gotten inside her skin.

When she finished talking, he was quiet for a minute. He said, "You could surrender yourself."

"You know that's off the table." Anger flared in her. "Maybe you had to suggest that, but no. Walk into some police station and submit to a potential murder charge? No."

He was quiet another long minute. "Can you get to New Mexico?"

That meant several hundred miles of driving, with a target painted on her back. "Yes."

"Then I'll arrange to have a friend meet you. What are you driving?"

"My boss's truck."

"Do the police know that?"

"Not yet." Then she said, "Michael . . . where will this end?"

"I don't know. But if we can keep you and Zoe safe, we'll have time to figure that out."

"We?" she said.

"You and me."

Her lips parted. He wasn't adding the rest, the words she loathed and feared and had hoped for: you and me and the U.S. Marshals Service.

"Thank you, deputy marshal," she said.

"Get some rest. You're going to need it."

Then he was gone. She leaned on the sink, hoping she hadn't just signed her death warrant.

20

In the first minutes after dawn, noise droned from the elevated freeway. Fell stared at traffic through a slit in the motel curtains. She had the night watch. She sat in a cheap chair by the window, knees drawn up, knuckles white, switchblade gripped in her right hand.

"All quiet," she said.

From the bed Grissom grunted. "Didn't think you knew I was awake."

"Your breathing changes," she said.

She was barefoot, in cotton panties and a white tank top. The tattoo, the cross with the comet's tail inked on her right hip, looked black in the dim light. She retracted the blade of the knife, her guard duties done.

Reavy lay in bed beside Grissom, blond hair feathered across her cheek. Her eyes were open. He propped himself on an elbow, pulled down the covers, and ran his fingers across her hip.

Fell and Reavy were not Grissom's ordinary wives. They didn't live with him or carry his name. But when Grissom took them on a job, they were wives of the wind, assigned to bond with him. And Grissom said only lovers could build the link required to know each other's thoughts, words, moves. If things came to a firefight, having sex could save your life.

Reavy dug it. Fell didn't mind standing watch. Fell had been a wife before.

She and Reavy were Eldrick Worthe's granddaughters. They were blood of the first blood, sealed in the blessing ceremony, bound, branded, and committed bone and soul to the clan. So said Eldrick, and Isom, and their mothers. They were obedient unto death.

In other words: fuck with the family, and they'd fuck you back twice as hard and four times as dirty. Fell knew that. That's why this job was so big. Get the kid back. Make the family whole. Nothing was bigger than that.

"DHL Attorney Services is owned by Danisha Helms. Zingasearch got me her address and phone number. Also her mother's address," she said.

Grissom stretched and stood up. He was

tan, his physique cut from working construction. "Good. You make coffee. I'm
gonna shower. Reavy?"

The angel's wings were sworn and dedi-
cated. They were skilled and merciless. But
they were also federal fugitives. And here on
the road, they outnumbered Grissom. He
liked to keep one of them within arm's
reach, hostage against the possibility that
the other would bolt or turn on him. The
trio was a team, but in math, two out of
three was a satanic ratio — two-thirds, .666,
number of the Beast.

Reavy headed sleepily to the bathroom
and turned on the shower. Grissom followed her. Fell got dressed, watching them
through the open door. Grissom didn't
worry about Reavy running, even though he
had no chattel hostage against her. Reavy
loved this.

He got the soap and scrubbed. He liked
to be clean before he embarked on a blood-
ing.

21

The fire in the fireplace had dwindled to a red glow. It was four-thirty A.M. in Oregon, the sky velvet-black and shotgunned with stars. Lawless stood at the plate-glass windows. The mountains loomed above the forest, sentinels, so old, and only sleeping. Sisters.

Michael.

Her voice had sounded strong. Smooth, and fierce, and urgent. She had said his name and trusted that he would know who was calling.

It had been five years. Yet when he heard her voice he exhaled as if he'd taken a punch in the gut. Sarah Keller. It couldn't have been anybody else. On the phone, her voice sounded exactly like her sister's. But Beth Keller's voice could only be heard in memory now. Sarah was still out there.

With each passing year, he had tried to convince himself that silence from Sarah meant she was safe, and safer, and out of reach. That silence meant everybody else had forgotten what happened at the cabin in the mountains, and had gone on with their lives, unmindful of her and the baby she had rescued.

He chided himself. *Is that what they taught you when you put on the star?* No.

He turned from the windows. The banked red glow of the fire cast devilish shadows across the room. He got his phone.

The number he looked up wasn't in his U.S. Marshals's official directory. It was part of his informal network. In the five years since Beth Keller's house turned into a torch in the snow, he had built a silent second roster of people he could rely on, separate from his colleagues and paid informants. Fugitive apprehension was the Marshals's long-standing mission, and sometimes catching fugitives meant searching the gullies and backwaters where people stayed out of sight.

He would have to hold off until a civilized hour to call his superiors in San Francisco. But this couldn't wait.

He punched the number. Sarah's words ran through his mind, clear as glass and just as cutting. *I'm blown. And running.*

Those were words no U.S. marshal wanted

to hear, much less from a woman with a five-year-old child. If he'd been quicker back then, everything might have been different. If he'd paid closer attention, he might have seen what was unfolding. He might have gotten there in time. He might have kept the whole fire from erupting. Beth Keller and Nolan Worthe might today be living their granola-sprinkled dreams.

Sarah might be living in California, sunny and free.

The call connected. It rang twice before a woman answered. "Good morning."

"Is the sun actually rising?" Lawless said.

Teresa Gavilan laughed. "Lauds, yes."

Lawless smiled. "It's good to hear your voice."

"Yours as well. But you didn't call to check that the sun still comes up in the east in New Mexico. What do you need, Michael?"

"A backstop. For a woman with a five-year-old child."

"You'd better tell me. Let me put the coffee on."

The prairie slowly brightened from gray to green. Sarah quietly packed up. The sky was clear. Glassy puddles from the thunderstorm were silver in the dawn.

Zoe lay asleep on her back, arms flung overhead. Sarah sat on the edge of the bed and stroked her hair.

"Time to get up, munchkin." She rubbed her daughter's arm until Zoe stretched and opened her eyes. "Gotta grab breakfast and run an errand, then pack up and hit the road."

Nobody was out. They hit a twenty-four-hour Walmart, got coffee and doughnuts and milk, and were back in the room twenty minutes later.

While Zoe covered her fingers and face with powdered sugar, Sarah laid out the clothes she'd chosen for her. Orange Texas Longhorns T-shirt, brown kids' cargo pants, and little lace-up hiking boots.

"I don't like that shirt," Zoe said.

"Put your sweatshirt over it."

"I want my daisies."

Sarah set her hands on Zoe's shoulders. "Not today. Today you need to do what Mommy asks. You can be mad, but you still have to do what I say. Got it?"

Zoe nodded. She looked up from beneath her long lashes. "Are we in trouble?"

"Yes." She'd learned early on that lying to this child always came back to bite her in the ass. "I'm afraid we are. We have to stay out of sight."

"Is this because of your job?"

"No."

"Is it because of the bus crash?"

"Absolutely not." She sat on the bed. "It has nothing to do with the bus accident. Why would you think so?"

"Because I saw the woman in the van talking on the phone and I knew she was going to run into the bus and I didn't tell anybody."

It sometimes felt as though Zoe saw everything. In crowd photos, more often than seemed accidental, Zoe was the only one looking at the camera. As if she'd been watching, anticipating the photographer's shot when nobody else did. Her eyes were always guarded and searching.

Sarah pulled Zoe against her side. "You did nothing wrong. The bus driver is the one who was supposed to look out for other cars."

"You mean nobody would believe me."

Sarah leaned her cheek against the top of Zoe's head. "I believe you. Always."

"But you're not always with me."

It felt like a blade through her ribs. "Then you have to tell me whatever you can, whenever you can. You have to pay attention to the people around you. You're good at noticing things about people. You can usually tell when they're honest."

"What's honest?"

"It means they tell the truth."

Zoe looked up. "I don't like it when people lie. Why do they do that?"

"Because they want to get away with something. Or they want to confuse you. Or because . . ."

"They're bad."

"Sometimes."

Zoe snuggled against her. Sarah said, "And we need to stay out of the sight of some people we don't want to talk to."

Sarah got the bag from Walmart. Took out the scissors and the hair dye.

"Are we going in disguise?" Zoe said.

"Kind of."

"Is that like lying?"

"No. It's keeping bad guys from seeing us."

"But we can see them."

"That's the idea."

Kid should be a spy, Sarah thought. Or a sorcerer.

When Sarah finished, they stared at themselves in the mirror, a couple of changelings. Zoe looked like an imp. Sarah's hair matched: cut spiky short and dyed Sith Black.

Welcome to the show.

Outside, not even the wind was moving. If Lawless had phoned the FBI or local police, they would already have raided the room. She'd be in custody. But he hadn't betrayed her yet. Five years, and he had never sent anybody after her. She was counting on that.

Zoe zipped her backpack. "Ready."

Sarah said, "Good. Now I need to get something straight with you. For today, and until I tell you otherwise, I'm going to call you Skye."

"Why?"

"Because it's important."

"Like a game?"

"Yes."

"Like a code name?" Zoe said.

"Exactly."

Sarah's phone rang. She rested a hand on Zoe's shoulder. "What's your name?"

"Zoe. But you call me Skye."

"Cool."

She smiled and it hardly felt forced. The phone continued to ring. A 505 Area Code — New Mexico. She picked up the call.

A woman said, "This is Teresa Gavilan."

Her voice was rich and round. She didn't sound young. "Michael Lawless asked me to phone. To whom am I speaking?"

"Michael asked you to phone?" Sarah said.

"Dark-haired guy, mid-thirties, quiet. Like Gary Cooper going, 'Yup.' You know him, I think."

That was both sufficient and amusing. "Sarah Keller."

"I understand you're on the move and need a place to bunk. My door's open."

"Where? And for how long? Is this a safe house you're talking about?"

"Let's call it that. It'll be safe. Who's after you?"

Sarah turned her back to Zoe and spoke in a murmur. "Cops and intensely motivated criminals."

"Does your ride have a full tank and a good engine?" Gavilan said.

"Yes."

"Can you get to New Mexico?"

Sarah took a breath. "It'll take most of the day."

"There's a music festival that starts this afternoon. Meet me there." Gavilan gave her the details. "Do you have another phone in case the one you're using is compromised?"

Sarah gave her a number. "How will I recognize you?"

Gavilan laughed. "You'll know me. Don't worry."

Sarah ended the call, bemused. "Saddle

up, kiddo."

"Where are we going?" Zoe said.

Somewhat baffled, Sarah said, "Roswell."

22

The morning was turning breezy. Noise from the highway gusted across the motel parking lot as Sarah loaded their things and buckled Zoe in the back seat.

"Where's Mousie?" Zoe said.

"In your backpack."

Zoe unbuckled the latch. "I want him."

"Hey, I'll get him." Sarah nudged Zoe back.

From the motel lobby, the high school band poured out. The kids chattered and laughed, nearly stumbling over all their gear, and headed toward their bus. Sarah pulled her ball cap lower on her head, climbed behind the wheel and started the engine. The kids were flirting, texting, sparking with energy. She edged across the parking lot. Her hands tingled on the wheel.

Nobody noticed her new haircut. The band director didn't wave her down to ask why, when she'd registered at the motel, under *Purpose of stay* she had written, "Teacher chaperone for Bowie High School Marching Band." She eased the truck onto the street.

Ninety miles west they hit Amarillo and she drove to a big box mall. Inside, she headed to Sweetheart Dolls. The walls and tables were a fluff of pink and porcelain.

Sarah asked a clerk, "Reborns?"

Toy stores rarely carried reborn dolls, but she hoped a specialty doll outlet might. Even if they kept them under the counter, like contraband. The clerk smiled knowingly and crooked a finger. Sarah followed her to a nook in the back of the store.

The reborns were nestled on the shelf, wrapped in blankets, like a retail nursery. They were sized and painstakingly painted to seem wrinkly and fresh, just like actual newborns. They had realistic hair, short and silky and swirling around cowlicks. They had mottled skin and eyelashes and veins drawn along their temples. They reminded Sarah for a moment of the magical way Zoe had felt in her arms, the first time she ever saw her. The clerk picked one up delicately, supporting its head as though it were actually human. Its eyes clicked open. Sarah tried not to grimace.

Quietly, as though not to wake the creatures in the vinyl creche, the clerk said, "Are you looking to adopt a particular baby? Someone to go with your little boy?" She glanced at Zoe.

"Birthday gift," Sarah said.

The clerk rocked the unlifelike thing in her arms. It had thick brown hair and wore a pink onesie. Its limbs flopped as the clerk bounced it.

"She comes with a birth certificate," the clerk said. "Of course, you'll get to name her before we print it."

Little Weirdo, Sarah thought.

The clerk smiled at Zoe. "What do you think, young man? What would you like to call your new friend?"

Zoe glared at it, and acid rose in Sarah's throat. Then Zoe said, "Her name is Sparky."

The clerk looked nonplussed, before laughing. "I'll ring you up."

Sarah bought the doll clothes and accessories. At the counter, she opened her wallet. And saw a photo of Zoe — wearing a dress and a hair band with a giant plastic sunflower. She handed over her prepaid card and flipped the wallet shut.

As soon as they left the store, she pulled out the photo and stuck it in her back pocket.

Zoe said, "She called me young man."

"Play along, honey."

"Why?" Zoe looked up at her. "Is this one of those things I'll understand when I'm a grown-up?"

"Definitely." Sarah checked her watch. It was nine forty-five. More than two hundred miles to go.

Harker walked into the Will Rogers OKCPD station at 9:50 A.M. The place was busy, but at a suburban pace — bustling and serious, but not on emergency footing. He flashed his credentials and headed to the detectives' pen. He didn't see Dos Santos or Bukin. He approached a young man who was on the phone.

"Hang up," he said.

The detective frowned at him. Harker pointed at the phone.

"Now."

Recalcitrantly, the detective told the caller good-bye and set the phone in the cradle. "Yes?"

"I need updates on the hunt for Sarah Keller," Harker said.

"I don't know —"

Harker leaned on the desk. "Then find out. Get Dos Santos."

The detective headed back into the build-

161

ing. Harker waited. He could outwait anybody, even the most obstinate. He held his fists at his sides and cracked his knuckles. When Dos Santos appeared, fresh and pressed and smelling of aftershave, Harker didn't let him speak.

"I see you got Keller's photo on the news. What else?"

"We've put out an APB. Keller's running. Her cell phone turned up in a diaper bag in some family's car in Kansas, and her satnav on an eighteen-wheeler near Little Rock."

Harker hid his surprise. "So she's an escape artist. She must have been planning to burrow underground for years."

"We contacted parents in Zoe's class and found Keller's house. Her Nissan pickup's in the garage. We think she's driving a vehicle registered to her employer."

"What else?"

"We have an issue with the Santa Cruz Sheriff's Department," Dos Santos said. "They have no record of Zoe Keller being reported missing, much less kidnapped."

"Ignore them."

"Not possible."

Harker leaned on the desk with his fists. "What are you going to believe, a California sheriff's department that overlooked a major crime or the evidence in front of your face?"

Dos Santos considered it. He crossed his arms. "The people Keller stuck with her phone and GPS — they both bought gas at a Love's Travel Stop on I-40 in southwest Oklahoma City."

"You got the surveillance video, interviewed the clerks at that Love's, right?"

"They may be back by now. Let me check."

He crossed the room and spoke to a colleague. The conversation seemed animated. They glanced at Harker and away again.

Harker waited. Let them speculate, and even gossip. As long as they kept investigating, kept the pressure on, kept the news loud. As long as they didn't contact any other federal agencies tasked with fugitive apprehension, such as the U.S. Marshals.

This was his.

For a moment he felt a ghostly arm around his shoulder, a hand clenching the back of his neck. He seemed to hear a friend's voice, torn and reproachful, whisper in his ear. *This has gone too far. Let it go, Curt.*

He shook the haunted visitation away.

Let it go? Not while the Shattering Angel ran loose, and Eldrick Worthe could sneer, *She's still dead. She'll stay dead.*

Harker had learned the hard way: He

couldn't count on friends to understand. He could only count on the power of the law. The people who would be coming out of the wind weren't ordinary humans. They would mutilate cattle and dump infected carcasses in reservoirs to punish people who hadn't paid their protection money to the Worthes. They thought that killing the families of apostate gang members was commanded by God. They were trash below all trash.

And he was there to get rid of it.

Dos Santos returned and handed him a thumb drive. "Video from the Love's Travel Stop. It shows Keller in the store, paying at the register. The child is with her."

"Vehicle?"

"Dodge Ram pickup, half-hidden behind a big rig. The rig blocks the view of Keller placing the satnav on the axle of another tractor-trailer."

"And you have the slightest doubt that this woman is attempting to evade arrest? She *knew,* detective. She planned this. She's been planning her escape for five years." Harker's blood beat hard in his temples. "You need to broadcast, as loud as possible, Sarah Keller's name and photo, and Zoe's, and let the world know they were last spotted here. You need to do that *now.*"

Dos Santos's gaze ran from Harker's clenched jaw to his clenched fists. "We're on it."

"Don't wait to talk to the Santa Cruz Sheriff's Department. They botched the investigation of Beth Keller's murder. Be bold, detective. Get the word out," he said. "Zoe Keller's life is at stake."

Back in his car, he headed downtown through sunshine and Saturday morning traffic to the Bureau's office in the Federal Building. He touched his wallet. He kept it in the pocket of his jacket, near his heart. Inside it were photos of Eldrick Worthe's victims. They were a reminder: The Worthes killed women. And it was his job to bring them to justice.

For you. He would never let it go.

With the sun behind her and green fields spreading around the concrete ribbon of the interstate, Sarah hooked up the hands-free phone and called Danisha. She knew the call would show up as an unknown number. She said, "It's me."

The pause on the other end seemed stunned. Danisha said, "Girl."

"You okay?"

"Is my truck okay?"

Sarah smiled. "It's rolling like a champ.

165

Who knows I'm driving it?"

"Nobody has asked, believe it or not. But I don't expect that piece of luck to last past lunchtime."

"No?"

"I sent one of the process servers to drive by your house. Cops were there. They had the garage door up — and I parked your truck inside. So they'll be checking registrations for DHL vehicles."

Sarah ran a hand through her hair. "Who's been to see you?"

"Two OKCPD detectives. You've seen your beauty shot on the news?"

"I hate that photo."

Danisha didn't laugh.

"None of it's true, Dani."

"You know I believe you."

"Thank you." The truck bottomed over a dip in the road. "You need to take care and watch out."

"I'll be careful, don't worry."

"The Worthes — they don't always come at people through the front door."

"I understand."

"Zingasearch, Dani."

Danisha was quiet a moment. "Understood."

Zingasearch was a skip tracer's dream. The search engine collated massive public databases — phone books, Department of Motor Vehicles data, property records — and published the results in a tidy package that included people's names, ages, phone numbers, and current and past addresses going back decades. Pay a fee, and you could get background checks and criminal history reports.

The site had a creepy habit of finding people in a few seconds — people who took excruciating care to protect their privacy, such as psychiatrists who treated violent psychotics, and judges who presided at mob trials. Their home addresses could be found at the click of a key, with a kicker: *Associated with,* followed by a list of relatives. Spouses, mothers, children. Zingasearch was a candy store for skip tracers and stalkers and vengeful criminals.

Sarah loved Zingasearch. She hoped it was outlawed, today.

A dull weight seemed to press on her back. "This is my fault. Dani, I'm sorry."

"Don't flatter yourself, Keller. I started this business and I knew it would win me no friends. Aside from lawyers, and who wants them for buddies?"

Brave words, and Sarah knew Danisha meant them. But she also knew she'd brought this down on Danisha like a black wind.

"I'll call back tonight."

"Watch your six, Keller."

"You too." She signed off.

Glanced in the rearview mirror. Zoe was coloring and humming to herself. Seated next to her, buckled into a car seat she'd bought at the doll store, was the reborn. Its eyes were closed. Sarah had wrapped a blanket loosely around its head, as though to shade its face from the sun.

Camouflage.

In Sarah's experience, people saw what they expected to see. That's why, when serving papers on prickly people in ritzy neighborhoods, she sometimes loaded a lawn mower into the cargo bed of the truck and wore a green work shirt. The ruse once got her past a gatehouse to the door of a 10,000-square-foot mansion, taken for a gardener come to tend the azaleas.

If you were a Finnish sniper who wore white in a winter forest, Russian soldiers mistook you for a snowdrift. And if you showed up with an infant in a Snugli and a kindergartner in hiking boots, people thought you were a mom of two: a baby girl and a five-year-old boy.

Zoe's lips moved as she sang to herself, a

lullaby about cowboys and horses. The lines she drew on the coloring book were ragged but somehow thoughtful. The little girl's head was bent forward, eyes on the page. Even with her hair cut short, there was no mark from where the microchip had been implanted.

Back at the motel, while Zoe slept, Sarah had researched RFID tags. Microchip capsules were biocompatible — nontoxic and nonallergenic. They were implanted easily, with a hypodermic syringe. But surgical removal was difficult. And the chips didn't expire or wear down. Bragged one veterinary website: They're good for the life of your pet.

At least RFID chips didn't send out a GPS signal. Generally, they simply stored information. They waited, completely inert, to be read. They couldn't, as far as Sarah knew, be used like a broadcast beacon to send out distress messages or tell the world where you were. You couldn't log onto some sophisticated computer network and ask it to find the tag and pinpoint its location.

Tech was a double-edged sword. Any smart skip tracer knew that. Especially any skip tracer who knew how to track missing people through phone records and credit cards. Tech could be used to conceal and to find. The real question was: Who's better at technology — you or the people hunting you?

She had to get the chip removed. She rolled west on the highway, counting the miles, watching the rearview mirror.

23

In downtown Oklahoma City the morning looked bright and blasted. Fell rode shotgun. Reavy sat in the back, pale and eager. Grissom drove, eyeing other drivers as though they were cockroaches. He rubbed a hand along his thigh. Fell knew his juices were flowing.

This city had been the scene of the most successful strike at the law in their lifetimes. FBI, ATF, IRS — all of them took body blows the day the Murrah Building went down. But they didn't have time to explore that battleground. They drove past the memorial, Reavy licking her lips, Grissom almost crackling with energy. They passed by a courthouse and yet another barbecue restaurant and yet another Baptist church, and finally by the simple brick building, shaded by an old sycamore, that housed DHL Attorney Services.

Grissom circled the block to check for

surveillance cameras and neighborhood watch signs. But it was Saturday morning on a holiday weekend and many offices were closed. Satisfied, he parked the rented Navigator a hundred yards from DHL. The blinds were down and the office looked dark.

"Maybe she left town for the weekend," Reavy said.

Fell said, "Office hours are ten to one Saturday."

And bang on time, a black Jeep pulled into a parking slot outside the DHL office. A woman got out. From beneath her old cowboy hat, dreadlocks reached halfway down her back. She wore a tight red top and turquoise squash-blossom jewelry that gleamed in the sun, blue and silver against her brown skin. She unlocked the office door and went inside.

Fell reached for the passenger door handle.

Grissom stopped her. "Ms. Dreads don't look like the kind of woman who's going to roll over. She'll take some persuading." He got out. "You and Reavy drive on over to the mother's house."

Fell climbed across the center console into the driver's seat. "What are you going to do?"

"Wait till you find Mrs. Helms senior. Then I'll have a chat with our Danisha."

He pounded on the roof of the Navigator and sauntered toward a coffee shop up the street.

Sarah spotted the Texas state trooper on U.S. 60, forty miles southwest of Amarillo. The countryside was as flat as a meat cleaver, the sky white with heat. She still had almost two hundred miles to the rendezvous with Teresa Gavilan.

She knew she wouldn't make it.

She checked the mirror again. The trooper was still cruising three hundred yards back. Zoe was staring straight at her.

It had long ago stopped unnerving her. Now it focused her.

At the next town she pulled off the highway. The trooper drove past the exit. She realized that her temples were pounding.

"What are we doing?" Zoe said.

She passed by towering grain silos. The electric poles along the roadside leaned at odd angles. "Need to run an errand."

Ten minutes later she stood beside a mechanic at Del's Auto Body, staring at the pickup. She had put on pink lipstick called Coquette, with a matching drawl. Unfortunately, they clashed with her Black Alchemy eye shadow. Still, the mechanic had tucked in his shirt.

She said, "My dad loves this truck. If he saw what happened to it . . ."

"He'd kill you."

She smiled sadly. "He'd die a little, trying to keep himself from wanting to kill me. And that would break my heart."

The mechanic shook his head at the nasty scratch along the driver's side. "People these days."

"I didn't think the guy would actually key the truck. Over a parking spot?"

The mechanic took off his baseball cap. Sarah waited.

"I'll have to sand it," he said.

She beamed. "Y'all just saved me. Thank you."

"And I can't match the color."

Better and better. "It's the scratch that matters, not the color."

"Even a rush job will take a couple hours. You and the kids can watch TV in the waiting room."

"We'll head down the street. Grab lunch and run some errands."

She handed him a prepaid card. It was a risk. But doing nothing would be even riskier.

While the mechanic prepared the paint

bay, she got Zoe out of the truck. Then she put on a Snugli and tucked the reborn doll into it. The thing was unnervingly heavy, especially its head. She patted its back as if to soothe it.

Zoe stared at her like she had gone dog-barking nuts.

Maybe she had. She took her daughter's hand. "Come on, firefly."

"I thought my name was Skye."

Down the street she found a Sonic. Half-way through her hamburger, Zoe eyed the reborn and said, "You should order Sparky some milk."

Two hours later, hot from walking around the little downtown and pushing Zoe on swings at the park, she climbed back behind the wheel, four hundred bucks down.

"Thank you," she said to the mechanic.

"Pleasure. Any guy who'd mess up a man's pickup, well."

She smiled. "He ever shows up here, sand his car down to the axles. He drives a red Porsche. His name's Derek Dryden."

She honked as she drove off. A minute later she pulled back onto the highway. Danisha might kill her, but the truck was now a darkly gleaming machine. Black Alchemy.

In the auto body shop, the mechanic walked

past the radio.

". . . seeking the whereabouts of Sarah Keller, who disappeared yesterday with a five-year-old girl . . ."

He stopped. Listened to the description.

". . . Keller is presumed to be traveling with the five-year-old. She was last seen driving a red pickup with Oklahoma registration."

He glanced toward the painting bay.

Woman wanting her red pickup painted, *right now.* Completely new color.

No, Keller had brown hair. She was traveling with a little girl. She wasn't a Goth with a boy and a tiny baby.

He stood there.

Woman wanting an emergency paint job. How likely was that?

But the truck — he shook his head. It had Texas plates, he was certain. Wasn't he? And when she drove away, with a honk and a cute wave, she had gone down to the highway and headed northeast. Toward Oklahoma. He was sure. He'd watched.

The phone rang. He headed to the office.

It wasn't her.

Was it?

Sarah turned off the radio. Zoe was settled with earphones and a kids' album on the iPod, coloring and singing tunelessly to Raffi. She hadn't heard. The white lines on the highway slurred past. Sarah held the speed steady just under the limit. She was staying within the law. Mostly.

Except for switching the plates on the truck. It now had Louisiana tags.

Three months earlier she had pulled a set of plates off an abandoned vehicle. During a skip trace she'd found the car half-buried in weeds beside a burned-out trailer. She checked the tags — the car was registered to the skip. It wasn't stolen. It was insured. But it had been abandoned when the guy blew town. She unscrewed the plates and added them to her escape kit.

The prepaid card she'd used at the auto body shop was another matter.

C. Kaler, the card read. Her handwriting on the application had been atrocious. But if the mechanic checked it carefully enough, it would come back to her.

She had to hope that after she honked and waved at him, he'd watched her turn onto U.S. 60 heading northeast. *Please.* She slowed, pulled a U-turn, and accelerated southwest toward the state line.

The wind rushed against the truck. The land ebbed to brown, as though slashed to the bone. By the time she sped past the sign that said, WELCOME TO NEW MEXICO, LAND OF ENCHANTMENT, the sky was a thin blue. It looked like it could blow away in an instant.

Grissom was halfway through a piece of hot blueberry pie when his phone buzzed. Fell's text said, *In position.*

He checked out the window of the diner. Down the street, the Jeep was still parked outside DHL. The black woman was inside the office building.

The sway of her hips as she walked had caused a stirring in him. The familiar feeling of *want.*

His anger rose quicker than a flame. *Fuck her.* The woman's cool confidence undermined the very pavement beneath her feet. It was insubordinate. Weakening him with want — that was a sin. Women were born not to power, but to obedience

Eldrick Worthe had taught him that. Eldrick had revealed many such truths.

Grissom had not been raised in the family. He had been nothing. Nineteen, a kid with fists searching for something to punch, until he walked into an Arizona minimart and interrupted the Worthe clan conducting a drug deal. *Screw off, dogface,* they said. *Out. Now.* So he got out. He waited for them to finish their business. And when they left the minimart he beat them unconscious with a two-by-four.

Normally, Eldrick would have had Grissom beaten in return, then dragged behind a truck and dumped in a ravine. But he saw potential in the kid. He saw initiative, a divine spark. He brought him onboard. Now Grissom was one of them.

He wiped his mouth, dropped a five on the table, zipped his jacket and walked out of the diner. He crossed the street and walked through the heavy heat of the afternoon to DHL. He felt a rush in his heart. It was like the beating of wings.

He approached the redbrick building. At her desk by the front window, head in a file folder, sat Ms. Dreads. He took the ski mask and gloves from his jacket and pulled them on. Then he gripped the military knife. Inside the office, a phone rang. Dreads answered.

"Mom?" she said. "What's wrong?"

He shoved through the door and walked toward Danisha Helms.

24

Danisha held the phone tight to her ear. "Mom. What's going on?"

"Nisha, they broke into the house. Through the kitchen door."

Danisha's blood pressure spiked to the red zone. She pushed back from her desk. "Who? Are you okay?"

"They told me I had to call you."

She heard, behind her mother's wheezing, the rush of road noise. "Where are you?"

She felt the way she had in Afghanistan, when the generators went funny and the lights flickered in the tent and the men who came through the flap from the desert heat wore uniforms but weren't allies beneath the clothing.

She was halfway to her feet. "Mom, are you safe?"

The door at the front of the office opened with a swish of air. She looked up.

The man coming toward her wore a black

ski mask and black leather gloves. His right hand gripped a military knife.

She lowered the phone and raised the SIG Sauer.

"Drop the knife," she said. "Get on the floor."

The man stopped. Beneath the ski mask his eyes popped with surprise. He backed up a step.

From the phone her mother's voice leaked into the room. "Nisha, they grabbed me, oh, my Lord . . ."

She steadied her aim on his center of mass. He was fifteen feet away.

She shouted, "I will not miss. *Drop your weapon. Get on the floor.*"

This time he didn't move. "Throw away your gun and you'll still have time to save her."

She inhaled, and he saw it. She set her cell phone on the desk and fumbled for the landline.

"Don't do that," he said.

She knocked it from the cradle and speed-dialed 9-1-1. From the cell phone her mother's voice rose to a sharp cry.

"Mom!"

He heard it at the same time she did: the engine of a heavy vehicle, revving, growing louder and higher in pitch. Whatever it was, it was coming in their direction.

"Hang up the phone," the man said.

She didn't move. "Mom —"

"Nisha, *run.*"

The engine noise grew intense.

He jumped away from the door. A blue Chrysler New Yorker appeared in the glass, heading toward them, chrome gleaming, bouncing across the road outside and the sidewalk and grass and parking lot, straight for the door.

Danisha screamed. *"No."*

She stumbled back, turning to flee. It was her mother's car. It crossed the blacktop parking lot before she could draw breath and rammed straight into the front door of the office and right on through.

The sun was low on the western horizon, the sky hazed red from sand, when Sarah cruised along a boulevard into downtown Roswell.

The city was sprawling yet tidy, with lawns struggling to find purchase and trees that crouched against the arid wind. She saw no overt signs of alien infestation.

At a stoplight, she texted Teresa Gavilan. *Here.*

A minute later, her phone pinged. *Medical Tent #1.*

Southwest of the city limits the Gate-crasher Festival rose from the desert like a kaleidoscopic outcropping of wild life. The immense parking lot was packed with cars and trucks from across the Southwest. The distant stage looked heavy with lights and Marshall stacks. There were thirty thousand people inside the chain-link fence. It looked like a Renaissance Fair that had been crashed by loggers and cowboys. Nobody was going to notice her.

She parked and got out. The evening air was bone-dry and hot, the sky folded with reds and golds. From the stage, loud guitars rang out.

Zoe hopped down from the truck. "Are we at a theme park?"

Sarah foraged in the glove compartment, found a set of airline earplugs and squashed them into Zoe's ears. "Music festival. And not Disney."

She strapped on the Snugli, lifted the reborn doll from the car seat, and tucked it in. Taking Zoe's hand, she pointed at the gate. "Lead on, scout."

She paid for general admission to the grounds, which used up her remaining cash. She looked around. This place had to have an ATM — rock 'n' roll was the most capitalist art form ever invented. She saw a

Ferris wheel and T-shirt vendors and a booth for ROSWELL UFO TOURS, which advertised visits to the site where the flying saucer crashed in 1947. On the counter sat an inflatable gray alien with eyes bigger than hockey pucks. Zoe gave it a searching look, like maybe it could be Sparky's new friend. Sarah spotted a portable ATM. She pulled $300.

By the time she found Medical Tent #1, the air-conditioning inside felt refreshing. At the check-in desk, she said, "Teresa Gavilan?"

A man pointed with his pen. "Saw her in the back."

Sarah led Zoe past examination bays jerry-rigged with paper curtains. The music from the stage was a battering drone. In the far corner of the tent, a woman sat on the edge of a cot, talking to a patient. The woman was in her late forties, with copper hair pulled back into a messy ponytail. She wore an Army-green T-shirt and combat trousers, like a character out of M*A*S*H.

"Ms. Gavilan?" Sarah said.

The woman patted the patient's hand and stood up. When she turned, Sarah expected the chain around her neck to end in dog tags. Instead, it held a crucifix.

Teresa Gavilan's eyes were a vivid blue,

framed by laugh lines. She looked like she'd spent her life outdoors, battling wind and weather with a hearty laugh.

"You made it," she said.

Zoe stared. "Are you a vampire hunter?"

For a second, Gavilan looked bemused. Then she touched the crucifix. "No, young lady. I'm a nun."

25

When Harker arrived, the auto salvage crew was hoisting the blue Chrysler New Yorker onto the flatbed tow truck. In the calm light of a spring evening, the mayhem had brought out the neighborhood to gawk. Harker took in the crumpled frontage of DHL Attorney Services, the bricks spilled around the gaping hole where the door had stood. It looked like a destroyed mouth, leaking wood and glass and office furniture.

He showed his credentials to a uniformed officer, signed the log-in sheet, and ducked under the yellow tape.

"Dos Santos," he said.

Inside, the detective glanced up. Harker climbed on a pile of bricks and through the hole in the building. At the back of the office, crime scene techs snapped photographs. Dos Santos handed him a pair of latex gloves.

"Seems you were right. Somebody besides

us is after Sarah Keller."

Harker pulled on the gloves and picked his way through the debris. Broken glass crunched and brick dust coated his shoes.

"Prints on the New Yorker?" he said.

"Plenty. We'll see whose."

He climbed over a smashed desk, feet sliding on Formica. "Witnesses?"

"Canvassing the neighborhood."

"Video?"

"Bank on the corner. Not in this building," Dos Santos said.

Harker nudged chunks of debris with his shoe. On the floor a broken piece of plywood was edged with blood.

"Whose?" he said.

"We'll find out."

Outside, a uniform called to Dos Santos. The detective trudged back to the door. On the floor, Harker saw the cell phone. Battered and dusty, lying beneath an office chair. He picked it up and slipped it into his pocket.

Dos Santos consulted with the uniform and returned. "Witnesses say the car raced up the street like a demon. Mounted the curb, took direct aim, and smashed through the front of the building without slowing."

"What about the woman who was carjacked?"

A female voice answered. "She'll live."

Harker and Dos Santos turned. Climbing through the hole in the wall was Danisha Helms.

"My mother's being held in the hospital for observation overnight. She has a heart condition and today nearly killed her."

Dos Santos said, "And what about you?"

In the dim office, Helms looked dusty and banged up. Her lip was busted. She had a butterfly bandage on her forehead, holding together a deep cut.

"Still standing. Sad to say, so's the bastard who threatened me."

Dos Santos said, "Had you seen the man before?"

"Haven't seen him yet. White guy, from what I could see around the eyeholes of his ski mask. Young, judging by his voice and physique. He was in shape."

Harker said, "Did you see the driver?"

She shook her head. "I saw that it was my mother's car. After that I was running. I scrambled out the back door with bricks flying and the grille of the car on my ass."

Dos Santos said, "Why do you think the car rammed the building?"

With a withering stare, she crunched past him into the center of what had been her office. "Man wanted me to turn over on my

188

employee. Instead, I defended myself. He took it badly."

Dos Santos said, "About that, Ms. Helms."

"Handgun license is here someplace." She swept her arm at the devastation. "Or you can find it in state records. Concealed carry."

Harker said, "This part of town has a neighborhood alliance, folks supposed to be watching out for each other. It has a reputation as a safe place. Or it did."

She gave him a cool glance.

"Of course, if you or one of your employees opened the door to violence, that would be a sad thing for the neighborhood."

In the middle of her ruined office, she looked tired and battered. But her voice was surprisingly firm. "What opened the door to violence were two psychopaths who carjacked my mother and drove her in a goddamn Chrysler through the front door," she said. "I'm going to see my mom at the hospital. Please get fingerprints and take your photos and find the sons of bitches."

Dos Santos said, "Yes, ma'am."

She turned and surveyed the rubble. "Has anybody found a cell phone?"

Harker climbed out the hole in the building and walked back to his car.

■ ■ ■ ■

Rolling along Northwest Expressway in the sunset, the rented Navigator was silent. At the wheel, Fell scanned the highway. Riding shotgun, Reavy pointed at the turnoff ahead. In the back seat, Grissom fumed.

Physically he was unhurt, Fell knew. When the Chrysler jumped the curb and plowed into the DHL office, he had thrown himself clear.

"Way she moved, she acted like she had military experience," he said.

His problem was Danisha Helms. She'd outgunned him. Made him need rescue. A woman.

"She's a dyke. We'll see to her," he said. "Yes we will."

Reavy hesitated, just a fraction of a second. "Course we will."

Fell echoed her. "Course, Grissom."

She sensed him twitch. With Grissom, hesitation equaled heresy. Women were required to demonstrate absolute obedience — in action, thought, and soul. It wasn't enough to submit immediately to a man's command. Women had to love their obedience. Anything else was rebellious.

What a lucky control freak Grissom was,

to have found himself a spiritual home with the Worthe family. And Fell knew the price of any slip: a life of chains.

She'd slipped once. She had asked *why.*

But all that was about to be made right. *Get the kid. Make the family whole.* Then, maybe, her chains would fall away.

She thought of the way Grampa Eldrick kissed her cheek after her husband Coffey died, and Uncle Isom told her she had to be strong. Yeah, well, she was doing that. She was going to get Nolan's kid back.

Reavy pointed to a strip mall beside a creek, overhung with live oaks. The UPS Store was at the far end. It was nearly seven, and inside a young man was closing up for the night.

Grissom opened his door while the SUV was still rolling. "Follow my lead."

He hopped out and strode to the door. In his hand he held a letter he'd scrounged from DHL after the Chrysler rammed the building. It was a Heart Association circular addressed to Sarah Keller at a street address on Pennsylvania Avenue. To their utter lack of surprise, the address turned out to be this UPS Store. They walked in and straight to the desk.

"I'm here on behalf of one of your mailbox owners," Grissom said.

The clerk wore a brown uniform shirt and a wary expression. "What can I do for y'all?"

"Box 2933."

The clerk nodded at the wall of mailboxes behind them. "Far left."

"I need access."

"Then you'll need a key."

"Much obliged."

The clerk looked perplexed. He was about twenty years old, a reedy boy with acne. "Beg pardon?"

Fell and Reavy slipped around opposite ends of the counter and approached him. Fell didn't know what convinced the boy quicker — Reavy's hand on the back of his neck, or the box cutter she found beneath the counter. But ten seconds later he unlocked the mailbox.

Sixty seconds after that, they had Sarah Keller's mail and were tearing out of the parking lot. The clerk had his life, and a warning that if he mentioned their visit to anyone, they'd come back.

Fell floored the Navigator along Pennsylvania, streetlights flashing past. Grissom punched the dome light and tore open an envelope.

"Would you look at this. It's Keller's credit card bill." In the looming dusk, he smiled. "This is our ticket to everything."

26

Sarah followed Teresa Gavilan's rusting Honda Civic up the gravel driveway, toward a clapboard house surrounded by scrub pines. Roswell had ended suddenly, as desert towns often did. One block was built up, with fast-food drive-throughs and storefront churches and ranch homes; the next was a tawny rolling plain speckled with stunted conifers, a freckled landscape that hinted of mountains beyond the horizon.

When Sarah killed the engine and opened the door, a sweet silence enveloped her. In the bright evening the only sounds were birds whistling, and her engine ticking as it cooled. Zoe was drowsy. Sarah unbuckled her seat belt and coaxed her out, but she sagged in the doorway of the pickup.

Gavilan approached and crouched down. "Piggyback."

Zoe climbed on. Gavilan huffed, snugged her arms around Zoe's knees, and straightened up.

Zoe said, "What do nuns do?"

Sarah flushed. But Gavilan smiled.

"Lots of things," she said. "And right now, this nun is going to see that you get a good night's sleep."

Sarah said, "Sorry."

"Don't apologize. I appreciate getting the chance to explain my vocation." She climbed the steps and opened the kitchen door. "There's a bed in the guestroom."

"Thank you." Sarah took Zoe and hoisted her onto her hip.

The house was close from the day's heat. The floor creaked beneath Sarah's feet. While Gavilan turned on a ceiling fan and opened the windows, Sarah laid Zoe on the double bed in an unadorned bedroom. She pulled off Zoe's shoes and socks. Quietly she said, "You sleep tight. I'll be in, in a little bit."

"Where's Mousie?"

Sarah went to get him and placed him in Zoe's hands. The girl barely noticed before she dropped off to sleep.

Sarah found Gavilan in the rustic kitchen, taking a kettle off the stove.

"Tea will be ready in a minute. If you want wine, it's ready now." She nodded at a bottle of Pinot Noir on the counter.

Sarah looked at the wine bottle longingly. But she needed to keep a clear head. "Tea will be great."

Gavilan poured two mugs, handed one to Sarah, and turned on a portable stereo player to mask their conversation. Bluegrass: mandolin and guitars and a fiddle.

Sarah took a long draft of the tea. "Thanks, Sister."

"It's Teresa." She sat at the kitchen table and nudged a chair out with her foot. "Sit."

Sarah dropped into the chair. She felt wound up, like a toy. Almost as if she'd spring apart if she let go. She was exhausted.

"Thank you for letting us come here tonight," she said.

"Not a problem. Do you want to talk, or do you just want to crash?"

For a second Sarah held it in. *Keep the spring pressed down tight.* But merely being in a room with an adult who knew something about what was happening to her felt . . . expansive. Strangely safe.

She said, "How'd you end up out here in UFO country? I'm sure New Mexico's glad to have a nun on duty, but ministering to the drunk and disorderly at a rock festival . . . what, no convent?"

"My order has chapter houses in several cities. And we have contemplatives. But we're mainly commissioned to go to rural areas and find a way to put our gifts to work."

"You have to earn a paycheck?"

"We get a stipend, but we need to make our own way. St. Paul warned against mooching, you know."

"Then I'll try not to mooch." She set down her mug. "And how did a nun get to be an underground confederate of Michael Lawless?"

Teresa pulled her hair free of the ponytail, finger-combed it, and refastened the hair band. "He didn't arrest me, if that's what you're asking."

"So you're part of his posse?"

"Michael and I have known each other for twenty years. Since before I joined the order."

"You were involved in the sanctuary movement, weren't you?"

"Among other things. Women's shelters. Similar work." She held her mug. "He told me something about your situation."

Sarah flicked a glance at her, unsure what she meant by *something*. "I didn't know who else to call. When everything blew up. I've had five years to be afraid of this happening, and when it did — I was ready, but I wasn't. I just . . ."

She leaned on her elbows and pressed her fists against her eyes.

Teresa said, "It's okay. You don't have to talk."

"I want to."

When she lowered her hands and opened her eyes, she saw compassion on the older woman's face.

"It's just — for so long I've kept everything back. Talking, I worry . . ."

"You've trained yourself to stay silent. It's become muscle memory."

Sarah nodded.

"And for five years you've been on red alert. Your fight-or-flight response is at DEFCON 1."

"Ready to launch. Seems it was wise."

"So yesterday, when things exploded, you ran. You didn't stay to sort it out."

"And I'm going to keep running until I can get Zoe someplace safe."

"Then what?"

Sarah's throat constricted. The brush of the wind outside pulled at her like spectral whispers. "If I had stayed in Oklahoma City . . ."

"I know. But do you have an endgame? You can't take Zoe on the road every time something goes bump in the night."

"Waiting for trouble was no answer,"

Sarah said.

But she knew: Zoe should be in school. She should be on a playground skipping rope with her friends. She should be cutting out paper daisies and learning how to use paste.

Teresa's silence felt both calm and portentous, like the quiet before a logger pulls the rip cord on a chain saw.

"Michael said he suggested you turn yourself in."

Sarah's heart skipped. Straight to *ignition.* "And I said no. That's not paranoia. It's a healthy instinct for self-preservation, and it's keeping Zoe safe."

In turn, Zoe was keeping her sane. Otherwise her grief over losing Beth, her shock at the violence that had stolen her sister, would have torn out all the circuitry that let her handle chaos and desolating truth.

"This is the real deal," she said. "I'm doing my damnedest here, in an extremely difficult situation."

Teresa seemed to mull that over. Then, letting it go, she smiled. "Sarah and Bethany. Lovely names. From scripture?"

Sarah's own smile was ironic. "From the places my sister and I were conceived."

"That's unusual."

"My mom was a travel journalist. She and

my dad spent three years in the Middle East and Africa."

"Bethany I recognize — a town outside Jerusalem," Teresa said. "But Sarah . . ."

"Sarah's my nickname. They were in Morocco, edge of the desert, but naming a kid Marrakech was a step too far, even for Mom. My full name is Sahara."

"How charming."

And useful, these last five years. Her Social Security card read SAHARA CARSON KELLER. Her driver's license, bank accounts, and various utilities read SARAH, SAHRA, or S.C. Confusion was her friend. If anybody asked about discrepancies, she told them, "It's misspelled." She didn't explain who had misspelled it.

"Sounds as if you have quite the family," Teresa said.

"I know nothing about my family. Mom didn't talk about our dad, and her background was . . . cloaked in mist."

"That must be frustrating."

"It's a puzzle."

And it had drawn Sarah into exploring the world's most enduring enigma: human history. In college she majored in archaeology. She studied the lost civilizations of Chaco Canyon and Mesa Verde. And she'd tried to trace her vanished relatives. The

Red Cross hadn't been able to find them, but it had convinced her to volunteer for a program that helped people locate family missing after wars and international disasters.

Later she worked part time for Past Link Software. The company's human anthropology programs let archaeologists and genealogists build a picture of history through census records, archaeological data, and DNA tracing. She had worked there on contract but they offered her a permanent job. Back before.

She smiled. "But puzzles intrigue me. Buried trails."

"Hence your avocation for skip tracing?"

"Maybe."

Teresa drank her tea. "So this wasn't where you intended to end up."

Sarah almost laughed. Five years earlier she'd had a round-the-world plane ticket. She had saved for years to buy it. She'd planned to stay at the American Colony Hotel in Jerusalem and the guesthouse where her mom and dad had stayed in Marrakech. She could still see the map of the world on her wall, pins stuck in it.

"Yeah, well," she said. "I'm here now."

She glanced around at the kitchen and the desert outside. The house was isolated. How much help would a religious sister be if the Worthe clan came crashing through the windows?

Teresa seemed to understand her qualms. "Michael is on his way."

A buzz ran through her head. She tried to speak, and her voice caught. She cleared her throat. "Is he on the clock?"

"He didn't say."

She nodded. No way to tell whether he was coming as an official emissary of the U.S. Marshals Service, or on his own dime and for his own purposes. That should have given her pause, but all she felt was an overwhelming sense of hope and relief.

Teresa said, "I should let him know that you're here and safe with Zoe."

"Okay." Sarah realized she was trembling. She took a quick breath. "Sorry."

"Don't be."

"Really, I'm okay."

Teresa put her hand over Sarah's clenched fist. Sarah gulped another breath and stood up. She couldn't risk emotional release. She walked to the window. The trembling diminished. The view over the edge receded. *Not yet.*

"Don't worry. I got this. I'll hold it together." She blinked away the stinging in her eyes and turned back to Teresa. "Lawless helped me get Zoe to safety when my sister died. I owe him."

Everything.

Teresa held out a hand. This time Sarah walked back, sat down, and took it.

"I'm scared," she said.

"Have you told anybody you were coming to Roswell?"

"Nobody."

"Have you used a credit card or a cell phone?"

"Prepaid card. Burn phone. They're as sanitized as I can make them, but no guarantees."

"This house has an alarm system. Doors, windows. And a perimeter alarm — motion-activated."

"Weapons?" Sarah said.

Teresa shook her head. "I took vows of poverty, celibacy, and obedience. I've added my own vow of nonviolence. I will not raise a weapon against another human being. But I'll do everything else to protect and defend you. And I certainly won't stop you from defending your life and your daughter's."

Sarah weighed her next words. Her impulse was to keep quiet and justify it with *What they don't know won't hurt them.* Her conscience, however, piped up. *At a nun's house? Honestly?*

She said, "I have a handgun. It's in a lock-box in the pickup."

Teresa considered her reply. "Do you consider that to be a safe distance from where you'll be sleeping tonight?"

"No." Sarah took a moment. "Bringing a gun into a room with a five-year-old is not ideal. If that's what you mean by *safe*. But leaving the weapon in the truck makes me see snakes in my head. I'd like to bring it inside."

"Thank you for your honesty."

"I'll get it before I go to bed."

"Leave it in the lockbox, please," Teresa said.

Sarah nodded. Teresa patted her hand and stood up. She lifted the phone from the cradle on the wall and called a number from memory.

After a moment, she said, "They're here."

Her body language was relaxed. She rubbed a crack on the kitchen counter with her thumb, seemingly with absentminded fondness.

"Tired but healthy. Zoe's tucked in bed. Do you want to say hello to Sarah?"

With a pleasant smile, she extended the phone. "Michael."

Sarah took the receiver. "We're both tucked up nice and tight in Sister Teresa's desert hideaway."

"Don't worry, she won't throw holy water over you, or force you to listen to the *Sound of Music* sound track."

His tone was offhand, almost reassuring, except for the undercurrent of urgency.

"Glad to hear it," she said. "Thank you. I mean it."

"Stick with Terry. Just keep your head down. I'm at the San Francisco airport, catching a connection to El Paso. I'll get a car there and be in Roswell midmorning tomorrow."

"Good." Tomorrow sounded too far away. "Will you be driving a company car?"

"I'll see you in the morning. We'll take things from there," he said.

"Gotcha." Though she didn't. "And . . ."

The distance over the phone line seemed to crackle and hum.

"Sarah?"

"Thanks, Lawless."

She replaced the receiver. The light in the kitchen had deepened to hot orange. The music formed an undercurrent in waltz time, a cello and mournful fiddle rolling through the room like a wave.

"He's halfway here," she said.

Teresa regarded her with seeming equanimity. Sarah felt like a bug under glass.

She picked up her mug. "So you weren't always a nun?"

"We aren't born wearing tiny habits."

"Sorry."

"I've been a farm girl. A mechanic. Social worker. Physician's assistant. In my thirties I finally stopped ignoring the call to take my life where it wanted to go." She smiled. "Now stop apologizing. Save your energy. And try to get some rest tonight."

She didn't add: *Because you're going to need it.*

As the sun slid toward the red horizon, Curtis Harker parked his Bureau car in the lot at the new Federal Building. Inside the airy, fortified structure only a few lights glowed. Government hours: the bane and blessing of his existence. He climbed from the air-conditioned car and the heat pressed in, invigorating. The hum of cicadas rose like a crazed buzz from the maples.

He leaned against the hood of the car and took Danisha Helms's dusty cell phone from his pocket. When he pressed the power button the display lit up. He smiled.

Tough little gizmo. *Takes a lickin' and keeps on harboring useful data.*

He thumbed the controls. Most of Helms's recent calls were to local 405 numbers. *City Courthouse* and *Mom* featured prominently. But what caught his eye was the text message from *Sarah K: Where r u?*

Helms had replied: *Rolling.*

"Gotcha."

If those messages were subpoenaed, and Helms was confronted with them in interrogation, she would squirm. But there was no time to get a subpoena.

Helms's contacts listed only one number for Keller — and that phone had been dumped in the diaper bag of a woman at a truck stop. But received calls showed several from numbers without caller ID. One of those might be Keller's burn phone.

He glanced up. In the fading sunset, the stars were coming out.

The clan had attacked DHL. They were *this* close.

They'd made one play for Sarah Keller. They would try again. Grissom Briggs. Reavy Worthe. Felicity Worthe, known as Fell. He could practically smell them in the heated evening, feel their wild and brimming hatred, hear their breathing — oxygen to their dead hearts. They should be corpses. They should be cold and buried.

Sarah Keller was the key to that. She was their costar in this misbegotten saga. Whether she had intended it or not — and he thought she was woven into their schemes in a deep and inextricable way — she was in this. She was the key. Because she had the girl.

Once the girl was located, the rest would follow, like iron filings drawn to a magnet.

He checked the time: 9:02. Danisha Helms would be leaving the hospital once visitors' hours were over. She might head back to her ruined office with a flashlight to continue hunting for her phone. It would be best if she found it.

He stuck the phone in his pocket and headed into the Federal Building to copy the data it contained. He was going to have a busy night tracking Sarah Keller down.

27

"Keller. K-e-l-l-e-r," Reavy said. "First name Sarah. Middle initial C."

In the motel room, she sat by the window with Keller's stolen credit card bill. She had the room phone on speaker. They heard typing as the card company's customer service rep accessed Keller's account.

In the corner by the door, Grissom crouched on his haunches, back to the wall.

Fell paced. The TV was on, the volume muted. She watched, fascinated.

Clan women who had undergone the blessing ceremony were normally forbidden to watch TV without their husbands' permission. The media was a firetrap, a series of IEDs buried every five feet in the outside culture. But tonight they were monitoring news channels for information about Zoe and Sarah Keller.

It was so flashy. Even with the sound off, the newspeople seemed loud and emotional.

Movie star attacked by chimpanzee. No way. *Second Amendment case goes to Appeals Court.* Footage of protesters and a judge — the same maggot who'd sentenced Eldrick. No *fucking* way. She hissed at Grissom and pointed at the TV. Sleepy-eyed, he looked, and spit on the carpet.

On speaker, the customer service rep said, "Ms. Keller?"

"Yes," Reavy said.

"Your date of birth?"

"August sixth." She added the birth year.

More typing. "The first line of your address?"

Reavy gave the UPS Store.

"Your sister's first name?"

"Bethany."

"Final question. The most recent transaction on your card?"

"Well, that's the problem. I'm afraid my card has been stolen. So I don't know what the last transaction was."

The rep said, "Then how about the last transaction you think *you* made on the card?"

Fell mouthed: *Play the odds.* Keller was running. She'd want to travel light. And for that she'd need greenback dollars.

Reavy nodded. "Cash withdrawal from an ATM. Yesterday around noon. Here in

Oklahoma City."

A pause. "Very well. How can I help you, Ms. Keller?"

Grissom smiled.

Reavy said, "My account has been debited several hundred dollars in the last day. I want to know if somebody got hold of my card number."

"Did you authorize a payment to Del's Auto Body in Greenspring, Texas?"

"No." Reavy wrote down the name and underscored it. "When was that?"

"Two-fifteen P.M. today."

"That's not a legitimate transaction." Reavy let her voice sharpen. "Got their phone number?"

"We'll deal with unauthorized transactions, Ms. Keller. They won't be charged to your account."

"Good. But I want to get in touch and see if they can tell me who's got my card. I'll want to give a description to the police."

"Of course. I don't have their number, but I'm sure it's in the phone book."

"What else?" Reavy said.

"A cash withdrawal from" — typing — "an ATM, but it's got an unusual notation on it. An ATM in . . ."

Fell walked over to her. Her skin felt cool with excitement.

210

The rep said, "Looks like a temporary ATM in Roswell, New Mexico."

Reavy's lips drew back.

"Oh," the phone woman said. "I bet it's at the Gatecrasher Festival."

"What?"

"The music festival. It's this weekend. A bunch of big acts are playing. Does that help you?"

Reavy locked eyes with Fell, and almost smiled. "Very much."

"Good." The keys clicked. "We'll cancel the card, reissue, and send you a new card with a new number. You'll have to alert —"

"No," Reavy said. "Don't."

"Excuse me?"

"Don't cancel the card. I think I know who's using it." She softened her voice. "My little sister. We've been looking for her."

"I'm sorry, Ms. Keller, but procedure requires —"

"Don't." Reavy's voice rose. "She's been missing for three weeks. If she's in Roswell, that's our first good news. Please — if you cancel the card, she'll know we've found her. She might run again."

"I'm not sure . . ."

"Please, we're all so worried — leave the card active. I'll call back every day to see if she's used it again. That's the only way I can follow her. And if she's at a music festival — she's only fifteen." She let her voice crack. "We just want Bethany to come home."

After a long second, the woman said, "Okay. I can do that."

"Thank you."

Three minutes later they headed out the door. Reavy said, "Keys. I'll drive. And Grissom, I need to stay awake."

He didn't balk at handing over the crank. He knew they needed to fly.

In the darkened guest bedroom, Sarah tiptoed to the window. She checked: It was locked. A sturdy sawed-to-measure broomstick was jammed in the casement to keep intruders from sliding it open.

But the broomstick wouldn't stop people from smashing the window — or slicing through it with a glass cutter. She took two books from a shelf and rested them against the pane, so if the glass moved, the books would dislodge and alert her.

Not that the police would come in that way. And not that the clan was partial to silent entry.

She closed the thin curtains. Zoe was far gone, lying on her back, arms over her head like a disco dancer in the middle of

"YMCA." Sarah changed into a T-shirt and gym shorts and slipped under the covers.

Moonlight sifted through the curtains. The silvery light fell on Zoe's face, almost snowy. Sarah couldn't help thinking of how Zoe had looked that day five years earlier, in her little cotton blanket and watch cap, face scrunched, as they ran from the cabin.

Teresa Gavilan had asked her whether she considered it safe to keep a handgun near a child. Sarah hadn't said anything then, but carrying a gun scared the Christ out of her. The only thing that scared her worse was the thought of not carrying one.

She had pulled a gun on a man for the first and only time in her life that day in the forest. Her hand had been shaking so hard that she could have used the barrel to chip ice from a block.

Michael Lawless. She rolled onto her back.

After she fled the forest, Sarah had driven down the mountain road, nearly hyperventilating. The baby strapped beneath a seat belt beside her, screaming, her face as red as a burning rose. Windshield fogged, wiping it with her hand. Snow outside, the road white, barely able to see. Beth. Beth.

Sobbing, she'd crossed the center line. Swerved back. Pulled over and pitched out the door into the snow and retched, falling to her knees. She stared at her hands. Covered in blood, sliced up, burning with pain. She plunged them into the snow and tried to wash it off. The snow soaked it up, blooming red. In her pickup Zoe screamed. God, what had just happened? What had she done?

She heard another vehicle and gasped and staggered to her feet. Jesus, gun in the truck — she'd left it under her seat. She ran to the open door.

The car that pulled up was the marshal's. He got out, his face hyperalert and full of alarm.

"What are you doing?" he said.

And all her words left her. She looked at the pickup. The baby screamed. "I don't know. I have to get her somewhere safe."

Her legs felt like yarn. He put a hand beneath her elbow. "Move. Keep going. Get out of the mountains and get out now."

She nodded.

"Can you drive?" he said.

She opened her mouth. She could see nothing but white and static and blood on her hands.

"Sarah." He put his hands on either side of her face. His eyes were all dark, one color. "Can you drive?"

She blinked. "Yes." She put a hand over

his. "I'll get her out of here. I'll take her home."

"Lock the doors. Stay there. I will get to you. Now go."

"Why . . . what are you . . ."

A black Suburban with a whip antenna raced past them, headed into the mountains. Lawless eyed it. Down the hill, a fire truck was speeding through the trees in their direction, lights spinning.

"Go," he said.

And she had. She'd gone hard.

Now she sat up. Moonlight flowed across the ceiling. She ran her hands through her hair, and was surprised again to find it short. She got up and opened her messenger bag.

Earlier, at the Gatecrasher Festival, she had shut off her first burn phone and removed the battery, so nobody could track its location to Teresa's house. Now she fired up her second burn phone — and called the voice mailbox for the first one. She keyed in her password. It didn't matter that the phone itself was dead. She could access messages without giving away who was calling, or where from.

One new message. She pressed Play.

"It's Danisha," the message began. Her night went to pieces.

28

Harker was the last to board the jet. The Oklahoma City airport — the Jetway, the MD-80 and its passengers and crew, the entire prairie — felt half asleep. The Sunday morning sunrise had barely cleared the horizon. Phone to his ear, he worked his way along the aisle.

"Southeastern New Mexico. Absolutely positive. I'd start driving," he said.

He ended the call, took his seat, and stared straight ahead, gripping the armrests. He visualized the flight and the mission. An hour to Dallas–Fort Worth, a change of planes, another hour in flight — with the time change, he would get to Roswell just after 10:00 A.M.

If he was this close, he could only hope that the clan was on the same trail.

Sarah woke up feeling as if she'd rolled down a hill inside a sack full of rocks. Her stomach was pinched, her neck tight, her eyes gritty. She had barely slept.

"Mom's at Southwest Medical Center. I'll be there till they kick me out, and back in the morning to get her. Then I'll be at the office. With the insurance adjuster and the biggest mofo of a bodyguard I can hire. After that . . . Sarah, don't call my cell phone. Can't find it. Don't know who has it. Don't call the office — the line could be tapped or bugged. Wait for me to contact you again."

Sarah pictured Danisha's mother, Corelle, in a hospital bed. Mrs. Helms was a woman of majestic presence, partial to floral dresses, wigs styled like whipped meringue, and quoting from the King James Bible and *The Hangover,* sometimes interchangeably. And according to Danisha's message, a young white woman had held a knife to her throat, forced her into her Chrysler, and driven halfway across town to ram DHL's office building.

Sarah pressed the heels of her hands against her eyes. It took the Worthes only a day to find her friend and her mother.

Danisha would not take this lying down. She was the human equivalent of a blowtorch. When something set off her temper, she didn't explode but would cut like a blue acetylene flame.

She turned over. Zoe's side of the bed was empty. Sharp morning sunlight streamed against the curtains. Voices in the kitchen sounded bright. The clock on the nightstand read six forty-five.

She found Teresa at the stove, in a terry-cloth robe and moccasins, cooking pancakes. Zoe sat on the counter, kicking her dangling feet. She was giggling, her little shoulders hunched with laughter.

"All the backpacks looked like they were lifting off the ground, and the sun *whooshed* down the side of the sky. All the kids too. They flew. Only they really were falling. Then the bus fell over."

Sarah took Zoe's hand and squeezed.

"I'm not scared anymore," Zoe said. "I didn't dream about it. I dreamed about an angel."

The air seemed all at once to feel like ice on Sarah's skin.

"It was flying from under the ground," Zoe said. "It had wings and they *whooshed* too."

Teresa gave Sarah a look. "How about Mousie? Did he fly?"

Zoe giggled again. "No, you silly." She tilted her head and pointed at Teresa's crucifix. "Does that protect you?"

Teresa brushed Zoe's hair gently with her

fingertips. "It's not magic. It doesn't work like that."

"What does it do?"

Sarah picked her up and set her in a chair at the table. "It doesn't *do* anything. It means she's a Christian."

Zoe said, "Mrs. Helms wears a cross but it doesn't have the guy on it."

"Jesus," Sarah said.

Teresa flipped a short stack of pancakes onto a plate and set it on the table. "It reminds me to live my life in a way that shines a little light on the cross. Coffee's ready."

She sat down. Beneath the chain of the crucifix was another one, half hidden by her robe. Sarah thought: Definitely dog tags.

"You were in the Army, weren't you?" she said.

Teresa eyed her quizzically. "Four years after high school. That's where I became a medic. How did you know?"

Sarah nodded at the chain. Teresa touched whatever pendant lay at the end of it, cosseted beneath the terry-cloth folds of her robe. "That? Oh."

Zoe picked up her fork like a stick and poked at a pancake. Teresa closed her eyes and bowed her head. Sarah took Zoe's hand and held it still. Zoe frowned, confused.

Teresa made the sign of the cross and smiled. "Eat. Come on. Don't hold back."

Sarah released Zoe's hand. The little girl dug in.

Teresa said, "I'm on duty at the medical tent from eight to four today."

Sarah felt conflicting impulses. The house was isolated, and inside it, nobody could see her. At the music festival there would be thirty thousand pairs of eyes and, possibly, police.

But the house was so isolated that nobody could see her and Zoe if they were attacked. On balance, if somebody was going to take her, it was better that it be the cops.

"We'll go with you."

"Today's the busiest day of the festival. Medical's likely to be swamped."

"I can help. I'm an EMT."

"In that case, welcome aboard," Teresa said. "But you don't work as an EMT."

"I got certified after we moved to Oklahoma. I thought it was a good skill set to have. Especially in Tornado Alley." And especially when she felt alone — and realized that for Zoe, she was *it*. She'd decided that if it came to survival, she'd better be a one-man band. She was her own little doomsday prepper.

"Sounds sensible," Teresa said. "Any other

skill sets you added?"

"Clearly I lack the how-to-explain-crucifixes skill set."

But she had plenty of hours at the firing range. And she'd taken self-defense classes taught by a former Army Ranger. She knew to go for the knees, the eyes, and the balls, if an attacker had 'em.

Teresa wiped her hands on a napkin and began clearing up. Sarah stood. "Let me get this."

"I'm going to say my morning devotions. We'll leave in forty-five minutes."

Sarah opened the fridge to put away the milk and syrup and butter. In the door, she saw a prescription vial.

Zoe said, "What are devotions?"

"Prayers, honey," Teresa said.

"You mean like, father, son, and holy ghost?"

"That's part of it."

"I thought the cucifisk didn't fight vampires. Does it fight ghosts?"

Sarah said, "No, munchkin. The Holy Ghost . . ."

"I don't say ghost," Teresa said. "Holy Spirit. Because God isn't a ghost, God's everywhere, a spirit that moves through our hearts." She glanced at Sarah, as if to say, *Is that how a five-year-old might understand it?*

"The father is how we think of God too. Because God is the creator of the entire universe. And God loves us like a father does."

Zoe kicked her feet. "Who's my father?"

Sarah's breakfast abruptly stuck in her throat. "Let's talk about that later."

"At the hospital they said my father is Nolan Asa Worthe."

Sarah couldn't turn away from Zoe's obstreperous stare. Or Teresa's curiosity.

"That's his name," she said. "And I'll tell you about him soon. Now let's get ready to go."

She led Zoe from the kitchen, feeling like an utter coward.

Lawless rolled out of Alamogordo, passing like a black shard near the White Sands Missile Range, a vast tract of dunes and desert that encompassed the Trinity Site, where the first atomic bomb was detonated in 1945. To the east, the sun crested the mountains of the Lincoln National Forest. The U-Wreck-Em he'd rented in El Paso pounded along the highway. The engine rattled but he didn't care if he drove it into the ground. He still had a hundred miles to go. At 90 mph, he'd be there in time for his next cup of coffee.

He called the Marshals Service again. He wanted to get protection approved for Sarah and Zoe. He needed backup, a team. But he was in bureaucratic hell, and it was a holiday weekend. The Marshals Service had a hot desk — but even so, contacting available people over Memorial Day was a nightmare. A guy he knew in New Mexico was on call, but had seemingly disappeared into Carlsbad Caverns.

"Dammit." He hung up. Called District again. Voice mail.

He had taken this to the supervisory deputy U.S. marshal, who said she would take it to the chief deputy for the judicial district — and that was all he'd heard.

Bureaucrats could have selective hearing as acute as any teenager. Meanwhile, Sarah's life, and Zoe's safety, hung in limbo.

He couldn't wait for the machine to grind into action. He'd rented the car on his own dime. He was carrying his service weapon. The star was good for many things, such as bearing firearms aboard commercial airliners.

He swung around a long curve on U.S. 70. This part of the Southwest was home to coyotes, both canine and human, and night skies that startled you into thinking the gods were flinging white sparks at the Earth. It was where the space shuttle had landed when other runways were shut. It was where J. Robert Oppenheimer saw the radioactive sunrise and recited from the Bhagavad-Gita: "I am become death, the destroyer of worlds." It was the birthplace of William Bonnie. This was Billy the Kid country.

Portentous, considering that Sarah might by now be a federal fugitive. Her photo had been on the news again. It was now officially a Story, a Thing.

He should have known all along that this would not stay under the radar. Not with the Worthe clan running loose. Not with Curtis Harker working the case for the Bureau.

He wondered how Sarah looked. On the phone her voice sounded clear and sharp. It no longer sounded young and lost, but determined, if desperate — like a flash of sunlight from a broken mirror.

He accelerated eastward. Once he crossed the mountains, it would be a rifle shot straight to Roswell.

Sarah wanted to get to San Francisco. There was no way to do that on a commercial flight, not without federal government resources being expended on her behalf. Unless he got a go-team with official clearance, and legal protections in place for her, he didn't want the government to know where she was. She needed to stay off the grid.

The road steepened. He put on his sunglasses against the morning glare.

He remembered spotting the flames consuming Beth Keller's house, crackling orange against the green of the forest. He had broken into a run. Heard another crack, sharp like gunfire, and drew his weapon. Out of the trees appeared a young woman, breath frosting the air, eyes hot with grief and panic and fury. Baby cradled against her chest. Glock in her right hand.

She saw him and brought the semiautomatic up, chest high, finger on the trigger. "Stop right there, or I'll kill you. I'll shoot you, motherfucker."

He stopped. He didn't doubt the death in her hand. But she looked so much like Beth, she had to be her sister. Her teeth were chattering.

He gambled. "If you want to stay alive, let me help you." Carefully he held up his star. "U.S. marshal. Lower the weapon."

She had a terrible gash across her palm. Her shoulders were heaving. The Glock never veered from a kill shot at his chest.

"I'm not staying here," she said. "I'm getting the baby out."

He looked at the burning house. "Beth?"

"No." Her voice broke. "The Worthes."

His chest felt hollow. "Nolan?"

"They're not getting Zoe," she said. "Hear me?"

He eyed the trail she had broken through the snow. He saw everything she had left in her wake: flames, death, blood where she'd fallen.

If the Worthes found her trail, they would follow her like a lit fuse.

He said, "I'll get you to safety. But lower the weapon."

She didn't. "Understand me. I'll protect Zoe. She's not leaving my arms."

She waited. She knew what she was asking of him.

"Understood," he said.

She held still an everlasting second longer. Took her finger off the trigger and lowered the gun.

He put a hand against her back. "Run."

He knew what she was asking of him, and he did it. He ran at her side, weapon at the ready, to the switchback where she'd parked her truck. Shaking, she climbed in. Fired up the engine. Waited for him to get in too. He turned back toward the forest.

"No." Alarmed, she opened her door again.

He shut it. "Your job is to protect the baby. Mine is to apprehend the Worthes. You want to have any chance of stopping them? Trust me."

She stayed icily still, the Glock in her hand. Then she swallowed and nodded.

"Go," he said. "Drive. Don't stop."

She spun the wheels, pulling away.

Trust me. Those two words, spoken in a snowy clearing, had echoed across five years and rung like broken glass in the hot New Mexico morning.

His phone buzzed. He read the message from Teresa Gavilan.

On our way to fairgrounds. Med tent #1.

He pushed the gas pedal to the floor.

29

Grissom drove the last sixty miles, while the women slept in the back seat. He checked the mirror. With their eyes closed, they looked like dolls, innocent and pliable. They looked perfect. On the seat beside him were the things he'd picked up from the dealer's house outside Amarillo. The man had been unhappy, stumbling out of bed at four A.M., but he was a sales associate of the clan. He handled dope and meth and occasionally sold firearms. He hadn't wanted to sell his personal weapons, but Grissom didn't give him a choice. A Smith & Wesson revolver was wrapped in a pillowcase. The Mossberg shotgun was on the floor with ten boxes of shells.

Ahead, the scrubby trees and scruffy billboards of Roswell pocked the desert horizon. When he pulled off the blacktop and bounced over the dirt into the parking lot at the music festival, he said, "Wake up."

Fell and Reavy roused themselves. For a second their eyes were vague with sleep. But then they snapped alert.

Time to unfurl the angel's wings and fly.

In the medical tent, Sarah set Zoe up with a coloring book beside a volunteer at the check-in desk. The morning crowd consisted of hangovers, a sprained ankle, and a suspected scorpion sting. In all, the festivalgoers seemed a ruly lot. They were having fun, but their idea of abandon seemed within bounds. Or maybe Sarah had grown used to people who thought boundaries were something to be snipped with bolt cutters and driven through with a stolen car.

She had the reborn doll in the Snugli. Zoe had on a blue T-shirt, jeans rolled up at the cuffs, and Converse All Stars. She looked like a kid out of *Father Knows Best.* Luckily, she was too young to understand either the fifties or irony.

Teresa handed Sarah a clipboard. "I'll let you take names. I imagine you're good at that."

"I'm good at matching names to the right people. And pinning them to a map."

"And then to the ground?"

"That's skip tracing. Anybody who's trying to stay lost, I find."

"Like a feral shepherd."

Sarah laughed.

Teresa began loading bottled water in a cooler filled with crushed ice. "This wasn't always the career you pined for, I sense."

"No."

The nun's expression filled with curiosity.

"You really want to know? I wanted to be a Secret Service agent."

"A shepherd indeed."

Sarah felt flustered. "I guess . . . I wanted the earpiece and aviator sunglasses, you know — getting to ride on Air Force One and all that. Have movies made about my badassedness." She shrugged, but nonetheless felt discomfited. "I wanted to live in the White House. I was eight."

"You've given up that ambition?"

Sarah made a face. *Whaddaya think?*

Teresa touched her arm. "I didn't mean to throw you off balance." Her expression turned kind. She glanced at Zoe. "You're a ferocious guardian already."

Sarah swallowed, unexpectedly emotional.

The tent flap opened and a young man came in, nearly dragging his girlfriend. "Little help?"

Danisha pulled her Jeep carefully into the carport at her mom's clapboard house.

"Here we are."

The place was painted sparkling white, like all the other clapboard houses on the street. A neat line of them, separated by chain-link fences, ran all the way to the river. Pecan trees were coming into leaf.

Corelle Helms was exhausted. She looked like she'd been beaten up. Danisha felt incandescent and ashamed.

This had come into her mother's life because of her. It wasn't her fault, or Sarah's. It was the fault of a bunch of sick patriarchal cocksuckers who wanted the world to burn, and wanted Zoe as some kind of torchbearer. Or as kindling. And to get her, they were willing to punch a widow in the face.

"The neighborhood watch is sending somebody to stay with you while I clean up the office," Danisha said.

Since her brother had passed three years earlier, Danisha had stopped by to see her mother every day. She hated the thought of leaving her this morning.

She killed the engine. "Wait here. Let me double-check that everything's ready for you."

"You be safe," Corelle said.

Danisha tried to smile, but her mother looked shrunken. Her glasses reflected her eyes, huge and shimmering.

"Lock the car doors after me," she said.

When she opened the front door, the emptiness, the lack of lights and noise, spooked her. She walked silently through the house, room by room, like clearing a building in Kandahar. Step by step, she began to feel calmer. Things looked all right. In the living room, framed photos on the side table had been knocked over. She set them back up, like a virtual choir, all smiling.

She brought her mom in and got her settled on the sofa with a glass of iced tea and a book of crossword puzzles.

"Thank you, angel," Corelle said.

Danisha went out to check the mail. The morning was nearly empty, just a jet on approach to the airport. She opened the mailbox, and stopped.

She drew out the eight-by-ten photo, her hands shaking. When she went back inside, she sat down beside her mom, fists clenched.

"I have to go out of town for a few days."

"Honey, no."

"I want you to stay with Yvonne and the boys till I get back."

There was a knock on the door. Through the frosted glass, she saw the neighborhood watch coordinator.

Corelle sighed. She knew that things weren't right. "Where are you going?"

Danisha wasn't about to show her mother the photograph she'd found in the mailbox. It was her brother Orrie's high school graduation photo. It had been in the lineup among the shining choir on the side table, and she hadn't noticed its absence.

A red *X* had been painted over Orrie's face in nail polish. Below, in black marker, was written *One down, one to go. You decide.*

The clan meant to terrify her into providing information about Sarah and Zoe. And if she didn't . . .

She patted her mom's hand. "I'll call you from the road."

Unless she helped take down the Worthes, nobody was safe.

"I'm going to New Mexico," she said.

30

Fell and Reavy walked side by side a step behind Grissom. The fairground looked like a vast dump in the morning light. Acre after acre of dirt, scuffed from tens of thousands of feet, speckled with beer cans. And speckled with thousands of people looking for breakfast or more beer. A cleanup crew was skewering litter with sharp sticks. The food court was open. On the stage, the load-in for the day's first act was in full swing.

Grissom paused. "They may not be here. May not even be awake yet."

Fell said, "They're awake."

"You contradicting me?"

"I'm speaking from experience." Damn, he was wound up. She hated having to watch every freaking word. "The girl's five. She's been awake for two hours."

On the long drive through the night they'd called all the motels in town. Sarah Keller had not checked in anywhere. The clan had outriders in this county — cousins who had been called and told to watch for Keller, for the girl, and for a truck with Oklahoma plates. Nobody had reported anything.

Reavy scanned the scene. "They're here. I know it."

Grissom nodded and ran the back of his hand down her arm. "Then they're here." He pointed at a booth a hundred yards away. INFORMATION. MEETING POINT. "Come on."

Sarah hung the IV bag while Teresa checked the young woman's vitals. It looked like dehydration, probably from a combination of sunshine, nonstop dancing, and vodka shots.

Teresa said, "Rest. Call if you need me."

She and Sarah walked to the check-in desk. From her perch behind the table, Zoe held up a picture she'd drawn. "Look."

It was Teresa, dressed in a nun's habit, her crucifix the size of a crossbow. She was riding a unicorn.

"Cool," Sarah said.

"Are my feet really that round?" Teresa said.

Outside, the P.A. amplifier whined to life. *"Sarah Keller to the Information booth. Sarah Keller."*

Zoe looked toward the tent flap. "Mommy, they're calling you."

Sarah stood frozen.

The volunteer at the desk was staring at her peculiarly. When she'd come in, Teresa had introduced her as Carson.

"Sarah Keller to the information booth."

Teresa put a hand on her arm. The volunteer looked back and forth between them, perplexed but peeling back the obfuscation. Her eyes widened.

That was their game, Sarah realized. "I should —"

Teresa held onto her arm. "You don't need to do a thing."

She felt the shakes begin, at her knees. "Right."

The aide seemed overcome with shock. Her cheeks were glowing pink.

Zoe said, "Mommy, aren't you going to the information booth?"

It was no use. Sarah said, "Yeah. Come on."

She took Zoe's hand and had her climb over the table. "Backpack. On." She looked at Teresa, feeling the beginnings of panic.

The volunteer stood up, clutching a clipboard to her chest. "You're the . . ."

"Teresa didn't know," Sarah said. Holding Zoe's hand, she ran toward the tent flap.

Zoe said, "Mommy, my colored pencils."

"We'll get more later." She looked over her shoulder. The volunteer had a walkie-talkie to her mouth.

Teresa was bustling after her, looking frustrated and determined. "This way." She grabbed Sarah's arm and pulled her toward the back of the tent.

"You don't have to do anything. This is on me," Sarah said.

"Faster."

At a corner of the tent the dirt peeked through. Teresa pulled up a tent peg and lifted the heavy plastic a foot off the ground.

"Hurry," she said.

"I can't ask you to —"

"Let me deal with my own decisions. Move."

Zoe stood by the impromptu exit, working her fingers together. "Where are we going?"

Sarah held back for only a millisecond. "Follow me."

She dropped to the ground and crawled underneath the plastic into the sunshine, then waved to Zoe. "Come on."

Zoe got on her belly and skinnied out, backpack scraping the tent.

Sarah jumped to her feet. In the Snugli, the reborn looked dusty. She hurriedly brushed its head. "To the truck."

"Sarah Keller to the information booth. Sarah Keller."

Inside the tent, voices rose. The volunteer said, "She went out the back."

"Mommy?" Zoe said.

She took her daughter's hand and ran.

As the highway neared Roswell, the land flattened out. Miles of sand and sagebrush rolled out ahead of Lawless, a view that looked like it would never end. He checked the clock. He figured he'd be at the music festival in fifteen minutes. He felt tired but wired. He phoned Teresa Gavilan.

Her number rang, and she didn't answer.

"Sarah. This way."

Running, Sarah looked back. Teresa had crawled beneath the tent flap and climbed awkwardly to her feet. She caught up. "The volunteer — she called Security. They'll call the police. I'm sorry."

Sarah's stomach cramped. Zoe said, "Mommy, what's wrong?"

Teresa led them down an alley between the medical tent and the food court. Vendors were piling crates out of vans and trucks, loading food in refrigerators.

"We have to get to my truck," Sarah said.

238

"My car's closer," Teresa said. "In the staff lot."

"And you have an official badge for that? They have your license number?"

Teresa grimaced. "Your truck. How far?"

In the center of the festival grounds, near the sound board, two stanchions were set up — girders for emergency lighting and the megaphones of the P.A. system. Fell climbed the stanchion as if it were the ladder for a high dive. Twelve feet up, she stared around the grounds.

Reavy was below, ready. Grissom said, "Well?"

Fell leaned out, one hand tented over her eyes. Hippies, druggies, children of darkness all around. And . . .

Two women, moving quickly, toward the parking lot. Pulling a child along.

She pointed.

Reavy moved.

31

Sarah held Zoe's hand and led Teresa through the crowd. People pressed in.

"Mommy, I can't go so fast," Zoe said.

Her backpack was bouncing up and down, her face confused and worried. Sarah picked her up and kept going. The parking lot was a quarter of a mile away. Sweating, she broke into a jog. Teresa put a hand on her arm to hold her back.

"Stay calm. Don't draw undue attention."

Lesson one, and Sarah had forgotten it. She slowed down.

Zoe said, "Where's Mousie?"

Sarah did not want to hear that. "In your backpack."

"No, he isn't." Zoe looked around. She looked at her hands. "I had him. I was holding him."

"We can't worry about Mousie right now."

Zoe's shoulders rose. "Mommy, I dropped him."

"I'm sorry."

"I dropped him. I want Mousie. Mommy, stop. *Stop.*"

She burst into tears and tried to squirm out of Sarah's arms. "I want Mousie. Go back. Go back."

"I can't," Sarah said.

Zoe's crying increased. *"I want Mousie. Where is he? Go back, Mommy. Go back."*

It was too much: Zoe had made it this far and hit her limit. She was having a meltdown.

Teresa peered back through the crowd. "What does Mousie look like?"

Sarah felt like her skin was covered in nettles. "He's about six inches long, white stuffed mouse wearing a red clown outfit, and . . ."

"Mousie," Zoe sobbed.

This was stupid. She couldn't have Zoe freaking out in public. She pulled the keys from her pocket and stuck them in Teresa's palm. "Get her to the truck. I'll find Mousie and catch up with you."

Instantly Zoe's sobs abated. Sarah set her down. Her shoulders shuddered and she wound her fingers together frantically, but the crying stopped.

"Go with Teresa. I'll be right there."

She rushed back toward the medical tent,

searching the ground through the ever-thickening crowd. Then miraculously, she saw Mousie. She rushed across a crowded patch of ground where he was being trampled underfoot.

He looked like a broken skydiver, flopping on the dirt. She bent and picked him up. People flowed around her.

Somebody stopped right in front of her. Hiking boots. She looked up.

A blond woman with glossy eyes stood directly above her. She had a tattoo on the inside of her right forearm. *Fiery Branch.*

She grabbed Sarah's hair.

Before Sarah could move, the woman dug strong fingers into her hair and twisted. Sarah tumbled to the dirt.

A man in the crowd raised his hands in a calming gesture. "Hey, not cool."

The blonde said, "Fuck off."

Sarah punched her in the groin.

She cringed and let go. Sarah scrambled away from her on all fours and stumbled to her feet.

She recognized her. She'd seen her once before in person, and many times in the newspaper and on wanted posters. Her name was Reavy Worthe.

Sarah plowed through the crowd, off balance. Ahead she saw nonstop people, a wall six feet high and six hundred yards deep. She looked back. Reavy was twenty feet behind her. And she was coming after her with a knife in her hand.

Sarah veered into a tent. People in black T-shirts wearing badges on lanyards, drinking orange juice and eating croissants. Somebody cried, "Hey — where's your credentials?"

"Help me," Sarah said. "A woman's chasing me — shit."

Reavy bulled into the tent. Sarah ran past a table laid with muffins and a kettle of oatmeal. She spun and upended the table in Reavy's path. A woman shrieked.

Reavy raised the blade over her head like a knife thrower in the circus, and flung it across the tent. It flicked end over end, flashing in the light. Sarah dropped low behind the upended table.

Somebody screamed. People dropped drinks and food and scattered.

A man cried: "I've been stabbed."

Sarah saw a young man on the ground, the knife sticking out of his calf. He looked astonished at the blood running down his leg from beneath his jeans. Sarah fled for the exit at the far end of the tent.

Behind her the young man screamed

again. "You fuckin' kidding me? Are you insane?"

Sarah ran out the exit into the sunshine. When she looked back, Reavy was coming. She had the knife in her hand again. She must have yanked it from the young man's leg.

Sarah jumped over tent pegs and raced into the crowd. Looked back. Saw only Goths and Emo kids and a few Rastafarians. *Maybe.* Maybe she'd lost her.

Then from the corner of her eye she saw movement. Her skin prickled. Another woman was running at her from an angle. Dark hair, dark clothing, pale skin.

Fell was here. Sarah pumped her arms and ran for the gate.

The angel's wings. If they were here, they weren't alone. They never attacked on their own. They were in the service of the Shattering Angel.

She sprinted toward the distant gate to the parking lot. Where was Grissom Briggs? He was the one she feared most. She could sense him — he was like a dark weight in the air. She pushed past concertgoers. Behind her, she heard shouts. She looked. Fell and Reavy were closing in.

She neared the chain-link fence that surrounded the festival grounds. The gate was straight ahead. All at once, she thought: *No.* She couldn't lead them straight to the pickup truck. She had to lose them again and get to the next gate down.

She veered left and raced along the fence. On the far side, a sea of parked cars shone in the morning sun. Her feet kicked up dust. Her breath came in long gasps. She chanced another look back. Fell and Reavy were closer.

They were going to catch her.

And the fence continued straight for what seemed forever. She was penned in.

Then she heard a horn honk, loud and long and hard. On the far side of the fence, beyond the first rank of parked cars, the black pickup appeared. At the wheel Teresa had one hand pressed on the horn.

Sarah ran for the fence, jumped, and climbed.

At the Roswell airport, Curtis Harker got behind the wheel of his rental car. The dry desert air was motionless, clear and warm. The sky seemed to gleam. It was a good day for hunting. He sensed it: The clan was here.

He opened his briefcase, took out the police radio scanner, and turned it on. On the flight he had studied a map of Roswell

and surrounding Chaves County. He rolled
out of the airport onto the blacktop, headed
toward town.

Sarah scrambled over the chain-link fence.
The cut ends of the steel mesh tore her
blouse and scratched her stomach when she
rolled across the top. She kicked out,
dropped to the dirt on the far side, and kept
running.

Ahead, the pickup jammed to a stop,
engine gargling. Sarah careened toward it
between parked cars. At the wheel, Teresa's
face was severe. Zoe sat behind her, hand
pressed to the window, looking stricken.

The fence rang as Fell and Reavy started
to climb.

Teresa shouted, "In the bed. Hurry."

Sarah heard the others hit the ground. She
grabbed the tailgate and climbed on the
back bumper. Teresa stomped on the gas.
Sarah pitched into the cargo bed, facedown.
The truck raced, jolting along the dirt lot.

Zoe shouted, "Mommy, look out."

Sarah heard the clatter of metal. She
rolled over.

Fell crouched on the bumper, hanging
onto the tailgate, staring at her.

32

Halfway into Roswell, the first reports scratched over Harker's police radio scanner.

"Request a unit at the festival. We've had a report of a stabbing."

Harker turned up the volume. Maybe one stoned hippie sticking a meth head. Maybe a feud over boy bands. Maybe not.

"Assailant is a white female, blond hair, early twenties. Witnesses report she recovered the knife and fled the scene in pursuit of another woman."

"Repeat that?"

"The assailant fled the scene of the assault to chase a woman with a baby."

Harker punched the accelerator. He pulled out and passed a line of cars on the two-lane blacktop, pressing on the horn. Opposing traffic swerved to avoid him.

Fell crouched on the bumper, knuckles

white. Her eyes were strange and mismatched. They seemed to burn, one hotter than the other. Around her neck hung a sheathed hunting knife.

Teresa bounced onto the blacktop and accelerated. Sarah looked around for something to throw at Fell. The bed of Danisha's truck was pristine. She didn't even have a piece of litter that could be used as a weapon.

From inside the cab Zoe cried, "Stop!"

For a moment, the truck stopped accelerating.

Sarah yelled, "No — *go.*"

Teresa punched it. Sarah let herself slide toward the tailgate. Fell perched on the far side like the *Twilight Zone* gremlin on the airplane wing. Her face was young and flawless. It would have been lovely, except for the murderous look in her mismatched eyes. She was staring straight through Sarah at Zoe.

With a surge of adrenaline, Sarah raised a boot and kicked at her face. Fell bobbed.

Distantly she saw a police car. The engine revved. They swerved across the yellow line as Teresa gunned it, passing traffic. Sarah glimpsed other drivers as they sped by. People were staring with open wonder. One woman had a phone out. Maybe the couple in the Toyota were taking a video. The word *cooked* popped into her mind.

Then she realized Teresa wasn't fleeing from the distant police car. She was trying to outrun a silver SUV that was barreling up the wrong side of the road at them.

"Oh my God," she said.

It could only be Reavy, with Grissom Briggs.

Sarah kicked again and hit Fell's shoulder. Fell's face contorted with pain but she held on. She swung and grabbed Sarah's leg.

Shit.

The drivers in the other cars stared open-mouthed as the truck raced by. They passed the ROSWELL UFO TOURS van, full of tourists with cameras, an insectile alien bolted to the roof. A sky-blue Pontiac Bonneville accelerated to pace them. The driver, a Latino in his forties, put down his window.

"Jesus, the baby," he shouted.

The baby.

The other drivers were staring at the Snugli and the reborn doll. They thought a mother with a newborn was kickboxing in the back of a pickup. *Great job staying under the radar.*

Fell gripped Sarah's leg, struggling for purchase. Sarah fumbled wildly at the Snugli and yanked the reborn out.

The thing weighed almost ten pounds. Its head was tough vinyl, filled with dense plastic beads to give it babylike heft. Sarah held its feet and swung it at Fell like a mace.

She hit Fell solidly in the face. Fell flinched and cried out.

A woman shouted, "Oh my *God.*"

The blue Bonneville honked and bounded up on their tail. The passengers stuck their arms out of the windows, waving to Fell. They wanted to rescue her.

Ignoring them, Fell drew her knife from the sheath. Its stubby blade glinted in the morning sun.

From the truck's cab, Teresa shouted something. Sarah couldn't make it out.

Teresa shouted again. Zoe said, "Latches, Mommy."

God — of course. Drop the tailgate.

Fell crouched like Gollum, black hair flying in the wind, looking ready to gut Sarah like a deer. The Bonneville rode their ass like the big American sedan it was, people now shouting to Fell: "Jump."

The latches were on the outside corners of the cargo bed. Sarah reached over the top of the tailgate, worked the first latch open and cringed back. Fell lunged, the blade flashing. Sarah swung the reborn like a sledgehammer at her head.

The driver of the Bonneville pressed on the horn. Behind him the headlights of the silver SUV grew bright. It was coming.

Sarah dived for the remaining latch, got her fingers under it, and flipped it open. Fell's eyes went round.

The tailgate dropped open and Fell keeled off the bumper.

She landed on the hood of the Bonneville. Fell hit the hood with a crunch and bounced into the windshield. It cracked. Everybody in the Bonneville screamed and the driver slammed on the brakes. Fell slid up the windshield and onto the roof and straight over, disappearing. Sarah sat in the bed of the pickup, staring out the open tailgate, watching the asphalt and white lines slew away beneath them.

She looked at the reborn doll. Its head was dented and its stomach sliced from Fell's knife.

Welcome to the fight, Little Weirdo.

She made her way toward the cab, her chest heaving, and pounded on the back window. Zoe squirmed around and slid the window open.

"Mommy, are you okay?"

"Fine. I'm climbing in." She tossed the reborn inside.

She wanted to get to the wheel. Teresa was

251

steady but Sarah feared that she was over-whelmed. Through the window she called, "Get someplace where we can swap places. I'll take over."

"You watch Zoe. Let me handle this." In the mirror the nun's expression flickered, briefly turning wry. "I'm good. I was a rally driver in a previous life."

"A what?"

"This truck is nowhere as tight as the Subaru Impreza I drove," she said. "But it'll have to do."

"Rally driving? Like races through forests and across the outback?"

"And the Inca Trail."

Teresa kept the pedal down. Through the open tailgate Sarah saw the silver SUV coming at high speed. Reavy and Grissom were bearing down on them.

33

Teresa called, "Sarah, come on. Get inside."

The truck raced through a yellow traffic light. As they cleared the intersection the light turned red. Behind them in the silver SUV Grissom and Reavy ran it.

"Shit," Sarah said.

She squirmed her head and shoulders through the narrow window into the back of the pickup's crew cab. Zoe reached up and tried to pull her in.

They were in a suburban neighborhood of sprawling ranch homes. Teresa veered across a vacant lot, vaulting the truck over the curb. Sarah shunted through the window on momentum and landed in a heap against the front seats.

Zoe's bottom lip was trembling. Sarah scrambled onto the seat and hugged her.

"It's okay."

Zoe buried her face in Sarah's chest. "That lady . . . she had a knife. What was wrong with her?"

"She's gone. She's gone now." Sarah thought: *Lying so automatically has become a bad habit.*

Teresa said, "Hang on."

She spun the wheel left and turned down an alley. The truck hit one trash can, then another. The cans banged like kettledrums and flew as they battered past.

Huddled under Sarah's embrace, Zoe went quiet. Sarah looked out the back window. The SUV was still behind them.

Harker followed the path of the car chase, vectoring thanks to information he heard on the police scanner. "Heading northwest toward U.S. 380. Reported that a woman in the back of a pickup truck is beating another woman with a baby."

"Repeat that?"

Eyewitnesses: notoriously unreliable. On the other hand: The clan brought out the most extreme in everybody.

He angled through morning traffic, past piñons and billboards, vacant lots and houses hunkered under the broiling sun. He didn't have a gumball light — the Bureau didn't go for sirens and flashing things; it wasn't running a disco — but if any local bubba in a black-and-white tried to stop him, he had his FBI wallet and would tear the guy's nuts out through his throat.

"Black pickup with Louisiana plates, heading into the Barnett neighborhood at high speed."

Barnett. Southwest Roswell, not more than two miles away. He laid a hand on the horn and cut the corner at an intersection.

Ninety seconds later he spotted the pickup. Two hundred yards ahead of him it flashed past, big Dodge Ram with performance tires, powering west into a residential neighborhood. He stomped on the gas just as a silver SUV raced after the Dodge in pursuit. Harker kept his hand on the horn. He keened around a corner and saw the Dodge and the SUV disappear into an alley.

He could get ahead of them. In the alley they had to slow for obstacles — if they didn't, they'd pinball off the concrete walls on either side. But he was on the blacktop. He could beat them to the far side of the alley and cut them off. He accelerated.

Sarah stared out the back window of the pickup, watching the SUV bearing down. At the wheel was Grissom Briggs. His face looked like a block of iron. Reavy was beside him in the passenger seat, blond hair hanging tangled in front of her face. She was

255

loading a shotgun.

Sarah's chest caught. "Teresa, they're armed."

Teresa shot a glance in the rearview mirror. Her expression didn't change, but she seemed to shift in her seat — to focus and stretch, like a racehorse being asked for a new burst of speed. This woman, Sarah thought, was braver than anybody she'd met in a long time.

The engine roared, a steady drone. They exited the alley back onto the blacktop.

Sarah felt dizzy. She wanted Zoe on the floor to protect her from gunfire, but the truck was going at death metal speed. She needed Zoe belted in, tight.

She pushed Zoe's head down. "Lie on the seat. Head in my lap."

But Zoe glanced around, a 180-degree sweep of the horizon. Sarah pushed her down again and bent over her.

"There's another man," Zoe said.

"Say again?" Sarah said.

From beneath Sarah's embrace, Zoe pointed out the window. "There's another man coming. In a brown car."

Sarah turned. The road was headed toward a fork, and they were on one of the prongs. Coming down the other one was a brown sedan. At the wheel was a man with short hair and sunglasses, wearing a suit.

A suit. Out here, the only people who wore suits were bankers and undertakers. And federal agents.

Teresa, voice strained, said, "Sarah?"

"I think it's an FBI agent."

"In pursuit?"

And I thought this couldn't get any worse.

"Of us. I presume so."

The truck bucketed over a dip in the road. Teresa steadied the wheel and kept racing toward the fork.

"Sarah? He'll have firepower."

"What are you asking?"

"Little backup wouldn't hurt."

Teresa was asking if they should turn themselves over to the FBI to save their lives. In Sarah's lap, Zoe huddled, tense and small.

"SUV's gonna be in range here in a second," Teresa said.

Surrender. That's what Teresa was talking about. Surrender and stay alive.

A cry escaped Sarah's lips. Teresa didn't know. She couldn't — could she? Could Teresa understand why she was hesitating?

The brown car drew nearer. The two roads were converging on a barren intersection of scrub and dirt. His side of the fork had a stop sign. He didn't look like he planned to stop.

"*Sarah.*"

She was asking permission. Sarah's throat caught, because she realized that Teresa had thrown all in: She was willing to risk everything, including herself, to run for it if Sarah only said the word.

Sarah clutched Zoe. If she died in a wreck or from a gunshot, what was any of this worth?

Teeth clenched, Sarah looked up. "Okay —"

To their left, the brown car was on a collision course. And with a high revving sound, the baby-blue Pontiac Bonneville reappeared between them and the FBI agent, accelerating like an arrow. Sarah gaped.

"The hell . . ."

Fell was at the wheel. Jesus, she had carjacked her rescuers. And how big an engine did that ugly old boat have under the hood? It was skiing along like it was on fire.

"Teresa . . ."

"See it."

The truck raced straight toward the intersection. Teresa was still waiting for Sarah's instructions. Stop, or go?

Then the blue Bonneville swung away from the pickup. It arced across the road, across the patch of dirt between the two forks of asphalt, and sideswiped the FBI agent's car.

It hit with a crunch and forced the brown car onto the far shoulder. Side by side, the two vehicles veered into the scrub.

Amid swirling dust, the agent's car slid sideways into a drainage ditch and dropped sharply to a stop. It was out of commission. The blue Bonneville limped away, the left side of the vehicle flattened, tires out of true. It could no longer give chase.

Behind the pickup, the silver SUV kept coming, lights ablaze.

Throat dry, Sarah said, "Drive."

Driving east along U.S. 380 into the morning sun, Lawless saw the first shimmering signs of civilization ahead: trees, dust, billboards on the empty highway. He saw a fork where the highway split in a Y. Left toward central Roswell, right toward the airport and music festival grounds.

Then he saw something else, coming straight at him. He saw three cars abreast, headed for him in all lanes on the highway. Fast.

A black Dodge Ram pickup. A pale blue big-ass sedan. A brown compact.

"No damn way . . ."

He turned the wheel and drove off the highway into the dirt. With a roar the three-car chariot race blew past him going the other way. His car slid sideways under a pale scrim of dust. He grit his teeth and steered into the skid. Dammit —

He braked to a stop on the sand near the fork in the road. Mouth dry, he looked west and saw the brown car canted into a ditch. The blue sedan was half-smashed but rolling away from the crash. It had no intention of stopping.

The black pickup was half-gone down the highway, headed west at top speed. Behind it followed a hulking silver Navigator.

Sarah was in that black truck.

He turned the wheel to give chase, but gave a last glance at the crashed brown car. The driver was still inside. He jumped out, ran to the ditch and pulled open the passenger door. And he saw Curtis Harker.

Lawless hung in the open doorway, one arm on the frame.

Harker sat tilted against the driver's door, which lay half-buried in dirt. He looked like he'd had his bell rung. With one hand he was fumbling with the seat-belt buckle. With the other he was trying to make a phone call.

He turned. His eyes were unfocused, his

teeth bared. But when he saw who was standing in the doorway, he seemed to snap to, like he'd been splashed with water.

"You," he said. "Don't look so unhappy to see me alive."

Still the same Harker. Bristly and brittle, even wrecked in a ditch.

"No head injury, then," Lawless said.

Harker groaned and popped the seat belt. He shook his head violently, trying to orient himself.

Lawless leaned in. "You okay?"

Harker batted his hand away. "What are you doing here, Lawless?"

"Are you all right?" He put a hand on Harker's shoulder and examined his eyes. They were clear and focused. His words were clear and focused. Lawless saw no blood or any sign that the man was in pain. "What's your name?"

"Screw you."

Lawless let him go. "I think you're fine."

Harker grabbed his arm. "She's not getting away."

Lawless pulled free. "I'll call the locals. They'll get you a tow truck." *And something to stanch the bile, maybe.*

He pulled back through the passenger doorway. Harker tried to climb over the center console and follow him.

"You're not going anywhere," Harker said.

Lawless turned and jogged toward his car.

Harker called, "Wait for me, you bastard."

"You shouldn't leave the scene of an accident," Lawless called back. In the air he heard the faint wail of sirens. "Help is on its way."

Lawless jumped into his rental. Harker lurched from the wrecked car, tripped and went down on all fours. He grunted to his feet and staggered toward the U.S. marshal.

"You leave without me and I'll have your star," Harker shouted.

Lawless fired up the engine. Harker broke into a sloppy run.

He yelled, "You can't save her, Lawless. She's mine. She's done."

Lawless spun the wheel. The back end of the car slid on the sand, scattering dust at Harker. Lawless took his phone from his pocket and thumbed Teresa Gavilan's number. He would bet his life savings that she was driving the black pickup. He straightened the wheel and punched it back onto the highway.

34

Under the heavy growl of the pickup's engine, Sarah bent over Zoe in the back seat. At the wheel, Teresa's face was set, lined and fierce. She drove down the center of the blacktop, straddling the line.

Out the window Sarah glimpsed the SUV. Grissom Briggs's dark bulk filled the driver's seat. Reavy's pale blondness and white shirt were bisected by the black gash of the shotgun.

Sarah climbed over the center console into the front passenger seat and hauled the lockbox onto her lap.

Teresa said, "What are you doing?"

"Defending us."

"I —"

"With a show of force if nothing else." God, not now, not pacifism — what kind of cast-iron balls did this nun possess?

Sarah said, "If I show them a loaded gun, they might back off."

"Good. Show it. Show them they can go to hell if they keep at it."

It sounded like a battle cry. Fingers trembling, Sarah fumbled with the lockbox. She could hardly see the combination. Another glance back: The SUV was closing in.

Teresa had her foot to the firewall. The road ran on into the endless desert, straight as a measuring tape. Here past the edge of town there was no cover. Sarah saw no out, no rescue, no sign of an off-ramp or any way to confuse their pursuers. The once-fearful sight of police lights had sunk below the horizon behind them. They were completely exposed.

She took out her Glock. It was loaded, but she followed procedure. Cleared the chamber, ejected the magazine, checked that it was fully loaded. Reinserted it with a flat *whack* with the palm of her hand to drive the magazine into place. She pulled back the slide to load the chamber.

She climbed over the center console again into the back of the crew cab.

"Mommy . . ."

"Stay down."

She knelt on the bench beside Zoe and braced her back against the front seat. She raised the Glock so it could be clearly seen through the rear window of the cab.

Grissom Briggs stared straight at her. The distance between the vehicles held steady.

Then began to diminish.

Reavy raised the barrel of the shotgun. Her hair whipped in the wind. The SUV veered into the opposite lane.

"They're coming." Sarah gripped the Glock two-handed.

The grille of the Navigator appeared outside her window. Then Reavy's pale form. The shotgun protruded out the window.

Teresa said, "Brace yourself."

Sarah pressed against the seat back. Teresa turned the wheel left and sideswiped them.

With a grinding crunch the Navigator veered, the sudden swerve causing Reavy to hit the doorframe. Grissom straightened out. Reavy lowered the barrel of the shotgun.

Sarah dived to the seat just as Reavy pulled the trigger.

The back passenger window shattered. Glass spalled and spewed into the cab.

Zoe screamed and grabbed Sarah's shirt. "Mommy . . ."

Get up. The gun was in her hand. The Worthes were right outside. *You've been here before. Get up. Shoot back.*

She pushed herself up, aimed the Glock

through the window, and pulled the trigger.

Just as Teresa turned the wheel left even harder. Her shot went wild. They slammed into the Navigator again. It caromed onto the shoulder. For a second Sarah thought Grissom was going to hold it, but he hit a bump and the Navigator fishtailed. He lost control, careened into a stubby pine tree, and bounced off. The SUV spun and wobbled to a stop.

Sarah's vision pulsed. "You got them."

Then she was shaking all over.

They crested a rise and the dust from the Navigator's spinout disappeared. Sarah dropped to the seat and pulled Zoe into her arms. Zoe clung to her like a spider monkey, shoulders jerking. Nuggets of shattered safety glass covered the back seat. Shotgun pellets were embedded in the back of Teresa's headrest. Sarah became aware that her face was stinging. Her forearms were stinging. Blood freckled her skin from tiny shards of embedded glass.

She called to Teresa, "You all right?"

Teresa kept the truck rolling like a freight train down the road. "Anybody behind us?"

"Empty blacktop."

Teresa braked, spun the wheel, and cut sharply through a break in a barbed-wire fence. She raced through a gate and over a cattle guard, tires ringing against the steel, and onto a furrowed dirt track. They barreled into the desert, blowing a rooster tail of dust behind them.

Five miles later they came upon an abandoned barn and trailer. Teresa finally stopped and killed the engine. She slumped back against her seat. Sarah put a hand on her shoulder.

Zoe said, "Are we there yet?"

"I don't know where we are. But we're all here together," Sarah said.

She reached into the Snugli, pulled out Mousie, and handed him to her.

35

Danisha was at the Avis counter at the Roswell airport when the tow truck pulled up, hauling a smashed rental car. She signed the rental documents absentmindedly. The car was wrecked but good.

She did a double take. Out of the tow truck climbed FBI Special Agent Curtis Harker. He grudgingly took some paper-work, slammed the door, and stalked toward the building.

Danisha grabbed the keys to her rental and hoisted her duffel onto her shoulder. Harker approached the door, his face a block of annoyance behind aviator sunglasses. She scooted around the corner before he could spot her.

She felt as if she had come down with a sudden fever. Harker — he had screwed with her phone. She'd suspected, but this proved it.

She'd found the cell phone in her ruined

office, under a pile of debris. A pile she had already sifted through. Yeah, the office was a disaster, but phones don't dissolve and re-appear out of empty air.

Harker. The asshole had taken it when he came to gloat and sniff. He was fanatical, like a dog with its teeth sunk into some-body's hamstring.

"Shit."

If Harker was here, it meant he had harvested the data on her phone. She felt a swell of fear and disgust, as if he'd fingered the panties in her underwear drawer. He was using the knowledge he'd gained to close in on Sarah.

Hell. She had been sloppy. She hadn't imagined that an FBI agent would palm her phone and illegally download everything it contained.

She pushed open a side door and stormed toward the parking lot. "Idiot."

She needed a new phone, a throwaway. She jumped in the SUV she'd rented and headed into town.

Dammit. Harker had already been in Roswell long enough not just to rent a car, but wreck it. What the hell was going on?

In the fallow field between the barn and the abandoned trailer, Sarah washed Zoe's face and hands with bottled water. She brushed glass from her hair. She carefully pulled the little girl's shirt over her head and got clean clothes from her go-bag. Zoe took it all in with limp silence, as if she had become a reborn doll.

"There you go, firefly," Sarah said.

Zoe stood in the sere yellow grass. It bent under the wind with a *skirr.* She looked very small beneath the sky.

The trailer sat on cracked and flattened tires, listing to starboard. It was a fifties-era model, all curves and porthole windows, now grayed and rusting into a Steampunk artifact. A few feet away was the car that must have pulled it out here, a decades-old white Chevrolet with a gull-wing rear end.

Teresa leaned against the pickup's front bumper. "1960 Chevy Biscayne. A classic."

The car was flat against the ground, wheel rims empty. It looked as if it had dragged the trailer halfway into the countryside and died.

Sarah said, "So this is where they keep the aliens."

"Some living quarters. Toothbrushes and probes, all lined up by the sink." Teresa smiled weakly. Blood stained the collar of her green T-shirt.

Sarah said, "You're a nun. Will you be able

to get out of trouble?"

"Not here. Not over this." Teresa spread her arms. "When the authorities look at me, they won't see a sister in a habit with a wimple, an obedient little woman."

"I never thought nuns were like that," Sarah said.

"We're not. Oh, I am obedient to Christ, as best I can be. But out here, in the Wild West? They'll look at me and see a radical in civvies, helping a fugitive."

Sarah's spirits fell. Overhead clouds skated past. Sunshine and shadow slid along the palomino ground.

Teresa touched her neck where a steel ball had lodged under her skin — buckshot from Reavy's sleek, black, Mossberg shotgun.

Death had been that close. Sarah heard a buzzing in her ears. "I . . ." she tried.

Teresa looked square at her. "You going to tell me?"

Sarah blinked.

"I mean, you going to tell me what's really going on?" Teresa's face grew stark. "Why'd you hesitate back on the highway, when I asked whether we should turn ourselves in to the FBI?"

The air in the shadows seemed to leach of all heat. Teresa's gaze was searching.

Sarah tried to clamp everything down, but

her circuits had fried. She put a hand over her eyes and took a hard breath.

"Sarah," Teresa said.

She seemed to feel the lick of snow on her skin. "The day my sister was killed . . ."

And she saw it again: the air white with swirling flakes, the forest nearly black, the house dead behind her. She had tripped over a protruding root and slid to her knees. Climbed back to her feet and saw her hand gashed. Zoe squirmed beneath her coat. She ran and thought, *God, no — don't cry, don't make noise* . . .

The figure appeared silently from the trees. He was tall and sturdy, a carpenter's build, his face raw in the snow and wind.

"Sarah, stop," he said. "Don't move."

Adrenaline flooded her system. She pulled up. Her skin felt electrified.

Nolan looked ragged and as terrified as she was. He stared at her and then at the cabin where he had once lived with her sister. His eyes, normally the carefree blue of an unclouded sky, looked chilly and strained, like thin ice.

She couldn't move. Her throat closed. "Beth . . ."

His faraway gaze snapped back to her. He didn't look lost and frightened anymore. He looked angry, like a cornered animal.

Then he spoke. And he didn't sound like the Nolan she knew, the devil-may-care dude who only wanted to live in the sun-sprinkled woods, hammering nails for new houses and playing his guitar. He sounded like an older man, a man of wrath.

"Give Zoe to me."

He sounded like his father, Eldrick Worthe.

Sarah found her arms tightening around the baby. The snowfall coated Nolan's head and shoulders. He held out a hand and gestured. *Gimme.*

Sarah backed up.

Nolan didn't look surprised. He didn't look frightened. He didn't ask whether Grissom and the girls were chasing her, or whether they should hide.

He didn't ask about Beth.

"Give the child to me," he said.

He might have been a puppet, a ventriloquist's dummy. His mouth was open, the words rolling out, but it seemed to Sarah that his lips didn't even move.

He reached into the pocket of his ski parka and walked toward her. "Let me have the baby."

Nolan eyed the bundle beneath her coat like it was his salvation. He reeked of desperation. He wasn't relieved to see his beloved child safe, but jittering to get hold of her because she was his last chance at staying alive.

He tugged a gun from his pocket.

Shaking, Sarah said, "A gunshot's going to be heard, even in this snow."

"The house is burning and nobody's going to notice any more noise."

Beth's words snaked through her head. *"Take her, Sarah. Protect her. Don't let anybody else touch her. Nobody. You understand?"*

She turned and ran.

He caught her after fifty yards. Snaring her arm, he spun her around. They fell to the snowy ground in a heap. The baby squealed. Nolan pawed at Sarah with his free hand, trying to rip the buttons off her coat and pry the baby away.

"Not yours," he said. "Give her . . ."

Sarah kneed him in the groin. He gasped and buckled. She scrambled out from under him. The baby wriggled against her, little chest going up and down, a tiny squall coming from her mouth. She staggered to her feet and got three steps and Nolan caught her again.

He swung, wildly, and smacked her in the face. Stung, she stumbled. He slammed her back against the trunk of a tree. And with one hand he grabbed her by the throat. Gagging, she clawed for his eyes.

He grunted, close, breathing harshly. Peripherally she saw the gun, black and ugly. Jesus. He'd shoot her to get Zoe. She was his prize, his lotto ticket.

She stopped clawing at his eyes and scrabbled for the gun. She couldn't breathe. She felt it, edges, warm metal. As they struggled, his grip on it loosened. She pushed it against his stomach.

The gunshot was so loud, so close, that Sarah cried out. The gun kicked and knocked her elbow back against the trunk of the tree. The barrel was buried in Nolan's gut. He slumped against her. His hand slipped from her throat.

He dropped to his knees and said, "Fuck. You shot me."

He toppled forward, facedown in the snow, and didn't move.

The white day turned red beneath him, a deep bloody pool seeping from his chest into the snow. The baby began to cry. Sarah stood over him, shaking. The snowfall seemed to turn to static, a hiss in her head. She pointed the gun at Nolan, but he lay motionless. Already new snowfall was sticking to the back of his coat and his jeans.

She heard a noise on the wind, and

jumped. She felt the Worthes like a sour breath on the back of her neck. A wail rose in her throat. Stifling it, she whipped around and ran.

And twenty feet ahead of her, from out of the trees stepped a man she didn't know.

She drew up sharply and raised the gun. Powered by fear and rage and her promise to Beth, she aimed it at his chest and said, "I'll shoot you, motherfucker."

He stared her down. Pistol in his hand. He looked so alert, she thought he might go off like a stick of dynamite. He peered through the trees and saw the flames. He saw Nolan facedown, his blood emptied into the snow.

He looked at the baby with open concern. He looked at Sarah again. "If you want to stay alive, let me help you."

He held up his star.

In the field outside the abandoned barn, Sarah swallowed and held back for one last second. The wind swept across the yellow grass. She lowered her voice so Zoe couldn't hear.

"I can never go to the police," she told Teresa. "I shot Nolan Worthe."

Then tears stung her eyes. "I killed him. And Lawless helped me get away."

36

Lawless rolled west on U.S. 380. He didn't worry about leaving Curtis Harker in the ditch. He did feel an itch at the base of his spine, like a creepy fingernail running up his back. Harker would not forget this. Harker held a grudge.

Harker would mark it in black against him, another point on the scorecard of shame and disappointment and *letting him down* that was part of his everlasting quest to destroy the Worthe clan.

But Harker was ten miles back, stuck with a twisted axle. What worried Lawless right now was the empty road. He saw no signs of the police, no signs of the silver Navigator or Sarah's black pickup. Where had they gone?

Ahead on the asphalt, glass glittered. He pulled over and got out into the heat.

The glass was clear and pebbled — auto safety glass. He walked the debris path. The glass was spread along the centerline of the highway. No skid marks accompanied it. It had come from a vehicle moving at high speed when the window exploded.

Teresa was at the wheel. Only an experienced rally driver would have kept the truck driving absolutely straight down a highway when the window shattered. She hadn't swerved. Not even when the Worthes shot at the truck.

He walked along the highway, phone in hand, pushing Redial every ten seconds.

How had Harker and the Worthes found Sarah so quickly? Things should never have unraveled this fast. Not if Sarah was half the woman he thought she was. Either she'd screwed up, massively, or both he and she had underestimated the resources and deviousness of the people pursuing her. No — the clan, and Harker, had lied, pressured, probably stolen information to track her to New Mexico.

He felt a pang, like a shard of metal in his gut.

He was the expert in fugitive apprehension. And he should have helped prepare Sarah better for what was coming down the pike. She'd had to learn on the fly, under intense pressure, with no training, no help, while caring for a newborn. He was the one who had told her: *Run.*

He'd sent her out here without any backup but a woman sworn to nonviolence, and the scorpions had caught up with her.

"Damn."

After five minutes he found a shotgun shell lying on the edge of the asphalt. A minute later he spotted where a heavy vehicle had run off the road into torn brush, sliding sideways, tires losing purchase and skidding to a messy stop. But whoever had spun out here was long gone.

Teresa — where are you? Are Sarah and Zoe safe?

He called her again and listened to the phone ring.

Danisha came out of the Roswell shopping mall with two prepaid cell phones. She waited in the shade of the entrance, eyeing the parking lot for law enforcement or anybody watching her. She was no expert in countersurveillance, but she thought she had good radar. And she didn't think she was being followed.

She turned on one phone and took the scrap of paper from her pocket, the one with Sarah's alternate burn phone numbers. She started with text messages, hoping that those were harder for the authorities to intercept.

Sarah, I'm here.

She hoped that was enough.

Harker sat for ten minutes in the new rental car at the Roswell airport. *This close.*

He'd been *this* close to them, and they'd gotten the upper hand. The silver Navigator — of course the clan had the means to rent a rugged beast of a vehicle. He was only surprised they hadn't bolted a bull bar to the front, or spikes mounted with human skulls. But the blue Bonneville that sideswiped him — that he hadn't foreseen.

Never underestimate the Worthes.

And that black Dodge Ram pickup — Sarah Keller was not alone. He'd glimpsed two adults in the cab. Keller had a confederate.

Scratch that — confederates. Michael Lawless.

Lawless always turned up at the wrong moment: just in time to rub salt in the wound and tell him, *Let it go.* Harker took out a packet of antacid tablets and popped two in his mouth.

Think it through.

Sarah Keller had help. Perhaps Lawless had hooked her into some underground

280

railroad for people who wanted to disappear. Lawless knew the dank and septic workings of Witness Security. After all, the Marshals Service had given new identities to around ten thousand federal witnesses — and not one of those in WITSec was a decent citizen. They were mob accountants and drug mules and the women who slept with them. Lawless knew all about scrubbing slime from the public record.

Harker was going to need more resources. Backup, tactical support.

This close. The Worthes were in the wind again, and now they knew he was in pursuit. But they wouldn't go to ground. They couldn't afford to. And, more to the point, they didn't want to. Lurking was in their nature, but once they had the scent of their quarry, they would never back off. They would finish it. They were animals.

He put his hand on the ignition and paused.

Why had Keller come to Roswell? To meet up with some hippie at the Gatecrasher Festival? Possible. Probable. But not just any hippie — somebody who knew how to handle himself at high speed. Somebody who had training in defensive driving and, possibly, threat evasion.

The music festival — that's where the

police call had originated. That's where he needed to start. He fired up the ignition.

37

Teresa stared at Sarah for an endless minute, then at the empty ranchlands that unrolled to the horizon, piebald with sun and shadow. She sat down in the doorway of the pickup, hands hanging from her knees.

She said, "I'm listening. You'd better talk."

Sarah talked. When she finished, Teresa looked up.

"Lawless left you at the side of the road that day? To fend for yourself?"

Sarah leaned against the side of the truck. "No. He said he'd find me, and he did. That night he came to my apartment."

At the time, she was living in a second-floor walk-up in Cupertino. When he knocked on the door she nearly jumped through the ceiling. She was pacing in the kitchen, rocking Zoe. The baby wouldn't stop crying. She knew now that her own grief had leaked into the little thing. But that night, when she let Lawless in, she just thought she was in Hell.

He shut the door and scanned the apartment, seemingly evaluating it for threats. "You okay?"

She simply stared at him. In her arms Zoe screamed and flailed. Sarah didn't even own a pack of disposable diapers. She'd pinned a pillowcase on the baby instead. She'd tried to spoon milk into her tiny mouth.

"What am I going to do?" she said.

He spoke in measured tones. "The Worthes fled the scene. We don't know if they saw you. Have no idea if they know your address. You should go to a hotel tonight. Get some things together."

"Done. Then what?"

That was when he noticed that she was already packed. A heavy backpack sat by the door. And he saw the map of the world that took up an entire wall. Pins stuck in it. Tokyo, Hong Kong, Chiang Mai, Bangkok. Mumbai, Jerusalem, Rome, Marrakech.

"My flight's tomorrow. Round-the-world ticket." She bounced Zoe. "Don't worry. I'm not going."

He shifted, seemingly surprised and impressed.

"I'm not supposed to be back for three months," she said. "Got a leave of absence from Past Link."

She'd planned to retrace her mother's journeys, then explore corners of the planet even Atlanta Keller hadn't managed to reach. She bounced the shrieking baby.

She wanted her mom, and Beth, and to go back twenty-four hours. But all her bridges were burned to ash. Her eyes shimmered with tears.

She'd killed a man. Killed Zoe's father. "I'm scared out of my goddamn mind."

Lawless had an incredible intensity about him, as if he had injected rocket fuel into his veins. But his voice was calm.

"You're going to be okay."

"How?"

He put a hand on her arm. "Listen to me. This is my job. I keep people safe."

"But Nolan . . ."

Behind his eyes, turbulence rose. "Yeah. We need to talk."

Somebody pounded on the door. She jumped again, like a crazed cat. "God."

He gestured her back and checked the peephole. Wariness overtook him. He opened the door. On the walkway were two men in U.S. MARSHAL Windbreakers.

He told her, "Sit tight."

He and the other marshals jogged down the stairs to the sidewalk. Sarah paced by the window, bouncing the screaming thing that Zoe had become, and watched them through a slit in the blinds. They stood under a streetlight, huddled in harsh discussion. Lawless seemed fraught.

Did they know she was the one who'd shot Nolan? What was he telling them?

Five minutes later he returned, subdued.

Her nerves knotted. "Are you going to arrest me?"

"No."

She nodded out the window. "Are they?"

"Nobody's getting arrested. They don't know it was you. They don't even know it was Nolan."

"I don't understand."

He stepped closer and tilted his head down to meet her eye. "Nolan's gone."

"You mean he's alive?"

"His body is gone," he said.

"Gone where? What are you talking about?"

"The clan buries its own, Sarah."

"They took him?" She still felt ready to short-circuit. "Are you sure? If he's gone, how can you know he's . . ."

Lawless shook his head. The look that overcame him was sad — as though he hated to deflate such a naive hope. She realized how much she wanted him to tell her that some miracle-working trauma doc had shocked Nolan back to life.

"After I helped get you and Zoe to the switchback, I went back to the house. He was still there — they hadn't found him yet. I stopped and checked his pulse."

He waited for her to absorb it. "But as far as everybody else knows, Nolan Worthe is simply missing."

She shifted the baby against her chest and walked to the map on the wall. It blurred in her vision.

Lawless approached. "Sarah. You have an opportunity here."

"To tell the police what happened?"

He shook his head. "That won't work. You don't have to convince me you acted in self-defense. But I didn't see the shooting. I heard the gunshot and then saw you running toward me. So . . ."

"You didn't see Nolan threaten my life. Nobody saw him with the gun."

Nobody saw him brutalizing a woman with an infant. Nobody saw her fighting for her life. Nolan was Zoe's father. He caught her running out the door of his house with his baby hidden in her coat — and his girlfriend dead in the kitchen. He confronted her. Thirty seconds later, she shot him dead.

The situation was vague enough that she might be arrested and put on trial.

Lawless said, "The crime scene will yield all kinds of evidence. The ejected cartridge casing. Signs of a struggle. And forensic evidence, especially DNA," he said. "But as long as you're not arrested, nobody can match that to you."

Blood. Not just Nolan's; hers. She'd fallen and sliced open her palm. Her blood was all over the scene.

She said, "Why are you telling me this?"

"Because I believe you're righteous. And that you mean it when you say you'll protect the baby. So you need to know the score," he said. "I know you acted to save your life and Zoe's. I will testify if called to do that — but it will be best if it never comes to that. A trial, publicity —"

"Will bring the clan after Zoe," she said.

A cold certainty settled on her. If she stayed in Cupertino, the cops would eventually come to her for DNA comparison — and they'd have her dead to rights. Zoe would be taken away.

In that moment of dark clarity, she understood. She had been praying, crying, imagining that she could conjure a way out: some excuse, some path back to the way things had been that morning. A lawyer, a confession, a miracle. But there was no way back.

And there was no standing still. Lawless believed in her innocence, but his faith wouldn't keep her safe. If she stayed put, soon enough the cops or the clan would batter down her door.

There was only one thing to do. Lawless stood close, waiting. He knew. He just couldn't tell her to do it.

"I have to go." She pulled Zoe against her chest. "I have to get her out of here."

Sarah told the story to Teresa in a monotone. Her voice, her emotions, were running on empty. She didn't try to explain or justify herself. Teresa would accept it, or not.

When she finished, Teresa brushed her hair away from her face. She stood up. She said nothing. She just looked at Sarah. Sarah's nerves were stretched taut.

Then Teresa's phone rang. When she answered, her fingers were beginning to tremble. "Michael," she said.

Phone to her ear, she walked past Sarah. As she went by, she set a hand on her shoulder.

38

At the information booth, the young woman in the bandanna shook her head. "Crazy, I'm telling you."

The noise from the Gatecrasher Festival stage sounded like an F-18 nosediving into the crowd. Harker put away his badge. "Describe the woman you saw running."

"Short black hair. Like, Goth. But jeans. And maybe cowboy boots?"

"What else?"

"The baby in the carrier. That was weird."

He already knew it was a decoy. "Who was pursuing her?"

"A girl with blond hair. Were they re-lated?"

"Why would you think that?"

"Both of them were running." She shrugged.

Harker knew the pursuer was Reavy Worthe. This wasn't helpful. He turned to leave.

The woman said, "I thought maybe they were trying to keep up with their mother."

Harker turned slowly back. "Who?"

She tilted her head. "The older woman, with the kid."

"Can you describe her?"

"Red ponytail. And . . ." She mulled it. "I think she was wearing a festival badge. A lanyard? Like this one?" She lifted the ID badge that hung around her neck.

Hers was yellow. Other festival employees wore green badges, white, blue.

"What color?" he said.

She considered. "Red? I think."

"What's that?"

"Medical."

Fell abandoned the blue Bonneville at the Roswell city dump. She drove deep into the landfill, rolled the car into a pit, and climbed out over half-spilled Hefty bags and rusted office furniture. She walked out past the curious eyes of men driving garbage trucks and bulldozers. She phoned Reavy and told her to pick her up.

She followed along the deserted highway unafraid of discovery by the police. Nobody at the dump knew who she was or that she'd carjacked the Bonneville. She was one of the angel's wings, and she was blessed. Battered and limping, stinking of garbage, but untouchable.

Nobody could damage her because she'd been torn apart years back. From here on out, there could only be restoration.

At a windswept crossroads, the Navigator stopped and let her in. She didn't comment on its beat-up right side, inked with black paint where Keller's pickup had sideswiped it. Grissom drove. Reavy sat with the Mossberg across her lap. For the first mile none of them spoke. Fell knew that the voice of revelation would come upon Grissom soon enough.

She hoped it didn't tell him to discharge lightning from his fists.

She waited for him to praise her for nearly killing Sarah Keller. To thank her for cracking the windshield of the Bonneville with her own body, and for stranding the car's owners in the desert without their phones or wallets or shoes, and for smashing the Bonneville into the federal agent who joined the pursuit.

He kept silent. They rolled along the blacktop through mirages floating in the heat.

Grissom put a hand on Reavy's thigh. "You nearly got Keller. Hit the driver, for damn sure."

Reavy said, "Not good enough. Couldn't get a steady shot, not when we kept swerving."

"Next time."

His voice sounded soothing and full of encouragement. Fell thought, *Give her a dog biscuit, why don't you?*

Fell said, "Next time, shoot the radiator. Don't shoot straight through the window."

If she'd shot the radiator, Zoe would be sitting in the back seat of the Navigator beside her right now. The emptiness, the space where a child should be, felt vast.

Grissom said, "Hey. Heat of the moment."

"She could have killed Zoe," Fell said.

Reavy turned, frowning. "You care about that now?"

The words seemed to hit every bruise on her body. "You're the one who wants Zoe for . . ."

Grissom glared at her in the mirror. She shut up.

"For what?" he said.

"Never mind."

"Finish what you was gonna say." He continued glaring. "*For the Fiery Branch.* That better be what you meant."

"Course, Grissom. For the Fiery Branch."

Reavy said, "Nothing matters more."

Grissom nodded. He rubbed his palm

down Reavy's leg, but his gaze remained on the mirror. His eyes, always sleepy, never closed. Reavy gripped the shotgun two-handed and stared at the desert, shoulders tight.

For yourself, Fell thought. *You want Zoe for yourself.*

She wiped her nose and tucked her locket inside her shirt. She leaned back. "They got off the highway."

"You see that with your own eyes?" Grissom said.

"They can't stay on U.S. 380. Too many people saw the pursuit. They got off the road."

Voice as tight as her grip, Reavy said, "They'll want to get rid of that truck."

"To get another vehicle they'll have to expose themselves," Fell said.

Grissom said, "We don't need to hunt for Sarah Keller. No, sir."

"What do you mean?" Fell said.

"The law wants her as much as we do," he said. "And they have more people, more technology, more resources."

Fell nodded. The clan had eyes and ears throughout the Southwest, but the law had more. And after this morning they'd be hyped up to capture her.

"So we let them lead us to her," Fell said.

"We watch and listen. And when they locate Keller and the girl, we close in," he said. "We need a place to hole up. We'll borrow a house for the day."

"We'll need a police radio scanner."

"You figure out how to get us one." Grissom nodded to himself. "We hunker down and listen, and we wait for the law to bring her to bay."

Reavy looked up. "Then Zoe's ours."

The young volunteer in the medical tent went rigid when Harker flashed his credentials. They generally did. The letters *FBI* froze people like a Taser.

The music pounded so loud that the walls of the tent vibrated. She hugged a clipboard to her chest. "They were here this morning. And last night."

"Twice?" Harker said. "And you didn't alert the authorities?"

She flushed. "I didn't know who she was. That she was in trouble."

" 'In trouble' hardly describes it. Sarah Keller stole that child."

Her knuckles whitened on the clipboard. "She had the little — you say it's a girl but she was dressed like a boy, I didn't know I should call the police . . ."

"Who did they come to see?"

She seemed to think about it. That was never good.

"If you withhold information, you can be charged with aiding and abetting a fugitive," he said.

Her face crumpled. "Teresa Gavilan."

"Is she local? Does she live in Roswell?"

"Yeah. But this Sarah, she never said the child's name, I'm sure . . ."

The volunteer looked like a sinner caught out and desperate to recite her penance. Harker pulled out his phone. The Bureau could obtain Gavilan's home address.

". . . I mean, it doesn't make sense."

He looked up. "What was that?"

The volunteer said, "Why would a nun get involved with a child stealer?"

Harker lowered the phone. "Tell me more about Teresa Gavilan."

39

The rental car angled across the countryside toward her, a black arrow through the tawny grass. It stopped outside the barn. The driver's door opened and Michael Lawless got out.

For a moment Sarah stayed in the shadows behind the Steampunk trailer. She lowered the Glock and cleared the chamber. Her heart drummed and an ache welled up inside it.

He stood beside the car, hands loose at his sides. As if saying, *No gun, no grudge, no worries.* He wore a black T-shirt and khaki jeans and black work boots. His hair, dark and wind-wrecked, was shorter than she remembered. His eyes were hidden behind Oakley sunglasses. The expression on his face was calm.

She stepped from behind the trailer. He didn't so much move as shift into a higher gear. He inhaled and his shoulders rose. She walked toward him, the Glock hanging from her hand, knowing the play of emotions on her face must have been like fireworks.

He came toward her and started to shake his head, maybe to smile, maybe to cover a welter of other emotions. For a second they faced each other.

Sarah stuck out her hand. He gripped it, as for a soul shake, and held tight.

Heat poured off him. It seemed to flow from his hand into hers, to sink through her skin, hit her veins, stop her breathing.

She felt like she'd been falling from a great height since the discovery of the microchip Friday morning — but that somebody had caught her just before she hit the ground. She knew that was untrue. He was a U.S. marshal, not an avenger. But she wanted to believe it, if only for a single second. She gripped his hand and told herself: no tears.

He said, "You've had a hell of a run."

The curve of his mouth should have been a smile, but his expression seemed to have too much pain behind it.

Sarah let go of his hand. "Take off those shades. Let me see what you're really thinking."

Lawless set them on top of his head. His eyes were hard and watchful and melancholy. The scar that ran across his eyebrow and ended below his right eye had faded in the last five years to a pale swipe, a parenthetical curve. Strangely, it didn't look fierce. It humanized him.

"Mommy?" Zoe approached from the barn, little feet scuffing in the dirt. She eyed Lawless with unabashed curiosity. "Are you Michael?"

"I am."

He shot Sarah a look, like, *Have you already trained her to get a skip to identify himself?* Then he crouched down to kid level. "Are you Zoe?"

She nodded. "People in a car shot a gun at us."

She knotted her hands together. All at once she looked ineffably vulnerable.

"That's terrible. I'm sorry," Lawless said.

Sarah spread her arms and Zoe leaned against her. She nodded at the barn. "Teresa got us out of it. But it was close."

He rose and set a hand on her shoulder. Pebbles of safety glass fell out of her shirt collar.

The adrenaline faded, and she felt like she was on a sugar crash. The wind funneled across the plain and shivered through the grass.

"It was Grissom, Fell, and Reavy. How did they find us?" she said.

"I'm going to check into that."

"Teresa has glass and buckshot embedded in her back. She needs medical treatment. And she needs your help to get out of this jam. She needs to walk away clean," Sarah said.

"I understand. It'll be done."

She waited, unsure what she wanted to hear in his voice. Rescue. A promise. She said, "I told her. Everything. She deserved to know."

He nodded. From the barn Teresa appeared.

Lawless headed straight to her. He had a way of walking, a slow stride, shoulders square, that reminded her of a wolf. In the face of it, Teresa smiled. She looked worn but was trying, gamely, to hide it.

"It's good you're here," she said.

"I wish it hadn't come to this."

"Of course." She held herself rigid, perhaps from pain. Then she looked at him as a mother might look at her prodigal child, come home too late. With great, irrepressible warmth. She sighed and patted his cheek.

"You need medical attention," he said.

"Soon enough. Sarah cleaned up the worst of it."

He looked over the minor repairs Sarah

had made, using the first aid kit in Danisha's pickup. She'd tweezered bits of glass and the buckshot and applied antiseptic and Band-Aids.

"We need to talk next steps," he said.

A gust of wind slithered through the grass. To the north, thunderheads were building. Sarah lifted Zoe onto the hood of the truck. She saw little reason to keep her sequestered from their discussion at this point — Zoe was too attuned to the emotional spectrum, and Sarah didn't want her to feel exiled, worrying and wondering what was going on.

Lawless said, "Harker's here. He got run off the highway about ten miles back."

"You saw him?" Sarah said.

"Had a conversation."

She leaned against the side of the truck. "What did you tell him?"

"That we should grab a beer if he ever gets done swearing at me."

"So he doesn't expect you to call in a task force from the Marshals Service to bring me in."

"He'd hate that." Lawless didn't have to say why: Harker wanted to be the one to stake Sarah to open ground, with the Worthes downwind and eager to find her scent. "And he knows I am not out here following protocol."

"Does that mean we're completely cut off from official resources and protection?" Sarah said.

Carefully, he said, "We're not cut off. But we have to move . . ."

"In the shadows?" she said.

"Silently."

"I think we blew that chance about an hour ago."

"We'll create another chance, Sarah."

She felt a wave of emotion, a fading sense that he was trying to buck her up, give her a locker room pep talk. Then she took his measure. Michael Lawless didn't mess around. He was here, and if he said it, he meant it.

"Let's do it," she said.

Of course, Michael Lawless couldn't control what happened outside this field, or disarm the world.

He got his phone to call the Marshals Service. She waved him toward the barn. "Come on. We can't count on wind shear grounding police planes and helicopters. Let's get the car and truck inside."

40

Harker drove cautiously along the gravel drive to the white clapboard house in the grove of scrub pine. In the passenger seat, the Roswell resident agent quietly scanned the scene. He was alert and curious, a kid named Marichal from Gainesville, Florida.

"Doesn't look like Gavilan's at home," he said.

Harker didn't respond. He didn't know whether the Roswell satellite office had sent Marichal with him as backup — or as a babysitter, a spy, or a mascot. He didn't particularly want to rely on an agent who looked twelve years old.

He parked and got out. The wind had risen, clouds in the north seeming to manifest from a void, a black curtain bringing rain and darkness. He peered through the kitchen window. In the house the lights were off.

Marichal climbed the steps to the kitchen

door. To his credit, he raised his eyebrows first, asking Harker's permission to knock. Harker nodded.

Marichal rapped, but nobody answered.

Harker said, "Try the knob."

Marichal shot him a look, perturbed. Harker nodded. "Go on."

Hesitantly Marichal tried the door. "Locked."

Harker drew his service weapon.

"What are you doing?" Marichal said.

"I have reason to believe that Sister Teresa Gavilan may be inside the house and in danger. Move aside."

"What are you talking about?"

"Sister Teresa was last seen at the Gate-crasher Festival, fleeing with a suspected murderer pursuing her."

"That's not what . . ."

"Sarah Keller is wanted for questioning in the killing of her own sister and the abduction of her sister's child. She may have targeted Sister Teresa as a vulnerable party who could be tricked into giving her refuge. We're talking about a nun — a soft touch when it comes to women who look down and out. Keller could have conned her into letting her into her home."

"They were seen running together from the medical tent . . ."

"When Keller was exposed, she wanted to stop Sister Teresa from calling the authorities. Sister Teresa attempted to get help, but Keller apparently caught up with her. Now the sister has disappeared. Stand back."

"We don't have a warrant," Marichal said.

"We don't have a choice. Cover me."

Harker raised his foot and kicked the door open.

Gun drawn, he swept into the kitchen. Marichal swore, but drew his own weapon and took up a position in the doorway.

One minute later they cleared the house. Marichal holstered his weapon. He looked like he was going to break out in hives.

"I told you. Nobody's home."

Harker surveyed the guest bedroom. On the floor was a child's drawing in colored pencil. He picked it up.

"But they were here."

He returned to the kitchen and rifled through the papers stacked on the counter.

"Agent Harker, you shouldn't —"

"Shouldn't what? Care about the life of a nun?"

He lifted the phone from the wall and clicked through the controls. When he got to recent calls, he said, "Write down these numbers."

He read them off. Marichal grabbed a pen

from his shirt pocket and scribbled them in a little notebook.

Pursing his lips, Harker pushed Redial. A number rang and went to voice mail.

"This is Michael Lawless. Leave a message."

Harker spun and threw the phone across the kitchen.

It hit the wall and clattered to the linoleum. Marichal stared at it. He stared at Harker. He didn't move.

Until the phone rang. On the floor it buzzed and lit up. As if tiptoeing through a field of rat traps, Marichal crossed the kitchen and picked it up.

"Hello?" He listened, and his face paled. "This is FBI Special Agent Ruben Marichal."

"Who is it?" Harker said.

Marichal looked at him. "It's the police. They received a silent alarm call for an intruder at this address. Officers are on their way." He held out the phone. "So I guess it's for you."

The garage was musty, overheated, and dim. Sitting in the Navigator with the doors open, Fell listened with one ear to the tears and pleading in the house, and with the other to the police scanner.

"*Quiet.* Don't make me tell you again," Reavy said.

Through the open door to the kitchen, Fell watched Reavy bind the woman to a chair with duct tape. She almost called out: *Start with the gag.* But it didn't matter. The woman was in her eighties and didn't have the lung power to alert the neighbors.

Grissom sat at the kitchen table, eating a plate of cold fried chicken from the fridge. The old woman's husband was in a Barcalounger in the family room, immobilized by Parkinson's and his oxygen tank.

Seizing the house had been easy. They simply waited in a supermarket parking lot until the old woman struggled out with her groceries. Fell offered a hand. She learned that the woman and her husband were on their own, that their children lived in Albuquerque and didn't visit. The old lady was glad for the conversation and for a bit of help from such a polite young woman.

She never noticed the SUV as it followed her home. The rest was just a matter of closing the garage door and all the curtains in the house.

Getting inside was always easy.

Hell, she'd been born inside, that's how easy — Eldrick's granddaughter. And his favorite for a time. He called her his little bird because she was quick, dexterous, and bold. She could climb and jump and nearly fly from tree to tree. And because, he said, she had a tender heart.

That didn't last. Her father fell afoul of Eldrick over money, and her parents came into disrepute. The shunning started, small at first. One day she was playing in Nolan's yard when his mother came out, pointed her toward the street, and said, "You get home and don't come around here no more." Nolan protested, and his ma gave him a switch across the back of the legs. After that Fell played alone, even at school. Then her dad was exiled from the family. Her mother was sent to a new husband. Fell started sharing a room with Reavy, her new sister.

That didn't last either. Not once Eldrick and her new dad decided she was marriageable. Fifteen — so old she was nearly spoiled goods. At least Coffey wasn't a bad husband. He was eighteen, desperate to believe and to become one of the clan's soldiers, shy and impulsive. The impulsive part was what got him killed, shot during a drug deal.

Fell's baby boy was born two months later. By then the family looked at her as twice cursed. She was put to work on enforcement, and little Creek was taken away for safekeeping.

Easy getting in. No getting out.

It had been impossible to refuse the bombing assignment in Denver. Because the clan had taken her child and told her she'd never see him again unless she did it.

In all honesty, she had a knack for it, and in a way liked it. The power. The thrill. Knowing they had beaten the Man. But afterwards, when she was on the run, the clan did not return Creek to her.

She still didn't know where he was. She knew that all the kids had that information embedded in their chips, but she had no access to any of the clan children.

Until Zoe Keller came into the picture.

In the kitchen Grissom drank from a carton of milk. Reavy ripped tape from the roll and bound the old woman's arms and feet to the chair.

"Why are you doing this?"

She sounded baffled. They always did. Acceptance of the obvious came so hard to most people. Why were they doing this? Because it was inevitable. They were the Worthes.

On her smart phone, the police scanner app bleated to life.

"Unit 9, report of a break-in at a residence

on Pony Trail Road. Silent alarm has been triggered."

"Dispatch, this is Unit 9. On my way."

Fell stretched and turned up the volume. Five dollar app, bought with Sarah Keller's prepaid card — not too shabby.

"Unit 9, report that two men are in the residence on Pony Trail Road claiming to be FBI agents. But the homeowner is not there and not answering her cell phone. Proceed to the residence with caution."

Fell leaned out of the Navigator. "Grissom. Reavy. We got the Feds."

41

The sun lay low in the west when Zoe fell asleep in the hayloft. The sky was split between glaring red sunset and a black curtain of rain that swallowed all light along the northern horizon. The evening bore the remains of the day's heat, but a chill came through the slats of the barn with every gust of wind. Sarah built Zoe a nest of coats and tucked her behind a bale of straw to shield her.

"Like a fort," she said, and Zoe smiled. Even though the little girl hadn't had a full meal since breakfast, she had dropped off to sleep quickly, heavily, with Mousie dangling from her hand. Sarah watched her for a minute and slipped across the planks of the loft to the ladder.

Below, the pickup and Lawless's rental were parked side by side. The doors at either end of the barn were drawn shut and barred. Lawless sat on a bale of straw, keeping watch through a crack in the wood. He was waiting for a callback from his superiors. Teresa sat opposite him on the floor, leaning back against a post.

Sarah paused and wiped grit from her eyes. She was exhausted, but feared that if she stopped moving she would collapse in the dirt, as inert as Zoe's stuffed animals.

Teresa's soprano, however, remained round and ringing. "Stop worrying about me. I've slept much rougher than this."

"El Salvador was twenty-five years ago," Lawless said.

"It's impolite to remind a lady of her age, even if I am supposed to have abandoned vanity when I took my vows."

"Sorry. I just want to make sure you don't need me to take you into town."

"I'm not going anywhere yet." Teresa coughed and settled herself. "You look strangely relieved to be here, Michael."

"I'm glad everybody's all right."

"And being in close contact gives you a sense that you can control the situation."

"Best I can."

Teresa said, "Sarah looks very much like her sister. As does Zoe."

The wind gusted. Loose hay swept through the rafters. Across the plains, thunder rumbled.

Sarah descended the ladder. "I didn't know you'd seen pictures of Beth."

Teresa's eyes were soft. "When Michael phoned about all this, I looked up your sister online. She was a lovely young woman. Her smile radiated generosity of spirit."

A pang went through Sarah. She thought of the family photos she had never shown Zoe. She'd been terrified that if Zoe saw pictures of Beth, she might talk about them to outsiders. Now she felt that she'd erased her sister and cheated her daughter. She stood awkwardly at the bottom of the ladder.

Lawless nodded her over. "Have a seat."

Sarah sat cross-legged on the ground in front of the hay bale. She wondered at the quiet intimacy of the conversation she'd overheard. Lawless seemed to regard Teresa as a nephew would a beloved aunt, with gentle concern and long-standing trust. The wind battered the walls of the barn.

"There's something I didn't want to talk about in front of Zoe," she said. "The RFID microchip."

Lawless glanced at the loft.

"Zoe knows about it," Sarah said. "The ER nurse scanned it and read the information aloud in front of her."

Teresa said, "It's so disturbing."

"A microchip. Like she's a *dog.*" Sarah pinched the bridge of her nose. "The Worthes had to have implanted it when Beth and Nolan visited them after Zoe was born."

"Yeah," Lawless said.

"You knew about that, didn't you?" she said. "About Nolan taking Beth to Arizona to meet his family."

"I did."

"How long had federal authorities been watching Nolan?"

"Ever since he left the clan and moved to California."

She exhaled. "Who watched them, and how?"

"FBI and ATF, as far as I know. I wasn't privy to their surveillance."

"What were you privy to? What do you know about how the clan chips its children? And what kind of information does that chip contain? 'Cause it's more than just Zoe's name and the names of her parents, I'm positive."

Lawless glanced at the hayloft again. There was no noise or movement from Zoe's little sleeping fort.

Sarah wasn't asking the one question that loomed beyond all others, like the wall of dark cloud erupting with lightning outside:

Why did you let me get away?

It frightened her. It made her grateful and terrified all at once. He had set her loose that day. And in so doing, he had seized control of her life. He held the secret. At any moment he could reveal it, or threaten her with its revelation. But he had asked nothing of her, had instead retreated into a background so deep that for years she'd wondered if he was still alive.

And now here he was, and here was her chance, and she kept quiet. Her situation was too tenuous to bring that up right now, as though mentioning it would rip open the door to a furnace and incinerate her.

Instead, she let her fear and disgust and rage come out in another question. "How do we get that chip out of my daughter?"

Teresa said, "You should have it removed by a physician in a sterile setting. Injecting a chip with a syringe is simple — the equivalent of an inoculation. Extracting it is minor surgery."

Sarah rubbed her eyes. "Anybody with a scanner can send information about her someplace else, right?"

"Yes," Lawless said. "Lots of stores, warehouses, transportation networks have RFID readers. Phone apps might be able to read it. The information in the chip can be transmitted to a credit card company or inventory control system for a store, an airline baggage tagging system, anything."

"Or to clan operatives," Sarah said.

"Yes. Unfortunately."

She looked at him. "The Worthes actually chip all their children? Every one from every polygamous liaison?"

His face was almost sad. "No."

Sarah's eyebrows and pulse both went up.

"Not all," Lawless said. "Just some. In a special ritual."

"Tell me."

He stood and walked to the door. His T-shirt had ruched up around his holster. He stared through the slats in the wood.

"Nolan wasn't the first clan member to leave. Others had walked away, and some of them talked to the FBI."

"They were arrested and interrogated, you mean," Sarah said.

"Some." He turned. "And some went back. Some thought they could balance their life in the outside world with their blood ties to the Worthes. Nolan did."

Sarah nodded sadly.

"Ever since Eldrick Worthe declared himself a prophet, his family has been developing an obsessive set of religious ritu-als. They celebrate Revelation Day, when the Holy Spirit descended on Eldrick. And they mark births with more than baptism," he said. "Baby boys are circumcised. Girls are taken to a ceremonial tent for a blessing ceremony. That's where they're chipped."

The wind spit through the slats of the barn. The door rattled.

"Why the girls?" she said.

"You know very well."

She shut her eyes. "Control."

"They chip the girls so they can track them and identify them," Lawless said.

"Are the girls ever told?" Sarah said.

"Once they reach puberty and are married off."

"What age is that?"

"Fourteen, fifteen."

"Lord save us," Teresa said.

Sarah said, "You sure you don't have a scalpel in your medical kit?"

Lawless said, "What information does the chip contain?"

"Names. *Worthe* names. Bethany Keller Worthe. Zoe Skye Worthe. I think Nolan told his family that he and Beth were married."

He thought about it. "That may have helped protect you these last five years."

"I realize."

"What else? A serial number?" Lawless said.

Sarah thought back. "I did see a number. A long one. At least one. What about it? Isn't it a factory-issued number to identify the chip?"

"Maybe. But it may be something else."

"Like what?"

Lawless turned from the door. "A password."

42

A password. The implications hit her, and hard.

Lawless said, "The Worthes are expert at hiding information — delivery dates, routes, contact lists . . ."

"Offshore bank accounts?"

He nodded. The sun singed the western horizon and soaked the desert with red light. Through the slats of the barn it fell across his face.

"Why would they encode that information in a chip implanted in their kids?" She ran a hand through her hair. "That's . . . cold. And weird."

"Because information like that is more valuable than gold," he said.

Even as Lawless speculated, she knew he was right. "It's the key to the vault that contains the gold. And the silver, and all their untraceable dollars."

"Exactly. Because computers can be con-

319

fiscated. From there, bank accounts can be identified and assets seized."

"Beyond that, somebody can take a sledgehammer to your computers or wipe them with a giant magnet and destroy your information and your organization."

"Disks, zip drives, thumb drives, even the safe they're stored in . . . all those can be lost too. And they're obvious sources of information," Lawless said.

"But a child is just a child."

They looked at each other. Sarah felt a deep cold flow into the barn. It had no source in the air, but in her fears. She glanced at the loft where Zoe slept.

"If you're right, this would be a perfect way to hide information," she said.

"Ruthless," Teresa added. "Calculated and ruthless."

Lawless said, "Eldrick and his council of prophets might call it holy."

Sarah shivered. "It also makes their children into currency. Doesn't it?"

Lawless grew pensive. Then for a moment his guard slipped. He looked like he'd been whipped across the back. And Sarah saw that his compassion was never more than a millimeter from the surface.

She stood up. "The Worthes assign their children to marriages as freely as the noble houses in Game of Thrones. Don't they?"

"They do. The men of the clan decide who will marry whom."

Teresa said, "These arranged marriages — am I correct in assuming they give young girls to older men in the family?"

"Yes," he said.

"And the favored men in the clan — Eldrick's thugs and toadies — get assigned the girls they want."

He nodded.

Sarah said, "So, if the girls have bank account information, or whatever, encoded in their microchips, that information goes with them to their . . ." She couldn't bring herself to say *husband*. "To the man they're handed over to."

"We have no proof of this."

"But it would make complete sense, from what I know about these people," Sarah said. "In the past five years I've spent a lot of time studying the Worthe clan."

And more. She'd spent an equal amount of time studying how to hide money — so she could track down deadbeats as a skip tracer, and so she could, in theory, hide money of her own, if she ever accumulated enough. Hide-and-seek was her specialty.

"It would be ingenious," she said. "In the most sinister way. But hell . . . drug mules swallow balloons of cocaine every day. Spies used to insert microfilm in suppository capsules. Why shouldn't the clan use a needle to inject bits of information into their children?"

She began to pace. "Does the clan send its girls away sometimes?"

"They send boys away all the time. Threats to the leadership. Excess Y chromosomes. In a polygamous community, only the most powerful or favored men get wives. The others are shunned and exiled. But girls . . ." He saw where she was going. "You're suggesting the clan might send a girl somewhere, to someone, so the information can be transmitted."

"Yes. And Zoe's been missing from the clan for five years. I think that chip contains information they want. Enemies lists, bank account information, evidence they'll kill to destroy. I think it's why they're so eager to get hold of her."

Teresa said, "If it's only the chip they're after, they'll take her alive or . . ."

They all fell quiet. Zoe didn't have to be breathing for the information on the chip to be valuable to the Worthes. She only had to be in their hands.

"We need to read the chip," Sarah said. "Where can we find an RFID scanner?"

"Most minimarts. If we can get to a 7-Eleven maybe we can pull the information."

Teresa said, "And what would you do with it?"

Sarah turned. "Save her. Save all of us."

43

The flashing lights of the Chaves County Sheriff's Department car lit up the walls of the house. Harker shut down the nun's computer. Agent Marichal came from the kitchen, looking so overtly relieved that the warrantless search was going to end, and so abashed, that Harker had doubts about the man's future in federal law enforcement.

Marichal said, "Something I found in the bathroom cabinet." In his gloved hand he held up a disposable syringe sealed in a sterile packet.

Harker took it. "Interesting."

He walked to the door. He opened it casually, as the two deputies hulked from their car and approached under the firework spin of the lights. Their weapons were holstered but their hands rested on the butts of the guns.

Harker pushed open the screen. "Gentleman. Come in."

"May we see some ID?" said one of the deputies.

Marichal nudged into the doorway and flashed his Bureau credentials.

The deputies said, "What's going on here?"

Harker said, "The woman who lives here has been taken captive by a federal fugitive."

"Want to tell us how you figure that?" the deputy said.

Harker shook his head. "I want you to tell me what resources the Sheriff's Department has and how it can use them to find her."

The sunset was a ruby slice along the horizon and Danisha couldn't get any answer on Sarah's burn phone. She paced outside the taquería on Roswell's main drag, her fingers itching, wishing she had a cigarette. Forcing herself to stay outside, and not even think about the vending machine inside the lobby of the restaurant.

"Come on, come on, answer," she said to the ringing phone.

Voice mail. Again. Her nerves gunned, like an engine stuck in overdrive. Had she made a fool mistake coming here? Was Sarah even anywhere close?

At the tone she exhaled. "Kid, it's me. We

gotta get you out of whatever's going on, and I'm here to say I'll help you do whatever it takes. Call me." Then, because she had become so paranoid that the sound of a horn honking or a songbird chirping made her want to jump and beat them to a pulp, she added, enigmatically, "I've always felt close to you, honey. I still do. Real close. Please consider me close enough to help."

She hung up, wondering if she'd sounded like she was speaking in code, or like a sick high school counselor trying to get a schoolgirl to open up. She hoped Sarah would get the point that she was here, nearby, and going off her freaking rocker.

She shoved the phone in her pocket and stared at the wide street and all its billboards and lighted signs and busy, empty commercial buzz. She took the phone back out and redialed and when the voice-mail announcement asked her to leave a message, she said, "And I'm driving a big-ass four-wheel drive with a 5.7-liter engine. It's new, it's fast, and it'll knock a longhorn twenty feet into the air before the steer knows what hit him. Just so you know."

She ended the call and pushed through the door into the taquería, from street noise and the desert evening to the cool hum of air-conditioning. She bought two packs of

Marlboros from the vending machine.

Nearby the cashier punched a sale into the register, talking with two customers at the counter.

"Crazy, I'm telling you," said one of the customers, a retiree in a checked shirt with red suspenders.

The cashier said, "You saw it? Actually, with your own eyes?"

The man handed over a bill. "Fighting. These two women, in the back of a pickup truck. They drove right past me, close as I'm standing to you. Going 'bout eighty down Main Street."

Danisha listened.

"I swear, the one in the back of the pickup was trying to kick this other gal off, right into the road. Craziest thing I ever saw."

His companion, even older, wearing a Caterpillar hat and blue suspenders, shook his head. "I swear I saw a kid in the cab of the pickup, but buster here says I hallucinated that."

Danisha said, "Excuse me. What make of pickup truck was it?"

The gents turned. Red suspenders said, "What make? I'm talking about a catfight on the tailgate, and you want to know what model pickup it was?" He shook his head. "As if this day hasn't been strange enough."

His friend said, "It was a Dodge Ram."

Danisha said, "Which way was it headed?"

"What next?" Sarah said.

Lawless said, "I need to check in."

"How many calls from here are you going to make on that cell phone?"

He raised a calming hand. "Don't worry. Cell towers are so far between out here, it's a wonder I can get a signal. Even if somebody tries to triangulate, at best they'll discover that this phone has registered with a tower attached to some rancher's windmill fifteen miles from here."

He punched buttons and listened for a while, seemingly to a voicemail message. By the time he hung up, he looked unhappy.

"What's wrong?" Sarah said.

"Intra-agency sniping. After FBI Special Agent Harker got his rental car towed out of the ditch, he called the Marshals Service in a snit."

"Complaining that you didn't stick around to draw a diagram of the accident for his insurance claim?"

He smirked. "Harker asked my superiors to track me and provide my whereabouts to the FBI."

"What an ass."

"I need to respond."

She held up a hand. "Wait — you're going to do it?"

"I need to deal with it."

She nodded at the door, indicating that Lawless should follow her out. Outside in the arid evening, the wind caught her hair. Her skin, and her anger, were heating.

"I am not stepping foot inside a police station or federal building and you know it," she said.

He stuck his hands in his jeans pockets. "You'll be safer."

"I'll be at the mercy of the government. And so will Zoe."

The dark wall of cloud in the north bristled with lightning. Sarah's nerves itched — it felt as if watchers could be anywhere. In the long grass, or on the rim of the golden horizon, sighting at them down the length of a scope. Or in the black void of cloud, readying to swoop.

He looked at her starkly. "What do you want from me?"

She pointed at the Chevy Biscayne. "In there."

She trooped to the car and crawled through the empty window into the back seat. He climbed in behind her.

He said, "You have to make some choices, Sarah. I'm sorry they're tough ones. But if you let me, I can try to improve your odds."

His eyes, dark and searching, seemed to be seeking a connection. She didn't think it was an act, a cover he had developed to gain trust from people he was coaxing to confess. She thought he was the real deal.

He'd better be. She was staking her daughter's life on it.

"I get it. And you've never let me down, Lawless."

She meant it as reassurance, but he looked like she'd just punched him in the head. His lips parted.

"That's . . ."

Perplexed, she said, "I'm trying to express my gratitude, Deputy Marshal. And my trust."

He looked away.

"What?" She shifted on the cracked vinyl seat. "Tell me. Is it Zoe?"

She glanced out the Chevy's empty window at the barn. It was a forlorn sight in the dusk, grayed and listing.

"Of course it's Zoe," he said. "Zoe and you and Teresa and all of it."

He looked pained. Beyond pained — stung. *All of it.*

She said, "It's about that day. The Marshals Service still doesn't know what happened, does it?"

"You want to do this now?" he said.

"No. I never want to do this. I want it all to go away." Her throat felt thick. She told herself: *Toughen up, cupcake.*

"Why were you there that day?" she said.

Another flash of lightning scored the horizon. The wind lowered to a chill sweep, flattening the grass outside the car.

"Michael. Why did the U.S. Marshals send an agent to Beth's house? For a long time I thought you were in hot pursuit of Grissom and Fell and Reavy. But that wasn't it. If you'd tracked them there intending to apprehend them, you wouldn't have been on your own."

He leaned on the front bench seat and hung his arms across it. In the distance, where the ranchland dipped into a hollow, birds began to cry. Chittering, squawking, a rude cacophony.

He took a long moment. "I came to talk to Beth."

She exhaled. "Why?"

He stared out the windshield. The squalling of the birds continued.

"Because of Nolan." He turned. "Because the FBI and ATF were determined to use him to bring down the Worthe clan and apprehend the courthouse bombers."

Sarah said, "I know the FBI wanted Nolan

to snitch on his family."

"They convinced him it was the only way he'd ever be left alone."

"Left alone by whom? His family, or the Feds?"

"Both. But one Fed in particular. We need to talk about the guy who's after you. Curtis Harker. You've got a heat-seeking missile on your tail."

44

Fell turned up the volume on the police scanner app. Reavy and Grissom came into the garage from the kitchen. Grissom wiped the back of his hand across his mouth.

"*Dispatch, this is Unit 9, at the dwelling on Pony Trail Road. No home invasion. It's two FBI agents.*"

"*Unit 9, Dispatch. Repeat?*"

Grissom grunted. "A-fuckin-men."

Fell had a map in her hands. "Pony Trail Road is in the boonies ten miles north of town."

"Who do we have within a hundred miles?"

Reavy took out her phone and scrolled through the contacts. "Jadom Simmons. Wyndham and his boys."

"Call them," Grissom said.

Fell said, "We need to find out whose house that is, and if Keller's been there."

He nodded at her phone, hissing with

police static. "We wait till all them filth leave the place. Then head out there."

She glanced past him and through the open door into the kitchen. "What about them?"

Grissom didn't bother to look back at the elderly woman slumped in the kitchen chair, half-silvered with duct tape.

"They won't say anything," he said.

"We gonna leave them?"

Reavy dialed a number. Under the hanging bulb in the garage, her blond hair shone like a corona. "Isom. It's the dawn of a new day."

Grissom leaned into the SUV, close to Fell's face. "What's wrong with you? Those folks mean nothing." He pointed two fingers at her eyes. "Focus. They got paradise coming. You got a kid to find."

Sarah pushed her hair from her face. "I know about Special Agent Harker."

"You know he's the guy who's trying to apprehend you. You don't understand how far he'll go to do that," Lawless said.

Lightning forked from the clouds, a pure and relentless white.

"He was a friend of mine," Lawless said. "We both worked in Denver. Federal agencies can be insular — you hang out with your own team. But Harker wasn't like that. He was always an independent operator."

"I didn't think the FBI liked independent types."

"They like incisive minds, and Harker has one. He saw connections where others saw only static. He solved cases. And he was reliable. A man who was as good as his word."

"You like this guy."

He hesitated. "I did."

"What did he do?" she said.

"It isn't what he did. It's what happened to him."

Thunder rumbled past.

"He's like a dog with a bone when he gets his teeth into a case. But tenacity is highly prized in the Bureau." He shook his head. "He was all about putting bad guys behind bars. I was too."

"Was?"

"I still am. But not *all* about it."

"What happened?"

He looked pained.

Sarah said, "Lawless?"

The county sheriff's deputies followed Harker and Special Agent Marichal through the nun's house.

The deputy said, "Sir? We're going to have to ask you to step outside until we can verify that Sister Teresa is, in fact, missing."

Harker said, "Get over it."

The deputy caught up and put a hand on Harker's arm. "Now, sir."

Harker shook him off. Did these men truly not get it? "Aren't you aware of the clown car parade that raced through Roswell earlier today? Not only was I engaged in the pursuit of the vehicle carrying Sister Teresa, but so was the Roswell PD and at least two other vehicles. Vehicles driven by members of the Worthe family who are federal fugitives. They forced me off the road."

The deputies looked at each other. They'd heard.

"We need backup. SWAT. And we need to move *now*. Because Keller is mixed up with the Worthe clan — with a trio who are wanted for the murder of a federal agent."

Both Marichal and the deputies sobered. One deputy said, "Excuse me, sir?"

She's still dead. She'll stay dead. For a second, Harker felt like he might gag. In his mind he saw Eldrick Worthe's unblinking eyes and heard his derision.

He turned to the deputies. "You want to understand the urgency of the situation? Want to know what they're capable of?"

He took out his wallet and removed a photo. He jammed it into Marichal's hand.

336

"When the Worthes set off an improvised bomb outside the U.S. District Court in Denver, they injured twenty-five people and killed two. One was prosecutor Daniel Chavez. The other was FBI Special Agent Campbell Robinson."

Marichal eyed the photo. Warily he looked up at Harker. "This is Special Agent Robinson?"

"They murdered her," Harker said. "They killed my wife."

The air pressure seemed to drop. Sarah said, "His wife? Oh my God."

"It destroyed him." Lawless scanned the horizon outside the wrecked Chevy. "He took two days' bereavement leave to bury Cam. Then came straight back, said work was his therapy. But . . ." He shook his head. "He could never rationally investigate the bombing."

"I can't believe the Bureau put him *on* the investigation," she said.

"They didn't. He's always been assigned to the racketeering investigation against the clan."

"But that hasn't stopped him from hunting for the bombers."

"Call it mission creep."

She sat back and ran a hand through her hair.

Lawless rubbed his eyes. "I tried to talk to him. He was in shock, a mess, I get that. But he was *feeding* on his anger."

"It was his link to Cam," she said. "Believe me, I understand how losing somebody to violence can make you burn up with rage."

It heated your life like a forge, until you shone with pain and hatred. For some people, such white fury became the thing that bound them to their lost loved one. It got them up in the morning and fueled their days. Eventually, the thought of relinquishing it became unbearable. Because, if you quenched the fire, how could you hold onto your sister?

"It nearly killed me — if I hadn't had Zoe to care for, I might have succumbed to the furnace," she said. "So Harker didn't want help or advice. How bad did you blow it?"

"I told him if he didn't back off he was going to implode and take the office down with him."

"Smooth."

"Mama told me my mouth would get me in trouble one day. I never listened." He leaned back against the seat. "He still looks like a successful agent on the metrics. But he's not the same man. His vision of the

338

law now brooks no dissent and no mercy. And it leaves collateral damage in its wake." He shook his head. "Guy also really doesn't like me anymore."

She swallowed. "How did this fit in with Beth and Nolan?"

"Ends justify the means." He looked like he was about to say something else, but glanced at the countryside. "Come on. Out of this wreck. We should check the perimeter."

They climbed out the window. The wind tugged at Sarah's clothing. Lawless headed for the barbed-wire fence that marked the edge of the field.

Sarah followed. "Harker's the one who convinced Nolan to snitch. Isn't he?"

He scanned the horizon. She caught up with him.

She said, "Beth told me an FBI agent promised they'd be safe. But that she and Nolan were tools." Her voice was dry. "It was almost the last thing she said to me."

He looked at her then. "So you must know, Sarah."

In the dimming light, Sarah felt her face flush. "Nolan was afraid of his family. And Special Agent Harker told him that if he returned to the fold and snitched on the clan, the FBI would put him in witness protection. Right?"

"Yes."

"You were going to take him into the program."

"Yes."

"You were going to take all of them. Nolan and Beth and Zoe."

"Yes."

"Is that all you can say?"

"You've got it figured out. What else do you need to hear?"

She felt the old anger kick through her system, filling her blood and bone. "That's how you knew about the blessing ceremony. Nolan told you about it."

"No." The wind made him squint. "I didn't know about the ceremony until later. I wasn't in that loop."

"Harker. He knew." Her stomach coiled. "He sent Nolan there to get Zoe chipped."

"That's the conclusion I've drawn."

"That was going to get Nolan his golden ticket to WITSec." Her vision swam. "That's Curtis Harker? He would put a baby's life at risk — Zoe's life — and Beth . . ."

"I told you, by that point he wasn't coloring within the lines anymore."

She looked at him. "You were going to help Nolan disappear with Beth and Zoe. And I would never have known what happened to them. What a fucking irony."

"That's the way it works," he said flatly.

"Where were they going to go? Who were they going to become?"

"That, I can't tell you."

"Why not? Have you given their life to somebody else? Is another family living in their ranch home in Missoula, playing Scrabble while the kids splash in the inflatable pool?"

"I can't say." His voice remained flat, but his eyes grew hot. "It was supposed to go down once Nolan testified under oath about the clan. I presume he was supposed to provide the chip as well."

"And Beth was onboard with the idea?"

"No."

Her heart untwisted. "Nolan conned her into going to Arizona. He didn't tell her until afterward that he wanted to take them underground?"

"That's the size of it."

She understood it then. "Beth went to Arizona and saw what the Worthes actually are. Creepy meth heads and polygamists. She freaked out. And when Nolan told her how they were going to escape from the creep show, she kicked him out."

"And Nolan told Harker that it was just a bump in the road, a tiff. That he'd get her to come around."

She crossed her arms and hunched against the wind. "And you were drafted to convince Beth to get with the program." All at once she felt exhausted. "But everything went wrong. The Worthes got to Nolan first, and then to Beth."

His face paled. "It all went wrong. When I drove up, the Worthes' SUV was in the driveway, empty, doors open." He looked like he'd been stuck between the ribs with an ice pick. "I didn't get there in time. What happened that day — it's my fault."

Marichal and the deputies went quiet. After a moment, Marichal looked at the photo of Campbell Robinson and said, "I'm sorry."

Harker took the photo from him and slipped it back into his wallet. "We're done screwing around. Deputies, you're done wasting time checking me out and wondering if Sister Teresa is in trouble. We're going to find out where she is before the Worthes catch up with her."

The deputies still looked uneasy. Harker walked past them to the kitchen counter. In the corner sat a small device that looked like a baby monitor. Plastic, the size of a bagel, with a speaker and an antenna. It had been half-hidden behind a stack of flyers from the local church.

He pulled it to the front of the counter and examined it. It had a blinking green light. A label read, *Life Sentinel.*

He held it up. "What's this? A burglar alarm control device?"

Marichal said, "It's a medical alert radio transceiver."

"What do you mean — like a radio alert for people who are sick?"

"It's a base station. Usually people use it who have a medical condition that could leave them vulnerable."

"And what do they do if they get sick — run in the kitchen and shout at this device?"

"No. They wear a transmitter on a chain around their neck."

Harker wanted to smile. "These transmitters — do they have GPS?"

45

Sarah turned and walked across the field, through the hard-blown yellow grass, back toward the barn. The first drops of rain spattered the ground and her face.

Nolan had been informing for the FBI. He'd planned to take Beth and the baby and disappear into witness protection after exposing his newborn daughter to his crazy relatives.

And Lawless was supposed to be their flight director. She kept walking. For five years, with a mix of faith and fear, she had counted on Lawless keeping silent about what she'd done. Had she been a fool?

She turned around. He hadn't moved. She walked back toward him.

"When Nolan's body disappeared from the woods, you encouraged me to run. Why?" she said. "For five years I thought you did it to protect Zoe from the clan."

"I did."

"Is that the only reason?"

"I'm telling you the truth."

She stopped in front of him, aggressively close. "I took a risk in contacting you Friday. Don't you understand? I didn't know if you could help me or if you would burn me. But when I realized that running alone wouldn't work, you're the person I called. Was that a mistake?"

"No," he said. "Please believe me. You did the right thing."

Thunder cracked from the sky. Raindrops beat on the dry grass. For a second she wanted to run. Then he reached out and wrapped a hand around her neck. He held on, a physical reassurance.

"You didn't make a mistake. I swear it to you."

His hand was hot against her skin. She put her own hand on his arm. "I believe you."

He nodded. "So what do you want from me?"

"Protection. Escape."

"Is that all?"

She didn't know if he was joking. He said, "It'll be hard. You don't want to enter WIT-Sec and you wouldn't be accepted in the program anyway."

"Then help me stay out of the clan's sight

until Harker captures them."

"Where? Overseas? You won't get a passport for Zoe." He raised a hand. "Sarah, I'm not trying to discourage you. Just to tell you how it is. Look, I'm here. I will protect you to the utmost of my ability. But you need to think about what comes tomorrow, and the day after."

"Immunity," she said.

"From prosecution?" His eyes were canny and doubtful. "For that, you need to have something to give the prosecutors."

"I do." She looked at the barn. "If we can get Zoe to a doctor who'll extract the chip, I have something invaluable to give them."

Slowly, he nodded. "That won't solve your problems with the clan."

"But it'll be a start."

He took her arm. "Come on."

They headed back toward the barn through the tall grass past the beached Chevy and the rusted trailer. He got his phone and made a call.

"It's Lawless," he said, and started talking.

She slipped back into the barn. He stayed outside, speaking with quiet urgency. When he hung up, he stood for a moment, the yellow grass swaying around his knees in the wind. He turned and pocketed the phone.

He came in the barn and scraped the door closed across the dirt. He glanced at the hayloft. There was no sound from Zoe's nest.

He put his hands on Sarah's shoulders. "They want me to bring you in."

Her nerves spit and she felt like sparks were jumping off her skin. "Arrest me?"

He squeezed. "That's not what I mean. They want me to put you and Zoe in protective custody."

"They want you to arrest *both* of us."

"Sarah, they know this is one giant clusterfuck and has been from the day your sister died. They want me to sort it out. Quietly."

Teresa said, "That's good news."

"It's great news," Lawless said.

Sarah felt, for the first time in days, a flicker of hope. She put a hand on top of his. "Okay."

"And it's getting dark," he said. "What do you say we get the hell out of here?"

By the time Harker and Marichal pulled into the sheriff's station in Roswell, Harker had the number for Life Sentinel and was on the phone with a supervisor in the company's El Paso headquarters.

"This is an official FBI request for the

GPS coordinates of one of your subscribers, Sister Teresa Gavilan."

The supervisor didn't hesitate. She had a crisp, professional voice. "May I have your badge number and the name of the agent in charge?"

Harker gave them to her. "I'm in Roswell. Phone the Chaves County Sheriff's Department and the FBI Resident Agency here if you must. But this is a matter of life and death. We need to locate Sister Teresa immediately. I'm talking minutes, ma'am."

"Hold, please."

Infuriated, he held. She was checking him out. In the station beyond him, the deputies were gathering. Marichal was explaining the situation. Soon a sergeant and lieutenant joined the discussion, and started making calls. Marichal gave him the thumbs-up. The sheriff's officers were going to call out the SWAT team and more.

The Life Sentinel supervisor came back on the line. "Agent Harker? I have authorization to provide the coordinates of Sister Teresa Gavilan's Sentinel pendant."

"Give them to me." He took out his notebook and a pen.

She read them off: 33 degrees 23 minutes 33 seconds north latitude, 104 degrees 31 minutes 29 seconds west longitude.

"Where is that on a map?" He waved Marichal over, shoved the notebook at him, and pointed to the nearest computer screen.

"It's . . ." The woman paused. "Looks like it's off-road west of Roswell."

Marichal typed and a landscape appeared.

Harker said, "Is the signal stationary, or is it moving?"

Another pause. "It's stationary."

Harker's hand curled into a fist. "Thank you."

He snapped his fingers at the sheriff's crew, beckoning. To the Life Sentinel supervisor, he said, "We're going to need your live feed from Sister Teresa's GPS signal. Stay on the line."

46

The wind picked up and rain spattered the barn. Teresa came calmly toward them. "We should get going before it turns completely dark and vile."

Lawless said, "I think the storm's going to blow through, but yeah. We don't want to get mired in mud or caught by flash floods."

Sarah said, "Which way are we headed?"

Teresa took a map from the pickup and unfolded it on the hood. "West across the fields to this ranch road. That'll take us back to Highway 380." She tapped the map. She sounded certain, but looked wrung out.

Lawless touched her shoulder. "You okay?"

"Absolutely. I should eat soon, but my levels are still acceptable." She looked at Sarah. "Diabetes. I need to monitor my blood sugar."

Sarah was taken aback. "You never said anything."

She looked at the chain around Teresa's neck, the one she'd presumed held dog tags. She thought about the prescription vial in Teresa's fridge. Insulin.

Teresa looked at her kindly. "Don't worry. It's well managed. And I have an injector pen in my pocket. I'm not an invalid."

"Hardly." She squeezed Teresa's arm. "I'll get Zoe." She angled to the ladder to the hayloft, and paused. "You thought I looked like Beth?"

Teresa nodded. "I can see it, yes."

"You sounded worried. My resemblance to my sister . . . does it add to the danger I'm in?"

"Why would you think that?" Lawless asked.

"The Worthes. They take sisters for wives, and they collect brides like Happy Meal toys. Would the clan take me as a replacement bride, or something twisted like that?"

Lawless said, "I don't know. But your likeness is one more reason to keep you out of their reach."

She started up the ladder. "We're not alike. I'm going to get out of this alive."

Fell whistled through the kitchen door. "Guys. Listen to this."

On the police scanner, the chatter picked

up. As Grissom came through the door, the sheriff's department voices said, *"Proceed to the scene. Code 10-26."*

Fell said, "They're moving. Something's going down."

Reavy whipped out her phone and started an online search.

Grissom grunted. "Get yourselves ready to go."

Reavy stared at her phone. "Chaves County Sheriff's codes. 10-26. Do not use sirens or lights."

Grissom said, "They're moving in on them."

The scanner bleated again. *"Code 3. Respond to the scene."*

Reavy said, "Code 3. Emergency."

Grissom banged on the roof of the Navigator. "We're going."

He nodded toward the kitchen. The old woman was slumped half-conscious in her chair. "Reavy, lock the house."

She ran inside. Grissom cracked his knuckles. He looked energized. He put a hand to Fell's cheek. "You are a beautiful, vicious creature. Good work."

She warmed. Covered his hand with hers.

He leaned close. "You pull this off, I'm gonna give it to you, real good. Make you scream, till you can't scream no more."

She froze. He tilted his head. His smile had mischief beneath it. And with Grissom, mischief always implied a victim.

"If you don't pull it off . . ." He shrugged. "San Francisco's the end of the line for last chances." His hand remained against her face, hot. "What's that look?"

"I'll pull it off," she said.

"You better."

Reavy dashed back into the garage, eyes alight. Backing away, Grissom turned, scooped her into his arms, and lifted her off her feet. He buried his face in her chest. Reavy's laugh sounded exhilarated.

Fell scrubbed the back of her hand against her cheek where he'd touched her. She fired up the engine and slammed the door. "Come on. This is it."

On the highway Marichal drove smoothly, his face intent. In the passenger seat, Harker loaded the shotgun. Behind them followed a Chaves County Sheriff's cruiser, along with an SUV and an armored command vehicle bearing the Sheriff's Department SWAT team. The wipers smeared the spotty rain across the windshield.

Harker had the Life Sentinel supervisor on the line, talking to her through a wireless headset. "Any change?"

"No. Sister Teresa's Sentinel pendant hasn't moved."

Traffic was nonexistent. The desert was empty, as if the sudden thunderstorm had scared away even the jackrabbits and antelope.

Marichal said, "We're almost at the county line. You sure about the GPS coordinates?"

"What do you mean?" Harker said.

"I mean, are we sure this crew behind us has jurisdiction?"

Harker glanced in the side mirror. The trail of dark vehicles and parking lights looked suspiciously like low-flying UFOs.

"We're fine. There's another Chaves County Sheriff's station west of us."

He had that on his phone. A text confirmation: Rio Sacado Station. Things were being coordinated.

In his ear, the supervisor said, "Still no movement. Sister Teresa hasn't called in an emergency, Agent Harker. Are you sure . . ."

"We presume the kidnappers have confiscated the pendant. Stay on the line."

To the west, headlights appeared. Harker sat up straighter. The empty road suited him — he didn't want surprises. Then, from out of the sunset, the lights rolled into clearer view. Along came a thinly disguised military convoy, trucks and a long flatbed big rig and outriding vehicles carrying men who were clearly not just Feds but former Special Forces, men with earpieces and mirrored shades, treating traffic like a target. The convoy cruised past and into the darkness to the east.

Marichal said, "Agent Harker, your body armor."

Harker spoke to the Sentinel supervisor. "Is Gavilan still in the same location?"

"No movement, sir."

Marichal said, "Agent Harker?"

Harker hadn't worn body armor in years. It was a point of contention between him and his superiors. But there was no point in wearing Kevlar. Nothing could hurt him anymore. If he took a round in the line of duty, he would feel nothing, and the Bureau could save itself his monthly paycheck.

He touched his wallet. It was in his jacket, over his heart. He didn't look at her photo, but he needed to know it was there.

Her face was as it had been. Before the bomb ripped it apart and left her shredded on the pavement outside the Denver courthouse. Before it took his spirit with her into the netherworld.

Campbell. Robinson on her FBI credentials. Harker on their wedding day. Campbell, who saw the world as it was and attacked it anyway. Campbell, who saw him as he was and loved him anyway. The woman who would do anything to see killers and gangsters brought to justice. The woman who had walked unafraid toward the U.S. District Courthouse in Denver that morning, ready to testify, to put Eldrick Worthe in prison for the rest of his life. Not knowing that she was moments from the rest of her life.

For you.

"I'm set," Harker said.

Marichal slowed. "That's the ranch access road."

He turned off and drove north across the countryside toward the thunderstorm. Harker gripped the shotgun.

47

"Come on, kiddo," Sarah said.

Loopy with sleep, Zoe tried to burrow into the nest of coats in the hayloft. "It's not even nighttime."

"You can sleep in the truck."

"Bring Mousie."

"Got him." She should staple Mousie to her own chest so he never got lost again. "Hang on tight."

Zoe clung to her like a koala and she made her way down the ladder. Teresa and Lawless had already loaded the vehicles.

Lawless said, "If you're okay to drive, Teresa can ride with me."

"Absolutely." Sarah wondered if he was protective, or genuinely worried about the nun's health.

Zoe climbed in the truck. With the window broken, it would be a cold and noisy drive. Sarah tossed her a jacket. "Button up."

Lawless walked over. "I'll lead. Stay close

behind. We don't know if the trio's out there so I don't want to use headlights if I don't have to."

"Got it."

He hesitated and held out his hand. She took it.

"Almost out of this," he said. "It's safer to get out of here and meet up with the hot team. Just a few more miles across hostile territory."

"I know." She squeezed his hand.

He climbed in the rental and fired up the engine. Sarah slid open the doors at the back end of the barn. The evening had grown weird with stormy light, a fading wash of orange along the horizon, the sky and fields shadowed with dusk and rain.

Teresa stood by Lawless's car. "Just keep an eye on our brake lights and dust."

Teresa slid into the passenger seat. Lawless put it in gear and eased out of the barn into the twilight. Sarah climbed into the cab of the pickup and turned the ignition. The truck's big engine fired up, strong and steady. She put it in gear and crawled toward the barn door, eyes on Lawless and Teresa ahead.

And she saw two men rise up from behind a scrim of rocks. They wore black, and carried long guns. They aimed the guns at

Lawless's car.

"No. Michael . . ."

Then outside the barn directly in front of her, two more figures dashed into view. A car drove over the rise in the ranchland off to her left, a big dark vehicle, bucking across the grass toward her.

She jammed the gearshift into Reverse and floored it.

Zoe squealed. "Mommy . . ."

"Get down."

She roared backward across the barn toward the closed door at the other end. The truck hit the rotten wood and splintered it. Zoe shrieked. Men shouted and broken boards spun around the truck and she gunned it outside. She threw the wheel and braked and jammed it into Drive. Looked forward.

In front of her were four men in black tactical gear and riot helmets, with rifles aimed directly at the windshield. A red laser sight veered up the hood of the truck and across the dash and came to rest on her chest. Behind the gunmen was a hulking truck with CHAVES COUNTY SHERIFF on the door.

A black sedan with an antenna on the back was stopped beside it.

At the passenger window, a man in a suit

appeared. He held a dark pistol two-handed, aimed directly at her.

"FBI. Don't move."

Behind her, somebody yanked open the door of the crew cab and hauled Zoe out into the night.

The stars were hidden, Fell thought. The black wall of cloud and lightning had swallowed them. She sat at the wheel of the SUV, parked at the side of U.S. 380, just west of the place Grissom and Reavy had spun out earlier in the day. Grissom sat beside her, flicking the safety of his semi-automatic on and off, on and off. In the back seat, Reavy cleaned under her nails with a card, maybe their hotel key, staring toward the countryside where the sheriff's caravan had turned off.

"Soon," Fell said.

"Better be," Reavy said.

The police scanner crackled alive. "Ten-fifteen."

"What's that?" Grissom said.

The dispatcher said, "Copy. Prisoner in custody."

Grissom inhaled and roused himself. "The Lord is good."

"I told you," Fell said, and started the

engine. "Now we wait to see which way they go and where they take her."

48

Handcuffed in the back seat of the un-marked government car, Sarah squinted against the last embers of sunset. The law enforcement convoy sped west across the darkening plateau, away from Roswell, into the vast nowhere.

"Where are we going?"

Special Agent Harker said nothing. Neither did the young FBI agent at the wheel, Marichal. Ahead, lights flashing, a sheriff's cruiser led them across the empty terrain at 75 mph. Behind, headlights glaring, the SWAT command vehicle hugged their bumper.

Further back, a Sheriff's Department Ford Expedition carried Zoe.

A sob welled in Sarah's chest. She shut her eyes and forced it down. She could not cry in front of these men.

The convoy passed a van broken down at the side of the road, hood raised. On top, a spray-painted silver alien glittered like stardust in the sunset. ROSWELL UFO TOURS.

The tour director waved frantically, trying to flag them down. The tourists were bunched miserably on the shoulder. The convoy blew by. The tour director flung his baseball cap to the ground in disgust.

Twenty minutes later, the convoy rolled into a crossroads hamlet. Gas station, feed store, minimart, faded stucco houses. And a sheriff's department outpost. The sign said RIO SACADO STATION. The cars and trucks rumbled into the parking lot like cowboys pulling their horses to a stop outside a dusty saloon.

Harker got out and opened Sarah's door. "Move."

She wriggled across the seat, hands bound behind her, and climbed out. It was near dark, the air fraught with electricity. The windows of the sheriff's station were lit with fluorescent lighting. In the back of a sheriff's cruiser she glimpsed Teresa and Lawless.

"Where's Zoe?" she said.

Harker led her by the elbow toward the door. A uniformed Roswell deputy pulled her daughter from the Ford Expedition.

"Mommy," Zoe called.

"I'm here, honey."

Harker tugged her off balance and over

the curb. She stumbled. The lights glinted from the glass in the door when he pushed it open. Inside, the desk sergeant came to the counter.

Harker held up his badge. "Interview room?"

The sergeant was in his mid-forties, a Latino guy packed solidly into his brown uniform shirt. His nametag read R. Butler. He eyed Harker and the crew that piled in behind him as if they were a dog-and-pony show, lost on their way to the circus.

A deputy brought Zoe in. Her shoulders were tight and shaking, her lips almost blue from crying.

"We've been waiting. Looks like everybody's finally here." Sgt. Butler spread his hands on the counter. "One prisoner?"

Harker said, "Interview room?"

"Are you going to book her?" the sergeant said.

"Soon enough."

Butler nodded down a hall. "Either door on the left."

Harker pulled Sarah through the lobby. Opposite the front counter was a Plexiglas wall that divided an area for desks. They walked past it and around a corner to a bare white door labeled INTERVIEW 1.

"In. Sit. Wait." He urged her inside and

turned to leave.

"Hey — the handcuffs. How about removing them?"

"Now, now," Harker said. "Will you be good?"

In the lobby she heard Teresa, and Lawless. He sounded irate. Then Zoe said, "I want my mom."

Harker barred the doorway. For a second he looked like Niedermeyer in *Animal House,* waiting for her to assume the position and to beg, "Thank you, sir — may I have another?" She felt a violent urge to headbutt him through the wall.

She looked at the floor. "Yes."

"Turn around." Harker got the key and unlocked the cuffs. "I'll be back."

The door locked behind him.

In the lobby Lawless waited, surrounded by men in uniforms and tactical gear. They hadn't placed him under arrest, but Harker had confiscated his weapon and his phone. He clearly wanted to strip him of authority and leave no doubt that he was suspect.

Teresa was taken down the hall to another interview room. They treated her gruffly, but with more courtesy than they did Sarah.

Zoe they placed on a chair in the lobby, watched by a deputy the size of a torpedo.

She sat, feet dangling, her face wan under the lights. She worked her fingers together, over and over, like tarantulas wrestling.

The desk sergeant beckoned Agent Marichal. "I know you and your big band here called ahead, but want to let me in on what's happening?"

"Special Agent Harker will brief you."

"Thought that's what you'd say." He turned to the Roswell deputies. "Gentlemen?"

One of the men said, "We seem to be the warm-up act. We're waiting for the briefing as well."

The SWAT team leader was behind the counter, speaking on the phone to their commander. After a minute he hung up and told his men they were headed back to Roswell. Their job was done. They shouldered their gear and filed out.

Harker returned. His color was high, his manner severe. He looked like a lit match, flaring and ready to set fire to the world.

"What's going on, Curt?" Lawless said.

"That's need-to-know. And you don't."

Sgt. Butler said, "We all need to know. Should I order pizza for this crowd? 'Cause it'll take an hour to get it here. Nearest place is in Alamogordo."

Lawless said, "You didn't take Sarah back

to Roswell for a reason. You wanted to isolate her in the middle of nowhere." He glanced at the desk sergeant. "No offense."

"None taken."

Harker said, "So it's 'Sarah' now?"

Lawless said, "You and I need to speak privately."

"You're in no position to make demands, Mike."

The senior Roswell deputy said, "But I am. It's time you briefed us."

Harker set his hands on his hips. "Very well. I've brought the prisoner here for operational and security reasons."

"What are those, exactly?"

Lawless said, "He wants to keep this out of the news."

Sgt. Butler looked at Zoe, surprised. "This is the little girl they were talking about on TV. You arrested the mother?"

"The abductor," Harker said. "And we don't want word getting out yet."

"Why not?"

Lawless felt a gnawing in his gut. "He doesn't want lights and cameras and reporters asking questions."

The deputies stilled. They could understand keeping it off the news until family members were notified. But Lawless was suggesting something else. They looked back and forth between him and Harker.

Harker said, "Go on, then, Mike. Why not?"

"Because lights and cameras and nosy reporters will scare off the wildlife." Lawless walked toward him. "They'll spook the Worthe clan and keep them from showing up here."

Butler raised a hand. "Hold on. The Worthes?" He nodded down the hall. "Does this have to do with our guest back there?"

Harker took a moment. He straightened his tie and smoothed his jacket. "Deputy Marshal Lawless is correct. The Worthe family is pursuing Sarah Keller, with the goal of taking the child into their custody."

Jesus, Lawless thought. Talking about Zoe while she was sitting right there. She went still, her hands knotted as if in prayer.

Lawless went and sat down beside her. Quietly, he said, "Hey." He held out his hand. Zoe took it. Her little fingers were hot. She was breathing rapidly, chest rising and falling.

Butler said, "And you want to draw the Worthes into the open?" He pointed at the floor. "Here?"

"It's safer than luring them into an urban environment like Roswell. The Worthes have no regard for life or the safety of innocent bystanders. They'll attack a protective detail or even a police station, and I want to minimize the chance of collateral damage."

"So you what, plan to let them attack us here?"

Harker shook his head. "With luck they won't get within half a mile of this station, because we'll see them coming. That's the beauty of holding the prisoner here. Rio Sacado has unobstructed views in all directions. The only two roads within miles cross right outside. You'll see anybody approaching with plenty of warning. Plus, we'll set up reconnaissance posts outside of town. And we'll deploy an FBI tactical team."

Butler said, "Are you sure they're going to come?"

"Positive."

" 'Cause we got people living around here. Only 'round a hundred, but they're my responsibility."

"Leave that to me," Harker said.

"I can't do that."

Lawless said, "One question, Curt. Without the media, how will you draw the Worthes here? How will they find out Sarah is in Rio Sacado?"

Harker offered a thin smile. "Same way they found out she was at the music festival."

He beckoned Special Agent Marichal. Marichal brought Sarah's messenger bag. Harker found her wallet and took out a credit card. He held it up.

"Does this town have an ATM machine?"

49

Tracking the law enforcement convoy was like tailing a freight train. Out here there was only one paved road. Fell stayed almost a mile behind the flashing lights of the cruisers and SWAT trucks. With their own lights off, the Navigator was nearly invisible against the black horizon.

Reavy said, "According to the map, the next town is Rio Sacado. If you can call it a town. That's the only place they can turn."

Grissom pointed out the windshield, like cracking a whip. "Close it up."

Fell accelerated. The white line on the asphalt was hard to see, but she pressed her foot on the pedal.

"Gotta be two deputies plus six SWAT and the two FBI agents," she said.

"Your point?" Grissom said.

She glanced at him. She would cope with being outnumbered, but did he really not see that they needed to deal with the arithmetic? "My point is, I don't want to waste ammunition having to take down so many useless cops. What's your plan?"

He turned his head, slowly, and glared at her. The dashboard lights reflected in his eyes. "You questioning me?"

"Never."

" 'Cause 'What's your plan' sounded like a question."

"It's dark out here, and I need guidance."

"The plan is, I lead, you follow."

From the back seat, Reavy said, "Course, Grissom."

"Course," Fell said.

Grissom took out his phone. "I'm on it."

The lights of the convoy vanished over a rise. The men in that convoy would know this vehicle. They'd be on the lookout for it. Deputies and FBI agents were as easy to kill as anybody, but they weren't as stupid as Grissom thought.

They passed a broken-down van by the side of the road. Man waving, passengers sitting in the dust.

She looked in the rearview mirror.

Locked in the interrogation room, Sarah could hear Lawless and Harker arguing in the lobby. The exterior walls of this sheriff's station might be cinder block and rebar, but the interior partitions were flimsy particle-board. The room measured six feet by eight, with a Formica table and two plastic chairs. She paced, rubbing her wrists.

The station was hardly bigger than a ranch house. This place was at the crossroads of tumbleweeds and jackrabbit junction. Why had they brought her here?

She leaned her ear to the door, trying to hear more clearly. *Zoe.* What were they doing with Zoe?

Lawless said, "No, Curt. Absolutely not." Another man, maybe the desk sergeant, said, "We need to coordinate with Roswell."

"With the Bureau in Albuquerque, you mean," Harker said.

She knew there was another interrogation room. She knocked on the wall. It made a cheap hollow sound.

"Teresa?" she said.

On the far side, a chair scraped on the floor. "It's me."

"You okay?"

"That word covers a lot of ground. But physically, yes."

Sarah rested her head against the wall. "Do you know where Zoe is? Who's got hold of her?"

"She was in the lobby with a deputy, last I saw."

"I have to get to her."

Teresa didn't reply.

Sarah said, "I don't know what they're playing at. They haven't put us in cells. No booking, no mug shot . . ."

"Who actually arrested you back at the barn?"

"Harker." She saw what Teresa was getting at. "He brought us here because it's a holding pen. He'll want to take me where there's a federal lockup to formally incarcerate me." Albuquerque, or El Paso.

But that wasn't the worst of it. "He's going to take Zoe. He's going . . ." She put a hand against the wall to steady herself. "I'm sorry. So sorry I got you into this."

"I don't know what's coming next. But I know we have to be prepared for anything. For that, you need to use whatever method works to hold yourself together. Right here, right now."

What Sarah wanted was a jackhammer to bore through the door and then through Harker's grimly satisfied face. She took a breath.

It seemed as if she'd been taking breaths to calm herself for five years. And look where it had gotten her.

From the other room came Teresa's voice, barely above a murmur. "My soul proclaims the greatness of the Lord, my spirit rejoices in God my savior . . ."

Sarah set her back against the wall and slid to the floor.

Lawless stood and walked toward Harker. "Why don't you splash Sarah with red paint, dangle her from the roof, and call her bait? You can't do this. You have no right to put civilians in the line of fire to capture Grissom Briggs and those women."

Harker's neck flushed. "I have no intention of placing civilians at risk. We'll set an ambush outside of town. The sheriff's department can put up a roadblock and keep local traffic from entering the area."

Sgt. Butler leaned on the counter. "You are not going to lure a bunch of homicidal maniacs into Rio Sacado. I will not let you endanger my officers or the prisoners and visitors you've brought here."

Harker didn't flinch. "None of this will be put into action until I have transported the prisoners to federal lockup. Did you not understand? I don't need Sarah Keller here. I just need her *to have been here.* Because once I use her credit card, it'll be like bees to honey. The Worthes will come."

Lawless didn't know whether Harker considered him a prisoner or not. But he knew he needed to get Sarah and Teresa and Zoe out of there. He needed backup from the Marshals Service, and that would take several phone calls — to his boss, who could call people in high places, who could then order Harker to stand down.

His most burning worry was Zoe. She shouldn't be here. She was in a sheriff's station, but extremely vulnerable.

He glanced toward her just in time to see her slide off the plastic chair. For a moment she stood staring at nothing, as though listening to sounds and vibrations none of the rest of them could hear. She looked around the lobby, slowly — at the desk, at Harker and the sergeant, and then past them, out the glass-fronted door.

Lawless said, "What is it?"

Her gaze lifted to meet his, gleaming and frightened. "Something's coming."

50

Lawless followed Zoe's gaze. Outside was nothing but darkness, seen through the reflected fluorescent lighting off the door and windows. But somehow the air in the room seemed to thrum.

"What's coming, Zoe?" he said.

She stared out the door into the night. Then she looked up at him. "I want to leave."

A high-pitched hum invaded his head. He held out his hand. She took it.

Outside, several hundred yards distant along the highway, headlights rose.

Sgt. Butler noticed their watchfulness. He looked out the door. A dark vehicle droned up the highway toward the crossroads and station house. Harker had taken out his phone and was scrolling through numbers. Lawless said, "Men."

The vehicle held its speed as it approached the crossroads. It rushed straight through, disappearing westward, maybe headed for Arizona, or Malibu.

Lawless swallowed, feeling bizarrely relieved. Harker gave him a disdainful look.

Zoe lowered her voice to a near-whisper. "I want to go. Please." She looked up at him again. "We should leave. Where's my mom?"

Another set of headlights appeared on the highway, high beams, coming their way. Zoe squeezed his hand.

The vehicle swelled into view, slowing at the crossroads. It was a van. It angled across the road into the sheriff's station parking lot and stopped sideways across the empty parking slots outside, parallel to the front wall. In the light leaking from the station's windows, the spray-painted silver alien glittered on top of it. It was the UFO Tours van.

Sgt. Butler walked back behind the counter. One of the Roswell deputies headed for a vending machine in the hallway.

Holding tight to Lawless's hand, Zoe backed up a step.

Faces filled the van's windows. The driver got out. Looked like the man in the ball cap who had been at the side of the road earlier, when . . .

"Harker. Sergeant," Lawless said. "Lock

the door."

Harker looked up from his call. Butler glanced at Lawless, perplexed. The driver walked along the far side of the van toward its rear end.

"Now," Lawless said. "Lock it. Deputies, watch him."

He grabbed Zoe and moved toward the hallway.

Butler said, "What the hell's got into you?"

"Sergeant," Lawless barked. "That van was broken down on the highway. Why is it here?"

The driver lifted the tailgate. Two other people climbed from the van and walked toward the station. In front was a chunky woman wearing an I BELIEVE sweatshirt. Behind her was a young woman. Close behind.

The tailgate slammed and inside the back of the van there was a bright flash.

One of the deputies said, "It's on fire."

He rushed to the door and ran outside.

"Where's the fire extinguisher?" Harker yelled.

Lawless shouted: "It's the Worthes."

The van seemed to *whoosh,* and filled with flame. The people inside it screamed. Lawless felt himself detach from the room and zoom out, as though seeing the scene from above.

Another deputy ran outside with the fire extinguisher.

The girl behind the I BELIEVE woman reached around her and brought up the matte black shotgun she'd been holding at her side. With one hand she aimed it at the deputy and fired.

He went down against the van. The girl shoved the I BELIEVE woman away. The driver came around the back of the van, pistol in his hand. The second deputy was trying to open the van door. He turned, hand on his holster. The driver shot him in the chest.

The van was roiling with flame, screams seeming to emanate from everywhere. Somehow the people inside lurched out the far side, some with their clothes on fire.

"Don't let them get through the door," Lawless yelled.

But Sgt. Butler was lumbering for the gun locker. He pulled at the key ring on his belt.

Lawless turned to put his body in front of Zoe. "Harker, where's my weapon?"

Harker had drawn his own gun. He and Marichal both. They turned to the front door just as the girl with the Mossberg kicked it open and came through, firing.

51

Sarah was already on her feet, brought up by yells from the lobby, when the gunshot boomed through the station. She gasped. The blast was deep and heavy.

"Zoe. Oh God."

She pounded on the door. "Harker, let me out."

More shouts from the lobby, and another shot. A man screamed.

"Zoe." She slammed her fist against the wood. "Open the door."

She yelled through the wall to the other interrogation room. "Teresa, can you get out?"

"No — door's locked."

Sarah looked around the room. She picked up one of the plastic chairs and started bashing it against the doorknob.

The shotgun blast missed everybody and tore chunks of wood from the front counter.

The man with the semiautomatic pistol charged through the station door and fired, hitting Sgt. Butler in the thigh. Butler cried out and fell to the floor.

Lawless hoisted Zoe onto his hip and backed around a corner. He needed a weapon and he needed it now. The little girl clung to him. He was barely aware of her, just chattering teeth and rapid breathing, little hands squeezing him around the neck.

The woman with the Mossberg swept the barrel back and forth. She looked impossibly young and absolutely bloodless. Blond hair and slim jeans and utter confidence with the shotgun. Butler dragged himself across the floor, trying to draw his service weapon from the holster on his hip.

The woman leveled the barrel at him and fired.

Harker and Marichal ducked low and ran into the desk pen, behind the Plexiglas wall. They crouched behind a desk and counted, synchronizing. On *three* they stood and fired through the glass toward the lobby.

Their shots sounded like ball bearings crunching into Glad Wrap. They punched neat holes in the Plexiglas. The blonde threw herself across the front counter and slid to the floor on the far side. She came up pumping the shotgun. Harker and Marichal ducked. She fired across the counter and blasted a hole in the glass a foot wide.

Lawless needed a weapon, but even more he needed to get Zoe out of there. He held her tight and ran down the hall. He heard pounding on a door. He threw it open.

Sarah stood inside with a chair overhead, ready to slam it down on his head.

"Wait," he said.

"Michael." She dropped the chair. Her eyes were wild. He handed Zoe to her. They ran.

Sarah held Zoe tighter than she thought possible. "How do we get out of here?"

Lawless rushed to the room next door and let Teresa out. She looked strangely calm. She had Zoe's backpack in her hand. She said, "What can I do?"

More gunfire echoed from the lobby.

Lawless pointed deeper into the building. "Find the back exit. Go."

Sarah ran, Zoe bouncing on her hip. She looked back and saw a man appear at the top of the hallway: Grissom Briggs. He had a silver gun in his hand. He raised it and fired.

Her skin seemed to spark. The shot hit the wall at the end of the hallway ahead of her. She skittered around a corner with

Teresa on her heels.

Lawless saw Grissom Briggs round the corner. He threw himself through the door of the interrogation room. Briggs fired and hit something solid — concrete. He retreated.

Across the hall, in the Plexiglas pen, Marichal and Harker were pinned down behind a desk.

Lawless said, "Where's my weapon?"

Harker glanced at him with regret. "Car. Outside."

From the parking lot came a low *boom* and an orange fireball filled the view. The walls and windows shuddered. The UFO Tours van had exploded.

Lawless could see it through the glass partition: it had flipped over the curb and landed against the front door of the station. Flames shot from it as from a rocket booster. They licked against the eaves of the building.

The weapons locker had to be close. Sgt. Butler had been headed for it. He looked at Butler's body on the floor twenty feet away.

He called to Harker: "Cover me."

Harker rose and fired two rounds through the hole in the glass wall at the front counter where Reavy was hiding.

Lawless burst from the interrogation room and ran to the sergeant's body. His heart was hammering. From the front of the building came the smell of smoke and the sound of flames consuming wood. The roof had caught fire.

Lawless scrabbled for the keys on the sergeant's belt. He saw Briggs lean out from behind a corner of the front counter. Sleepy eyes and a T-shirt that said STFU.

"Harker," Lawless said.

Harker fired another round. Briggs retreated. Lawless scrambled to his feet and ran down the hall. Tried the keys in the door labeled FIREARMS STORAGE. He got it open just as the shotgun fired at him.

He pitched inside. A gun rack greeted him. Four rifles, four shotguns, and storage for handguns. Opposite wall: ammunition.

He unlocked the rack and took a shotgun. It was a Remington 870, a law enforcement favorite, and it felt reliable in his hands. He got two handguns, stuffed one in his holster and the second in the small of his back. Grabbed boxes of ammo. In the hallway more shots rang out.

He loaded the shotgun magazine to capacity and racked a shell into the chamber. Took a breath, and pressed his back to the wall by the door. Just as the fire alarms rang and the sprinkler system kicked in.

52

Sarah ran to the end of the hall. It split in a T. She ran right around a corner and threw open a door. It was a windowless storage room. More shots echoed from the lobby. The fire alarm blared. A second later the sprinklers popped down and sprayed the station, but the smoke and crackle of flame continued.

"We have to find the back door," she said.

"Mommy, I'm scared."

"Hold on." She gripped Zoe, her own arms shaking.

She tried another door: locked. They would have to go back and cross the hallway, putting them in view of the lobby. Teresa put a hand on her arm.

"Let me go first."

She led them back to the hallway and peered around the corner. Pulled back. A second later a shot punched through the opposite wall. Sarah's legs felt like water.

Then, in the distance, another shotgun blared. Lawless shouted, "Harker, with me. Marichal — cover the back. Find Sarah."

Agent Marichal skittered around the corner. He was panting, his face dripping water from the sprinklers. He looked as angry as Sarah had ever seen a man.

He held his service weapon at his side. "You okay?"

It was the most ridiculous thing anybody had ever said to her. "Super."

He handed over her messenger bag. "Weapons, ammo."

Out in the hall, voices rose. Harker and Lawless were shouting at each other.

"We have to find a way out the back," Sarah said. "I thought it was this way, but . . . gotta be around the corner and past the interrogation rooms."

Marichal nodded. He looked at Teresa. "Sister, can you run?"

"I can do whatever you need," she said.

The sprinklers sputtered and shut off. The flicker of orange flame still reflected in the wet walls and floor. The fire had crept under the eaves and into the space above the ceiling. The sprinklers had done nothing to quench it.

Marichal looked at Zoe. "You're being awesome. Stay brave, kid."

Sarah's throat caught. Zoe looked at him, lip quivering, and might have nodded.

"Follow me," he said. "Single file, right behind me."

He took a breath, leveled his weapon, and spun around the corner. When there was no gunfire, Teresa followed, then Sarah.

Marichal hurried along the hall until they found another turn. He paused and held his gun level toward the lobby. "Go."

Sarah and Teresa ran around the corner. At the end of the hall was a fire door.

Sarah beckoned. "Marichal, this way."

She ran to the end of the hall and stopped. Teresa pulled up alongside her.

Marichal caught up. "I'll go first."

"When we get outside, what do we do?" Teresa said.

"Run. Run for cover and don't stop."

The sheriff's station should have been cover. It should have been the place to run for safety. Sarah had no confidence that any other structure in this little crossroads would be better.

Marichal said, "We have a lucky break. Harker and Lawless have both hostiles pinned down. Head northwest — the building will block their view of us."

He took a hard breath, raised his weapon, and put his shoulder against the door.

Sarah said, "What do you mean, both hostiles?"

There were three of them. The Shattering Angel and his wings.

"Marichal, wait —"

He rammed the door open and shouted, "Go."

A shot and a muzzle flash emanated from the night. Marichal huffed like he'd been hit in the gut with a sledgehammer and fell to the ground in the doorway.

Lawless kept his back to the wall. Black smoke churned along the hallway ceiling and boiled through the holes in the glass wall of the Plexiglas pen. The sprinklers hadn't put out the flames. Harker coughed.

They couldn't stay where they were. The building was going up.

But Briggs and Reavy were hunkered behind the front counter. If they could be pinned down for one more minute, maybe he and Harker could get the advantage on them.

He whistled. "Harker."

The FBI agent glanced across the hall. Lawless explained with hand signals.

One of them had to pin down the hostiles with covering fire while the other went out the back. With the fire and lights reflecting from the windows, people in the building couldn't see out. But a shooter outside in the dark would have a clear view into the lobby.

Harker got it immediately. He pointed at Lawless, a jabbing index finger. *You.* Then he jerked his thumb toward the back of the building. *Go.*

Lawless slung the shotgun over his back by the strap and drew the pistol from the small of his back. Harker stood up from behind the desk into billowing smoke. He leveled his weapon at the front counter and fired.

Lawless dashed from the interrogation room, spurred by Harker's bravery. He ran toward the back of the station, caromed off the wall, and slid down the corridor.

Marichal lay splayed in the doorway, legs inside the building, his chest across the threshold. The fire door slowly closed on its pneumatic hinges and hit him. Another gunshot spit from the darkness outside the back of the station.

He coughed and tried to lift himself off the concrete. He couldn't.

Sarah set Zoe down. She pointed at a water cooler a few feet away. "Get behind that. Hurry."

Zoe ran and crouched low behind it, clutching her knees. Sarah was shaking so hard she could barely see.

"Teresa, help me," she said.

They each grabbed one of Marichal's legs and pulled, trying to drag him back inside. A shot cracked from the dark and rang against the door. Sarah jumped and blurted out, "Jesus Christ." They kept pulling but the door closed with them, pinning Marichal against the frame, his shoulders and arms outside.

"Roll, Marichal," she said.

He groaned and shuddered and couldn't manage it. "Weapon . . ."

Sarah saw his gun outside. He'd dropped it. And damned if she was going to leave it there. It was only a foot outside. She took a breath, took two, and three, telling herself: *Do it.*

She lunged, grabbed the gun, and jerked herself back inside. Teresa kept trying to pull Marichal through the doorway.

"Roll," the nun said. "Come on, man."

Another shot. It hit Marichal in the shoulder with a sickening thud.

"Goddammit," Sarah said. She held the gun, but her hand was shaking like a hummingbird.

Marichal was still conscious but now immensely worse off, and jammed in the doorway, unable to move. They couldn't get him inside from where they were. And if they left him . . .

Sarah got to one knee, steadied herself, and thought: *Straight back at the firing point. Where I saw the flash.*

She squeezed the trigger. Marichal's weapon fired, kicking heavily in her hand. She steadied her hand, braced her right in her left. Exhaled and fired again.

Hitting anything would be a one-in-a-thousand shot, blind luck. But she didn't need to hit the other shooter, just suppress her fire. And the night outside went quiet. "Now. Pull," she yelled.

She grabbed one of Marichal's arms and yanked him half-upright. Teresa hauled on his legs. He slid awkwardly through the doorway, moaned, and flopped back on the tile floor. The door shut.

Teresa rolled Marichal on his back. His body armor hadn't protected him. Beneath it his shirt was soaked red, blood pulsing from a hole in his shoulder. And the leg of his trousers was sopping.

The fire alarm continued to ring, relentless and loud. Did this crossroads have a fire station? Did it have a volunteer fire department? The smoke was billowing from the front of the building, infiltrating the hallway like roaming dirty fingers.

Teresa pressed her hand to the wound in Marichal's shoulder.

Sarah heard the crackle of flames. "The building's burning down. We need to leave."

The nun didn't take her eyes off the young agent. Marichal was breathing raggedly. His eyes were glazed.

"Mommy, I see the fire." Zoe's voice was threaded with fear.

"Teresa, *now*. Anybody who stays in this building is going to die," Sarah said. "I need to get Zoe out. Pull him if you have to, but we have to find another door, or a window, we gotta move right this second."

She turned to the water cooler and grabbed Zoe's hand. She wanted to cry, wanted to scream, saw her daughter's eyes and wanted to kill everybody who'd put a look like that on a five-year-old's face. She ran down the hall, nearly dragging Zoe. Behind her she heard Teresa grunting, pulling Marichal along the floor.

She found an empty room, some kind of storage for office furniture. It had the only thing she needed: a window.

"Me first, then you," she said to Zoe.

The smoke billowed into the room. Zoe said, "Hurry, Mom, hurry."

The crackling sound intensified. Black smoke rolled along the ceiling, bulging and coiling. She opened the window, hopped on the sill, and dropped to the dirt outside. Raised the gun.

Nobody fired at her. She felt as if she were lit up with nerves, a fiery wraith, a huge target. She waited for the gunshot to tear through her, rip her skin and muscle and bone. When no shot came, she took the biggest risk of her life.

"Come on." She waved to Zoe.

Zoe scrambled onto the windowsill. Sarah grabbed her under the armpits and lowered her to the ground. Inside, into the dark room, Teresa dragged Marichal. She slammed the door and hauled him toward the window.

Sarah took Zoe's hand and prepared to run. But Zoe stared back through the window. Then she looked up at Sarah. In her eyes was a simple, blinding question.

Sarah's breathing snagged. She scrambled back inside and helped Teresa pull Marichal to the window.

"Let's see if we can get him out," she said.

Lawless banged around a corner into a back hallway filled with smoke. He threw open a door. It was a break room. Incredible heat met him. The window was open, air rushing through. Flames writhed along the ceiling and walls. Outside a figure huddled, staring at him.

The ceiling tiles flared into flame and collapsed. The gush of air that followed slammed the door shut in his face.

What in hell?

Behind him Harker issued more covering fire. Lawless turned and backtracked. What in *hell* had he just seen? He slipped in a slick of blood on the floor. Looked up. Ahead was a fire door.

He ran to the exit, paused, and slammed through, firing two shots into the night. He ran along the side of the building in the dark, eyes on the lobby.

Inside the storeroom Agent Marichal was barely conscious. The door was shut but around the frame smoke leaked in, and behind it an orange glow cut a deathly rectangle.

Sarah said, "The two of us can get him out the window."

When she picked him up under the arms, he swiped for the windowsill, trying to help, but couldn't grip it. Outside, Zoe watched.

Sarah climbed on the sill. "Come on."

Together the two of them managed to lug

Marichal through the window. They dragged him away from the building and set him on the lawn.

Around them was the empty desert night, maybe the lights of a trailer home a quarter-mile away. Nothing but sand and stars and wolves. Nowhere to hide. The fire threw orange light onto the ground.

And then she heard a truck roaring toward them.

Marichal said, "Run."

She stared at the night. Could see nothing. She crouched and placed his service weapon back in his hand. He gripped it feebly. She looked at Teresa. The nun knelt at Marichal's side, putting pressure on both his wounds.

"Go," Teresa said.

Sarah grabbed Zoe's hand. Reaching into her messenger bag for the pistol Marichal had stashed there, she ran away from the building, her shadow and Zoe's stretching ahead, wavering.

In the dark beyond the reach of the lights inside the station, Lawless took a position outside the lobby windows. All he saw were flames. At the station's main door, the UFO Tours van was engulfed.

Inside the station Harker fired another

round. How the man was holding his position in the heat and smoke Lawless couldn't imagine. He swung the shotgun off his back and leveled it at the lobby windows.

Then he heard a vehicle coming fast. Running without lights. The engine sounded heavy, revving, headed straight at him.

From behind the front counter Reavy and Grissom Briggs stood up, weapons in their hands.

Grissom fired at Harker in the Plexiglas pen. Reavy spun toward the windows facing directly out at Lawless.

He fired the Remington through the window.

The glass was reinforced but spidered white. Reavy and Grissom leaped out of the line of fire.

Outside the station, fifty yards from him, headlights flipped on, lighting him up. An SUV roared toward him.

Reavy racked the slide on the Mossberg and aimed it at Lawless. She unleashed one shot, then racked it and fired again, directly at the window, blowing two holes in it side by side. Lawless had nowhere to run, except backward, firing. Grissom threw himself at the window, rolling to hit the fractured glass with his back. He punched through, landed, and came up unloading shots from his pistol.

Reavy climbed out after him.

Lawless yelled, "U.S. marshal. Don't move."

Grissom ran for the street. Reavy got to her feet, racked the slide again, held the shotgun low by her hip, and fired toward him. He threw himself to the ground.

The SUV bounced over the dirt, headlights glaring, straight at him.

53

Outside the burning sheriff's station, the silver Navigator bumped across the dirt, heading at Lawless. He rolled, scrambled to his feet, and jumped out of its way.

Harker came running out of the fire door. The Navigator blew past him and he fired, again and again.

The Navigator jumped the curb and roared onto the street.

Harker stood, arm extended, chest heaving, aiming at taillights that had diminished to hot red pinpricks. The Navigator raced north on the crossroad into the night.

Lawless looked around. "Where's Marichal? Where are Sarah and Zoe?"

"Who was in the SUV?" Harker said. "How many? Did you get a head count?"

Indistinctly, Lawless heard a voice calling out. A woman's voice.

He ran toward the building. "Harker —

this way."

Sarah heard the blare of a truck engine drawing near. "Run, Zoe."

Her daughter said nothing. She had nothing left to say. But her feet moved, little steps racing at Sarah's side.

The truck slewed up next to her. She raised the pistol.

And heard a familiar voice. "Get in. Hurry."

At the open driver's window, a man stared at her. "I mean it. Come on."

She didn't move.

He said, "You want to keep breathing? Get in. You gotta get out of here. There's three of them here tonight. By the morning, there'll be more."

The building was a boil of orange flame. She tossed Zoe into the cargo bed and leaped in after her. The truck pulled out, racing west down the highway away from the station.

The flames burst through the station's windows. Beneath their roar the voice sounded thin. "Back here. Help!"

Lawless and Harker ran around the building, where smoke was pouring out an open window. Nearby Teresa knelt on the grass, bent over Marichal.

She coughed. "Hurry."

Lawless ran up. "Sarah and Zoe."

"Gone."

"Where?"

"Away."

Harker ran over and dropped to one knee. "Backup?" Lawless said.

Harker leaned over Marichal. He nodded. "Phoned the sheriff's office in Roswell. They're coming. And paramedics."

Along with the FBI team from Albuquerque, Lawless knew. The FBI team that had coordinated with Harker and thought they had plenty of time to get to Rio Sacado. The team the FBI thought would conduct an ambush. Not clean up after one.

Teresa leaned over Marichal and put pressure on his wounds, but she was hacking, shuddering, ready to fall over herself.

Lawless said, "The paramedics are coming from Roswell?"

"Closest county rescue unit." Harker looked empty. He knew Roswell was seventy miles behind them.

"We need air evac," Lawless said.

Harker shook his head. "Air ambulance is en route to a multivehicle accident outside Roswell."

"Alamogordo's thirty miles west," Lawless

said. "Give me the keys to the car."

Harker looked baffled. "I need the car. We have to initiate pursuit."

"Harker." Lawless grabbed his arm. "We can't drive any of the sheriff's cruisers parked out front. The keys are all inside a burning building."

"Where did they go?" Harker stared into the night, north, where the silver Navigator carrying the trio had disappeared. "Why did they leave?"

Teresa said, "Because the people they're after are gone."

Harker looked at her, momentarily confused. He looked like a boxer who'd taken a hard punch to the jaw and gotten his bell rung.

"Gone?"

"Sarah and Zoe are gone. And they're the only reason those others attacked the station. Once Zoe left, the attackers had no reason to stay. They weren't here just to burn it down and shoot at you."

From the far side of the building, somebody called, "Hello? Is anybody in there?"

The tourists from the UFO van staggered around the corner. Lawless waved to them.

He said, "Harker. The keys."

As though in a trance, Harker handed them over. Teresa looked at Marichal. She released the pressure on his wounds.

"It doesn't matter anymore. He's gone."

They stared at the young agent under the lurching light of the flames. The wind had come up, or maybe that was just the fire eating the sky, wanting them as well.

Teresa made the sign of the cross and began to pray.

Harker stumbled to his feet. He swayed and wiped soot from his face with the back of his hand.

Lawless put a hand on Teresa's shoulder. Teresa folded Marichal's arms over his chest, pressed her hand against his as if offering him comfort, as if telling him *Sorry*.

She looked up at him through the reflected orange light of the flames. "I can't fight any more."

He nodded. "Will you be okay?"

She gave him a sorrowful look and managed a nod. He turned to go, and she held out a hand, stopping him. Groaning to her feet, she embraced him.

"I'm sorry," he said. "I'll be back to get you."

She touched his face, almost a blessing, and whispered, "Finish this. Find them, Michael."

He held her gaze a second, her gentle eyes made fierce by the firelight. He nodded.

Then he turned and half-staggered away.

Harker called after him. "Where do you think you're going?"

"The Worthes are gone. All they want is Sarah and Zoe, not you, Harker." He tried to swallow. His throat was raw from smoke.

He wanted to get a thousand miles from Curtis Harker. But he turned back. "While I was looking for the fire exit I stumbled into a break room. It was fully involved but I saw somebody outside the window."

Harker stared at Marichal's body. He touched his jacket pocket, as though checking that a heart pacemaker was still ticking.

"Harker," Lawless said. "What the hell is going on? Who was that?"

Harker didn't look at him.

"I opened that door and you know who I saw," Lawless said.

Harker shook his head. "It was Marichal."

"No," Lawless said. "That's not who I'm talking about." He approached Harker and grabbed his arm. "You arranged for him to come here? What the hell?"

Harker pulled free. "I had to."

"Are you crazy?"

"It's a necessary part of this operation." He snapped out of his confusion. "Information, Lawless. How do you think we're going to bring down the clan without gathering information?"

"What are you talking about?"

"Passcodes. Routing numbers. It's encrypted," Harker said. "Blood money, man. Who else do you think can help us trace the blood money?"

Under the flames he looked crazed. Lawless backed away. He felt absolutely undermined, lost, and hopeless.

He wiped soot from his face. He turned away from Harker and his crazy plan, and walked away. He didn't care anymore. Even if it meant he would risk losing his marshal's star.

"Where are you going?" Harker said.

"I'm done with this," Lawless said. "You set off a chain reaction. And you can't stop it."

"I said, where are you going?"

"After your fugitive. The clan still wants Sarah. Her only chance is for me to get to her first."

54

Lying in the cargo bed of the big pickup, holding Zoe tight, Sarah stared at stars that sprayed the sky like blinding ice. Rio Sacado receded. The fiery sheriff's station shrank to a shivery glow at the crossroads. The night turned dark and vast, empty again, nothing but the desert and a flat strip of road bearing them to freedom.

At the wheel, Nolan put the pedal down.

Her breath caught in her chest. *Alive.* Nolan. Alive and involved and *right there.*

She reached up and beat on the back window of the cab. The truck kept going, one minute, three, roaring along, wind scouring the bed. Zoe didn't move or speak or cry. Sarah thought her heart might break.

They crested a long, curving hill and coasted down the far side. Only then, when they were far gone from any sight line to Rio Sacado, did the truck brake and pull onto the shoulder, bounce across the scrub for a minute, and finally come to a halt.

When they stopped Sarah felt as if the entire sky kept racing. Zoe clung to her, balled up and tense. The driver's door opened and Nolan climbed out.

"You got in," he said.

He stood, waiting. For whatever it was she was going to deliver — a blow, a smile, a scream. She turned the gun in her hand so it caught the moonlight. It was an FBI standard-issue Glock 22.40-caliber semi-automatic.

She said, "This time I won't struggle with you for it. This time it won't be an accident or a lucky shot. This time I won't leave you wounded, Nolan. I'll kill you."

She glanced back toward Rio Sacado. The stars fell all the way to the horizon.

He said, "They went the other way. I saw their SUV beat it heading north."

She hopped down from the cargo bed, lifted Zoe out, and led her to the cab. "Let's go."

A minute later they were rolling hard along the empty two-lane highway, with ghostly sagebrush sliding past. Nolan checked the mirror. Nobody was behind them. He turned on the headlights.

His breathing sounded rough. He was solid, not something hallucinated —

narrow-eyed under the dashboard lights, unshaven, wearing a Grateful Dead T-shirt that smelled of smoke. Sarah felt as if she were falling toward spikes. One after another, every turn simply brought her deeper toward ruin.

They raced past a sign. WELCOME TO OTERO COUNTY.

"One set of cops down," Nolan said. "Wonder how many more are waiting to welcome us."

"Where are you headed?"

"Wherever we can get to before the tire goes flat. I picked up a nail back at the crossroads."

Great. Just what they needed. Sarah found a map in the glove compartment. Under the map light she saw vast tracts of land unmarked by road or civilization. Forest, desert, military installations, national parks. Just this one little line, a road like a black piece of thread, wobbling toward Alamogordo and on west.

"Find an arroyo with tree cover," she said.

Zoe looked at him. "I heard your name. You're Nolan Worthe."

He nodded. "But you can call me Scott Williams."

"Why?"

Sarah wanted to snirk. *Tell her. Tell her*

everything. He just shrugged.

"Are you my dad?" Zoe said.

Sarah's entire body tightened. She saw pinprick stars. "He is."

Zoe examined him like he was a specimen in the terrarium in her kindergarten classroom — maybe one of the geckos.

"I don't think I look like you."

He tried to laugh. "You look like your mother."

"Beth," Zoe said. "Her name was Beth. That's what it says on the microchip."

His lips parted.

Zoe leaned against Sarah. "She was my mother. This is my mommy."

Sarah rubbed Zoe's arm. *Don't cry.*

The road unrolled like a cable across the desert. All the way across the sand and mountains and hundreds of miles of flats, burning ground, arid, scarred, ruthless. And now everywhere was enemy territory. San Francisco lay at the end of it, twelve hundred miles away.

She'd been holding onto that image since this began. *Get to San Francisco.* San Francisco meant the edge of the continent, and somehow, at least in her frayed imagination, it meant jumping off. It was a place where nobody could chase her anymore, where Zoe would float free and serene under cloudless skies. It meant purging herself of this five-year nightmare.

That, she now saw, was a dream. That was the power of denial. She, who had trained herself to paranoia par excellence, had left open a gaping hole of wishes and impossibility, and she'd driven her child and friends right into it.

She choked down a sob. Turned her head and looked away.

She had thought she'd slipped up at the barn — that she hadn't been careful enough, and because of that the FBI and sheriffs had found them in the middle of nowhere. But now she knew: This was not about how careful she was.

She could never be careful enough. Not with the Worthes on her tail. Not with the FBI after her.

She watched the white lines slip past, leading her nowhere.

In the living room of the trailer, the twin babies squalled. Their mother walked up and down the carpet, one on each hip, trying to shush them. Fell thought the noise would drive her mad.

"Grissom, want to get them to shut up?"

He was standing in the doorway, sweaty, a silhouette that stank. His Smith & Wesson gleamed in the light from the kitchen.

"Mind at least shutting the door?" Fell added.

He shuffled away, pulling the door closed behind him.

On the bed in the cold bedroom, Reavy lay panting. "Get to it."

Fell ripped open the roll of gauze and set it on the nightstand beside the tweezers and the X-acto knife. She'd given Reavy two Valium to numb the pain. Her sister was bleeding from a gunshot wound to her hip.

"Pray to God or curse the bastards and bitch to kingdom come," Fell said. "Just don't scream."

Reavy's hair was matted with sweat and she was shaking. But the bullet hadn't gone deep, hadn't hit anything vital. It had ricocheted off the rivet in her jeans. Fell could see it lodged beneath her skin, in the big muscles along her flank.

This place belonged to their Worthe cousins, Jadom and Lolly. The two were nineteen and had four kids, which worried Fell, because little eyes came with little mouths and the urge to talk. But for tonight they were safe in this trailer in the mountains east of Ruidoso. Jadom and Lolly worked in the business. He cooked. She minded the home and handled the finances, ran a payroll service for family members who were less successful.

No, Jadom and Lolly wouldn't talk. The Shattering Angel was standing in their living room. World without end, fiery wings alight, amen.

"Stay quiet."

She jabbed the X-acto knife into the wound on Reavy's side, deep enough to see the bullet. Reavy breathed hard, like a weight lifter. Blood swelled a bright and healthy red all around it, spilling across her sister's haunches. With the tweezers, Fell dug the bullet out.

She held it up. "Prize of the night, girl."

Reavy held out her hand. Fell dropped the round into her palm.

"This is not the prize. Zoe is," Reavy said. "Keller has no right. Zoe isn't hers."

Fell threaded a needle and began to stitch. "No. She's not."

"She's been blessed. She's a Worthe."

Fell worked the needle. "If you want Zoe —"

"You don't. You want the chip."

"If you want her," Fell continued, "don't ask permission. Get her. Own this."

Reavy pressed her lips tight. She blinked and looked at the closed door.

Fell said, "If we rescue Zoe, we're heroes.

413

You bring her home in your arms, Isom has to let you keep her. So get her. Claim her. Then maybe Grissom'll make you his full wife. Maybe not."

"I'm not gonna have kids any other way. I got to."

Fell finished stitching. She knotted and cut the thread. "Nobody knows and I'm not telling."

"I haven't had kids. That's telling."

Chlamydia, or the abortion — one or the other had probably left Reavy infertile. God had punished her. And unless she got a kid some way, the family would punish her too. Fell brushed her sister's damp hair back from her face. Reavy reached up and touched a finger to the locket that hung from the chain around Fell's neck. It glowed in the dim light.

"Creek," she said.

"Yeah."

Reavy fingered the locket, but said nothing else. Nobody ever did. The only person in the family who'd spoken one word about it was Nolan, right before he took off for California. Murmuring to her: "Ain't fair. Taking a kid. Ain't right."

Fell got up from Reavy's side and opened the door. "Grissom."

The view into the living room was chaotic.

The babies shrieked. Jadom sat at the kitchen table, playing solitaire, his wispy mustache looking verminous. Lolly walked back and forth, eyeing Grissom with undisguised fear.

Grissom came into the bedroom. "Done?"

Reavy held up the bullet. "Gonna pay back the bastards twice and then some. The bitch too."

"Amen," he said.

Fell wiped her hands on a dish towel. "We can stay here tonight, but only to let Reavy rest. We need to put out the word to everybody we've got, within a two-hundred-mile radius."

"You think Sarah Keller's gonna get that far on foot, after all she's been through? And with a five-year-old? Don't think so," Grissom said.

"You didn't see her disappear," Fell said.

Reavy lifted her head. "I did. She got in a truck. She's got help."

"You sure about that?"

"I'm shot, Grissom, not blind. And not stupid."

He walked over to her then and stared at the stitches. With his thumb he pressed down on the wound.

"You shall not speak thus to your lord husband, girl."

Reavy breathed heavily, staring at the wall. In the living room, Lolly stopped and stared. Fell stood with bunched bloody rags and the X-acto knife in her hand.

Grissom turned to her. "Nothing to say?" He waited, daring her to step out of line. When she didn't, he said, "Where'd Keller go?"

Reavy looked up, her eyes deadly. "West. I saw Sarah Keller get in a pickup truck headed west."

He looked at her for a second. "First light, that's the direction we head. And we watch the news. Reporters will be sniffing around the Rio Sacado Sheriff's Station like dogs."

Fell took the rest of the rags and bunched them up. She would need to burn them, but for now she held them like badges of honor. "I was ready to stay and finish off the FBI man. You're the one who said to pull back."

"Because Keller was gone. That's twice you've let her escape."

He watched Fell's face. Slowly she wiped the blood from the X-acto knife. She sheathed it and slipped it into her back pocket.

"They won't get away," she said.

Grissom loved his own life. He cared less about hers, or Reavy's. In the 60-watt trailer light, she saw him anew. The sleepy eyes and bad boy lips, the ripped body, the eager fists. Protector, enforcer, user. He only cared about the angel's wings because they supported him. Fair enough. Let him think he was the center of God's own whirlpool of blood. She tucked her locket inside her shirt.

"They won't get away. I'll die before that happens," she said, and Grissom smiled. As he always did when somebody mentioned death.

55

Under the morning sun, the ruined Rio Sacado Sheriff's Station smoldered. It stank of charred wood and burned plastic and worse. Inside, forensics techs walked the grid, white bodysuits ghostly amid fallen slabs of the roof and twisted girders. The county sheriff prowled the parking lot, a grizzly ready to rip her long claws into whoever had killed her men.

Harker stood inside the yellow tape in yesterday's suit and shirt and tie. Two FBI special agents from the Albuquerque office flanked him. One murmured into his phone, describing the scene. The other took photos and notes and tried to keep from looking at Harker.

Harker pressed his lips together tightly. They would convene an inquiry into the attack on the station. They'd interrogate him and question his tactics. They would lose sight of what mattered. Deputies, dead.

Special Agent Marichal, dead.

Dizziness swam through him, with a sound like waves breaking on a beach. Fatigue and adrenaline depletion, he figured. Maybe the sun. When he looked at the station, it hit his eyes. He turned sideways to avoid it.

The sheriff walked over, her boots kicking shrapnel from the UFO Tours van. She was in uniform. That was a signal — solidarity. In one night she had lost three men, more than the department had lost in the previous century. Harker realized he didn't know the deputies' names.

"How did they know the Keller girl was here?" she said.

"Not from me," he said.

"You brought this operation into Chaves County, Special Agent Harker."

He straightened. "Sarah Keller brought this into Chaves County, Sheriff. And she dragged the Worthe clan with her, into Roswell and to Rio Sacado. I've been in pursuit, trying to stop it."

He eyed the station, briefly, the dizzy sensation lurking. "But somebody let the word leak. And the Worthes attacked."

"Somebody," the sheriff said.

"Not I."

The sheriff's tone cut through the reticence of the other two FBI agents. They put away their phones and shouldered up beside him.

Harker said, "I was in secure communication with the Bureau in Roswell, Albuquerque, and in D.C. Repeat: secure. It's impossible that information leaked to the Worthes from our end." He set his hands on his hips. "But Roswell law enforcement broadcast information over the radio from the first moment Sarah Keller was spotted at the music festival."

"You're saying my department led the killers to Rio Sacado?" Her voice was sharp. "Do you understand what's going on here?"

"Do you?" Abruptly the dizziness receded. "This morning an elderly Roswell man crawled out of his house and flagged down a neighbor, saying his wife was duct-taped to a chair in their kitchen. The Worthes had held them hostage while they tried to figure out what local law enforcement was up to. Do you record your police band comms? I'd listen in, and see who was talking too much. Names, places, times — God knows what they gave away in open communication."

One of the Albuquerque agents, the murmuring phone guy, said, "The SWAT team was pulled back before completion of the operation as well."

She turned on him. "Don't. Do not."

"We need to call in FBI tactical? That's the way it's looking now."

Harker held up a hand. "We need fire-power. We need broad-brush authority. We need to attack this from every angle. We have to get these people."

He touched his hand to the wallet near his heart. "The Worthes are not going to slink away. This was a skirmish. They've seen their prize and they know it's close. They will redouble their efforts to seize it."

"It," the sheriff said.

"Zoe Keller," he said. "The clan knows this is their chance to grab her. Believe me, they're close by. They have extended family scattered around New Mexico like poison-ous weeds. They're holed up, preparing to take another crack at the child." He tight-ened his tie. "Which is why it's critical to apprehend Sarah Keller."

"We have conflicting reports on whether she has, in fact, abducted the girl. Oklahoma City sent us a report —"

"Sarah Keller is a fugitive. Following her lawful arrest last night, she escaped from the custody of the Chaves County Sheriff's Department. She broke out of this station and ran, taking a minor child with her. And she is risking the child's life."

He nodded at the desert. "She took a five-year-old out there, knowing full well that the Worthes are in pursuit. That's so reckless it's homicidal," he said. "If she's not actually working with them. This could all have been a ploy."

The sheriff looked incredulous. "You're suggesting that Sarah Keller let you arrest her, so that SWAT and the FBI and my deputies would all be gathered in one place — a big fat target?"

"They're cop killers. Ambushers. When they bombed the Denver courthouse, Reavy Worthe dropped the improvised bomb and strolled *into the building* to get away. It's all distraction, misdirection. They're masters. They pull people in, Sheriff."

"That sounds far-fetched," the sheriff said.

"Sarah Keller's spent the past five years playing cat and mouse with the authorities, and now she's bolted, leaving a trail of destruction across your state. She's armed, she's dangerous, and God knows who she's going to get killed next. We're going to bring her in."

He held the sheriff's stare. She said nothing. He turned to the Albuquerque agents.

"Come with me."

They followed.

■ ■ ■ ■

The truck stop was nearly empty, a diner and gas station sixty years old, straight out of a James Dean movie. Standing outside, Lawless watched the morning sun crest the mountains, gold through the dark boughs of the pine forest. He tried again to contact Sarah. Her phone just rang. He left another voice-mail message.

"Me again. Get in touch. Please."

He hung up. He wondered where she was. Whether Zoe was holding it together even a little bit. He raised the paper coffee cup to his mouth, but couldn't manage a swallow.

He felt desperate to explain. He knew she would flay his hide. He deserved it.

The sky was a cloudless blue, empty and scoured, promising heat. He felt none of it. He might as well still be in the snowy woods where he had first seen Sarah Keller. He might as well never have left that forest.

At first, he'd thought it had just been a deadly day in a career that unavoidably took him into violent situations. He thought that day would fade.

Why, he couldn't imagine now.

When he first drove up that mountain road and saw an empty SUV parked in

Beth's driveway, doors open, engine running, he knew things were wrong. When he rushed silently through the forest toward the house, heard muffled shouts and saw Nolan — Nolan, who he was supposed to extract — confronting the woman he thought was Beth, he knew he was in a shit show.

He had moved toward them, but the pair ran and Lawless lost sight of them. Then, beneath the crackle and snap of the fire, he heard a gunshot. A minute later the woman ran raggedly into his path, clutching the baby. Her face was Beth's and not quite. It was younger, more beautiful, incredibly frightened and nearly homicidal.

Behind her, Nolan lay facedown in the snow.

And he took her arm and said, "Run."

She clutched the baby and raced beside him through the trees, toward the switchback where she had parked her truck.

"He tried to kill me," she said.

Her voice was shaking. Her hands were shaking. Where her jacket hung open at the collar, red marks ringed her throat — Nolan's handprint.

"They're coming," she said. "The clan."

The way she said it, four simple words, chilled him beyond measure.

When they reached the switchback, he helped her buckle the baby in the truck, and turned to pursue the Worthes. But Sarah thought he was about to go collect evidence against her. She opened the truck door and said, "No."

He shut it. "Your job is to protect the baby. Mine is to apprehend the Worthes. You want to have any chance of stopping them? Trust me."

She looked at him. "Who are you?"

"Michael Lawless."

She held his gaze a moment, seeming to memorize not just his name but his face, his bearing, the frost swirling in the air around him, fixing him in her mind.

Then she spun the tires and drove away.

Telling her to run was a snap decision. She said she'd acted in self-defense and, given the circumstances, he was willing to accept her at her word. What wasn't in doubt was the imminent danger. Sarah needed to save the baby.

The truck faded to a faint gray form in the snow, as insubstantial as a wisp of smoke. He heard the distant crackle of flames. By the time he ran back through the pines, the cabin was a screaming streak of red fire. He knelt beside Nolan's body, weapon drawn, listening for the clan, the

Worthes, and their Shattering Angel. Almost a single organism. One that killed.

Nolan Worthe was not one of them. He had accepted the FBI's offer to become a confidential informant. The clan might be a pathogen, but Nolan had agreed to become a virus within, and betray them.

The results lay before him, covered with dusty snow, still and cold in a pool of blood.

He called for backup. Then he put his fingers against Nolan's neck to confirm that he had no pulse, looking at his watch to fix the time.

"Shit," he said.

He rolled Nolan onto his back. Nolan breathed and opened his eyes.

He said, "Sarah shot me."

"I know," Lawless said. "How'd that happen?"

Nolan didn't answer. He said, "Beth?"

Lawless shook his head.

Nolan's face crumpled.

By then there was no sign of the Worthes, aside from tire tracks on the driveway. They had fled. A team from the Marshals Service quietly evacuated Nolan to San Jose and got him hospitalized under an alias. To the Marshals it quickly became apparent what had happened: Nolan had been sloppy, and Harker's FBI operation flawed. The Worthes had never been convinced by Nolan's sudden conversion. So they came after him, planning to kill him and Beth, and take Zoe.

But Nolan was going to survive, and would have to live with the consequences. What a sour lemon of a prize.

Lawless drove to Sarah's apartment to tell her. A minute after he got there, two other deputy marshals showed up and called him outside. They had his supervisor on the phone. Instead of Lawless telling Sarah the good news, they told Lawless how it was going to be.

Let Nolan be declared missing.

"It's the only way," his supervisor said.

It was, in fact, almost perfect. Beth was dead. The baby was taken care of. There were no messy issues to worry about.

"You mean, lie to Sarah? Let her think she killed him?" Lawless said, disbelieving.

"She can't know. If anyone discovers Nolan's alive, he's done. You might as well put a gun to his head and pull the trigger."

It was WITSec logic. The only way to save Nolan's life was to let Sarah and the clan believe he was dead. And if Sarah ever broke down and confessed to shooting him, her confession would serve to bolster his cover.

Lawless climbed the stairs back to Sarah's apartment.

He followed the rules that day. He wore the star. He carried out the mission.

He lied, big-time, and put a two-ton weight on Sarah's back. *Nolan's dead. I checked his pulse.* Carry that, Sarah. Hold onto that baby and don't ever tell her you killed her father. Carry it all.

At the same time, Lawless used this misconception to keep her under the radar. She thought she'd killed Nolan, and that gave her a huge incentive to live quietly and protect Zoe.

What a crock. He had convinced her to close off options she should have felt confident to take advantage of. Like the cops. Who wants to make a law-abiding woman fear the cops?

He stared at his coffee. He poured it on the ground.

Trust me.

Yeah, he was a big-time liar. That night at her apartment in Cupertino, he'd told her there was no reason she should fear being arrested. As long as she kept quiet.

"As long as I keep quiet," she said.

He nodded.

"Because . . ." And her face fell, everything came in, all the light and horror of the truth. "Because if I stay here with this baby, the Worthes will come back. They want her."

"I wish I could tell you different," he said.

She stared through him, and at her apartment — the backpack, the map of the world, the adventure she was supposed to embark on. For a moment she looked ready to fold.

Then she steadied herself. "I have to take Zoe and go someplace they can't find us." She hugged the baby tighter. "I can cash in my round-the-world ticket."

He had sent her on the run. He had seen the fear and determination in her eyes, cradling the baby, a young woman with no experience, thrown overboard from her own life, little more than a girl, really. She wasn't part of the WITSec deal. He had left her to sink or swim.

The girl she'd been was nothing like the woman he'd met yesterday. This Sarah, five years older, was something fierce. And loving, and clear-eyed. This Sarah was a warrior.

How could he face her now?

He looked at the mountains. To face her he had to find her. But everybody was scattered to the wind, with no protection and no relief. Marichal and three deputies were dead. Teresa, at least, was safe, having spent the night in a hospital for observation. But Sarah and Zoe were gone.

Fear ran like a scalpel along his spine. The clan had found her once. So had Harker. They'd find her again. They might have found her already. He stared out across the desert, the sand, the blue hills in the far distance. This was the Worthe clan's native territory. If they hadn't already captured Sarah and Zoe, they would be closing in on them.

He took out his phone and tried again to call her, without any luck.

56

Dappled sunlight flickered through the windshield of the truck. Sarah stirred and squinted at the sunrise. Stiff, bruised, she straightened and looked around.

The truck was well hidden in brush under a cluster of cottonwoods in an arroyo off the highway. The Glock rested on her lap. In the back seat, head pillowed on her backpack, Zoe was still asleep.

Outside, Nolan sat under a tree, eating a granola bar, staring at her.

She didn't move.

In the daylight Nolan looked more than five years older, mid-thirties but his hair in a ponytail salted with gray. The lines around his eyes looked deep. From stress, maybe. She hoped. He took another bite, calmly watching her.

While Beth was still dead.

The hairs on her arms stood up. She seemed without volition to inch sideways, to block any possible view of Zoe in the back seat.

How could he do it?

How could Lawless?

How could Lawless have kept this from her for five years? How could he have let her think she had shot Nolan to death? Who the hell was he?

The same deputy U.S. Marshal she'd seen that day in the snow, calm and focused, who never hesitated to tell her: *Run.* He had taken charge. He knew what to do. She hadn't objected or even questioned what he told her. He saved her. Freed her. Or so she'd thought.

And Lawless thought Curtis Harker was the one who was too driven and devious?

Nolan finished the granola bar. He pocketed the wrapper and brushed his hands together.

She unlocked the doors of the truck and got out.

He was waiting for her, distant, almost skittish. Let him worry. She tucked the Glock in her belt.

She was relieved that he hadn't made a fire. She was relieved that he hadn't run away or called the FBI, or his cousins. She realized that she trusted him, at least on some gut level. It wasn't merely exhaustion. Though she knew she couldn't have stayed awake without becoming psychotic and useless. She had closed her eyes, and now she was walking toward him, seemingly unscathed.

He said, "The spare tire's a doughnut — one of those little temporary tires that'll only last fifty miles. And it won't take much abuse."

"What happened, Nolan? What happened that day outside the cabin?"

"Thought you'd figured it out by now."

She resisted the urge to slap him in the face.

He looked away. "You got there too late. Or too early, that's what happened."

"You were going into Witness Protection that day?"

"No. I was going to tell Beth I was going into WITSec and she needed to come with me. I'd been working on it for months."

"She never knew."

"She knew about the FBI. Not about the aftermath."

"Who approached whom?" she said.

"The FBI came to me."

"Harker. How did he convince you to work with the Bureau?"

He looked at her like, *Come on.* "He told

433

me what I already knew. That I'd never be safe as long as my family knew where I was. Witness Security was the only way to save me. And Beth and the baby."

Sarah nodded, encouraging him to go on.

"And the only way he'd arrange for us to enter WITSec was for me to provide evidence against the family — evidence that would lead to criminal convictions."

"And he asked you to obtain evidence by letting Zoe undergo the blessing ceremony."

"Yes."

"You must truly, deeply hate your family," she said.

He couldn't meet her eye. "I've been in WITSec for five years. You think I was scared that day? I've been scared every day of my life since then. That's why I never reached out to you, or tried to contact Zoe."

"For fear of discovery?"

"And that it would expose Zoe to the family again. If I ever surfaced, I'd lose my U.S. Marshals protection. The family would come not just for me, but for her."

"Then why did you show yourself now?"

He didn't answer.

She crouched down in front of him. The Glock was jammed in the small of her back. "I want to know — why did you try to grab Zoe from me that day? Because you did.

You were crazed, and I knew you were going to do something bad."

"I didn't know where Lawless was, I just knew Beth was in trouble and Fell and Reavy and Grissom were coming for me. So I went crazy."

"I thought you were planning to turn Zoe over to the clan."

"Holy shit, no." He looked horrified and actually, truly, hurt at the accusation.

"I think I believe you. You just wanted to take her with you into WITSec. And you wanted the information from the microchip, because you thought that, without it, the FBI might renege on your deal."

He straightened. "I loved Beth. I never wanted to hurt her or Zoe."

He looked like a whipped dog. At some level, he now felt ashamed. And he was deeply unsettled around Zoe. He didn't know what to do or what to say, and he sensed, correctly, that if he got too close Sarah would cut his balls off.

"Don't lie to me, Nolan. Did you want to get her chipped?"

"Yeah." He seemed to sag. "I knew they'd give her a chip with a number in it."

"And you could then turn that over to the FBI."

"Yeah."

"What's on the chip? Bank account information?"

"At least."

"What do you mean?"

"They don't just want Zoe for the chip. They think she's special."

The cold buzz began at the base of Sarah's skull. "What kind of special?"

"Her birthday has spiritual significance, by their reckoning. January third. One-three. It maps onto a New Testament verse about 'worth.' Second Peter, chapter 1, verse 3. 'God's divine power has granted to us all things that pertain to life and godliness, through the knowledge of him who called us to his own glory and excellence.' "

Sarah could hardly swallow. "They think that verse proves that the Worthe family is special. Divinely appointed."

"Absolutely. They think her birth was their sign from heaven."

She felt barbed wire tighten around her chest, squeezing, pricking at her heart.

Nolan said, "What are you going to do?"

"Tell me the rest."

"A few days ago Harker convinced me to come in from the cold."

"How did he find you?"

"How else? He's FBI. They wangled it out of the Marshals Service." He rubbed his hands along his thighs. "And I was so tempted. These last five years have been tough. Sarah, you have no idea. It's been lonely. I've been so isolated."

She sat on her haunches and stared at him. He was describing everything she'd been living through — but while raising Zoe and keeping her safe, without the protection of the Marshals Service.

"So when Harker called and told me I'd be able to live openly again, and see my daughter . . ." He shrugged and his expression curdled. "But I was just another pawn in Harker's grand plan to place every flavor of bait in front of the clan."

And Nolan was an extra shiny pawn — Harker thought that, if captured, Nolan would be well placed to get lots of info from the family.

"He promised you liberty — in return for what?" she said. "What did he tell you you'd have to do?"

"Show up. Talk. I thought."

"Harker's taking extreme measures. I don't know what he was going to ask you to do, but it wouldn't be pretty."

"I don't know." Though he was sitting down, he looked wobbly.

She had a bad feeling. She wondered if Harker planned to implant a new chip in

Nolan, a listening device. Like a wire, but undetectable. At the very worst, Harker would get a recording of Nolan being murdered by the clan.

"What's the plan?" he said.

"I'm going to figure out what to do."

"You mean how to survive?"

A breeze stirred the cottonwoods. Their leaves shivered like a thousand tiny wings preparing to fly.

"No," she said. "How to win."

57

At eight A.M. Harker got the first reports.
No sightings of Sarah Keller or Nolan
Worthe. No sightings of the clan. He led
the Albuquerque agents into a two-bit diner
down the road from the burned-out sheriff's
station. No other customers were there but
a TV was on, news being broadcast from
right outside.

Harker flipped the sign on the door to
CLOSED. He called to the waitress: "Coffee
and your biggest breakfasts — three of
them."

One of the Albuquerque agents ended a
call. "Got it. Driver's license for the protectee. Under his new name." His phone
beeped. He showed the photo to Harker.

Harker nodded. *Scott Alan Williams.* "Yeah,
it's Nolan Worthe. Find out the make and
model of any vehicles he owns and get the
tag numbers. Check rental agencies at the
Roswell airport. The clan was driving a

silver SUV. I saw it up close —"

"They flew into Oklahoma City," he said. "A Barry Briggs rented a Silver Navigator. OKC's sending us the info. And two female passengers on the same flight used a similar name — Riggs. Could be an alias."

Harker nodded. "Good. Get the sheriff to put out a BOLO. State police as well, all counties."

"You think they're still in New Mexico?"

"They're after Zoe Keller. If she's here, they're here. And Zoe's nearby."

"But probably on the move by now."

The remark sounded casual and annoying, and Harker nearly said so. But he paused. The agent was right.

"We need to make sure that she can't go any farther," he said.

"And how are you going to do that?"

He gazed out the window of the diner across the plain, at the empty vista, toward a jutting mountain far to the west. It rose from the desert like a hatchet, blue with shadow. Roadblocks? He needed to mobilize a large law enforcement response, in a rapidly expanding search radius.

"We need to distract them. And we need to clear out civilians," he said.

He needed something quick and dirty. He needed a sideshow. An effective sideshow,

440

which would contain both Sarah Keller and the clan. And which would not reek of FBI involvement.

He recalled the military convoy that had passed him on the road yesterday — trucks and a long flatbed big rig and outriding vehicles with men inside who were clearly not just Feds but former Special Forces, men with earpieces and mirrored shades, treating civilian traffic like targets.

He pictured the New Mexico map he had studied earlier. Holloman Air Force Base was sixty miles west, and the White Sands Missile Testing Range, and the Trinity Site. The U.S. government owned nearly half the land in this state, and liked to store deadly and secret materials in desert bunkers. He thought of how fast that convoy had been moving, and the fact that even with skilled drivers, highway travel could end in a ditch. Out here, it didn't even take a crew of God-addled rednecks to send you off the road. You merely crested a rise and came face-to-face with wandering cattle.

"What's the agency that handles nuclear transport?" he said.

"Office of Secure Transportation?" The agent looked at Harker with suspicion. "Headquarters is in Albuquerque. Why?"

"What happens if there's an accident?

There's a protocol, right?"

"The area around the accident is shut down and quarantined." The man's suspicion turned to something between shock and excitement. "OST won't like it."

"The OST doesn't have to be involved."

The agents glanced at each other, and back at Harker.

Harker stared across miles of blinding sand at the morning sun. "It only has to last for a couple of hours. We're close. They're here. This is the only way to activate a multiagency response on short notice."

"There's an incident command system in case of emergency."

"Extreme emergency can override the command system. And this is one. Any normal roadblock will tip off the Worthes that we're trying to corral them. This will actually keep the officers enforcing the cordon safer." He got out his phone. "Look — if the Worthes get stopped by a cop in a cruiser, they'll open fire. But if they're directed back with everybody else because they hear a nuke has crashed up the road? We'll pen them in. And tighten the noose."

Harker had to admit: Sarah Keller had far more savvy and survival skills than he had foreseen. But they weren't playing tag. It was past time for her to surrender. There could only be one winner, and it had to be him.

Because if he lost, so would she. The Worthes, Grissom Briggs, these sick child-women Reavy and Fell, were sadistic psychopaths. They wouldn't hesitate to kill Keller. Her only chance was to surrender to him. For her sake, and for the child's.

"I'm afraid we're about to have an accident. And we're going to have to declare a nuclear transport emergency."

58

"This way."

Sarah climbed up the slope of the arroyo through chaparral, boots swishing on the soft dirt. She kept the truck in view. She had the keys in her pocket, the Glock in her hand, and Nolan within range. They reached the lip of the arroyo and stopped. The view spread for fifty miles.

The aircraft graveyard was off the highway ten miles south of Alamogordo. It was the size of a university campus, covered with a hundred acres of abandoned airplanes. In the stark sunshine they gleamed silver and white and red and green and black, tail livery fading in the heat. The road was adjacent to White Sands National Monument, the Sahara of white dunes that rose a hundred feet high and flowed across the desert floor for twenty miles. It was thirty miles as the crow flies from the site where the first atomic bomb was exploded by the

Manhattan Project in 1945. It was at the heart of ancient Apache lands. And it was just down the road from the mountains where Billy the Kid was born, and hid out when he was on the run.

The perfect place to make a last stand.

She stood in the morning sun staring at the white desert to the west, an arc of sky behind it so blue it seemed to look straight through to nothingness.

She couldn't run anymore. Running would only exhaust her, endlessly, until they brought her down. That was no life for Zoe. Run, and she would destroy the child she had sworn to save.

She had to turn the situation around. She could no longer let Zoe and herself serve as bait.

How, she thought — how could she do this?

She climbed on a boulder and sat, hands hanging from her knees. She stared and thought. The sun heated her back and warmed the dun-colored slope. Below on the desert floor, mirages began to glimmer.

The sun was higher in the sky, shadows shorter, when she finally climbed down from the boulder. Nolan was still sitting nearby, waiting. She walked past and waved for him to follow her back down the arroyo to the truck.

"Well? What's the plan?" he said.

"Multistage. Like a Saturn rocket."

She just hoped it didn't blow up in flight.

"What are the stages?" Nolan said.

"You won't like them. But you'd better understand them," she said. "One. Eliminate Grissom, Fell, and Reavy. I don't care if they end up in prison or in the ground. But take them off the board. Permanently."

He nodded. He looked pale, but he wasn't disagreeing. They trooped down the slope.

"Two. Convince the family to give up trying to grab Zoe. Make her of no interest to them."

"How the hell are you going to do that?" The look on his face said: *Unless you hand her over to them and satisfy their craving.*

"I have to convince the bosses of the family she's no longer useful to them. If I can do that, they'll give up on pursuing her."

He looked at her askance.

"Isom," she said.

She would never have the time or ability to bring down the entire Worthe clan. But she didn't need to.

"Isom controls the clan's day-to-day operations. Your father's in prison so Isom's the de facto family manager. If I convince him that Zoe is of no value to the family, he'll stop hunting her. He has the authority to call off the search."

Nolan seemed uncertain, but said, "Go on."

"Three. I get the FBI off my back."

"You get it off both our backs. Agree with you totally there."

She bet he did. They reached the bottom of the arroyo. Beneath the shade of the cottonwoods, the truck remained cool. Inside, snuggled on the back seat, Zoe had balled up like a little rabbit. Soon she'd stir.

They continued out of earshot to the bottom of the arroyo where a thin stream shimmered over rocks.

Nolan said, "So how you gonna light this multistage rocket?"

"I implicate the trio in a betrayal and lay it all at Isom's feet."

"Implicate? Wait, what . . ."

"The people who care about getting hold of Zoe are Isom and the trio. Isom runs operations — he has to be the one who gave the order to capture her. Grissom and the women are the ones under orders to do it. Hell, they're having the time of their lives. They think they're on a treasure hunt," she said. "The point is, those four constitute the clan's power structure and center of violence. Nobody else has the knowledge or incentive or homicidal mania they do."

"I have to agree with you there." He looked, for a brief moment, isolated and afraid. "How are you planning on doing that?"

"I have to get rid of the money in the clan's secret account — in a way that convinces Eldrick the trio has stolen it."

He gaped. "You're nuts."

She shook her head. "It's the only way."

"No it's not. There's another way — keep running."

"Not going to do that anymore. That way leads to a dead end, with me and Zoe and probably you getting run down. Nolan, you know this. We have to take another path."

"We."

"I need your help." She bent and picked up a rock from the stream. "You have the name of the bank."

He clenched his jaw. His lips were pressed together, pale.

"That's what I lack. Not to mention the FBI," she said.

"The microchip." He glanced at the truck. "It has an account number. But not the name of the bank."

She nodded. "That's part of the reason Harker wanted to draw you out of hiding. To get the name of the bank, so he could

448

track the money."

"Jesus."

"What I need is the bank, the account number, and the name of the account holder. Or is it a numbered account?"

He hesitated. Bright thoughts seemed to flicker behind his eyes. He was calculating. *The money. All that money.* Or what he thought was all that money.

"Nolan. I need the name of the bank so we can commence wiring and transfer instructions. And if it's not a numbered account, I'll need the name of the person who is authorizing the transfer." She frowned. "You want a percentage?"

"No, I . . ."

"Finder's fee? Maybe we can arrange that. But you'll get stiffed, or get a bullet in your head, unless you tell me the name of the bank. Don't you get this? Your family is all about blood and money. And you're already a turncoat. If you take any part of the cash, they'll treat you like an accountant who has stolen from the mob."

He opened his mouth to talk. She shook her head. "We need to use the money to screw them, badly, permanently. It's our only chance, Nolan."

As though pulling his own tooth with a rusty pair of pliers, he said, "All right."

"Okay then. What we have to do is make it look like one of the trio has taken it."

"Or all three."

"Or all three. But I suspect we'll do better if we turn them against each other."

"They're solid."

"Really? There are no cracks? In that threesome? Come on. Not between the sisters who are expected to take turns in Grissom's bed?"

He thought about it. She raised an eyebrow. "What?"

"Maybe . . . but I wouldn't count on it."

"Spill."

"Fell — her dad got on Eldrick's blacklist over money. It put an invisible mark on her. Nobody was to trust her. Nobody was to *play* with her. At recess one day our cousins threw fruit at her. I told them to knock it off and she got away, but . . ."

"What godly little assholes."

"Don't feel sorry for her. That was the last time she cried. After that she learned to fight like a velociraptor," he said. "Point is, the mark of distrust can never fade." He glanced at the stream, as though the rocks had ears. "The other thing is, Reavy has always wanted Grissom. Top dog, bad boy, fresh set of genes, don't ask me why. But she does, and he knows it. And he'll use it to get what he wants out of her and Fell."

She threw the rock upstream, thinking.

"What do you have in mind?" Nolan said.

"Turnabout. They obviously stole my mail and pretexted my bank card company to find out where I'd withdrawn cash. That's how they tracked me to Roswell."

"Pretexted?" he said.

"Spoofed my identity. Pretended to be me. They lied," she said. "It's time to repay the favor. What's the name of the bank?"

"First Royal Bank of Antigua."

Offshore. In a time zone a couple of hours ahead. But in a country that might have lenient banking regulations — and where it wasn't a holiday.

"There's a branch in Houston," Nolan said. "That's how the family opened it. They don't have passports, you know. Mark of the Beast and all."

"Passwords?"

Nolan hesitated. His shoulders dropped, seemingly with resignation. "You're right. It's the only path for me now. I won't go back into WITSec after this. The Feds won't want to protect me on the same terms as before — I ran off with a fugitive." His smile was wan, but had a bit of grit in it. "This is for Beth. And for you."

He pulled his Grateful Dead T-shirt over

his head.

Sarah had seen his tattoos before. They were a cross between Manga and DC Comics. A sleek school of fish gliding across his shoulder. A flock of birds diving along his ribs. Vivid reds and blues, yellows and a deep green, etched with black, work that she'd rarely seen done so well outside of Japanese art magazines. It must have made it difficult for him to stay subterranean — no beach parties if he wanted his identifying marks to stay hidden.

He turned around.

"Oh," she said.

On his back, rising along his spine and spreading toward each shoulder, was a tree. Wound in among the branches were lines from scripture — or so it seemed from a glance.

"I am the password," he said.

"Your family arranged for you to get this one?" she said.

"They called it my homecoming ceremony. Had a tat artist from Phoenix come up when I returned to the compound with Zoe. They were trusting me."

She scanned the tattoo. It was darker than the others, stark, words sharp and black.

"Which one's the password?"

He turned back around. "They didn't tell me."

So they didn't trust him all that much.

"Security measure," he said. "I couldn't blurt it out inadvertently."

But somebody with time and patience and the skill to kidnap him could figure it out.

She read the verses. "Any clues? They tell you anything?"

"No. But seven is their lucky number. Presume the password's seven characters. Can you take it from there?"

"Maybe."

She snapped photos of the tattoo. He put his shirt back on.

"What's the plan?" he said.

Her stomach tightened. She would be leaping into the deep. "I call the bank. When I do, I presume it'll send up a red flag. The family must have automatic alerts when somebody accesses an account. Or am I wrong?"

"They never trusted me with that level of information."

But the Worthes were as careful with money as they were insane with scripture.

"If the bank pings them that somebody is trying to siphon money from the account, I imagine they'll go to battle stations. And if the evidence indicates that it's the trio trying to steal everything . . ."

"That would not go down well."

Sarah's head buzzed. Hunger and nerves were working on her. She had to think this through, had to be convincing.

"Give me a few minutes. Let me work on the password."

She stuck her hands in her jeans pockets. He nodded and ambled toward the shade. She pinched the bridge of her nose.

"Nolan, wait." She took a beat. "One more thing." Last item on the list, and most important. "Zoe."

Nolan's gaze broke from hers. He stared up the arroyo, his eyes pained.

He said, "I made a mistake five years ago. I need to rectify it."

Her nerves spun like a turbine. He looked like he had grown taller in the last five years. He looked tougher than the frightened, fawn-eyed boy she'd met in California.

He walked back to her. "I know I need to stand up."

She saw it on his face: He knew he could give Sarah her life back. She could free herself with a single nod. She could slip away and retrace her steps to the bright stream of plans she had laid out for herself before Nolan ever met her sister. Round-the-world trip. Working for Past Link or a similar software firm, keeping up with Mesoamerican archaeology as a hobby. Filling in the blanks in her family's history. She could reset the game.

If she gave Zoe to Nolan.

As she stared at him, she realized that it had been years since she'd thought of her ruined dreams. Teresa's question had reminded her about her girlhood idea of becoming a Secret Service agent. If she gave in to fantasy, she might entice herself with it again. But she realized that she no longer thought of her former wishes as ruined dreams.

She looked at the truck, where Zoe slept. She had her dream.

"What would you do, if . . ." she said.

"Return to Witness Security, if I have to. She'd be safe with me. The Marshals Service would create a new, bulletproof identity for her."

Sarah nodded. Her heart seemed ready to rupture from pain.

She tried to see the truth of it in his eyes. He looked solid. He wasn't wavering.

Nolan was Zoe's father. If they got out of this alive, later they would have the time to think about legal papers and adoption or visitation or absence.

She said, "If you can get her out, and keep

her safe, and there's no other way . . ."

He looked like he was on a high wire, trying to stay upright, about to get shoved off.

"If it's her life, take her," Sarah said.

He looked tough for one second longer. Then his jaw trembled. His eyes filled. He nodded and looked away, inhaled, and finally stepped forward and wrapped his arms around her.

"You're a champ," he said. "Beth was right about you."

She stood rigidly. "Nolan."

He stepped back. "I can't . . . she's . . ."

"Please, what?"

"If it comes to that — I'm here," he said. "But you've become her mother."

He turned and walked off, running the back of a hand across his eyes.

After a long, frozen second, she walked to one of the cottonwoods and leaned her forehead against the trunk. The leaves shivered all around her. She put a hand against the bark and stood still.

"Mommy?"

Zoe stood in the doorway of the truck. Sarah blinked and smiled. Zoe hopped down and shuffled over to her. Sarah sat and pulled Zoe onto her lap. She held her close and rested her cheek against the top of Zoe's head.

Cuddled against her, Zoe said, "Are you going back to sleep? It's breakfast time."

"Then we'll get you some breakfast."

"Mommy?"

"In a sec." Wiping her eyes, she lifted Zoe off her lap. "Granola bars are on the dashboard."

Zoe scooted back to the truck. Sarah sat and waited until she stopped shaking.

She took out her burn phone and sent a text to Danisha. Then she closed her eyes. She only had to wait a minute before her phone buzzed. It had been getting calls all night from Lawless. And it was ringing now.

She opened her eyes and answered it. She said, "Get here."

Lawless hung up the phone. Ninety seconds later he was headed west, spitting dust from beneath the wheels.

59

They heard it long before they saw it coming up the arroyo: a big-ass four-wheel drive that could knock a longhorn twenty feet into the air. They were camped in a ravine two miles off the highway, in a county where the population density was less than ten people per square mile. Aside from the squeal of hawks, the rumble of the 5.7-liter engine was the only sound they'd heard for the last hour. Sarah walked out from under the cottonwoods. The rental tank bumped into sight, suspension shuddering, and stopped by the glittering stream. Danisha hopped down from the cab.

She set her cowboy hat on her head and sidled toward Sarah.

Smiling, Sarah jogged over, grabbed her friend, and hugged her. "I am so . . ." She choked up.

"*Grateful* is the word you're looking for."

"I was going to say sorry. But that doesn't

even begin to cover it." She shook her head. "I really can't believe you're here. It's . . ."

"Get over it. And get over yourself," Danisha said, and smiled.

Sarah hugged her again. Danisha was wearing a sleeveless buckskin vest and boots so worn down at the heel she might have pulled them off a rider from the Seventh Cavalry. She looked like she should be carrying a saber and a six-shooter.

Zoe skipped up. "Hi, Danisha."

"Hey, rugrat." She ruffled Zoe's hair and shook her head at Sarah. "I was hanging around downtown Roswell sending you text messages, when I overheard people talking about a wild-ass Road Warrior car chase. Where's this baby I hear you were beating people around the head with?"

"The doll's up the highway in your pickup, parked outside an abandoned barn. Unless she was summoned by her coven of reborns and drove away."

Zoe said, "Mommy painted your truck."

Danisha did a double take. "Woman?"

"Temporary." Sarah pressed a hand to Danisha's shoulder. "I should have known you'd be close. But why . . ."

"I'm here for you, and for me." She raised her eyebrows. "You understand? They came after me and mine. They put my mom in the hospital. They destroyed the office. And they'll mow me down to get to you. So I can't step aside. The Worthes are going to keep coming back. I have to help take them down. Else I won't be safe."

"I understand."

"And I am also your friend. I don't want you to handle this alone. I see where it got you."

Sarah inhaled. "Got everything?"

Danisha took two bags from the rental. "Everything you asked for." She took out the radio mike and transmitter. "Including the wire."

Sarah played with it. "It'll fit under my shirt."

"You aren't worried about getting frisked?"

"By an FBI agent? Normally, yes. But not in this situation."

Harker had only touched her once, when he took her by the arm after he placed her under arrest. He barely even looked at her when she was in his presence. She was little more than an object to him. An annoying, slippery object, something to pin to the ground.

She said, "Ready to make the call?"

"Say the word."

Danisha looked up the arroyo. Under the

trees Nolan was hanging back. He raised his chin in greeting. Danisha stared at him with open curiosity.

Sarah said, "It was even more of a surprise to me, believe it."

"How . . ."

"Harker. And the U.S. Marshals. But now" — she smiled at Nolan, feeling like a shark — "he's helping us."

Outside the diner in Rio Sacado, Harker paced, waiting for the Albuquerque agents to make their calls. His own phone rang.

"Special Agent Harker? Detective Fred Dos Santos, in Oklahoma City."

"Detective," Harker said.

"I have Danisha Helms on the line. She wants to talk to you."

He stopped. *My, oh my.* "Conference her in."

A moment later, with a click, Helms came on the line. "Harker? Sarah Keller wants to talk to you."

He felt amazement — and doubt. "About what?"

"Coming in. If you can guarantee her safety."

"She wants to surrender herself? Tell her to come to Rio Sacado. Immediately."

"Not so fast," Helms said. "She needs

guarantees. Last night she was in Rio Sacado, and she was far from safe."

"Her safety, and Zoe's, are my paramount concern, I assure you."

"Hasn't looked that way," she said.

He heard the anger in her voice, and the strain. He wanted to take her by the shoulders and shake her. "Every minute Sarah delays makes things worse. The people who are pursuing her will show no mercy or remorse."

"You don't need to educate me about the Worthe clan, Agent Harker."

"Then let me be blunt. On her own, Sarah has no chance to make it out alive. She either surrenders herself at the nearest police station, or you tell me where I can find her in the next half-hour, or she's dead by sundown."

Helms paused. And sighed. That was good.

It didn't really matter whether Sarah Keller agreed to come in — if she used her cell phone, he could pinpoint her location.

"What's Sarah's number?" he said. "I'll call her personally."

"Yeah, right."

"Then you phone Sarah. Tell her it's vital she get in touch with me." He gave her his number.

"Got it," Helms said. "Sarah will meet with you — but she wants an FBI tactical team backing you up, and helicopter evac to take her and Zoe to a secure location. Such as NORAD."

"NORAD?"

"You get my point. If you guarantee that, then she'll agree to come in."

"Fine. Call her," he said.

"I'll get back to you."

Helms hung up. Dos Santos remained on the call. Harker said, "You got her number?"

"OKC local number." Dos Santos gave it to him. "I'll seek a pen/trap order — I can be in front of a judge in half an hour. We'll get Helms's call records."

"Make it twenty minutes, detective. Sarah Keller's on the move, using a burn phone. I need that number to locate her."

He hung up and stood at the crossroads, sun beating on his head. Even twenty minutes was too long to wait. But he didn't have to. He had Helms's phone number, right in the palm of his hand.

Sarah's phone buzzed. She let it go to voice mail.

Sitting in her rental SUV twenty feet away, Danisha waited for the tone, took a theatrical breath, and left a message. "Sarah. Agent

Harker says he'll provide the protection you requested. He wants you to call him. For Zoe's sake. For yours." Eyeing Sarah through the windshield, she rattled off his number. "Call me as soon as you get this message. Hold tight. It'll be okay. It's almost over."

Danisha hung up.

Sarah smiled. She waited a long minute, counting to sixty in her head, and phoned Danisha back. Danisha, in turn, let the call go to voice mail.

"You have reached the office of DHL Legal. Leave a message after the tone."

"It's me," Sarah said. "All right, if Harker's giving me a guarantee, I'll go in — if you think it's the right thing." She paused. "It had better be. I'm out of time. This is my last play."

She ended the call. She shook off her faux-theatrical attitude and gave Danisha a thumbs-up. Danisha hopped out of the SUV.

She knew that Danisha had set up her phone for call forwarding, so that the calls she'd just made would register as originating through DHL's office in Oklahoma City. She presumed the FBI was monitoring Danisha's phone. Even if they weren't, she presumed Harker had stolen the pass-

code for DHL's voice mail when he took
Danisha's phone from the wrecked office.
He could call in, listen to the message she'd
just left for Danisha, and capture her burn
phone number. She was counting on it.

Nolan said, "What was that?"

"That," she said, "was my opening move."

60

Twenty minutes later, after wolfing down the sandwiches and juice Danisha had brought, Sarah walked to the shady spot by the stream where her friend sat cross-legged beside Zoe, finishing a Thermos of coffee.

"Time," Sarah said.

Danisha stood and brushed off her jeans. "Last chance. You don't have to do this alone."

"Yes I do. I need you to monitor the wire. And to keep watch on her."

She looked at Zoe, building a little fort for Mousie out of rocks from the stream.

The air seemed charged with light. She crouched at Zoe's side. "Time to go, firefly."

Zoe looked up. "Where?"

"You're going with Danisha this morning."

"Is Nolan?"

He was out of earshot, sitting on the tailgate of the truck, scarfing a ham sandwich. "No, honey."

"Where are you going?"

"I'm staying here for a little while."

Zoe stood up. She let Mousie fall to the dust. "Don't, Mommy."

"I have to." She bit down and breathed through clenched teeth. "Come here."

Zoe leaned into her arms, small and warm. She put her cheek to Sarah's. "I can stay with you. I can be quiet, you'll see. I'm good at whispering. Like this." She turned her lips to Sarah's ear. "I know the password."

Sarah nearly jumped. "What?"

Quieter than a breeze, Zoe said, "I heard you talking to Nolan. You need a password. I know it."

"How do you know it?"

"But it's not secret. The password is Zoe Skye."

Sarah leaned back. "Why do you think that?"

"It's in the tree on Nolan's back, in the tattoo." She curled against Sarah's chest and whispered again. "But that's not the real password. For you and me."

Was she thinking of her school pickup password? "What?"

Soft as sunlight, she said, "I love you, Mommy."

Sarah seemed to feel the light in the air condense and surround them. She held Zoe close. "I love you too."

For a moment she doubted herself and everything she was about to do. But she knew if she backed out, Zoe's chances would be nil. Keeping Zoe within arm's reach had only convinced the FBI and the clan that if they cornered Sarah, they captured their prize. She had to take a risk, and change course.

"Right now you need to go with Danisha."

"Mommy, don't. Please."

Her face looked close to crumbling. Sarah got a hitch in her breath. *Don't lie.*

"Staying with me right now won't be safe. You need to be far away for a little while."

"What's a little while? A little while was how long we were going to be on this trip."

"I need you to do this for me."

Zoe tipped her chin down and looked up from beneath her long lashes. "Are you going to tell me to be a brave girl?"

Sarah almost laughed through a sob. "You're already brave. Now I need you to put that bravery into action."

Zoe's shoulders started to rise and fall. "When will you be back?"

"As soon as I can. Maybe a day. Maybe tonight." And though she knew it was tough, she said, "Hold on and know that I love you more than anything that's ever been, ever."

Zoe's dark eyes held hers, searching for lies. Finally, lip trembling, she whispered, "Okay."

Sarah stood, holding Zoe's hand. Danisha came over, a messenger bag in her hand. She took out a little device that looked familiar. It was an RFID scanner.

"Ready?" Danisha brushed Zoe's hair off the back of her neck. "Hold still a sec, sugar."

She scanned the chip. With a beep, a set of names and numbers appeared on the scanner's display. Using her phone, Sarah snapped a photo of the data.

Danisha said, "Wait — there's more."

She scrolled through the display. More names. Birth dates. Sarah felt off balance. "What the hell?"

Sarah took more photos. She and Danisha glanced at each other. Danisha said, "Don't know what all that is, but you want to forward those snaps to one of your other burn phones, and to your e-mail somewhere in the cloud."

"Yeah."

Increasingly uneasy, she helped Zoe get buckled in Danisha's rental SUV. Before she lost control, she squeezed her daughter's hand and kissed her little palm. She handed Mousie to her and shut the door.

Danisha fired up the engine. Sarah walked around to the driver's open door.

"Hit the highway and drive straight through Alamogordo," Sarah said. "Get to the front gate of Holloman Air Force Base and talk your way in."

"You sure about that?"

"Not even the Worthe family has the stones to attack an American military installation."

"Then I'll get inside the wire. I have my Army ID. Sergeant Danisha Helms reporting to the Base Exchange for discount steaks and M&M's."

"You're the best. You know that, right?" Sarah said.

Danisha's eyes were fiery. "I know. Trust me."

Sarah blurted out a laugh, desperate and hopeful. She kissed Danisha's cheek. "Godspeed."

She shut the door and knocked on the roof of the SUV with the flat of her hand. Danisha drove away.

As the dust settled behind it and the scrunch of the tires faded, the quiet came upon them. Nolan stared at her.

"What?" she said.

"You just look like Beth. That's all."

"People keep saying that."

"I loved her. I really did."

"Then let's make it up to her," she said.

Ten minutes later, Lawless drove up.

She stood still and waited for him to approach. He looked tired, squinting, unshaven. His black T-shirt and khaki jeans were the same ones he'd been wearing yesterday.

He came straight up to her, ready for whatever she dealt. He said, "If you want to hit me, go ahead."

"I do. Later."

"I —"

"Later." The air pressed on them, heated and dense. "Just tell me whether you still have your star."

"I've got it. And nobody knows I'm here."

She had asked him not to tell anybody — yet. "Good to know."

She didn't mean to sound cutting, but he took a breath.

"After last night, I won't blame you if you never trust a federal officer again. And I won't lie — your safety has never been a priority for the Marshals Service. They knew about you from the start, and declined to take any jurisdiction or responsibility."

"They were told that my actions didn't warrant law enforcement attention?" she asked.

"By me."

"That's why the Santa Cruz County Sheriff never investigated Nolan's disappearance —"

"They still have him listed as a missing person. But the case isn't active."

"And Beth?"

The pain in his eyes was acute and honest. "You know how her case was handled."

"Open. But you pressed them to leave it that way."

"I did. Her records are sealed. They presumed Nolan disappeared into WITSec with their baby."

He glanced behind her. "This is a surprise, to say the least."

Nolan ambled forward. He looked uneasy, not sure how to deal with Lawless. "Deputy Marshal."

Lawless didn't smile. "You know that the Marshals Service has never lost a protectee in all its years . . ."

"That's one of the reasons I went into the program."

"That is, never lost a protectee who stayed with the program and didn't try to return

472

to his former life."

"You have no idea, man. It's a cold way to live."

Sarah held up a hand. "And we're back to 'later.' "

Lawless hadn't moved, maybe still waiting for her to punch him in the jaw.

She said, "Danisha has Zoe. She's headed west to Holloman Air Force Base."

His eyes widened. He seemed to realize that the scope of her plans had changed.

"What's going on?"

"A setup."

"Against?"

"Harker. And the clan."

"Why are you planning to do that, exactly?" He looked like he was facing a wild dog, waiting for it to bite. "And how?"

"I'll explain later, but right now I need Nolan to phone Isom."

If Nolan had looked pale before, he now looked like Crisco. "Isom Worthe."

"I want you to tell him you're ready to come home. You want to return to the family."

Lawless took a step back. "The family thinks he's dead."

"The family thinks he's missing. They think he got away."

"I'm not going back," Nolan said. "No

way. You're crazy."

"I don't want you to go back." She put a hand on his arm. "I want to get you and me and Zoe out of this mess once and for all."

"And I'm gonna do that by telling Isom I'm alive? Isom's running things for the whole bunch. I tell him I'm alive, they'll track me down and kill me."

"You want to make it up to your daughter?"

"You know I do."

"Then you can atone right now."

Lawless said, "Sarah, can you please explain?"

"First, Nolan's not actually going to turn up. He's going to make a couple of phone calls and then he's going to vanish back into the mist. Because you're going to provide him with a fresh WITSec identity. Aren't you?"

Lawless simply stared. As if thinking, *When did you get appointed my boss?*

"Nolan, you're going to call Isom. First off, I know you have his phone number in your contacts. Because you're smart."

She didn't care how safe he'd been in Witness Security — she figured he had kept the family's numbers as a fallback. They terrified him, but if all else failed he would have no option but to throw himself on their mercy.

"Don't deny it."

He didn't. He tightened his arms across his chest.

"And in any case, you have to convince Isom that there's a reason you want to come back, and for them to keep you alive."

"Which is?"

"You're going to bring the prize. Zoe."

Lawless looked deeply unsettled, but only for a moment. "I know you don't have any intention of letting that happen. But even to suggest it . . ."

She held up a hand. "Bear with me. Nolan, it's important that Isom think you're willing to become the prodigal son and crawl back begging forgiveness. Because I want him to agree to bring you in."

"He'll agree. He'll agree with a 12-gauge fired into my face," Nolan said.

"You're never going to see him. All I need you to do is be convincing," she said. "And one other thing. Get him to have Grissom call you."

Nolan had started to look like he was ready to jackrabbit. But that stopped him. "I don't want to talk to that rattlesnake."

"I know. I don't either. And you won't have to. All I need is Grissom Briggs's phone number."

Lawless said, "What are you going to do with it?"

She smiled. It felt grim and righteous. "I'm going to screw Grissom and the clan into a hole so deep, they'll be dirt. And they won't be able to come after me again — even more, they won't want to."

61

They took two vehicles down the twisting mountain road from Ruidoso. Grissom in Jadom's Ford F-150 pickup, Fell and Reavy following not long after in the silver Navigator. Reavy's wound had left her sleepless. Her eyes darted around the vehicle. She was edgy, hurting, and angry. She was eager to hurt somebody back.

Others were coming. Grissom had contacted cousins up in Durango, across the Colorado line. The cousins had been driving all night; Grissom, Fell, and Reavy since dawn. Everybody was going to meet near Alamogordo. There they would wait and listen and vector whichever way the police scanner and Sarah Keller's bank card pointed.

"We need to get the girl today," Reavy said. "I'm tired of this shit."

"We will," Fell said. *Get the kid.* Trade her for Creek. Fair was fair. She ran her tongue over her lips.

"Gonna shoot Keller where the round hit me, then six more times."

"We'll see." She pointed at Reavy's phone. "Try again. If you can get a signal, call the prepaid card company."

Danisha was twenty miles down the highway toward Holloman Air Force Base when the state troopers flagged everybody to a stop. She rolled down the window and stuck her head out.

Ahead, two cop cars sat crosswise across the road, blocking it. A trooper was setting up a barricade. ROAD CLOSED.

Zoe said, "What's happening?"

"Don't know."

She tried to see if they were searching cars, asking for ID, looking for a mother with a missing five-year-old. She wouldn't pass muster. The color scheme in this car didn't match.

Ahead, a Toyota pulled out of line and turned around. It drove back the way it had come, passing them. A minute later another car did the same. Danisha waved. The driver slowed.

"What's going on?" Danisha said.

"Some kind of accident. Hazardous material, cops say. They got a radiation symbol on the barricade. Nobody gets in or out."

He drove away. She stared at the roadblock. Nobody got in *or* out? What kind of
accident was that?

No accident.

It was a trap. Even if it wasn't meant for
her, it put her in a pen. Ahead, a trooper
walked from car to car, leaning down to
speak to each driver.

She didn't wait for him to reach her
vehicle. She turned it around and headed
back the way she'd come.

The hairs on her arms stood up. She was
driving on the only paved road to be found
for fifty miles. She turned on the radio.

". . . the entire area is being quarantined.
There is no confirmation from state or
federal authorities, but we have it on reliable authority that it requires an emergency
nuclear response."

She got out her phone.

In the line of cars and trucks behind the
roadblock, Grissom drummed his hands on
the wheel and tried to see what the cops
were doing up ahead. This road was lightly
traveled, but already there were a dozen cars
and SUVs and a big rig idling in the white
desert sun.

A truck drove past headed back the other

way, driver's window down, man leaning out to call at the vehicles he was passing. Shaking his head. He cruised up beside Grissom.

"Accident," the man called. "Bad juju, man. They're talking nukes."

He accelerated away. Grissom waited. Nukes would be too lucky. Nukes would mean the chance of a lifetime for him to steal his dream weapon. No more scrounging dynamite, or stalking government stooges at federal courthouses. Just . . . boom. But this had none of the markings of that fulfillment. This had the markings of a police setup.

Another car pulled out of line ahead and turned around. It was a red SUV that made a wallowing turn across both lanes and the shoulder. It gunned back this way and passed him.

He sat motionless. Looked in the mirror.

Danisha Helms was at the wheel.

He waited for a yellow VW to pull out of line and turn around. Then he spun the steering wheel with one hand and pushed a number on his phone with the other. In two seconds, he was driving east, in the Helms woman's dust.

"You're not going to steal the money —

you're going to throw it away and pin its disappearance on Grissom?" Lawless said.

"If you have a better idea, tell me. It's my shot. And I have to take it *now.*"

Lawless looked like he was trying to work it out. "Where are you going to transfer the money?"

"The Marshals Service must have an account for seized assets."

He cut a glance at her, as though glimpsing a dimension that could only be seen from the corner of his eye — a view into the sly. He brightened.

"We can't use an obvious account. Figure the Worthes will try to trace the transfer. You don't want it going straight into a government account."

"Then a way-station account. A slush fund." She gestured in Nolan's direction. "With a fee sent on to whatever local bank he'll be using in his next WITSec existence."

Lawless stood thinking, loose limbed, watchful. "Shall we include the Bureau in this transaction?"

"Of course not."

"What are you going to do?"

"Call the Worthes' offshore bank. As soon as Nolan gets Grissom's phone number, I'm going to call Antigua and move the money."

Nolan said, "Assuming I do this, how

come you need Grissom's phone? You call
the bank, they're going to know it's not
him."

"On the contrary." She dug in her messenger bag. She came out with two cards.
She held them up. "Calling card. To keep
from showing my own number. And this"
— she raised another credit-card size item
— "is the ticket."

Lawless said, "Spoof card."

"Damn right."

"How legal . . ."

"I don't see you walking away."

He let out a near-laugh. "You bought the
whole shebang?"

"My employer considered it a worthwhile
investment in skip tracing. Possession of the
spoof card is fully legal. The company's
registered in Panama."

He did smile then. She felt his encouragement as reassurance.

A spoof card allowed you to disguise your
phone number when making a call. It
replaced your actual number with another
— a number you entered into the system
before you connected the call.

"You got the voice alteration package?"
Lawless said.

"It'll lower my voice to a male register. I'll
sound just like Grissom Briggs. *Man,*" she

said, adding a lazy drawl to her voice. "I'm going to trick the bank into thinking Briggs is making the transfer."

His smile seemed admiring. "To the slush account. We'll have to disguise that."

"Can you put a name to the slush account?"

"Reavy Worthe?"

"Joint account. Reavy, Fell, and Grissom. For their trousseau."

"I'll work on that. But if you can't convince the banker that you're Grissom —"

"I don't have to. The banker's not going to know exactly how Grissom sounds. All he has to do is say, 'Yes, I spoke to Mr. Briggs,' when Isom Worthe or the family's accountant calls the bank to ask who the hell emptied the account."

Nolan said, "About the joint account."

She tensed. "It can't have your name on it."

"Not what I meant. Fell and Reavy used to use aliases. They had fake IDs. The names were Jade and Opal Riggs."

She smiled. He was in. Lawless was nodding.

She nodded at Nolan. "Make the call."

She wanted him to do it while he was ragged and hoarse and tired, and before he chickened out. He got his phone. As she'd known, he scrolled straight through his contacts and hovered over a number. His eyes had a gleam of fear, but he called.

He put the phone to his ear and closed his eyes. Took a sharp breath. "Uncle Isom? It's me. It's Nolan."

And he burst into tears.

In her pocket, Sarah's phone vibrated.

Danisha kept the radio on, loud enough that Sarah should be able to hear.

"Road's blockaded west," she said. "I can't get to the Air Force Base."

She heard nothing in reply, just open silence.

"Sarah?"

Sarah stood chilled and hot. Road blockade. She snapped her fingers at Lawless. Mouthed, *News. Phone.*

She couldn't have Danisha and Zoe come back here. She couldn't have them anywhere within shooting distance of her and Nolan. She ran her knuckles across her forehead.

On the phone, Danisha repeated, "Sarah? Can you hear me?"

Nolan was talking in hesitant teary bursts to his uncle Isom, sounding abject and wheedling. She walked along the arroyo downstream, behind a cluster of boulders.

Danisha said, "Radio says it's a nuclear spill. They're cordoning off this area in a thirty-mile radius. Nobody gets in or out."

Harker. He was penning them all inside, and planning to drive the trio straight at her. She was inside a noose. Firewalled.

She said, "Where are you? Could you get to a police station — or even one of those cops at the barricade?"

"I'm miles away from the barricade. And I don't want to turn around. Bunch of other vehicles pulled out of line right after I did. Maybe they all just want to avoid traffic, but if one of them's following me . . ."

"Yeah." If that was the case, then doubling back would put her directly in their path. She pictured the landscape. "The airplane graveyard. Get there and get as deep inside as you can."

"Then what?"

She glanced around the boulders. "Lawless will come to get you. I'll call the FBI. Tell them where you are. Maybe they can airlift you to safety."

"Sarah, I don't like this. You don't want to mess with the FBI."

"We're running out of choices."

She didn't think Harker had the resources on scene to protect Zoe. Danisha could take care of herself, but Zoe needed more. She needed an assault team, with air support and missile defenses. She needed the Death Star.

Sarah had one handgun and one U.S. marshal. "Call back when you're in the boneyard."

"I'm two miles away. I'll get back to you."

She hung up. Danisha sounded rock-solid but stressed. *God help her,* Sarah thought.

Queasy with apprehension, Sarah hurried back to Nolan and Lawless.

Nolan squatted on his haunches, head down, speaking into the phone. "They didn't put me in witness protection for *giving* them anything, Isom. They put me in 'cause Beth was planning to tell the FBI everything she learned about the family. The Feds were coming to the cabin that day. They were going to take her into protective custody so she could talk into a recorder until she ran dry."

It was a good lie. He listened, eyes shut. Isom, Sarah guessed, was not playing the cuddly uncle.

"Like you would have believed me?" he said. "Isom, just listen for a second. You want to know why I disappeared? Because Sarah Keller shot me."

He held still, balanced precariously on the balls of his feet. Though listening to Isom, his lips moved. He seemed to be praying, or mumbling, *Come on, come on.*

Then he stilled. "Shot me and left me there for dead. And she took Zoe. I tried to keep her from taking my baby girl, but she shot me right in the gut. When I came to, the marshals had me handcuffed to a hospital bed in a federal jail facility. Told me I could cooperate and continue into WITSec, or I could go my merry way back to the family — and after I'd been disappeared for a week, maybe the family might not believe what I was telling them about my innocence. So what was I supposed to do?"

He listened again, his fears reeking from his posture. "And you want to know the ironic part? The FBI — they're the ones convinced me to come out of hiding this week. They're the ones showed me I was a fool to believe anybody in the government this whole time." He laughed. "They're the ones who got me my kid back."

Two more seconds. Then he stood. He clenched a fist. "You heard me. I got her. Zoe's with me."

He looked at Sarah. His eyes were bright.

"But I need help to get to you. The Feds, they got agents everyplace around here. They see Zoe, they'll go nuts. They're searching every car, every truck, they're gonna go house-to-house and tree-to-tree before long." He paused. "I need Grissom."

Sarah walked to Lawless's side. They watched, barely daring to breathe.

"This number?" Nolan said. "Yeah, I'll be on it. I got a signal. But hurry. No way I can keep under the radar much longer. I need Grissom here, *now.*"

He hung up. His hands were shaking.

"Grissom'll call," he said.

62

No guard at the gate, Danisha thought. No gate. She drove through a gap in the fence where a rusted chain-link barrier listed against the shining white sand.

She had a prickling sense of foreboding. The sky above was so blue it looked glazed, but she felt the darkness lowering.

From the back seat Zoe said, "These planes look all broken. Do they fly?"

"Nope. So we're going to explore them."

She eased the red rental tank past endless neat rows of 737s and DC-9s and into a military section, F-4 Phantoms and then a destruction yard, ranks of B-52 intercontinental nuclear bombers bigger than Mc-Mansions, eight-engined terror machines sitting dry and empty. Their wings had been guillotined from the fuselage and lay smashed in the sun, left there for orbiting Russian satellites to photograph and verify.

When she found a narrow rut in the sand

between two columns of planes, she turned carefully, thinking, *Sarah's little girl, Sarah's little girl, in my hands.*

In the rearview mirror, sunlight flared behind her. She glanced up but saw nothing. She looked out the window. Everything was flaring in the sun — aluminum fuselages, cracked cockpit glass, curving canopies. She checked ahead: the rutted path ran straight for nearly a mile, directly through the center of the boneyard, and intersected another road that ran along the inside of the fence at the far end. If she had to, she could get out that way. She drove halfway down the path and pulled the SUV beneath the shade of a blue KLM jumbo. A ladder leaned against the wing but it looked as dusty and forgotten as everything else in the boneyard. Nobody was around.

She parked under the wing. "Out you go, pipsqueak. Let's play fighter pilot."

They climbed up the ladder. At the top Zoe balled her hands in front of her eyes to shade them from the silver glare off the wing surface. Danisha led her through the open emergency exit into the jet's gaping, gutted interior.

Danisha paused. All the plane's windows and doors had been removed. The view to the west looked out across a moonscape of

490

white sand to black-ridged mountains. There wasn't any wind, just an oppressive stillness. She listened, wondering if she heard an engine in the distance, or whether it was the pounding of her own heart.

The insistent ringing wasn't what made Grissom pull over and stop in the middle of the aircraft graveyard. What made him pull over was the insistent ringtone that told him Isom Worthe was calling.

He seemed to feel a hot punch, like a match being lit in his gut. This job wasn't done yet. Which meant this call couldn't be congratulations.

"Isom."

"Drop what you're doing. We got a lost sheep says he wants to return to the fold. And says he's bringing a little lamb with him."

Grissom listened, and the lit match feeling eased and spread into a sense of warmth and well-being. "What's Nolan's number?" he said.

Nolan held his phone like it was a baby dragon, ready to breathe fire. He wiped the back of his hand across his forehead and leaned against his truck.

Sarah rubbed his shoulder. "You did great."

"I need a drink."

Lawless was on his own phone, talking to somebody in cool, muffled tones. She approached and he finished the call.

"They can put two names on the account. I told them Grissom, plus Jade Riggs. They're working on it."

"They. Your people. Does that mean they're still willing for me and Zoe to enter protective custody?"

"They're also working on that."

She tried not to scratch at her arms, or his throat. He looked like a rock, maybe one that was about to splinter off a cliff and crash to a valley floor. He looked as if he wanted to comfort her, or kiss her. She still wanted to punch him.

He put out a hand, palm up. She gripped it, just for a second. When she let go she felt steadier.

Quietly she said, "If Grissom calls, Nolan doesn't need to answer. Asking him to hold it together may be too much."

Lawless eyed Nolan, who was rocking back and forth beside the truck. "Agreed. All he needs is the number. He can let it ring."

And it did, a clear chime in the dry air.

Nolan twitched and before Sarah could speak, said, "Grissom. Hello."

Grissom heard the weasel's voice on the other end of the line. Five years, he hadn't heard it, certainly hadn't missed it, didn't care for it, and had no doubt who it was.

"Nolan. Where are you?"

On the passenger seat, his second cell phone buzzed. It was a text from Reavy, replying to the message he'd sent her a minute back, telling her he was at the airplane graveyard.

15 min out.

He panned the view up the white sand road, to the turnoff where the Helms woman had driven.

He spoke calmly. "Nolan? I'm going to bring you in. Tell me how to find you."

Hesitantly, Nolan said, "How long's it gonna take? I need you here ASAP, man. The cops are crawling all over the place."

"Then tell me where to find you."

The pause in Nolan's response sounded like, *duh.* "Oh. Motel at a town on Highway 82. The Atomic Inn. I'm afraid to open the door, man. I registered under another name but I don't trust the front desk. Just get here."

"I'll be there within thirty minutes. Sit tight."

"Good. Okay, cool," Nolan weaseled. "Thanks."

"I'm on my way," he said. "Oh, and Nolan — let me talk to Zoe."

The look in Nolan's eyes turned to open panic. Sarah got halfway to his side and he said, "Why?"

The way he listened, she thought his hair was going to ignite and slough off. She mouthed, *What?*

He mouthed back, *"Zoe."*

The panic became contagious. Her skin heated. She shook her head. Made slashing motions. *Refuse. Tell him no.*

Cringing, he said, "Not going to do that, Grissom. There's no need. And, frankly, you'd scare her."

He listened.

"She's a wreck, that's why. I don't need her crying again. Walls here are thinner than Saran Wrap. I gotta keep her quiet."

He closed his eyes again. Nodded and said, "I'll be here."

When he hung up he crouched by the truck, breathing hard. Sarah knelt beside him.

He held up the phone. "Here's the number."

"Thank you, Nolan."

He nodded again, quick, jerking motions. "He believed me. We're okay."

Grissom put away his phone. He stared up the road, into the forest of planes where Danisha Helms had driven.

Why was Helms hiding? She wasn't wanted by the law. She wasn't afraid of some nuclear disaster.

She had something with her. Or somebody. And there was only one person that could be.

He started his engine.

63

Sarah's heart beat like a drum in her chest. Grissom Briggs had provided a phone number. It set up everything she needed to set them free.

But he had asked to speak to Zoe.

Grissom Briggs called himself the Shattering Angel, but he was a snake in the grass.

"He knows," she said.

Lawless said, "What do you mean?"

And she had let Zoe go with Danisha. She had let go of Zoe's hand, let her out of her sight. She'd thought that made sense, that it put Zoe in a safer position.

But Briggs.

"He wanted to talk to Zoe. He knows."

"Knows she's not with Nolan?" Lawless said. "He might suspect."

"He knows it's a trick."

"Then get on the phone to the bank. Right now."

Her heart drummed, rapid-paced, a

rhythm of dread. She seemed to hear a dry sound, the rustle of scales, a rattler sidewinding toward them.

"Why else would he ask about Zoe?" she said.

Lawless put a hand on her back. The touch nearly made her jump. "Sarah?"

"What if he . . . Jesus."

Vision thumping, she phoned Danisha.

Her friend answered on the second ring. Hushed, whispering. "Sarah, what's going on?"

"You okay? Safe? Out of sight?"

"A mile deep in the aircraft boneyard, surrounded by the Cold War. But Sarah . . ."

"What?"

"Is there any chance somebody could have followed us?"

A moan rose in Sarah's throat. "Stay put. Stay quiet. I'll get the FBI there. And the cops."

"You sound worried."

"You have a weapon. Right?"

"You know it."

"Safety off."

The quiet on Danisha's end lasted a long heavy beat. "Call me when the law's on its way."

Sarah ended the call, hands trembling. "I have to get to her."

Lawless was shaking his head, already dialing a number. "I'm on it." He looked up. "You call the bank."

"I don't . . ."

"Call them. Do it. This is your one chance. If we arrest Grissom before you get through to the bank and move the money, you've blown that chance."

He was right. She crossed to the truck, leaned against the hood, and laid out all the information. She checked her watch. She looked west, toward the white sands and blazing sky where her little girl was shielded only by friendship and grit. *Hang on,* she thought.

She took out the calling card and dialed.

64

In the shade of the withering trees, deep in the arroyo, Sarah made the call. She accessed long distance through the calling card. Then she dialed the access number on the spoof card.

An automated voice answered. "Welcome. Please enter your PIN number."

Hair hanging in her eyes, she thumbed in the PIN. The automated voice told her she had 85 credits remaining, and prompted her to place a call.

"Press the destination number, followed by the pound sign."

She entered the number of the First Royal Bank of Antigua.

"Now enter the number you wish to display on caller ID."

She entered Grissom Briggs's cell phone number.

"To use your normal voice, press one. To

alter your voice to sound like a man, press two."

She pressed two.

Lawless had his phone pinned between his shoulder and ear and was scribbling on the inside of his wrist with a pen. He jogged over and held out his arm. Written on it was a string of numbers and the names Grissom Briggs and Jade Riggs.

"If you would like to record the call, press four."

She pressed it. The number rang.

"First Royal Bank of Antigua."

She began.

Harker had a map out and was checking the radius of the quarantine cordon. He was tired, felt like sand was scratching his eyes. There were only three roads he could see on the map. It was a USGS topographical map, highly detailed, every creek and goat track labeled.

If the Worthes wanted to get out of the quarantine zone, they'd have to take a paved road. They might have resources, but not enough to go through the outback. And if they did try . . .

When his phone rang, he answered with annoyance. "Harker."

"It's Lawless. What assets do you have for

air support?"

Harker's ulcer flared. "Now you want my support?"

"Curt. I need to know."

Harker continued to look at the map. Air support was coming, but from Albuquerque — a hundred miles away.

"Inbound. Why do you ask?"

"Zoe's with Danisha Helms, taking cover in an airplane graveyard near Alamogordo. And Danisha thinks Grissom Briggs may be closing in on her. We need to extract her."

Harker straightened. "Give me the precise location."

He stared at the map. He was twenty-five miles from the airplane graveyard. He had a small crew of FBI agents and deputy sheriffs. The SWAT team was in Roswell, as were the Roswell PD's helicopter and the state police's traffic airplane. All the rest of the law enforcement assets under his command were arrayed at the perimeter of the quarantine zone. Helms and Zoe were in the dead center of it, as far from all of them as it was possible to get.

"I'm on my way," he said.

"How long?"

Waving at another agent, he ran for the car. "Twenty minutes."

Lawless said, "I'll be there in fifteen."

■ ■ ■ ■

"That's right, hon," Sarah said, stretching her words, giving them a hard edge. "B-r-i-g-g-s. Now read that account number back to me."

Though to her own ears her voice sounded as female as ever, she knew that on the other end of the line, the bank manager heard a male voice, maybe with a threatening undertone.

The woman read back everything, in her own lilting voice: the transfer instructions, the account number, the name on the account to which the funds would be credited.

"And the amount?" the woman said.

"All of it."

"The entire amount?"

"That's what I said."

There was a clicking of keys. Behind Sarah, Lawless ended his own call and whistled at her and Nolan. He ran to his car.

Why was Lawless suddenly in a rush?

"Mr. Briggs?"

"Yes," Sarah said.

"That will be three million, four hundred ninety-one thousand U.S. dollars and twenty-seven cents, transferred to your account at the Bank of the West. Minus our transfer fee of fifty-one dollars."

Three *million*? Finally she said, "When?"

Lawless started his engine. He eyed her through the windshield. Waiting. Impatiently. Something was going down.

The bank manager said, "The transfer will be effective by close of business today, pending confirmation."

"Confirmation of what?"

"Per instructions put in place when the account was opened, I will call you back to verify all details before the transfer is executed."

What? "No."

"I'm sorry, but those instructions must be followed."

The landscape, the arroyo and dry creek bed and the thirsty trees, seemed to shimmer in her vision. "I'm going to be out of phone range this afternoon. I'm in New Mexico, and cell coverage is unreliable. I'll need you to e-mail the confirmation to me."

The manager paused. "I'll have to check whether that will be acceptable."

Lawless waved to her, beckoning. She gathered her things and ran to the car. Nolan was already in the shotgun seat.

To the bank manager, she barked, "Get with the twenty-first century. The e-mail will come through ten times more reliably than a call. Let me give you the address."

Hesitation. "Very well, give it to me. But I'll have to verify whether that will be satisfactory."

She slammed the car door and Lawless took off. Tossed back against the seat, she said, "The address is Worthe-dot-Briggs at Gmail. Worthe with an *e.*"

"That's —"

And phone reception died. The call was cut off.

"Dammit," she said. "Get out of this arroyo."

"Did you do it?" Nolan said.

"Almost. Not yet. Maybe. Get into clear air, where I can get online. I have to set up a Gmail account." And pray that the address wasn't already taken. "Where are we going and why so fast?"

"Harker's sending men and air support to get Zoe and Danisha. But they're all on the periphery. I think the airplane graveyard's ground zero, and we have to assume Briggs and the women are closing in. We have to get there first."

65

At the listing chain-link gate, Lawless stopped the car. The gleaming expanse of dead airliners and warplanes stretched on far beyond their ability to see, hulking sarcophagi, some six stories tall, desiccated and steely under the morning sun. The white sand made the light unbearable. Sarah put on her sunglasses.

Nolan said, "What are you waiting for?"

The car idled, sunlight glaring off the hood. Lawless stared through the gate. Sarah turned in her seat and scanned the view up and down the highway. She saw nobody on the road, not even glints off distant windshields. She felt as isolated as she ever had.

"One of us needs to stay here and watch for anybody coming. The FBI, SWAT. Or the clan," she said.

She needed to get to her little girl. She felt an ache like a magnetic force, pulling on her to get inside and get hold of Zoe.

Lawless said, "It'll be best if you stay here, Sarah."

Because he was armed. And trained. And good at extracting people, clear into new lives.

"I'll stay." She pointed at a jetliner parked next to the road just inside the fence. "I'll climb in the cockpit of that 727 and watch the road. It'll be high enough to see for miles in all directions." She checked her phone. "And I have a signal."

She also had a live e-mail account for Worthe. Briggs. She hoped she'd get confirmation from the bank in Antigua soon.

Lawless said, "If Grissom and the women are already inside, they might hear us coming. We have no intel, no way to know where they are. If so . . ."

"Call me if you can."

She had her Glock, in her messenger bag, with a full magazine and two extra clips. "I hit the target's head thirty straight times at the range in OKC. I'll come if you need me."

Lawless held her gaze, silently reminding her: hitting a paper target was different than hitting a live opponent who was firing back. As if she could ever forget that, with Nolan sitting in the front seat.

She opened the door. "I'll come if Zoe needs me."

She climbed out into the rising heat. Lawless drove through the gate. She strode through after him. The ground, once she stepped off the asphalt, was powdery and white.

The back stairs of the 727 were down. She jogged up them and into a murky interior, lit by striped light through empty windows. The passenger seats were gone. She made it to the cockpit and climbed into the cramped pilot's seat. It was hot, close, the sun screaming off the nose of the plane. But, facing east, it was also reflecting off the windshield. She didn't think she could be seen.

The dead planes weren't the only equipment in the graveyard. In the distance sat a gigantic crane. Hanging from its tall arm on cables was a dark metal blade the size of a kitchen counter. It was an airplane guillotine. Beyond the crane, looking like a mechanical Tyrannosaurus rex, was a demolition excavator. At the end of its long neck were jaws four feet wide, with a set of heavy steel teeth. It was designed to rip jetliners apart.

She took the Glock from her bag. She shoved her phone in her back pocket. She watched.

Ninety seconds later a glint on the horizon turned into a silver Navigator. It slowed at the gate and turned in.

Fell was at the wheel.

Fell nursed the Navigator through the half-torn gate into the airplane graveyard. Beside her, Reavy dialed Grissom.

"We're here," she told him.

Reavy sounded thin. She looked pale. She'd been drained, Fell knew. But it all combined to give her the look of a cut piece of glass, clear and sharp and ready to slice.

"Okay," she said into the phone. "You got a definite bead on where they went?"

She listened some more. "Then we need to cut them off. Pinch them between us so they can't get away."

A few seconds later she hung up. "Half-mile ahead. Turn left, he'll meet us and we can close on them front and behind."

Reavy wiped a hand across her forehead. Though the AC was blasting, she was sweating. "We're gonna get Little Miss Golden Eyes. We're gonna get her, and I'm gonna stick Keller like a pig."

Sarah scrambled from the pilot's seat. She cast a last-gasp look out the windshield and past the fence at the highway. She saw nobody else coming. Not Harker, not the state police, not a wayward longhorn. And no air support. She was lost among a thousand airplanes and not one had the power to lift her and her baby out of there.

She ran down the length of the jet, pulled her phone out, and called Lawless. He answered while she was running down the back stairs, from shadow into blinding light. Silver, white, blue sky throbbing above.

"Sarah?"

"They're here. Reavy and Fell, driving the silver Navigator. Headed your way."

"Call Danisha. Where are you?"

"Coming."

She ran.

Briggs put the pickup in low and eased forward, creeping up to the turnoff where Helms had gone in with the red SUV. When he reached it, he stopped, idling. The rutted path ran deeper into the boneyard between two rows of heavy aircraft. It ran for a good mile, but he could see that it ended at the fence. There was no gate down that way. They were still inside.

His phone rang. He ignored it.

He didn't see Helms but he knew which way she'd gone. He turned the wheel.

In the heated interior of the jetliner, Danisha took off her hat and tossed it aside. On her hip was the holster carrying her SIG Sauer. She kept hold of her phone. She listened. She heard only the ticking of metal as it warmed in the sun, and the hiss of sand hitting the fuselage in the breeze.

Zoe watched her, solemn and observant. Danisha tried not to let her face show her fears and concern. This had to end. Zoe needed out of this, and right damn now.

She crooked a finger. "Come here, Boo."

But Zoe tucked her chin into her chest and didn't move. Her little stuffed mousie hung from her hand. She turned and climbed over metal floor struts and leaned against the fuselage to peer out an empty window.

"They're all gone," she said.

Danisha climbed after her. Gently she put a hand around Zoe's waist to nudge her back from the window.

"Who, honey?" she said.

"The birds. Look." She stared into the sea of sun-burnished aluminum outside. Her voice waned to a murmur. "They all flew away. Everything's gone."

■ ■ ■ ■

Lawless tossed his phone to Nolan and turned down a hard-packed gypsum trail between two rows of planes.

"Call Danisha. Warn her," he said. "And tell me if you spot Fell and Reavy."

Nolan fumbled with the phone, shoulders crimped. "Jeez. They're . . . Jesus, they're here?"

"Sarah just saw them come through the gate."

He drove past one airplane and another, wheels and landing gear flashing by the windows like picket fencing. "And try to get directions from Danisha."

This was a dry forest of metal, a ruin that extended for miles. He didn't have Danisha's precise location. He didn't want her to make a run for it without him there to provide cover. But if he couldn't find her, that issue was moot.

Nolan dialed, and a moment later said, "Danisha, they're in here. We got to get you out. Where are you?"

He put it on speaker. Danisha's voice came through, quiet and clear and strained. "Half a mile in, there's a crossroad. Left, another half mile to a soft sand track."

511

Damn. Lawless realized he had gone too far — he'd passed the crossroad. "The track, does it come out anywhere?"

"Yeah, it intersects the hard sand road that runs along the inside of the fence."

The fence was not far ahead. "We're nearly there. Coming."

"Do we need to move?" she said.

"Are you out of sight?"

"Yes."

"Stay put for now."

At the fence he turned left. Along the road just inside it, the hard sand rushed beneath the tires. And too late he saw the intersection, the soft rutted track, ninety degrees to the left, a narrow lane between jumbos and a row of military bombers. He drove past it, Nolan saying, "Hey, hey . . ."

He braked, reversed, skidded backward to the turn.

About four hundred yards along the rutted path sat Danisha's red SUV, under the wing of a KLM 767.

Beyond it, at the far end of the path, was the white F-150 pickup driven by Grissom Briggs. It was turning down the track, headed straight for them.

66

Fell roared along the hardpan toward the center of the boneyard, bouncing so hard that the wheel bucked and Reavy guttered low cries of pain. Planes flashed by on either side. Reavy reached between her legs and picked up the shotgun from the foot well.

"Watch for them. All of them," Fell said.

Grissom wasn't answering his phone. That meant he was on the verge of action. It also meant he couldn't tell her exactly where to find him. She looked for breaks in the crowd of dead planes, checking for signs of where Zoe was being hidden. She drove past heavy construction equipment, cranes and diggers with chomping steel teeth.

Reavy pointed. "Try that way. Right."

Fell skidded around a corner. Sand flew into the air. She roared through a herd of Army-gray bombers with their chopped wings lying beside them on the ground.

Reavy ducked and peered below the bellies of the jets. "Stop — I see a car."

Fell swerved to a stop. About a quarter of a mile away, parked beneath the wing of an airliner, was a shiny red SUV. Reavy tossed open her door, hopped out, and headed for it, limping hard, the shotgun at port arms. Pistol in her hand, Fell broke into a run and caught up.

She said, "I can't see anybody in the SUV."

"Ladder's leaning against the wing of that jet," Reavy said. "Bet they climbed up and hid inside."

Distantly, Fell heard an engine. "Grissom's coming."

Beneath the field of jets she glimpsed rolling tires and blowing dust. From far away the F-150 was barreling along a rutted sand track toward the empty SUV. But she heard a second car. It was closing in on the SUV from the opposite direction.

"Not just Grissom. Somebody else," she said.

They kept running. Along the rutted track a black sedan skidded up and stopped next to the jet and the parked red SUV. Out jumped two men.

The first was the U.S. marshal, the dark-haired man who had shot at her when she tried to run him down outside the sheriff's station last night. The second . . .

She slowed. Reavy limped past her, wheezing, her face set.

"It's Nolan," Fell said.

Reavy grunted. Fell ran, off balance, stunned, seeing everything in painfully bright detail. He wasn't dead. He was here. Alive.

"Nolan?" she called.

He looked around and saw her.

Reavy turned to her, face flat. "Shut the hell up. He's with the marshal."

Grissom's truck drew nearer, roaring along the track. From the black sedan the U.S. marshal lifted out a Remington 870. He racked the slide and motioned Nolan behind the car. Then he stretched across the roof and leveled the shotgun at Grissom.

For a second Nolan stood motionless, gazing at Fell. He raised his hands together and steepled them in front of his lips.

Prayer, greeting, plea . . .

Reavy groaned with effort and pain and started to lift the Mossberg. Nolan saw it. As if he'd been fired from a slingshot, he ran, ran like a crazy animal, to the ladder that leaned against the wing of the 767. He began climbing.

Fell kept running. "Nolan," she yelled. He

wasn't dead. He was . . .

He was going after his little girl. He was trying to get Zoe.

He was halfway up the ladder to the wing of the jetliner when Grissom leaned out the window of the truck and started firing.

Running flat-out, through shade and light beneath the wing of a dead airliner, Sarah heard gunshots. *Pop, pop, pop, pop.* She gasped and her skin shrank.

Zoe.

She heard more shots, from a different gun, deep and sharp. Gripping the Glock, she ran out onto a rutted path. She saw a scene of converging chaos.

Ahead, Danisha's red SUV was parked next to a ladder propped against the wing of a blue jumbo jet. Just beyond it, Lawless was pinned behind his car. He crouched, his back against the wheel well, reloading a shotgun. Nearby, a Ford F-150 pickup was awkwardly stopped, driver's door open, steam blowing from the grille. It looked as if Lawless had shot out the radiator.

Grissom Briggs was halfway up the ladder, firing repeatedly at Lawless as he climbed. He was going after Zoe and Danisha.

Above him, on the wing, Nolan was making his way unevenly toward the fuselage.

Sarah ran.

Grissom reached the wing at the same time Nolan reached the emergency exit door. Their footsteps clattered on the aluminum surface. Nolan glanced inside the jet, put a foot on the exit door, and paused. He turned. Grissom was coming at him, ten feet away. Nolan pulled his foot back down, put his back to the exit, and blocked it with his body.

Grissom raised his handgun and fired.

Nolan collapsed with a thud, rolled off the back of the wing and dropped like a bundled carpet twelve feet to the sand. He hit and lay still.

"Oh, God," Sarah said.

Grissom kept walking toward the emergency exit.

Lawless broke from cover and ran to Nolan's side. Sarah sprinted across the sand toward the ladder.

Lawless dropped to his knees and leaned over Nolan. "Hold on, man. Hold on."

He heard her coming. Jerked up, swung around, shotgun in his hands.

"Michael, no," she yelled. "Grissom. Zoe . . ."

Above her, footsteps cranked on the wing. Lawless nodded her toward the ladder.

She ran to it and began to climb.

In her pocket, her phone buzzed. She kept going. She heard the metallic footsteps reach the fuselage and a grunt as Grissom climbed through the emergency exit. He was inside.

Fell nearly stumbled. Nolan lay splayed on the dirt. Grissom had shot him like a dog. Shot him without a word or a pause while Nolan stood in front of him unarmed.

Reavy let out a cry. *"Done."*

Fell turned her head. Reavy was lagging, her face still striated with pain. But her eyes were alight, her lips drawn back. She grunted with effort, bringing up the shotgun in the general direction of the blue jumbo jet.

Grissom edged into the gloomy interior of the jet, a tangled hole of torn-out seats and tumbled wiring. He looked up one way and down the other. No sound, no movement. Where were Helms and the child?

He ran forward through the plane. He saw no sign of them. Not in the cockpit, not in the remnants of the galley.

Outside, footsteps rang on the ladder.

He looked around again.

They weren't here.

He glanced to the far side of the plane. The emergency exit on the other wing was also open. It had been tossed out, and on the wing were fresh scratches.

And footprints in the thin coating of sand on the wing surface.

They'd gone.

They'd climbed out the other exit and split. And Nolan, in an act of fool misloyalty, had tried to keep him from seeing their escape path.

He spun around and fired the revolver back through the door he'd come through, at the ladder. Then he jumped out the far door and ran along the wing.

Sarah cringed on the ladder, her mouth so dry she couldn't spit, fingers gripping the hot rungs. The shot had grazed the wing. It echoed like a wire being pulled.

Beneath it she heard running footsteps, distant and receding.

Grissom had gone out the far side of the fuselage and was headed along the other wing. Why?

Her phone buzzed again. She pulled it from her pocket. "Danisha?"

"We gotta go."

"Where are you?"

■ ■ ■ ■

Danisha looked out the window of the wrecked B-52 where she and Zoe were hiding. She was facing back toward the blue KLM jumbo where she'd left the SUV. Three planes were parked wingtip-to-wingtip between the KLM and the B-52, like a chorus line. She and Zoe had walked along those wings and jumped from one plane to the next, never leaving footprints on the ground. She thought they'd been safe. But outside, it wasn't birdsong that echoed. It was gunshots, and now footsteps. In the distance a man appeared at the top of a bomber's hulking fuselage. He had a weapon in his hand. He balanced and skidded over the roof of the craft and kept coming, headed in their direction.

"We're in the military section. I parked and we jumped from plane to plane. We're in a B-52 and somebody's coming. A man."

"Get out of there," Sarah said.

Danisha took Zoe's hand. And she saw his face. The Shattering Angel.

Sarah yelled, "Lawless. They're not here. They're in another plane — a bomber. And Briggs is headed for it."

She looked down. Lawless had dragged Nolan back to the black car and propped him up. He was holding him in place, one hand on his shoulder, another supporting his head, talking to him.

She hesitated on the ladder. A pang took her in the chest. Nolan was staring at nothing, his shirt a sopping mess of blood.

"Michael," she said.

He held onto Nolan's face a second longer, talked to him a second longer, as though as long as he spoke, he could keep a conversation going, and Nolan would still be alive. Then Lawless's shoulders dropped. He gently lowered Nolan to the ground.

Lawless looked up. He didn't need to shake his head.

Sarah clung for a second to the ladder, strangely stung. Then behind Lawless, somewhere under the mass of scrapped planes, a woman cried out.

Fell and Reavy were coming. Sarah scrambled onto the wing.

"Lawless, come on," she yelled.

He didn't move.

"Lawless."

He stood and hoisted the Remington and faced away, toward the angel's wings. "Run, Sarah. I'll cover you."

She ran to the emergency exit door. She

was halfway through when someone fired a shotgun.

67

Sarah scrambled inside the fuselage, yelling, "Lawless!"

The blast of the shotgun was followed by return fire, terrible sounds, flat and ripping. She plunged across the interior of the plane, out the emergency exit on the far side, and ran along the wing.

At the end of it, she saw a gap. Three feet, maybe, to another wingtip, another commercial jetliner. She accelerated and jumped and landed half off balance. She slid to her knees.

"Jesus."

Ahead, now two hundred yards distant, Grissom Briggs crested the top of a B-52, looking like a mite on the back of a beast. He slid onto the far wing and charged away.

She got to her feet and clunked across the wing after him. She climbed through an emergency exit into the jet and out the other side. She paused to look back, hoping to see Lawless bringing up the rear, but nobody was there.

Sarah put on a burst of speed and aimed for the wingtip. There was another short gap — but she could make it. *Zoe* had made it. She watched her balance and leaped.

Below her, between the wings, on the blinding white sand, stood Reavy. She held a shotgun, aimed skyward.

Holy Christ. Sarah yelled, a crazy shocked cry, midflight, unprotected. She landed and behind her, close, a shot echoed.

The wingtip twelve inches back whanged and split.

She ran, the Glock swinging. Below the wing, Reavy pumped the shotgun.

Sarah got through the door of the plane a second before the shotgun blew another hole in the wing. She kept going, her mouth dry, her legs shaking so hard she thought they might buckle beneath her. She looked back and still saw no sign of Lawless.

And heard no more shots. She realized that Reavy was running along the sand beneath the jet, trying to get ahead of her. She climbed out onto the far wing and ran, eyes on the bombers ahead.

Fell dropped to her knees by the marshal's car. Nolan lay slack on the ground like a marionette whose strings had been cut. His chest was still. His blood soaked the white sand beneath him.

She tried to say his name, and no words emerged. She'd seen so many dead, but her uncle, the one person who had always been kind to her, the only one in the family who had taken her side when times got tough, who thought it was wrong when her baby was taken away . . .

She didn't touch him. She stared, and didn't understand the stinging sensation behind her eyes. It burned.

Grissom had shot him. The marshal had dragged him here and laid him down and she supposed that meant Nolan had slipped into the arms of the law. But Grissom had shot Nolan without so much as speaking to him. All because Nolan had blocked the wing door with his own body, to keep Grissom from getting hold of his child.

Grissom had declared war on anybody who was standing in front of him, and decided his gun was the purifying force of the universe. Grissom had decided he didn't need scripture to show him the way — he was the way, and if you were in his path, good-bye.

Reavy had smiled. Limping along, shotgun at the ready, Reavy had smiled when Nolan fell from the wing and hit the ground.

In the distance, she heard people running across the wings of a jet. Grissom was after Zoe.

She needed to get her first. She stood and ran after them.

Sarah ran along the drooping wing of the B-52. Beyond it lay the airplane abattoir. Bombers sat chopped, their amputated wings and tails lying on the sand beside them. An enormous crane loomed in the distance, the heavy steel blade of its guillotine hanging high above the scene. Excavators with grappler claws were parked nearby. Around them the carcasses of commercial jetliners lay ripped and strewn across the desert floor.

In her pocket, the call with Danisha was live and on speaker. Danisha said, "Somebody's coming. Think it's him. Sarah . . ."

Sarah saw Grissom a hundred yards ahead. He was climbing a ladder to enter the front door of a 747.

"I'm coming," she said.

Below her came the sound of the shotgun being pumped. She shouted and ducked and kept running. The gun fired, blowing shards of aluminum from the wing in front of her. Below the hole Reavy limped into view.

Sarah pulled to a stop. *Not without a goddamn fight.* Nerves crackling, she swung the Glock around and aimed straight at the hole in the wing. She fired. The pistol kicked. She ran.

Metal twanging beneath her feet, she thumped to the end of the wing. As she leaped to the hard white sand, she fired another shot straight down. She landed hard and rolled. The air felt charged with static electricity. When she came up, she saw Reavy on the ground, taking cover beneath the wing. She was trying to stand but one of her legs wouldn't hold. She was using the shotgun to haul herself up. Sarah steadied herself, thinking, *It's Reavy or Zoe.* Both hands on the weapon, she fired. And hit nothing — she was out of range. Reavy didn't even flinch. Instead, she rose and took more shells from her pocket and began to reload the shotgun. Sarah ran again, hot, nearly insane, to the ladder. She started climbing.

From inside the jet came a muffled gunshot. Danisha cried out.

"No," Sarah said.

She kept climbing, the gun clanging against the rungs of the ladder. The door above her drew nearer. Ten feet, seven, four. Sarah squirmed up another step and threw herself inside. She squirreled into the plane and lay in the sudden shade, panting.

She held the Glock with both hands and rolled to her knees. It took a moment for her eyes to adjust. Her nerves felt afire. Where was Grissom?

Just for a second, she thought she heard a little voice near tears. Every last bit of adrenaline in her body poured into her bloodstream.

Outside came heavy breathing and limping footsteps. Sarah scuttled to the doorway, grabbed the ladder, and began pulling it up into the jet. It was flimsy but awkward as hell. She heard Reavy jump, trying to grab it. She missed and landed with a moan. Frantically, Sarah manhandled the ladder inside.

She paused, breathing hard, trying to quiet her heart and lungs so she could hear. When she turned from the door, her eyes adjusted to the gloom.

The giant jet was half-gutted. Rows of seats had been torn out. But the stairway to the upper deck was still in place. And that's where she heard noise, the sound of somebody shoving aside debris. The sound of Danisha crying in pain.

Silence from Zoe. Sarah ran for the stairs.

68

Sarah edged up the stairs of the 747, deep in shadow, the Glock growing heavy in her hand. From above her came a repetitive thudding. Somewhere a heavy diesel engine gunned. Near the top of the stairs, she crouched and peered gingerly at the upper deck. It stretched forward a good fifty feet, past rows of seats and a narrow passageway to the cockpit.

The cockpit door was closed and bolted. Outside it Grissom stood battering it with his shoulder.

On the floor between his feet lay Mousie.

She stood and raised the Glock. She steadied her aim with a two-handed grip. Her vision pulsed. She took a breath — and held still.

Was the cockpit door armored? Zoe and Danisha were on the other side. She couldn't risk firing .40-caliber rounds into old plastic and plywood.

With a metallic shriek, the entire aircraft lurched.

Sarah grabbed the staircase railing. Below her at the bottom of the stairs, where the main deck had lain in gloom, a blinding strip of sunlight now poured across the floor. In front of the wings, a gaping hole had been torn in the fuselage.

The excavator's grappling arm swung into view. Its claw attacked the airframe again and with a diesel roar ripped out a new six-foot hole. The plane shuddered and rocked. Reavy was tearing the jet apart.

Heart thundering, Sarah raised the gun again toward Grissom's back, and tried to see whether the cockpit door had been reinforced with locks and a spyhole. The claw opened and spilled vast chunks of metal and insulation and wiring on the ground. It rose again, aimed for the door Sarah had come through, and sank its teeth into the floor of the main deck, shaking the jet like a predator with a rib cage in its teeth. Thrown off her feet, Sarah stumbled down the stairs. She hit hard, slid hands out like Superman, and smashed against a bulkhead. A chunk of insulation and airframe spilled on her, trapping her arm underneath a pile of debris. She tried to worm free. The Glock was tangled in wiring. She twisted and pulled, but couldn't dislodge it.

The claw rose again, jaws opening.

"Shit."

She yanked again, but the Glock was firmly entangled. *Shit.* She let go of the gun, withdrew her arm from the debris pile, and rolled aside. The claw ate the debris, Glock included, and scooped it away with a six-foot chunk of the floor.

She scrambled to her feet, barely able to breathe in the abrupt plume of dust and fiberglass that swirled from the torn airframe. Upstairs Grissom was still battering the cockpit door, trying to get past Danisha's barricade, but now it sounded like he was attacking the door with a heavy object.

And she remembered her phone. Heading for the stairs, she pulled it from her pocket. "Danisha."

She heard hard breathing, and more distantly, the sound of Grissom battering on the cockpit door with something like a lead pipe or sledgehammer.

"Danisha," she repeated.

The diesel excavator roared again and the grappling arm appeared. But this time it opened its claws and reached into the interior of the jet.

It swung toward Sarah, blind and raging, its teeth dripping torn metal and cabling.

She jumped out of its reach across piles of debris.

"Danisha!"

"Sarah . . ." Danisha was nearly whispering. "Door's not gonna hold. So listen."

Then, audible from the deck above, Danisha yelled, "Aft. Get aft. Cargo hold — she's . . ."

Sarah stilled. What was Danisha doing?

"Aft, there's stairs down to the hold. Hurry, Sarah."

Then she knew — or hoped she knew. And she gambled.

She took a big breath and shouted up the stairs. "Zoe?"

"Go," Danisha shouted.

She turned and ran down the length of the jet, climbing over jumbled seats and ripped ribbons of carpet and buckled sections of the floor. She ran for the back, loudly, shouting and stumbling. And listening.

She heard reckless footsteps pound down the stairs. Grissom was coming.

Every hair on her head prickled to attention. She thought, *Okay, come on.* She put the phone to her ear.

"He's coming."

"Good," Danisha said.

Sarah's heart leaped. She shoved the

phone in her pocket and scrambled past tilting lavatory doors and a set of beverage carts that had come loose from a galley.

She glanced over her shoulder. Grissom was down the stairs and charging after her. Behind him, the grappling arm rose again. Crouched on top of its clenched claw was Fell. She was getting a lift.

Reavy nudged the grappler to the edge of a hole she'd torn in the airframe. Fell jumped through it.

Reavy ripped another hunk from the jetliner and spat it on the sand. Sarah kept going.

Let 'em come. All of 'em.

She just had to get them to follow her, and keep herself alive long enough to let Danisha escape with Zoe.

Zoe wasn't in the cargo hold. She was in the cockpit with Danisha. That's what her friend had been trying to tell her. She'd been trying to misdirect Grissom into following Sarah. Sarah was sure of it — she'd seen Mousie on the floor outside the cockpit door. If Zoe had run from the cockpit on her own, she wouldn't have left Mousie there. She would have picked him up. The only reason he got left behind was that Danisha had hauled her to safety behind the cockpit door.

Grissom shoved debris aside, blundering through the jet. Fell, farther away, was quieter. That scared Sarah more. And now the excavator had subsided to a low idle.

Then a new engine fired up, a rolling drone. Another big machine.

At the back of the plane, still twenty yards away, was the aft galley. Like everything else, it looked like it had been looted in a riot.

Outside, the new engine revved up and a creaking sound twanged through the air.

A second later, a towering shriek tore through the wing of the 747. The jet rocked and outside came a hideous collapsing sound. She looked out the empty windows. Dust was billowing, huge white swirls of sand. Then she saw the blade of the guillotine rise slowly on its cables.

Reavy had gotten into the crane. She'd dropped the blade and severed the right wing. She was chopping the plane into sections.

Why? Cutting off any more safe exits?

The plane creaked, suddenly unbalanced. Sarah felt close to hyperventilating. Outside a whipping sound filled the air. The blade hit the roof of the jet, directly in front of the wings. It sliced through and rammed all the way through the floor. *Jesus.* Dust filled the interior. A moment later, the cables tightened and the blade rose, disappearing skyward through the rip.

Dimly, muffled by the sound of the crane's engine, Fell shouted something to Reavy. It sounded like, *"Again."*

Please. Sarah saw Grissom emerge from a crouch and climb past newly created piles of twisted metal and clamber toward her. Fell was at an empty window, waving at Reavy, directing her where to aim the guillotine.

Sarah paused one second longer, to make sure Grissom saw her. *It's okay,* she told herself, trying to maintain her nerve. Just lure him and Fell to the back of the jet. Keep them on this side of the chopping block.

Because Zoe was with Danisha on the other side. And with every fall of the blade, it became nearer to impossible for Grissom or Fell to get to them.

He caught her eye just as the blade dropped again. With a hellacious shriek it slammed through the roof behind him, slicing it and rocking the plane like a toy. A toy in a magnitude 8 earthquake. The roof was torn from wing to wing, and the floor of the plane was shattered all the way across the cabin.

For a short second, the tear in the floor looked like a moat, impenetrable, a safety barrier. Then the plane groaned, a twanging moan of metallic pain. The slice in the roof began to gape, an inch at a time. The plane was being torn in half.

And if it was, the cockpit door wouldn't protect Zoe. The cockpit was three stories above the ground. If the plane toppled, it would be akin to dropping a house thirty feet to the dirt with her little girl inside.

Danisha was going to have to get out.

And Sarah had to keep Grissom and Fell from going after them. She turned and clattered through the mess toward the back of the plane.

Ordinarily, 747s didn't have access below the main deck. But this jet, half-disassembled, had a hole in the floor, with a rickety ladder descending. Beneath it was a dusty splay of sunlight. Somewhere a door was open or missing — a cargo door, something. There was a way out.

She became aware that Grissom had stopped shooting at her. Maybe he figured Zoe wouldn't come out of a hiding place unless Sarah called her. Good. Let him think so. Except that probably meant he had plenty of rounds in his gun.

She clambered past toppled dinner carts

and open cabinet doors through the aft galley. Outside the windows, the guillotine blade swung past and edged upward, rising again on its cables.

One more slice and the plane would disintegrate. She wedged herself into the hole and set her feet on the ladder. Glanced back. Grissom and Fell were coming, scuttling like gargoyles through the wrecked guts of the jet. Behind them, near the front of the plane, she glimpsed the staircase.

A little hand held onto the railing, coming down. So did a woman's hand, raggedly, leaving a streak of blood.

They had one way out: the emergency exit over the remaining wing.

Look away. Don't let Grissom know something's caught your attention. She turned her head. She heard the crane outside, its engine revving.

Hurry, Danisha. They had to pass near the point where the blade had been falling. They needed to get out before it dropped again.

She waited for it. Grissom and Fell loomed nearer. She held poised on the ladder, nerves writhing, and waited for the blade to drop.

From outside came two booming gunshots.

The crane's engine revved wildly. The

blade didn't fall. Sarah looked outside. In the cab of the crane, Reavy had been flung back against a window. She'd been shot. And was deathly still.

Lawless pulled himself into the cab and shoved her from the seat. He leaned over the controls.

The cab of the crane swung around. He swayed and put a hand on the seat to steady himself.

In the cabin of the 747, Grissom let out a long animal moan. He was staring at Reavy.

The moan turned to a scream. *"Fucker."* He put a hand on his head. "Reavy." With his revolver he pointed at Fell. "Kill him. Gut him, Fell."

Then, at the bottom of the stairs, Danisha stumbled and crashed to her knees. Grissom turned at the sound. He forgot Reavy, and Lawless, and saw his prize. He saw Zoe holding tight to Danisha's bloodied hand.

Danisha struggled, trying to get her feet under her. Grissom headed toward them. They were almost two hundred feet away, past buckled flooring and collapsed ceiling panels and tangles of wiring and ripped-up seats. But he was intent. He raised his handgun and clambered after them as if forging against thigh-high water in a riptide.

69

Grissom forded through junk toward the gap in the floor of the jet. At the bottom of the staircase, Zoe pulled on Danisha's hand. Danisha slumped, collapsed. Zoe was trying to get her up, but Danisha wasn't moving.

Sarah plowed after Grissom. He might not be able to jump across the ragged hole in the floor of the plane and reach them, but if he got close enough he could shoot them both.

The airframe groaned again and the rip in the roof gaped wider. The floor gained a slight but noticeable tilt. Sarah fought her way uphill. She didn't see Fell. Her nerves whined. Maybe Fell had gone after Lawless. Maybe not.

She heard Zoe. "Danisha, come on."

Her chest cramped. It looked like Danisha was unconscious. Zoe was tugging on her arm.

Sarah shouted, "Zoe, run. Run away."

Her child looked up at her. Her face was pale and her expression perplexed. It seemed to say, *How can I leave Danisha here?*

"Go," Sarah yelled. "I'll get Danisha. Go to the front of the plane. Hurry."

Silently, Zoe turned and ran.

Grissom climbed on all fours over wrecked rows of seats. Sarah passed the galley. Cabinet doors hung open. She foraged. In an unemptied trash container she found a Perrier bottle. She slammed it against the counter and shattered the end off.

Ahead of her Grissom reached a half-wrecked lavatory. The door hung by one hinge. He jammed his gun in the front of his waistband, ripped the door free, and carried it with him toward the tear in the floor.

Zoe disappeared near the front of the jet, little legs flashing. Grissom hoisted the lavatory door and tossed it across the gap in the floor as a bridge.

Sarah ran up the aisle, raised the broken bottle, and lunged at him. With both hands she jammed the bottle down into his shoulder.

He yelled and buckled and they went down together onto a floor covered in dust and metal filings and tufts of insulation. Grissom hit facefirst. She raised the bottle again and slammed it down onto his right wrist. She put all her weight behind it and twisted and ground the glass into his arm. He screamed and clenched and tried to throw her off.

She brought the bottle up again and swung it at his bloodied face. She slashed and he flinched and she grazed his cheek. She swung again and he brought up his left hand. She twisted the bottle and felt it dig into his palm.

The pain took him then, channeled into rage. He flung her off and turned on her. His hands were a wreck, torn useless. But he swung at her as though flailing with dead meat and knocked the bottle from her hand. Then he turned back to his makeshift bridge.

She got to her knees. *"Lawless,"* she yelled.

Above her the jagged rip in the roof slowly yawned wider. Sunlight flooded through. In the sky above hung the blade of the guillotine, swaying on its cables. The engine of the crane continued rumbling.

"Lawless. *Help.*"

Grissom staggered against a bulkhead and aimed dazedly for the bridge. She clawed to her feet and dived at him.

Got him around the legs and brought him down in a heap.

Grissom was two hundred pounds of dense muscle, damaged but still powerful. He cocked an elbow, his face gleaming with fury, and clocked her in the temple.

The view erupted like sparklers and a loud hum filled her head. Her hands went numb. *Hold onto him,* a voice seemed to say.

"Hold onto him," the voice repeated. It was Danisha.

She clung to his legs. He kicked, but she wedged a hand under his belt. He couldn't shake her. He couldn't move his fingers enough to grip the gun.

But he could beat her to death with his bare knuckles. It was only a matter of time.

"Hold him, Sarah." Danisha struggled to her knees. She had her SIG, but in her left hand, and couldn't get to her feet to get a shot.

Through the gash in the roof, the sun caught the blade of the guillotine. It hung directly above her and Grissom, swinging, almost eagerly.

Sarah tried to breathe. Watched it sway. She felt Grissom's bulk and strength gather itself beneath her. Grunting, he pulled himself toward the bridge by his elbows and free leg.

The dust and noise seemed to clear. She heard only her own voice, the words carrying through the desert air.

"Lawless — Drop the blade."

Danisha gasped.

"Lawless, do it!" Sarah screamed.

Grissom grasped what was about to happen. He redoubled his efforts to crawl free and cross the bridge. He squirmed and kicked and elbowed her again. She felt herself slipping.

"Lawless. Now. *Drop the blade.*"

Grissom fought and groaned and began to pull her with him up the tilting floor onto the bridge. He was getting away. She wasn't going to be able to stop him.

With a thump, somebody landed on him. A wiry body, clawing into his hair with her hands, biting him in the back of the neck. It was Fell.

Too shocked to complain, Sarah held her bare grip on him. One last time, she cried, "Lawless — *Do it.*"

Before the words left her mouth the cables twanged and there was a rush of air overhead. An image of Zoe filled her mind. Of laughter, a gap-toothed smile, small warm arms wrapped around her neck.

The blade of the guillotine, two tons of dull steel, fell through the rip in the roof and passed in front of her eyes with an apocalyptic noise.

70

The dust and debris billowed in a yellow cloud, choking everything, everything but the sight of the blade buried in the floor in front of her, everything but the sound of the fuselage giving way, groaning and shrieking. With a final rip, the airframe tore in half.

Tail heavy, the back of the plane dropped and the section where Sarah was clinging tilted up.

She was too shocked at being alive to feel frightened, until she and Fell and all the debris and what remained of Grissom slid loudly toward the aft of the jet in a jumbled slow-motion catastrophe.

She shouted, alarmed. Her hand was still wedged under Grissom's belt. She pulled it free, tumbled past the galley, and plowed to a stop against a wrecked bunch of seats. Stunned, she held still, as though moving would set the plane thrashing again. Fell was five feet away, battered, covered in dust and blood. Grissom's feet protruded from under a collapsed pile of overhead bins. Fell stared, as if she wanted to kill him again.

Sarah tried to stand. Her legs wobbled. She seemed like nothing but one giant tremor.

Fell pulled herself painfully to her feet. She swayed. Then she hawked and spit at Grissom's feet.

"Shattering Angel," she said hoarsely. "Got his due. Thought he was God." She grimaced in pain. "Hubris."

"I've heard of that," Sarah said, chest heaving.

Fell slumped against the wall of the plane. "Keep that in mind." She wiped the back of her hand across her mouth. It came away bloody. "That was for Nolan. So you get a pass."

Fell looked toward the cockpit and pushed away from the wall. A locket swung from the chain on her neck. It had opened. Inside was a faded photo of a small child.

"Your son?" Sarah said.

Fell touched it. "My boy. Creek," she said. "I don't want Zoe for myself. I need my boy."

Sarah raised the revolver she had pulled from Grissom's belt. She aimed it at Fell.

"Live to fight another day," she said.

For a moment Fell glared at Sarah with her strange mismatched eyes. She seemed to think about it. Then, turning, she stumbled down the aisle toward the tail of the plane. She slipped through a break in the airframe and disappeared.

Hacking, Sarah lowered the gun. After a second she broke open the cylinder. As she'd feared, the gun was empty.

Being a cast-iron liar had its advantages.

She climbed to her feet, eyes gritty, muscles shuddering. The jet creaked and settled. The phone was ringing. She grabbed it from the floor and made her way through the break near the tail of the jet, into a day so full of white sand and sunlight that she nearly vomited. The phone continued to ring.

The nose section of the 747 had tipped forward into the sand, like a bird that had done a facefirst landing, and keeled on its side. She staggered to it and climbed on all fours up the hot metal of the fuselage to the open forward door.

"Zoe," she called.

She hoisted herself through the door, dropped onto a bulkhead, and crouched, looking around. The light followed her, strange beams broken by the long line of windows overhead.

"Zoe."

A rustling sound came from behind the first row of seats, tipped vertical, right at the nose. "Mommy."

Zoe unbuckled her seat belt and crawled out onto the wall of the plane that lay against the ground.

Sarah jumped off the bulkhead, braced herself, and took her girl in her arms.

"I gotcha, kiddo. I gotcha."

"I got you too," Zoe said.

Sarah held Zoe tight.

"I buckled up," Zoe said. "Like you always tell me."

She should have been too shattered to walk, but with Zoe on her hip Sarah seemed to have all the strength in the world. She held her close, breathing the scent of her hair, warmed by her lithe, smooth arms around her shoulders.

She found Danisha a minute later. She was slumped against the wall of the jet near the stairs, half-conscious and weak with pain, applying pressure to a bloody wound in her shoulder.

"Bastard got me. Wasn't quick enough," she said.

Sarah set Zoe down and crouched at her

side. She set a hand against Danisha's cheek.

"Thank . . ." She couldn't get the words out. "Dani, thank . . ."

Danisha put a finger to Sarah's lips. "You're welcome. Now stop being all syrupy and get me to a goddamn hospital."

A minute later Sarah boosted Zoe through the door and climbed out after her. In the distance she heard helicopters and the faint wail of a police siren.

Overhead, the crane loomed, its cables loose, dripping down into the body of the 747, where the guillotine blade was embedded. The crane's engine was silent.

Then she saw Lawless, sprawled in the sand beside it. A chalky pool of blood spread from beneath his back.

She skidded up next to him on her knees. "Michael."

His hand moved. He breathed, jaggedly.

She touched him with care, her hands shaking. "What . . ."

"Reavy. She . . . it's not bad."

He was a terrible liar. "Hang on."

"Zoe?" he said.

"Safe. I've got her. We're okay."

The helicopters drew nearer, rotors beating the air. She stood and waved her arms overhead.

A medevac helicopter that had landed just outside the fence loaded Lawless and spooled up its engines to take him to the trauma center. Sarah stood poised outside the door as the life flight crew hung an IV and locked the gurney in place. They scrambled around, professional and calm, but their care was edged with alarm.

In the boneyard, the crime scene was being secured. In an ambulance nearby, paramedics were attending to Danisha. Zoe sat on the back bumper, drinking from a water bottle.

Lawless managed to turn his head toward her. "You," he said.

"Hold on. You're in good hands," she said.

"You — Sarah, I wish . . ."

She swallowed. "I'm okay, Lawless. We're okay. We're good." Her eyes were swimming. "You did good."

The flight crew urged her back.

Lawless raised his head. "Reavy. Had . . ." He touched his shirt pocket, tapped it. "Angel."

"What?" She tried to get closer. "Angel's wing?"

"Searched her." He tried to hold her gaze. "Key is — she had . . ." He grit his teeth.

"Blew . . . it . . ."

"Blew it? What? You didn't blow anything."

"No. Angel . . ." Pain took him and his head fell back.

"Lawless? I don't understand."

The crew shut the door. She ducked away from the spinning rotors and downwash as the helicopter lifted off. It rose, the nose tilted down, and it swooped away, leaving quiet in its wake.

Standing on the other side of the landing zone was Special Agent Curtis Harker.

He looked wrung out, but his eyes were as keen as ever. Squaring her shoulders, she walked toward him.

"It's over," she said.

He squinted at the landscape. His gaze settled on Lawless's black car, and Nolan's body lying beside it. Though his suit was neat, his tie smooth, it seemed to Sarah that he was being picked at by invisible crows.

"There were three of them. Where's the third?" he said.

"She took off while the plane was falling apart. If you haven't found her, she's long gone."

"She'll come after you," he said. "They all will."

"I'll take my chances."

"That sounds either brave or fatalistic.

What does it mean?"

"It means I'll take my chances with the Worthe clan," she said. "But I'm done running. And you're done chasing me. You're done putting out bulletins calling me a child thief. You're done using my daughter as bait."

His jaw tightened and his lips pressed tight. He continued to gaze at Nolan's body.

Sarah said, "You can hunt Fell down and try to bust the entire Worthe family, but Zoe and I are out of it."

"I can't guarantee that," he said.

"You can and you will. Because every sheriff's deputy and FBI agent within five hundred miles knows what happened last night at the Rio Sacado Sheriff's Station. You dragged Zoe there to lure the clan into attacking — and because of that people are dead." She stepped closer. "Now you're going to ensure that I am publicly cleared of any charge that I abducted Zoe. I'm her only family now. You know that. You know why I rescued her that day."

"Every war has its casualties," he said.

"You know. Say it."

He finally looked at her. "I know. You didn't abduct Zoe. You rescued her. But you put yourself in the middle of something far bigger than yourself."

"And now you're going to extricate me. You know I am completely innocent. Don't you."

He sighed. "Yes. What's your point?"

"I want an affidavit of my innocence filed in Federal Court. You can do that. People who have their identities stolen get it done all the time. Well, I'm getting my identity returned." She felt a lump in her throat. "Beth can't have her life back, but you can make it possible for Zoe to live a normal life."

He hesitated.

"Harker," she said.

He stared at the scene, the chaos, the quiet, the end of everything he'd been trying to capture for so long. He hadn't been the one to finish it. She sensed that he felt robbed.

"It's not closure. Closure doesn't exist," she said. "But you're going to let me go."

He stared past her shoulder. Sand scraped along the ground on a gust of wind. It whispered like static, ghostly.

Harker said, "There's no such thing as letting go. But there's looking away. You want an affidavit? Fine. I'll sign it."

She nodded. "I'll e-mail you the readout from the microchip. It includes names, initials, and birthdates. I think it's a list of the children the clan has taken from their parents as hostage. You can get to work on it."

She walked away.

It didn't matter whether he acceded to her demand or not. The FBI wouldn't bother her again, ever. Harker could hang on to his grief and rage, and try to build himself a future out of ashes. But he couldn't have her and he couldn't have Zoe.

She felt the wire she was wearing, taped to her midriff beneath her shirt. It had recorded everything.

Standing at Sarah's side, Zoe waved at the ambulance when it pulled away. Sarah glanced around for a ride. She wanted to get to the hospital. Danisha looked like she was going to be okay. Sarah wanted to get to Lawless.

Zoe said, "Can we go home now?"

Sarah nodded. "I think so."

"Then we need to find Mousie."

She almost broke down then, almost laughed and cried all at once. "Mousie's in the plane, honey. I think he may have to stay there."

The phone rang again. On emotional autopilot, she answered it.

"Mr. Briggs?"

It was a woman's voice. Sarah looked at the phone. She'd picked it up in the 747, but it wasn't hers. She shuddered, repulsed. It was Grissom's.

The woman said, "Hello. Mr. Briggs?"

The voice was familiar. It had a lilt. Sarah stared at the broken jet on the white desert floor and put the phone back to her ear.

She said, "Mr. Briggs has already boarded his flight. Your call's been forwarded to the office — this is his P.A. Is this Lucinda from the First Royal Bank of Antigua?"

"It is, miss."

"Excellent." She looked up at blue sky. "If you're calling to confirm the funds transfer, I can verify all the information for you."

71

The sand under her bare feet was hard and wet. The waves broke with a roar and rushed toward them in barreling foam. Up the beach, the Golden Gate Bridge shone in the sun. Zoe raced sandpipers along the waterline, laughing.

Sarah tilted her head to the sky and let the wind lift her hair from her neck. The breakers ran over her feet and receded with a hush. The water was cold. Her jeans were rolled up to her knees but got splashed anyway. She didn't mind.

Zoe skipped up, surrounded by birds taking flight. She wrapped her arms around Sarah's waist.

"I think there are dolphins in the water," she said.

"Definitely."

"And sharks?"

Surfers in wet suits sat beyond the break line, rising and falling, waiting for the right curl. It had been ten years since Sarah had come to this beach. More than a lifetime. Forever since she'd stood here and gazed past the Marin Headlands at the blue horizon.

For too long she'd thought this edge of the continent would be the jumping-off point. This would be where she lifted Zoe into her arms and disappeared, westward, vanishing into clouds and nothingness, becoming vapor.

Instead, she enjoyed the feeling of solid earth beneath her feet, the rugged cliffs of the Presidio behind her back, the city beyond. Loved the sun on her face, Zoe's smile and ricocheting energy. It had been six weeks since the fight in the airplane graveyard. Six weeks since Danisha had gotten the all clear. Six weeks since Sarah had given a copy of the wire recording to the FBI, since an affidavit of her innocence had been filed, since Harker had disappeared from her life.

And it had been six weeks since Zoe's RFID microchip was removed. Sarah had forwarded some of the chip's information to the FBI. As she suspected, the chip contained more than just Zoe's name and the clan's bank account number. It had revealed the names of clan children who'd been taken from their parents. Many of them had now been found.

Many — but no boy matching the description of Fell's son, Creek.

Fell remained at large. The deaths of Grissom Briggs and Reavy Worthe had been heavily reported. So had the death of Isom Worthe. His body had been found in a field in northern Arizona, picked over by vultures. He'd been shot twice in the back of the head.

Gangland war, the papers speculated. Intrafamily feud.

Eldrick's wrath, Sarah thought. Isom had failed to protect the family's profits, and he paid for it.

It had been six weeks since the money vanished from the clan bank account. Nobody had come after Sarah. Nobody had come for Zoe. They'd been living openly. Nobody cared anymore.

"Yeah, there are sharks in the water," she said. "But we don't need to worry about them today. They're busy chasing fish for lunch."

Zoe bounced. "Can I go in?"

"With me. Up to your knees." She didn't want to explain riptides yet.

They'd been in San Francisco for five days, decompressing. Zoe was edgy and prone to nightmares, but she no longer stuck to Sarah's hip, silent and watchful. She was seeing a counselor.

And, with Sarah, she had been to see Beth's grave, nearby in the coastal mountains. A headstone was a hard thing to show a little girl. But that cold marker of Beth's end was also a beginning: the opening of the story Sarah was telling Zoe about the young mother who gave up her own life so that Zoe could have one. The flowers Zoe laid on the grave were a vibrant, messy bouquet she'd gathered herself. Beth would have loved them.

And Sarah had begun formal adoption proceedings.

Zoe threw her hat in the air and caught it. Sarah smiled.

A voice behind her said, "You'll turn blue."

She glanced back. Lawless limped toward her across the sand.

He was pale, his hair scruffy. The walking stick he was using gave him a rakish air. He was only two weeks out of the hospital. He'd lost his spleen and part of a lung. His fibula had been fractured. He was barely into physical therapy, facing a long slog in rehab. But he was alive.

He stopped at her side. His eyes, always

alert and guarded, for once seemed open.

"Want to catch some waves?" she said.

"Tow me on an inner tube behind a jet ski and provide me with a case of beer."

"The time off's doing things to your head."

He smiled. "What's it doing to yours?"

She brushed her hair back from her face. "I haven't decided."

She could continue to work for Danisha in Oklahoma City. Her desk was waiting. Her house was waiting. A jerry-rigged life was there. Lawless was here. The rest of the planet, rising and falling on the tide, was here, and beyond.

"People are going to keep disappearing, wherever I work," she said. "Some of them need finding. And some of them need help erasing their old lives."

The waves washed over her feet. Lawless took her hand. He ran a finger along her palm, down the scar left from falling in the forest and cutting her hand, many years earlier. It followed her lifeline.

She smiled. "I always thought mine was untraceable. But what do you know."

She hung onto his hand. Some people needed to vanish. And some needed help to retrieve bits of their past. "Anything more come back to you?"

He eyed the horizon, where it faded to blue mist and met the sky. "Fragments."

He had almost no memory of the final minutes at the aircraft boneyard. Shock and blood loss had stolen most of his consciousness. He didn't recall telling her about Reavy and an angel. He didn't even remember searching Reavy's body.

"The key," she said, not for the first time. "The clue. The source. The secret."

"The Shattering Angel. Angel's wings. Nope. Nothing," he said.

No key had been found on Reavy. No items whatsoever had been found on her body or in the crane. Not even the Mossberg shotgun. They knew Fell must have taken that — and cleaned out Reavy's pockets before she fled the boneyard.

They knew the trio had been in San Francisco, at least for travel. Their flight into Oklahoma City had originated at San Francisco International. The T-shirt Lawless had seen Grissom wearing in Rio Sacado turned out to come from Tank Up, a Bay Area coffee chain. There was one on Mission Street in San Francisco, but another at the airport — he could have picked up the shirt anywhere. Beyond that, nobody had yet been able to backtrace the trio's movements. Whether Lawless's rambling, urgent attempt to tell Sarah something had meant anything at all . . . no luck.

Zoe tugged on her arm. "Let's get in the waves."

"In a sec." She held onto Lawless's hand. "If anybody blew it that day, it was Reavy. Not you."

He scanned the surf.

Zoe continued to tug. "Come on, Mommy. I want to see you turn blue."

Her smile was beguiling. Sarah looked at her and went still.

She looked at Lawless. "Michael, I misunderstood you."

Blew it? What? You didn't blow anything.

No. Angel . . .

"You said *blue.*"

He glanced at her sideways. "Say again?"

"You said *blue.* I heard *blew it,* but that was wrong. Which is why you said, 'No. Angel.' "

"Blue." He looked dubious. "Blue Angel?"

A cold wave ran over their feet and retreated. Sarah said, "It's worth a shot. Reavy had a key. For the Blue Angel Apartments. Car rental. Adult movie studio."

He got his phone. The look on his face hung between *You're nuts* and *What the hell.* But after a minute he looked up.

"Blue Angel Hotel's on Market Street

near the Civic Center."

"What do you know," she said. Her smile stopped, half-formed. "How close to the Civic Center?"

He accessed the map. "Six blocks." Pensive, he zoomed in. His face grew even more pale. "Three blocks from the San Francisco Federal Building."

Under his breath he said, "Damn." He zoomed in again. "Tank Up coffee, on Mission — it's just around the corner."

Sarah leaned in to see. The map listed a congresswoman's office, complete with phone number and antigovernment rants. Across the street, filling the block directly between Tank Up and the Blue Angel, was an imposing granite building.

"What's that?" she said.

Lawless zoomed in again. Sarah straightened. It was the U.S. Court of Appeals.

"That's the Ninth Circuit Courthouse." Her lips stayed parted. "It looks like it's in the crosshairs." Damn. She pulled out her own phone. "That Second Amendment case."

"What?" Lawless said.

"You've been sidelined. The Ninth Circuit is hearing an appeal on a big gun control case. Every Uzi-hugger and pacifist in the continental United States has been yakking about it. Hell, Sister Teresa's probably standing on the courthouse steps with a protest sign."

"And?"

She typed a search. "The judge — the one who presided at the Denver trial of Eldrick Worthe."

"Partyka."

The search result appeared. The entire day went chilly. "He's now a justice on the Ninth Circuit, here in San Francisco. He's on the panel hearing oral arguments." She looked up. "Later this week."

Lawless punched a number and put the phone to his ear. "Jesus. They could be planning another attack."

He pulled her against his side and rested an arm over her shoulder. She wrapped an arm around his waist. She felt his heart beat.

"It's Lawless," he said into the phone. "We have an emergency."

The fourth-floor window overlooked the alley. She sat on the windowsill, watching the protesters and TV news crews down on Mission Street. Directly across the alley, the parking lot at the U.S. Courthouse was ringed by a spiked steel fence. But it exited where the patriots and hippies and reporters were gathered, on a sidewalk plaza guarded by wispy trees and concrete car-bomb protection bollards. Justice Partyka's car was parked in the lot today. It was close, so close.

The protesters sounded energized, but they were just warming up. Later in the week, when oral arguments began, there would be more of them, and they'd be riled like hornets.

Justice Partyka deliberately varied his schedule. He never arrived at the same time in the morning or left at a predictable hour at night. He was accompanied at all times by his U.S. Marshals protective detail. But no matter what, later this week he would have to drive right past the protesters to reach the street.

Close, so close. She could feel it in her fingertips. Close, and soon.

On the bed Cinda sat cross-legged, hunched over a Sudoku book. It was the way Fell had found her when she arrived here three days earlier, after hitchhiking her way across the west from New Mexico, hiding out with cousins along the way. But apparently Cinda had been like this for the past six weeks, ever since Grissom was killed. Ever since she quit work at Tank Up and took to hiding in this room, crying, and reading *Tiger Beat,* then getting the guilts over that and reading the Bible.

At least Cinda didn't know how Grissom came to die. Fell saw no need to tell her.

Over on Mission Street two police cars pulled up. Silent approach: lights flashing, no sirens. Officers jumped out and hustled into the courthouse.

She turned her head toward the hotel room door. The hallway outside had gone quiet.

The Blue Angel never went quiet. It was a fleabag dump, always noisy with European doper tourists and bums a few steps from the Tenderloin and Skid Row. Silence meant death.

She stood, grabbed her go-bag and opened the window. Cinda looked up.

"What —"

Fell put a finger to her lips.

She waited a painful moment, hoping she was wrong. She heard footsteps on the stairs.

"Move," she said, but Cinda stared, dumbfounded. "Split, or kill yourself, but don't sit there. Move."

Cinda stared fearfully at the door. "What do we do?"

"Live to fight another day."

Fell climbed onto the fire escape and ran.

ACKNOWLEDGMENTS

My thanks to Jessica Horvath, Ben Sevier, Brian Tart, Jamie McDonald, Claire Zion, Kara Welsh, Jhanteigh Kupihea, Nancy Freund Fraser, Sara Gardiner M.D., Kelly Gerrard, Adrienne Dines, Mary Albanese, David Wolfe, Tammye Huf, Justine Hess, and Paul Shreve.

Those interested in skip tracing or in methods by which, even in a hyperconnected technological society, it's still possible to vanish, might enjoy two books I found helpful while writing this novel: *How to Disappear,* Frank M. Ahearn with Eileen C. Horan, and *How to Be Invisible,* J. J. Luna.

Those familiar with New Mexico and the Texas panhandle might wonder about a couple of towns and several highways that appear in the novel but not on any maps. I hope you'll forgive me for altering the landscape to add fictional locales. The

Southwest is a big place, and I figured there was room for them.

ABOUT THE AUTHOR

Meg Gardiner is the author of *Ransom River* and four Jo Beckett thrillers, as well as five novels in the Evan Delaney series, including the Edgar Award–winning *China Lake.* Originally from Santa Barbara, California, she divides her time between London and Austin.